BOOK

4

THE COMPLETE SERIES

VOLUME 4

CONTAINING THE NEXT FOUR STORIES:
DEVILS OF DARKNESS
TALONS OF TERROR
THE CORPSE CAVALCADE
THE GOLDEN GHOUL

WRITTEN BY
PAUL CHADWICK, EMILE C. TEPPERMAN
& G. T. FLEMING-ROBERTS

BOSTON
ALTUS PRESS
2010

© 2010 Altus Press

Devils of Darkness originally appeared in
Secret Agent "X" (March 1935)

Talons of Terror originally appeared in
Secret Agent "X" (April 1935)

The Corpse Cavalcade originally appeared in
Secret Agent "X" (May 1935)

The Golden Ghoul originally appeared in
Secret Agent "X" (July 1935)

Printed in the United States of America

First Edition — 2010

Visit AltusPress.com for more books like this.

EDITED AND DESIGNED BY
Matthew Moring

THANKS TO
*Brian Earl Brown, Will Murray,
Ray Riethmeier & Bill Thom.*

ALL RIGHTS RESERVED

No part of this book may be reproduced or utilized in any form or by any means, electronic or mechanical, without permission in writing from the publisher.

TABLE OF CONTENTS

Introduction .... *by Will Murray* i

Devils of Darkness.................... *by Paul Chadwick* 1

Talons of Terror .... *by Emile C. Tepperman* 121

The Corpse Cavalcade .... *by G. T. Fleming-Roberts* 231

The Golden Ghoul................... *by G. T. Fleming-Roberts* 357

INTRODUCTION

WILL MURRAY

THIS FOURTH VOLUME of the chronological adventures of Secret Agent "X" is a true cornucopia of pulpy action-horror.

Secret Agent "X" originator Paul Chadwick opens the grim proceedings with one of his most relentlessly intense efforts, "Devils of Darkness" from the March 1935 issue. The formula editor Rose Wyn devised for "X's" exploits insisted on a suffocating dose of terror and horror infusing the requisite action-adventure plot. So it is not enough that the unknown "X" squares off against a band of the most diabolical bank robbers ever conceived. They happen to be whip-wielding torturers as well!

The superscientific premise of "Devils of Darkness" is not original with Chadwick. It's lifted from Doc Savage creator Lester Dent's 1932 *Detective-Dragnet* novelette, "The Sinister Ray," which featured Dent's first scientific detective, Lynn Lash. Detective-Dragnet was published by Magazine Publishers, Periodical House's parent affiliate. So the story was in the family so to speak. However, the basic concept may go back to the Dean of Science Fiction, Murray Leinster, and his 1929 *Argosy* stories, "The Darkness on Fifth Avenue" and "The City of the Blind."

Whether editor Wyn fed author Chadwick this plot germ, or Chadwick—a *Detective-Dragnet* contributor himself—simply borrowed it, is unknown. But it doesn't matter, "Devils of Darkness" takes Dent's idea to a far more horrific level than the creator of Doc Savage ever dreamed. It's not beyond speculation that Dent himself might have offered Chadwick the idea. Lester was famous for helping other writers plot stories. He was forever trying to teach his secretaries to write. One of them was Dorothy Lester, Dent's secretary in 1933-34. She subsequently married Chadwick. Of course, Dent knew Chadwick from the American Fiction Guild, to which both belonged.

INTRODUCTION

"Talons of Terror" (April 1935) is the work of Emile C. Tepperman, who penned the occasional "X" adventure, while writing short stories in the back of the magazine under his own name and those of Anthony Clemens and Jordan Cole. This is a particularly good one, which evokes the classic vampire theme, and boasts a great villain in the devilish Doctor Blood.

Tepperman ghosted many pulp heroes in the years to come—among them Operator #5, Dan Fowler, the Spider, The Avenger and the Phantom Detective before moving over to radio in the 1940s, where he wrote for such major shows as *Suspense, Inner Sanctum* and *Gang Busters*. Here, he closes out his contributions to the ongoing adventures of the faceless "X" after only four fascinating change-of-pace novels.

After *Secret Agent "X"* once again mysteriously skipped an issue, a new author makes his debut with a clever concoction. (Did one of the star contributors blow a deadline?)

With "The Corpse Cavalcade" (June 1935), G. T. Fleming-Roberts assumes the mask of Brant House, and "X" has a new major scribe. Fleming-Roberts would also move on from this series to originate the Ghost, the Black Hood and Captain Zero. But *Secret Agent "X"* is where he learned to write series novels.

With its echoes of early Shadow novels like "The Silent Seven" and "Circle of Death," "The Corpse Cavalcade" manages to continue the standards set by Paul Chadwick while injecting a strange new flavor to the series. Where Chadwick laid on a heavy oppressive atmosphere transplanted from his Wade Hammond series, Fleming-Roberts injected other elements—a stronger emphasis on clues and deduction, more imaginative plot twists, and a deeper view of characterization. A greater emphasis on some of the Agent's operatives will also hallmark this new exciting phase of "X's" career.

Fleming-Roberts' "The Golden Ghoul" (July 1935) shifts the action to a classic Shadow staple locale—Chinatown. Here another creepy supervillain joins the long parade of arch-fiends the Man of a Thousand Faces went up against. And yet another weird "death"—the Amber Death—takes untold innocent lives. No pulp series ever pitted its indefatigable hero against so many bizarre and gruesome murder methods as did Secret Agent "X." By pulp standards, the Amber Death is probably the most imaginative and realistic of them all.

After this pivotal sequence of stories, Emile Tepperman fades out of the series, while Paul Chadwick remained content with penning the odd novel. From here on out, *Secret Agent "X"* will be G. T. Fleming-Roberts' domain.

Turn the page and watch it all unfold as the three primary ghostwriters behind the house name of Brant House strut their individual stuff as Secret Agent "X" careens from one figurative house of horror to another, with all the square-jawed determination and chameleon cunning that made him one of the most indefatigable pulp heroes of the 1930s.

BOOK XIII

DEVILS OF DARKNESS

Black as night, black as hell itself, the "devil-dark" descended upon a fear-crazed populace! Men and women shrieked in agony beneath the lash of bloody, torturing whips. The mangled bodies of innocent children lay in the streets, while human fiends emptied the city of its wealth. And into this chaotic and hideous fog of darkness went Secret Agent "X" to wage a life-and-death battle with unseen criminals.

CHAPTER I

TERROR'S CALL

LIPS TIGHTLY COMPRESSED, eyes clouded with growing horror, a man in a black press coupé knifed into upper Broadway. His hands on the vibrating wheel before him had the steely tautness of curved talons. His foot fed gas recklessly to the roaring motor. And in his brain beat the mad words of an amazing message he had received a few moments before.

"Come, boss! Hurry! It's getting dark—dark as night. Dark as hell itself. I can't see the sun any more—because it's gone out. And all over the block, people are screaming, fighting—looting! Come—for God's sake!"

The words had been uttered with the frenzied hoarseness of one gripped by terror of the unknown. They had transmitted some of their horror to the nerves of the man in the careening press coupé. And, incredible as they seemed, he couldn't ignore them. For that message had come straight from the lips of an operative trained and employed by one of the shrewdest criminal investigators in the world.

Others evidently had received word of this madness. On all sides of the rocketing press coupé was movement, turmoil, a frenzied medley of sound and action as the city stirred itself into unwonted activity.

Near by, an emergency squad truck, siren shrieking, hurtled forward like a berserk green monster trying to shake off the human leeches that clung to its swaying body. On an avenue running parallel, a clanging ambulance kept pace. Farther ahead, a regulation police prowl car added a persistent thinner note to the din.

Excitement was in the air. Excitement with an undercurrent of nameless fear, lashing the spinning wheels of a dozen vehicles to a more furious pace—as all raced forward toward the same objective.

As Agent "X" struggled to seize the gun, a bullet passed screamingly close to his chest.

But the man in the press coupé was making the best time of all. Hunched forward to the seat, tense in every muscle, he tore past intersections with the horn button held down. He drove with death-defying abandon; swung by the ambulance, cut in ahead of it, ignoring a cop's whistle that shrilled at him to stop.

He took a time-saving detour through a narrow side street. This got him ahead of the police cruiser. Another five blocks, and he trod abruptly on his brake pedal and brought the coupé to a slithering, screeching halt. This was as far as even he could go. The street was blocked by jammed traffic and crowds of frightened human beings, milling, shouting, jostling each other.

As he leaped out of his coupé he heard snatches of conversation from the bloodless lips about him:

"The dark!"

"The terrible twilight!"

"The world—coming to an end!"

"The devil—is on earth!"

Superstitious fear showed on the faces of some. A woman was weeping hysterically, fearfully, wringing her bony hands in a paroxysm of awed fright. An old colored man who looked like a preacher was down on his knees at the edge of the curb, praying, his body swaying, his eyes rolling toward the sky above, his deep-toned voice quavering in religious fervor.

"Oh, Lord, save us! Save thy chullen from the hands of Satan! Save the blessed earth from his wiles and wickedness!"

His words seemed an echo of the stark terror that was stamped on the features of everyone in sight—terror of the unknown.

The man from the press coupé strode ahead grimly, slipping unnoticed through the milling mob, moving on toward the spot from which the nameless horror seemed to have radiated. And then he glimpsed one face upon which no fear was registered. It was the face of a white-haired, shabbily dressed beggar standing in a doorway with a tray of chewing gum tied around his middle—a blind beggar whose sightless eyes had mercifully been spared the horror of the darkness which had cast its dread spell over every one else.

The blind man leaned forward abruptly, listening to the approaching footsteps.

Suddenly he called out: "Mr. Robbins! Mr. Robbins!"

Only for an instant did the driver of the press coupé pause. He laid a friendly hand on the blind man's shoulder, uttered a name quickly: "Thaddeus Penny." Then he plunged on through the crowd which at this point had begun to thin.

A hundred feet from the spot where he had been forced to park his coupé, he came upon ghastly evidence that the mysterious terror which all had mentioned wasn't imaginary.

Two big delivery trucks, coming out of side streets, had met in a fearful, head-on collision. The motors and front wheels of both were telescoped into a tangled mass of shattered junk. Water from their cracked radiators had spilled into the street, running away in rusty rivulets.

THE driver of one truck was visible. Yet he was hardly recognizable as a man. An inert, flattened figure, he lay pinned under the side of the cab—beyond the aid of ambulance or interne.

The man from the press coupé stepped jerkily around the telescoped trucks and moved forward. But the accident of the crashing trucks was only the beginning. Twenty feet farther on he paused to stare with widening eyes into the gutter. Here, too, the Grim Reaper had struck.

The bodies of four people, three women and a man, lay in distorted postures, trampled to death by the onrush of many frenzied feet, their clothing torn and soiled. Bundles they had clutched before the fear-crazed mob had wrought its horrible havoc upon them, lay scattered and broken. Then the coupé's driver came to the most gruesome tragedy of all—a thing so horrible that it made breath hiss between his clenched teeth.

For a school bus, filled with small children, had swerved and crashed into a lamp post. It had cracked open down its whole length, and turned on its side, spilling the crushed and mangled forms of its small occupants into the street. Tousled curly heads and tiny faces lay still under a mass of broken glass and debris. Three who had succeeded in dragging themselves from the wreck had fallen, pitiful victims to the frenzied mob's feet. Only one, a little girl with chestnut hair, had managed somehow to reach a doorway on the street's opposite side. Huddled in a corner, she sobbed in confused terror.

The man from the press coupé walked to her, bent down and whispered quiet words of reassurance until her crying ceased. He picked her up, comforted her still further, and gave her into the temporary care of an old lady who was peering fearfully from a first floor window.

Something else attracted his attention then. Faces stared out at him from the glass front of a big store, men and women with fear shadows in their eyes, gaping like frightened, wondering animals, too dazed to move.

He strode toward them, opened the store's door, and when he entered they backed away. But he raised his voice harshly, authoritatively, and began quick questioning. As he did so he drew a press card from his pocket and held it up for all to see. This bore the name of A. J. Martin.

The store's proprietor was the first to find his voice and answer the queries that were flung at him. Yet what the man said seemed hardly to make sense, any more than the statements of the milling people at the edge of the mob. For he was trembling, his hand waving toward the littered street, and his speech came haltingly.

"The dark!" he croaked. "The dark—out there! Even our lights were no good. The sun must have gone out. It was—an eclipse, I guess. But I don't understand—about our lights not shining."

A pause followed his startling words. Then a frightened woman spoke:

"No—you're wrong. The sun didn't go out. It was a fog—a black fog that filled the street. The people ran screaming. I saw them—and then—It was terrible—like a night when nothing can be seen."

The man who held the press card nodded tensely. Fog, or an eclipse, or the falling of night—these people couldn't explain the thing that had come to pass. Yet something infinitely strange had happened, something under the influence of which nightmare tragedies had occurred—cars smashed, men trampled, small children killed.

A moment of silence passed while his sharp eyes hovered over a dozen fear-strained faces. Then he said: "Thanks," turned and hurried back into the street.

THOSE whom he had questioned weren't aware that no syndicate or newspaper had sent him. They weren't aware that his plainly cast features were part of a brilliantly clever disguise, natural as living flesh. They didn't guess that behind it lay the face of a man whose identity was hidden from all the world—the identity of Secret Agent "X."

Norman Coe

Strange rumors had been built up about this Man of a Thousand Faces. His name had been spoken in awed whispers throughout the underworld. There he was feared as a swift, relentless human scourge who seemed to hear all and know all. Yet the police of many cities had been ordered to investigate his activities, trace him down, trap him. For the law regarded him as a desperate criminal. Only a few on earth knew that the direct opposite was true, that this man of strange destiny and mystery was one of the most daringly ingenious criminal investigators alive. For where crime appeared in its most threateningly hideous form—there, also, Agent "X" made a habit of appearing.

Yet his arrival now seemed oddly inconsistent. Darkness had fallen. Fearful accidents had occurred. People had been trampled, killed. But Nature, not man, seemed the guilty one.

The Secret Agent left the store, strode on down the block, and a figure suddenly stepped from a doorway and accosted him.

"Mr. Martin!"

The man was tall, redheaded. There was on his face a look of strain, as there had been on those others in the store. "Mr. Martin," he said again. "Listen—the sun's shining now. But it wasn't a few minutes ago when I called you. It got dark, black as hell!"

The Secret Agent didn't answer. There were lights of strange intensity in his eyes. Wild and fantastic had been the description of the people in the store, and the snatches of hysterical conversation in the street. Nightmarish they had seemed. But now the man before him, Jim Hobart, his own operative, whose powers of observation he trusted absolutely, was repeating the same thing. Darkness, as black as night, as black as hell, had fallen. And those fear-stricken people, those dead men and women and children, proved that under its cloak hellish things had happened.[1]

"There was looting," Hobart continued, "like I told you. I could hear windows smashing and people yelling. What a story it will make, chief! Better hurry before the other sheets get in on it."

The Secret Agent made an angry, impatient gesture. Hobart hadn't seen those children, those slain innocents back there. He didn't know how horribly death had struck in this street of mystery.

"Wait!" he said harshly. "First I must see—" He left the sentence unfinished, gave no indication of what it was he hoped to find. But there was a bank building in the precise center of the block. The Agent hurried on toward this.

Dignified marble columns rose above the pavement. Granite steps led up to the bank's facade where polished bronzed plates were set. It, too, had apparently come under the dread shadow of the terror fog, the darkness that none could explain. For when the Agent climbed the steps he stiffened abruptly.

The glass in the big front doors was broken, shattered. Behind them there were other signs of ruin. Windows along the tellers' cages had been smashed. No employee of the bank was in sight. But at the far end of the main corridor, a crowd of depositors stood huddled, men and women who turned their fear-blanched faces at him, like dazed and frightened cattle herded into a pen.

The Agent strode swiftly toward them, and suddenly stopped in shocked amazement, clenching his hands at his sides. For these people had been treated like cattle. Searing welts showed on the features and hands of many. Plainly they were the marks of whips. Whips that had streaked out from behind that cloak of darkness. Whips with metal studded ends that left not merely welts, but jagged crimson cuts. And they had been plied ruthlessly.

A half-fainting girl cowered against a wall desk, her dress torn to ribbons where the sharp lashes had fallen, her white body was a crisscross of angry welts. She had been struck again and again as though some fiend had held the whip. One blow had landed on her cheek, laying it open, making a cruel wound that might disfigure

---

1   AUTHOR'S NOTE: *To aid him in the secret daring work to which he is pledged, Agent "X" has built up two unique organizations. Jim Hobart, former police detective, dismissed from the force on graft charges trumped up by an underworld czar, heads one. A man named Bates heads another. Neither they nor the men and women under them know that they are working for Secret Agent "X."*

her for life. She could only whimper now, and cower, dabbing a handkerchief to her crimson-stained face. But a man in the trembling terrified group addressed the Agent with hysterical shrillness.

"The police!" he screeched. "Get the police! This bank has been robbed. Those devils who whipped us—while the darkness came—have looted the vaults! They've murdered the tellers!"

A noise sounded as he spoke. It was a man's groaning curse. Agent "X" whirled. A bank employee in a gray coat was getting up, reeling into sight. He had been lashed into helpless, pain-racked terror. And behind him the great door of the main vault was open, papers scattered across its floor, every metal compartment emptied of currency and coin.

A second depositor spoke then, words grating bitterly from between bruised and lacerated lips. "They grabbed my wallet!" he snarled. "The bank's cash wasn't enough! They took even the money I'd drawn out."

Others nodded agreement, complaining that they had been robbed of all they had. Agent "X" stood tensely silent. He was not thinking of the reports of robbery—except that they confirmed his startling suspicion. Man, not nature, had made this hideous darkness!

Mysteriously, abruptly as it had fallen over one whole block in the very heart of the city at high noon, somehow human hands and human brains were responsible for it. A great theft had taken place. Ruthless raiders had gone about their sinister work, unseen, yet able to see.

Those accidents, those stampeding crowds, those pitiful, trampled bodies had been only indirect results. Back of this inhuman carnage—was human greed.

CHAPTER II

LASHING DEATH

AGENT "X" LEFT the bank quickly before police detectives arrived. They would have their opinions. But there was one whose opinion "X" wanted to hear even more. He returned to the spot where the blind beggar had stood. The sightless man, Thaddeus Penny, was still there, and once again his face lit up as he heard the Secret Agent's steps.

Months ago, in the disguise of "Robbins," Agent "X" had done Thaddeus Penny a great service. And Penny had become his friend for life. He had helped "X" often with his power of identifying men by their steps, his trick of never forgetting the tone of a voice, his strangely acute intelligence. He was one man the Agent could come to in any disguise, since it was "X's" speech which identified him to the blind man, and the Agent was always careful to use the same voice in addressing him. Yet in spite of this "X" sometimes suspected that Penny knew more than he let on, and was aware that the man called "Robbins" was a unique and mysterious being.

The Agent asked an abrupt question, "Tell me just what you heard as you stood here, Thaddeus. Exactly what were the sounds?"

The blind man was silent for a moment. His expressive face showed that he was recalling unpleasant impressions. He spoke slowly, sadly. "There are things a man would rather not hear, Mr. Robbins. People were hurt. They screamed, trampled each other. And I, a blind man, could do nothing. They spoke of darkness. But I am not afraid of the dark. I told them not to be afraid, but they wouldn't listen."

"But the bandits?" "X" urged. "Did you hear them come?"

Thaddeus Penny looked puzzled. "I heard them talking. I heard one give orders to the others. But they didn't sound like crooks, Mr. Robbins. They spoke like gentlemen—men like yourself."

"I see," said the Secret Agent. "Thank you, Thaddeus."

The blind man clutched his arm suddenly, seemed to be looking off into space with his sightless eyes. "There's one thing, sir, that I almost forgot to tell you. It seems—funny! All around me I heard people shouting that it was dark, pitch dark. And yet—the sun was shining all the time."

Agent "X" stared at the sightless face. "The sun—but how could you be sure of that, Thaddeus?" he asked sharply. "This is winter. The sunlight is weak."

"Those who have no eyes must learn to feel many things, Mr. Robbins. I always know if the sun is out or not, no matter how feebly it shines. My skin tells me. And the sun was shining today at noon, while people screamed about darkness. I swear to that."

Agent "X" was tensely silent. What utter madness was this? The sun shining, while a thousand human beings cried their terror in abysmal darkness, while his own operative Jim Hobart spoke of the fearful night. Was it the product of Thaddeus Penny's brain—or had a blindman's delicate senses "seen" what normal eyes could not?

LATER that day Secret Agent "X" crouched over a desk in the small office of "A. J. Martin." He was alone. Newspapers were spread before him. Black headlines screamed the story of the bank robbery which the metropolitan press had rushed into extras. A dozen theories had been put forward to explain the darkness under which such hideous things had happened.

A smoke screen, vaporizing quickly, some said, had been thrown over the block. Still others claimed that a restricted, radio-induced solar eclipse had occurred. That the thing was man-made all agreed.

But the press and the police were equally baffled. There was no inkling as to the fiendish criminals' identity—no clues save those bloody welts on the faces and bodies of those who had been close to the scene of the crime.

The accidents, the stampeding, trampling mobs, could be easily explained now. Autos had crashed because their drivers could not see. Crowds had run in panic from Stygian blackness that seemed to presage the end of the world.

The fingers of Secret Agent "X" clawlike in their tenseness, reached forward, took a clipping from a pigeonhole in his desk. It told of a similar phenomenon, the coming of darkness at high noon, which had occurred a week before in a small town upstate.

Only a few people had seen it, a hundred or two at most, and because of the quiet of the rural community and the absence of traffic, there had been no accidents or riots.

The big city dailies, when the story reached them, had made light of it, called it the mass phobia of people who had deluded themselves into seeing something which had no existence.

But Agent "X," ever on the watch for strange occurrences, had saved the item. A profound student of physical science, he had never before heard of such an occurrence. He had been suspicious that it was somehow man-made. And there had even been in his mind the thought that such a veil of darkness would be a perfect cover for a band of criminals to work beneath.

Now, in the light of today's robbery, Agent "X" understood. The coming of this darkness in the small town had been merely a preliminary test. There had been a bank in the town, and it had not been robbed. But undoubtedly the criminals who had created the darkness had also made a careful study of the situation—to see whether or not a bank could be robbed. The test, having turned out favorably, they had moved their operations to the neighborhood of a bank in a big city where a daring crime would pay.

AGENT "X" tossed the clipping aside. He searched through the newspapers again, reading over the appalling lists of dead and injured that the accidents during the period of darkness on the block had caused. He looked methodically to see if any of the thousand or more witnesses had enlightening data to give. Perhaps strangers had been seen prowling around the section. Perhaps some odd activity had been noted by some one previous to the darkness. But there were no such reports. The criminals had operated with organized efficiency, with complete secrecy.

Then the Agent came upon a brief item which made him instantly alert, though it was tucked away at the bottom of an inside page. It said:

GIRL SECRETARY MISSING

> Craig Banton, president of the Guardian Bank, gave notice to the police this morning that Ellen Dowe, a girl secretary employed by him, was missing. The police were asked to institute a search for the girl after she had failed to report for work, and when her friends and family disclaimed knowledge of her whereabouts. Efforts to locate her have so far failed.

As a news event it was unimportant, vastly overshadowed by the robbery and accidents that had taken place. But to Agent "X" it seemed vital. His alert mind, trained to probe for the hidden seeds of crime, saw in it a possible sinister significance. He wondered instantly if it presaged another hideous robbery such as that which had taken place today. The bank raided during the noon hour just past had been wealthy, but the Guardian was of even more importance, one of the city's soundest financial institutions, patronized by scores of thrifty workers.

The Agent reached for a telephone on his desk and dialed the number of the Hobart Detective Agency. His own unlimited resources, drawn from a fund subscribed by ten public-spirited men at the outset of his career, had gone into building it up. It was his to command in any way he wished under the guise of A. J. Martin. Often it, and the Bates' organization, working independently, had been of service to Agent "X," running down minor leads which left his own time free for the missions that only he could undertake.

Hobart answered quickly, eagerly, recognizing his employer's voice.

The Agent read the clipping concerning Ellen Dowe over the phone. Then he snapped an order:

"Find her, Jim. Put every man and woman you've got on the job. See how she went to and from the bank. Find out who her friends are. Learn where she ate her meals. Get some trace of her!"

There was a brief pause at the other end of the wire. Then Jim Hobart spoke hesitantly: "I thought, boss, you wanted me to comb the crook joints to see if I could pick up any news of that bank gang! I've got half the boys out now and—"

"Recall them!" snapped Agent "X."

Jim Hobart didn't argue. Often before his boss had moved swiftly, changed his tactics in the twinkling of an eye, working at times on hunches alone. All this Hobart had attributed to "Martin's" insatiable thirst for news. Now there was an edge in "X's" voice which demanded quick obedience.

Hobart immediately promised to round up the men and women under him and start the quest for the missing Ellen Dowe.

THE Agent snapped up the receiver and opened a locked compartment in the bottom of his old-fashioned desk. From this he took a black box that was the size of a small valise. He raised the cover, drew out a length of flexible electric cable with a pronged plug at its end. He thrust this into a wall socket, and bent over the open box.

It was one of the most compact radio transmission sets in existence. Its efficiency was proof of the Secret Agent's ability in the difficult field of radio engineering, for he had built the set himself. Speech or code could be broadcasted from it. The Agent used a small sending key now, reeling off dots and dashes with the touch of an expert wireless telegrapher.

Sully

The message he sent out was in a five-letter code known only to one man in the city. This man was Harry Bates, head of the Secret Agent's second investigating group. Bates had never seen his mysterious employer. He got his instructions by mail, phone or radio. To him, "X" was known only as the "chief."

At all hours of the day and night Harry Bates kept a small receiving set within hearing, so that when his personal signal was called he might give instant attention. The insect buzz of that secret code generally meant that the chief was beginning one of his startling campaigns to unearth the cryptic details of some hideous crime. And "X" had built and sent by mail to Bates a portable radio set so small that it could be carried inconspicuously on the operative's person.[2]

When the Agent was sure that the signal code word had been picked up, he gave Bates instructions to send men drifting through the underworld with an ear open for word of the ruthless bank bandits. There was little likelihood that anything would come of it. Criminals clever enough to use such a thing as this curtain of darkness to aid them in their crime would hardly leave traces behind for underworld gossips to talk of. Yet it was a stone that must not be left unturned.

Hours passed, and neither the police nor the Bates organization turned up anything of importance. It wasn't till the next morning, shortly before noon, that a message reached Agent "X". It was from

---

2 AUTHOR'S NOTE: *Readers will remember that this set gave valuable assistance when Agent "X" was battling the extortion-terrorist, Monte Sutton. On it, Bates received a call sent by "X" from Sutton's yacht, the "Osprey," in time to summon the police and catch Sutton red-handed.*

the excited, triumphant red-headed Jim Hobart. He said:

"We've found her, boss. We've got the gal you want, but—" Hobart's tone became slightly mournful—"she's been croaked. Hurry, anyway, and you'll make a scoop on the yarn. Even the cops don't know about it yet. Dwyer and Lancy Streets, right behind the fence in the vacant lot."

Agent "X" asked no questions. A strange, harsh light had leaped into his eyes at the news. He got into his car, made rubber burn as he sped through the morning streets. Dwyer and Lancy—that was on the west side of town. Not a nice neighborhood, either.

He saw the red-headed detective lounging on the corner as he turned into Dwyer street. A cigarette hung placidly from Hobart's lips, but his eyes were snapping. He was proud of the thing his organization had accomplished, proud that he'd been able to fulfil the mission his boss had imposed upon him. The fact that the girl was dead was only a minor disappointment, all in the day's work. He had seen many corpses in his grimly practical career.

Agent "X" brought his car to a skidding stop, leaped out.

"It was a neat job, if I do say it," Hobart stated buoyantly. "We found she drove a car, got the tire tracks in her own garage. One of my men located the same tracks in some mud out here. Her own bus was used for the job. Maybe she had a crazy boy friend who did it."

"Where is she?" asked "X."

JIM HOBART turned and sauntered into the vacant lot. He moved along the inside of the fence, stopped, and indicated a pile of old boarding that had been shoved away. Under it, a rough hollow had been scooped in the ground, and the body of a girl lay there. Her dress was torn to pieces, like that of the cowering girl he had seen in the bank. On her face, neck and shoulders the cutting marks of the metal-tipped whips showed. Pain and horror were registered on her set face and in her glassy eyes.

"We saw where the car had stopped," Jim Hobart went on. "Then we found footprints at the edge of the lot and saw somebody had shifted that lumber. Only one guy brought her. He wore number ten shoes. He must have weighed about a hundred and seventy, judging by the depth of the tracks. I knew it was the right gal as soon as I saw her, because one of my boys wangled a picture from a friend. Looks like a crime of passion, boss. Lovers these days—"

But Agent "X" instantly shook his head. The marks of the whip had told him what he wanted to know, confirmed a theory that lay like a black shadow on his mind. This wasn't the result of a lovers' quarrel. Cold-blooded purpose had been behind that merciless beating. The Agent turned and snapped quick orders.

"Tell the police about this girl at once, Jim. But say you were employed by a member of her family to find her. And here's another job for you. Go to my office as fast as you can and get the movie camera you'll find there in the closet. There's film in it. You know how to work it. Go to the Guardian Bank where this girl worked. Find a window somewhere across the street overlooking the front entrance. Don't let anyone see what you're doing. If the darkness should come again today the way it did yesterday—crank that camera for all you're worth!"

Jim Hobart's jaw dropped and he stared in amazement at the man he called Martin—stared as though he thought his chief had suddenly gone crazy.

"You don't mean, boss—you don't want me to take pictures in the dark. It wouldn't do much good. Why—"

The Agent's answer was low-voiced, grim, with a note in it that Hobart had learned to obey unquestioningly. "You heard me, Jim. Take pictures—no matter how dark it gets. Understand?"

"O. K., boss."

The Agent turned on his heel, strode to his parked coupé and sped away. He glanced at the clock on the car's instrument panel. It was twenty minutes of twelve now. Twice the mysterious darkness had descended at high noon; and the second time panic had occurred, grisly accidents had taken place and millions of dollars had been stolen. If what he feared was true, the darkness was about to descend again—and he might be too late to prevent the hideous catastrophe that would surely follow.

CHAPTER III

UNHEEDED WARNING

YET AS AGENT "X" raced on his self-imposed mission, he made one swift detour. This was necessary. His disguise of A. J. Martin was valuable. He must run no risk of having it linked with the activities of the mysterious Agent "X." More important still, it would not serve the purpose he had in mind.

He stopped at a hideout, one of several he maintained, and there made a swift change of disguise. He removed the plainly cast features of A. J. Martin, which formed a carefully molded, flexible covering of plastic material. This had a pyroxyline base, but contained other volatile substances in a compound known only to Agent "X."

Disguise was the backbone of his strange power, just as it had been of many another great crime hunter, from the incomparable Vidocq on down the line. But Agent "X," studying the methods of predecessors and contemporaries, had made of disguise an exact science. The skill of a character actor on stage or screen had gone into his work. The art of the sculptor was manifest in the genius with which he caught men's likenesses.

After the removal of the Martin disguise, including the perfectly fitted sandy-haired toupee, Agent "X" appeared for a moment as he really was. Here was the face that a score of police heads throughout the nation would have given a small fortune to look upon; the face that none, not even his few close intimates, had ever knowingly beheld. For the Agent's true identity was a jealous secret, guarded with his very life.

The features exposed now in the seclusion of his hideout were as remarkable in some respects as the man himself. Youthful, powerful—they were filled with character and understanding. A forceful, original mentality showed in the clear brilliance of the eyes. Kindness and even a trace of grim humor were combined in the mobile lips. The curve of the nose held hawklike strength. But perhaps the most extraordinary thing of all about his face was its odd changeability. Seen in an oblique light it seemed to grow more mature; planes and hollows were brought out, the indelible marks of a hundred strange adventures and experiences.

Seated before a collapsible, triple-sided mirror, Agent "X" quickly built up a different personality. From a small bottle he washed on darkish pigment that dried almost instantly, owing to its highly rarefied benzine base. Over it he spread a volatile substance that quickly assumed the appearance of ruddy, living flesh. This he molded into the cast of a firm-jawed, stern-looking man of fifty.

He darkened and thickened his eyebrows, slipped a toupee shot with gray over his head—and the transformation was complete. He had aged at least twenty years.

From a small cabinet he took a card bearing the name of Frank Hearndon, agent of the U. S. Department of Justice. This he slipped into his wallet. When it suited his purpose, "X" never hesitated to act as a representative of the law, for, though neither the police nor the D. C. I. suspected it, he had the secret sanction of one of the highest government officials in the land. Messages had often flashed between Agent "X" and a man in Washington, D. C., who preferred to be known only as K9.

The change had taken Agent "X" exactly eight minutes. He slipped into another suit, hurried to the street again. But now he ignored his black coupé, which was registered under the name of Martin. He summoned a taxi instead, and, with a five-dollar bill, bribed the driver to law-breaking speed across town till the Guardian Bank hove into sight.

As he had feared, it was crowded. For this was the first of the month, and at least a hundred depositors jostled at the tellers' windows, some drawing out cash, others depositing part of their salaries.

"X" strode toward the bank's rear where a short flight of steps led to a balcony lined with the offices of the officials.

A big man in a blue uniform barred his way by placing a determined hand on the small gate across the steps.

"Sorry, sir," he said. "We don't allow—"

"I must see President Banton," the Agent snapped. "It's vitally important."

"Sorry," repeated the bank guard, "but you'll have to wait. Mr. Banton is engaged. Take a seat over there. I'll let you know when you can—"

There was pompous assurance in the guard's tone, but it vanished in a surprised gasp, as Agent "X" impatiently brushed the man out of his way, snapped open the metal gate, and sprang up the steps.

"Hey—you can't do that! Mr. Banton is—"

His words fell on unheeding ears. "X" was already half across the balcony. He swiftly passed a dozen doors lettered in gold. The bond department. The trust officers' rooms. The chambers of the vice-presidents. He yanked open a door marked, "President," entered a small, luxurious outer office.

An angry voice reached his ears, not Banton's, but that of a man who stood before the desk of the girl receptionist. "X" paused an instant to stare. A dispute was obviously in progress and the two engaged in it were too excited to notice his entry.

THE man was firm-jawed, powerful, with a face that was familiar to Agent "X"—a face that had the stubborn cragginess of rough-hewn granite. He was Norman Coe, head of the Citizens Banking Committee, an organization representing the claims and complaints of depositors in a dozen closed banks, and a man who had made life unpleasant for more than one shady banker.

"I tell you," he shouted, "that Craig Banton can't treat me like this. I've waited for twenty minutes now, and I'm going in or—"

The girl at the desk was stubborn also, with the scared determination of one eager to make good on her job. She shook her head. "It can't be helped. You've got to wait—like any one else. Please be patient."

Norman Coe broke into another angry tirade, pointing a shaking finger at his watch.

"Twenty minutes, I say—twenty minutes. My time is worth—"

Agent "X" took the opportunity to cross the room swiftly. Coe heard him and whirled. The girl at the desk gave a startled shriek, putting her hand to her mouth. But Agent "X" had already flung open the door of the president's office. It might serve as an adequate barrier even to such an important person as Norman Coe, but it couldn't stop the Man of a Thousand Faces when the threat of crime spurred him on. He saw at once, however, that the girl at the desk hadn't lied. Craig Banton was busy—very much so.

A fashionably-dressed woman was seated close to his side—a woman whose face was familiar to the Agent, just as Norman Coe's had been. While Banton let Coe cool his heels in the outer office, he

As the Agent leaped, one corner fell with a rumbling crash, and flames volcanoed upward.

was having a tete-a-tete with Vivian de Graf, society beauty, whose sensational affairs had formed front-page gossip for the scandal sheets. Only recently her name had been connected with that of Roswell Sully, millionaire utility magnate, called the most hated man in America.

Arresting, exotic, Vivian de Graf was the type to attract men wherever she went. And she made a point of doing so. Her tailored clothes subtly accentuated the perfection of her statuesque figure. Her beauty was carried with poised arrogance. At the front of her gown, contrasting with the dazzling whiteness of her throat, were the spread petals of an orchid, yellow as saffron, spotted like a leopard's coat. The flower was as exotic as its wearer—and had something poisonous in its loveliness that seemed symbolic of Vivian de Graf's spotted career.

The caressing smile on her crimson lips, the coyly arched eyebrows, and the confiding closeness of her chair to Banton's, indicated to "X" that he had broken in on a very intimate conversation.

Craig Banton, red-faced, bull-necked, looking a little foolish at the moment, raised glittering eyeglasses and made an angry sound in his fat throat at "X's" informal entry.

"How the devil did you get in here?" he barked. "I thought I told—"

Secret Agent "X" strode forward sternly, plucking the card of Frank Hearndon from his wallet and thrusting it under Banton's nose.

THE bank president's beefy face got redder still. "Hearndon!" he spluttered. "Hearndon, eh! What in thunder do you want? Why do you come in like this? I don't understand and—"

Agent "X" spoke a single swift sentence. "I want you to close this bank, Banton."

At his blunt words, Craig Banton gasped; then gaped, thunderstruck.

"Get every depositor out of here as fast as you can," the Secret Agent ordered. "Shut and lock the doors. Get the vault closed."

"You're mad!" Banton found his voice in a scornful exclamation. "Do you know what you're saying? I've received no orders—"

"Never mind orders!" the Agent snapped. "This bank must be closed—at once! Do you understand?"

Vivian de Graf gave a silvery, rippling laugh. "It's just too thrilling!" she drawled. "Like a motion picture!"

Watching Agent "X" amusedly, she opened her small handbag. Her slender fingers, conspicuously scarlet-tipped, reached for a cigarette. Stray sunlight from a high window danced and shimmered on a mirror on the inner edge of her bag as she snapped a small lighter into flame, touched it to her cigarette. She leaned back and blew smoke through her nostrils. Still smiling, she said:

"Go on with the show! I came here expecting to be bored with a lot of business details, but all this is vastly entertaining."

Craig Banton made a gesture of annoyance. He cleared his throat harshly. "This may be amusing to you, Mrs. De Graf," he said sourly, "but it hardly amuses me!" He stared at the Agent tense with irritation. "I say again you must be mad! What you ask is utterly impossible! Don't you realize that closing the bank would be taken by the depositors as a sign of weakness, that—"

Agent "X" struck the desk. His eyes snapping, he glared into Banton's face. "If you don't get every depositor out of your bank," he said slowly with, grim emphasis, "if you don't close up at once without further quibbling, you may regret it to the end of your days!"

Speechless, impressed in spite of himself with the Agent's words, Craig Banton stared uncertainly at the man who had come in like a human cyclone and made his astounding demand. He started to protest again. But the words died in his throat, and an expression of stark terror replaced the sneer on his face. Slowly, woodenly, he turned his head. And Vivian de Graf dropped her cigarette. The sunlight streaming through the window seemed suddenly to have grown dimmer.

Agent "X" felt a sudden, faint sense of giddiness. A humming sound buzzed in his head. Pinpoints of colored light danced abruptly before his eyes. Then they stopped—and he saw that dimness was filling the office as though twilight were swiftly falling.

Craig Banton spoke thickly, harshly, clutching the edge of his desk with shaking hands. "Good God! It—it's getting dark!"

Vivian de Graf, close beside "X", gave a small, stifled shriek. Her aplomb, her smiling amusement, had vanished. Agent "X" took one step toward the window and stopped. He could hardly see at all now. Uncanny, awe-inspiring darkness was descending like swift night, blotting out the sunlight, making the luxurious office of Craig Banton a sightless cavern.

And Agent "X" knew what it meant. He had come too late. The ruthless devils of darkness had arrived.

CHAPTER IV

BLACK HELL

A SMOTHERED EXCLAMATION burst from his lips. He had been prepared—but the stunning actuality of the thing was beyond all reason. The silhouette of the window had faded before his eyes. The last vestige of light had disappeared from the street outside. The glare of the sun, high overhead, shooting its bright beams straight down, had vanished as though a total eclipse had taken place.

Blood pounded in the Agent's temples. His throat felt constricted. He whipped a small flash from his pocket, clicked it on. He couldn't see it at all. He brought it to within an inch of his eyes. For an instant a faint, cherry-red glow was visible. Then that diminished, too—like a coal dying out. The terrible blackness was complete!

There was noise, mad confusion in the big bank. Girls screamed. Men were shouting. Agent "X" could hear the clatter of running feet. There would be another stampede, bringing horrible death in its wake, as when the first bank was robbed. He turned, groped his way toward the door of Banton's office, flung it open. At the top of his voice he shouted a warning:

"Quiet—everybody, quiet! Don't run—and you'll be safer!"

Some few heeded. There was a momentary lull. The Agent shouted again, hoping to avert the horror that panic would cause. But even in that he was too late. Glass snapped and crashed in one of the big doors, giving way before the thrust of wedged, frantic humans. Then came a louder crash. A scream, piercing in its intensity, sounded from Banton's own office.

"X" whirled, turned back and stumbled through the door. That scream had come from the lips of Vivian de Graf. The crash he could not identify at first. Then, as the odor of gasoline and hot oil reached his nostrils, he realized that some vehicle had crashed into the side of the bank, smashing the window of Banton's office.

Vivian de Graf screamed hysterically. Obviously she was unhurt, but the sound of the accident had unnerved her.

"Better stay where you are," said "X" harshly. "You'll be safer—all of you."

He couldn't see, any more than they could. For once the Man of a Thousand Faces was helpless. But his nerve had not been shaken. He felt no fear—only dread of the horror that might lash out at the innocent people caught beneath this curtain of dark.

The sounds from the main floor outside had risen into a frenzied uproar. Men and women, crazed by fear, were shrieking, stampeding. Aghast at the possibilities of death and destruction in that mad bedlam, "X" started toward the door again, to make another desperate attempt to recall the mob to sanity.

But on the threshold he froze, listening. The milling of frenzied feet had abruptly stopped. The cries that rent the air had taken on an added shrillness. They rose in a piercing crescendo of sheer terror. Coldness clutched the Agent's heart. For above the horrible confusion he detected another sound. The spiteful, vicious cracking of whips.

Like miniature gunfire the crackling of metal-tipped lashes echoed through the bank. In its wake came stark cries of pain, like those of wounded animals. The blackness, fearful enough in itself, had become a living, lurid hell.

In Banton's office there was no sound now beyond the echo of horror and the scrape of hoarse breathing. All stood frozen, listening to the blood-curdling drama being enacted outside.

Driven by pain and fear, a man in the depositor's corridor broke into a tirade of frenzied curses. The answer to that was a whip crack like a tongue of vicious lightning singling out a place to strike. The man's curses rose to maniacal pitch, then diminished beneath a salvo of crackling torture, to die away in a whimpering, long-drawn moan.

Little by little the snapping of the whips died away. Agent "X," in total darkness, could vision graphically what was taking place. He could see the depositors, their clothing torn, arms and faces lashed into bloody streaks of torment, cowering back, falling over each other to escape the metal-tipped whips. He pictured the raiders' slow, methodical advance, as they plied their lashes till the floor was clear.

But how could they see, when the darkness was more complete than any night? Agent "X" was as baffled as he was appalled by the course of a crime more astounding than any he had ever known.

THE whip cracking was hardly audible at all now. That meant that the crowd of scourged men and women were huddled like dumb beasts in pain-racked passivity. It meant that the raiders had achieved their purpose—cleared the way for robbery.

A moment passed. Then came the faint clank and clatter of metal boxes. Compartments in the great vault were being opened and dumped out. Then, as Agent "X" stood desperate and helpless in the impenetrable darkness, his ear detected footsteps approaching Banton's office. Ghostly and measured, they moved across the outer room. The girl at the reception desk gave one terrified cry. Her chair clattered as it overturned. The steps passed her, entered Banton's inner sanctum.

Agent "X" stood frozen like the others. Not with fear, but with sheer amazement at the thing. It was uncanny, beyond belief, that any eyes could penetrate this darkness which seemed almost to have a substance of its own. But a voice spoke to them—low, harshly evil.

"Keep your seats—all of you. You who are standing, sit down!"

Agent "X" did not move.

The voice challenged him harshly, proving beyond doubt that the newcomer could see. "Sit down!"

Agent "X" stepped back slowly, found an empty chair and sank into it. His eyeballs ached, as he strained his eyes toward the spot whence the voice came—the voice of a man whom he could not see but who, somehow, was able to see him. A harsh chuckle sounded.

"It is fortunate, Banton, that the vault was open. Otherwise we would have had to blow it up—which would have been inconvenient for us and troublesome for you. As it is, everything is going nicely. We shall soon be away from here."

The laugh was repeated. Then silence followed. Slowly the steps moved away. The faint noise of the raiders methodically at work filled the black hole of silence in the room.

A moment later Agent "X" lifted his head alertly. There had been an infinitesimal stir in the air. He had felt it—and his nostrils caught a faint whiff of perfume. The scent was exotic, cloyingly sweet. He crouched forward in his chair, every nerve taut. And in the silence he caught the sound of whispering. A very guarded whispering, as though two people were in secret conference, and anxious not to be overheard.

Who was it? Who in the room had moved?

Pulses racing, "X" slid cautiously from his chair. Though he could not see, his mind retained a photographic picture of the arrangement of the office. He knew where Banton's desk was, where Banton sat, and where Vivian de Graf had been.

His fingers reached oat, groped lightly. He took a few steps forward. Banton was sitting in his chair, rigid. Then the Agent stepped to the right—and grew tense, for the chair where Vivian de Graf had reclined languidly was empty!

Either she had left in fright, to huddle in some other part of the room. Or it had been she who—

The Agent was given no time for speculation. A curse, sounding in the darkness at his left, cut it short. "X" could not see anyone approach, but his acutely alert senses warned him that the man who had cursed was striding in his direction. Instinctively he raised his arms over his face.

As he did so there was a hiss and a snap—and the serpentlike end of a whip snarled about his arm. Its metal-tipped end, fanglike, bit into the flesh of his wrist. He wrenched his body sidewise and pulled his arm clear. The whip came back at him. It struck his neck this time, coiled about it like a loathsome snake. A scalding brand, the metal tip licked up at his cheek.

AGENT "X" did not cower away. Taunt as steel, eyes blazing in the dark, he reached out and grabbed the leather lash. He pulled it toward him and plunged straight at the unseen figure wielding it.

The man with the whip gave a startled, angry cry. Furiously he tried to wrench free. Again the whip was a snake, coiling frenziedly in the Agent's grasp to free itself, to strike at him again. But his hands moved tenaciously along its pliant length until they encountered human fingers.

His own hand closed over the whipman's arm. He swung savagely with his clenched left fist. But he could not see. The other could, and eluded the blow, struck back. "X" closed with his unseen adversary, driving home body blows, and they fell to the floor together in a fighting, clawing heap.

He was conscious again of a scream from Vivian de Graf. He felt the breathing of the man he fought. His opponent had dropped the whip now, was trying to break loose from the Agent's hold. But

"X's" hands, vicelike, did not yield.

This was no darkness he was fighting now. No whip that struck treacherously from behind a curtain his eyes could not penetrate. This was a living, vicious man—one of the raiding gang. And "X" fought with the bitter anger of one who remembered the pain-racked screams of those innocents outside. He fought with punishing blows, craft and science disregarded for the moment in the primitive joy of meting out justice to one who had caused the torment of others.

Then his right hand, lifting for an instant to clutch at the other's throat, tensed uncertainly. He had felt something—a mask or hood made of a substance that felt like pliant rubber. It covered the man's shoulders and head. And across his face were heavy goggles. In a flash Agent "X" had the answer, incomprehensible as yet, as to how the raiders saw their way about in the darkness. Somehow they had protected themselves against the night they created.

With fierce eagerness "X" sought to tear that hood from the man's head. He was sure that without the hood his opponent would be as helpless as he himself.

But the other apparently sensed his purpose, and began fighting like a living fury. Lifting a knee, he gave a savage, treacherous blow, twisted and turned on the carpet. Agent "X" thrust his knuckles against the man's heart in a jiu-jitsu blow, which, if he had not been handicapped by his cramped position, would have ended the fight then. As it was, it struck with only half strength, and his own movements weakened. Air whistled from between his teeth.

Then, through the thunder of his own pulses, "X" heard the clatter of feet on the tiled corridor outside. He strove desperately to deliver another blow. He must knock this man out, take off his hood before help came. If the hood enabled him to see, he might be able to do something. The labored breathing of his opponent told him that victory was almost within his grasp.

But at that moment a new voice snarled an oath, and before the Agent could leap away in answer to the warning of his senses, something struck him heavily beside his ear. Something that made lights dance before his eyes, and seemed to bring the black room crashing down about his head. He stiffened, gave a choked gasp, and collapsed senseless over the man he had almost mastered.

CHAPTER V

THE TORTURING LASH

A SWAYING VIBRATION accompanied the slow struggle of the Agent's senses back out of the black pit into which they had been plunged. The dark in his brain, coming on the heels of that other dark in Banton's office, had left a blank page in his memory. He was dazed, uncertain.

Then, without conscious effort, his will fought to regain its poise, aided by the balanced nerves of a perfectly coordinated body.

The swaying which seemed part of some hideous nightmare became gradually familiar. His ears picked up sounds that registered in his brain. He was in an auto, traveling swiftly. The swish he heard was the sound of tires. That rumble was the throaty voice of a heavy engine. He was in an auto, and these criminals who worked behind the black fog were taking him away, bound hand and foot.

"X" discovered then that he still was unable to see. But it was not the unearthly darkness this time—only a prosaic strip of adhesive taped across his eyes that shut out the light. He knew, of course, why he had been made a prisoner instead of being killed on the spot. Some one had found out that he had warned Banton of the raid. And his attack on the man with the whip, his refusal to be cowed by fear like the others, had frightened the raiders. They thought he must know something about their activities, and they wanted to find out exactly what.

Twisted and cramped on the car's floorboards, an old wound in the Agent's side, made long ago by bursting shrapnel in a field in France, gave him a twinge of pain. Eminent doctors had told him at the time that the wound must kill him. Yet he had gone on living, his magnificent vitality triumphant. The pain from that wound invariably acted as a spur to a steely grimness of intent. And, curiously enough, the cicatrix of the wound took the form of a crude

"X"—a living, pulsing symbol of the Secret Agent's indomitable spirit.

His fingers curled tensely, reached back and touched the ropes binding his wrists. Given time he could get those bonds off. But there was no time for that. The auto was slowing already. The rumble of the motor diminished and the vehicle turned lurchingly with a grate of shifting gears. It entered some sort of drive or alley, and stopped. Garage doors rumbled back, the car plunged forward a few feet, came to a standstill. The doors clanged shut.

Voices sounded, clipped and indistinct. A second of silence, then rough hands abruptly reached in and yanked the Agent out. He made no attempt at struggle. Feigning complete unconsciousness, he let his body sag.

Every sense was active, every nerve alert as they carried him into a building and down a flight of steps. A short, straight passage was traversed, a door was opened, and warmer air told him that they had entered an inside room. His captors dropped him to the floor as though he had been a sack of grain.

He lay inertly while other doors slammed and feet moved by. Then voices sounded behind an adjacent wall. He strained his ears, but even to his acute senses the words were unintelligible. If only he had his hands free, and could use some of the strange devices he carried. Pressing his elbows experimentally against his sides, he could tell that these things, worn in secret pockets inside the linings of his garments, were still intact.[3]

Swiftly, surely, his finger ends touched and tested the knots that bound him. But before he could loosen even one, a door opened close at hand. A heavy tread crossed the floor toward him. "X" lay still, not knowing who it was that stood above him. It might be some grim murderer commissioned to blot out his life with knife or bullet. But "X" was gambling on the premise that he wouldn't have been brought here unless his captors wanted him alive.

Not by a single quiver did he betray himself. He was as one plunged in an abyss of sleep. The man moved to the wall of the room, returned, and flung a bucketful of icy water into "X's" face.

---

3 AUTHOR'S NOTE: As readers who have followed the chronicles of Agent "X" will know, he carries many odd devices with the magic of applied science behind them. A sound amplifier no larger than the smallest pocket camera. Sets of tools which can probe the secrets of any lock. A hypodermic needle containing an anesthetizing drug, and hidden containers of various kinds of gas. These he changes from time to time, in his effort to be always prepared for any emergency.

The Agent did not stir.

An outthrust toe followed the water. It prodded, then delivered a brutal kick. Dizzying pain almost drove the breath from his body. But the groan that escaped his lips was calculated; the groan, apparently, of a man whose senses were still lost in a daze.

A voice above him sounded, barking a sharp order.

Shuffling footsteps responded, those of at least three men. They entered the room, walked to "X's" side. He was jerked roughly to his feet and flung into a chair.

"Wake up! Wake up!" He was shaken roughly.

This time the Agent didn't even groan. He let his head hang forward, lolled and slumped in the chair.

"Maybe he's finished," a cold voice said. "That bruise behind his ear—"

THE man who seemed to be in charge spoke again. The Agent recognized the voice as the one he had heard in Craig Barton's office.

"Don't be a fool. Untie his wrists. Work his arms and get him breathing. And look out for tricks. You, Fritz, shoot him in the leg if he tries anything. We don't care if he's crippled."

There was utter callousness in the tone. Yet neither this voice nor those of others, were the voices of underworld criminals. No slang was here, no thickness of accent. It was the smooth, precise speech of educated men.

The Agent's arms were freed and moved forcibly from side to side as though he were drowning. He could feel blood coursing through his veins, prickling in the stiffened flesh of his wrists. Keeping up his part, he groaned again. The working of his arms continued. Slowly he let his body stiffen, closed his mouth which had been hanging slackly open.

Something struck against his face with a ringing smack that nearly made him jump. *Crack, crack!* It was the leader, slapping him with flattened palm. Fury surged over the Agent, but he forced it back with iron will. The blows stung painfully, even through his flexible disguise.

He stiffened a little more, feigning the behavior of a man returning slowly to consciousness. The man who had slapped him laughed harshly. "Wait," he said, "here's something else. That ought to fix him."

Agent "X" doubled up his knuckles and delivered a famous jiu-jitsu blow.

A pain like a knife thrust curled the nerves of "X's" wrist, as a cigarette's lighted end was pressed into his flesh. But the Agent had schooled himself to stand pain. Spartan courage had saved him in more than one perilous situation. Torture had been his lot before. He opened his mouth, emitting a sudden hoarse cry, exactly as a man resuming consciousness might be expected to do. He lashed out wildly with one arm, mumbling incoherently.

He was instantly pinioned on either side. The grim voice of his torturer spoke in front of him.

"So—you're back with us again, Hearndon!"

Agent "X" let his mouth gape with mock surprise.

"Yes," the other sneered, "we found your card. We brought you with us just for a friendly little visit. We think we're going to find your conversation most entertaining."

Agent "X" stiffened, lifted his head toward the speaker. The adhesive tape still covered his eyes and no move was made to tear it off.

"You're going to talk, Hearndon," the other continued. "Talk is cheap, and won't cost you anything. But remember that silence comes dear! Now—what were you doing in the bank? Why did you give Banton a tip? And who sent you to meddle?"

The Agent kept silent a moment, marshaling his thoughts. There was some inconsistency here. They had found his car, addressed him as Hearndon—and yet wondered why he had warned Banton. Did they doubt his disguise as a Department of Justice man? He tried a quick rejoinder in his chosen role.

"You can't do this! You can't buck the government. We found the girl you murdered, Ellen Dowe. Not so smart—leaving her there! It wasn't hard to figure out why she'd been tortured. You birds are washed up now. You're in a tight spot!"

A harshly sneering laugh was his answer. Then the unseen questioner spoke again, gloating evil in his tone. "A good line, Hearndon! A nice bluff you're putting up! But drop it now! Talk straight. You're no D. J. man. You've been checked on that. You got away with it at the bank, but not with us. You're a fake. But I want to know who sent you, and what's behind it. Understand?"

A COLDNESS stole over Agent "X." These men were clever as well as ruthless—super clever, keeping track of the Department of Justice lists, guessing so soon that he was a fraud. Had they penetrated his disguise, too? But no, the speech of his questioner had shown they had not done that.

He growled a sullen curse, squared his shoulders, thrust out his jaw. Let them think, if they wanted to, that he was a hard-headed dick from some private agency, posing as a government man.

"All right, Hearndon," said the mocking voice. "You found the girl we murdered, you say. Ellen Dowe. But you aren't a dick. You didn't bring any cops to the bank with you. How was that?"

Agent "X" remained stubbornly silent. A note of icy anger crept into the other's voice. He thrust his head so close that "X" could feel the man's warm breath against his face.

"You'll talk, damn you! We'll have no snoopers getting in the way. You were at the bank. You heard those cattle screaming under our whips. You found Ellen Dowe—and know what happened to her. Well! Now you're going to talk."

The man paused abruptly in the midst of his furious shouting, and when he resumed his threatening of Agent "X" his voice was an insinuating purr, more deadly than the bellowing rage that had preceded it.

"You were a kid once, weren't you, Hearndon? Maybe your parents whipped you sometimes, too. But not the way we do it. Oh, no! Not with our kind of whips. No man can stay silent under the lashing we give them. Ellen Dowe couldn't. She told us all we wanted to know. We whipped the truth out of her. Unfortunately our man got over-enthusiastic. Maybe he liked the way she screamed! When I talked to her she was all through screaming. She couldn't even stand. I promised not to whip her any more if she talked—and she did. It wasn't our fault if she decided to talk—too late! So you see, it may be too late for you—if you don't talk now!"

Secret Agent "X" maintained his stubborn silence. He knew, too, that nothing he could say would appease them. Unless he told the truth. And that would mean death—the end of his campaign. They wouldn't let the Secret Agent go. Even by men like these he would be feared. And what men fear, they kill.

"All right—you asked for it! Let's see if you can stand as much as Ellen Dowe!"

Two men sprang forward and jerked "X" from his chair. His feet were still tightly bound. No move was made to untie them. They dragged him by the arms across the floor and spread-eagled him on a narrow cot. The two men pulled his arms in opposite directions, almost yanking the bones from their sockets. A cold something was pressed against his scalp by a man at the head of the cot.

"The same way we handled Ellen Dowe," the cold voice said mockingly. "Except for the gun. You ought to be flattered, Hearndon. I've given instructions to shoot you through the brain if the whipping makes you too violent. Now, boys—go to it! Let's see you tear his coat to pieces!"

The snaky head of the whip was like miniature lightning in the air. The metal tip struck with a vicious *crack*. Its nipping bite, directly between "X's" shoulders, proved that the whipman was an expert—as sure of his aim as those professional performers who can snap a cigarette from between human lips on the stage.

Crack! The whip landed again, and the cloth beneath it ripped. In a moment it would be gnawing at the Agent's quivering flesh. They could not make him talk—but slow, torturing death faced him on that cot.

CHAPTER VI

THE AGENT TRAPPED!

NEVER HAD AGENT "X" been closer to complete disaster. Never had the hand of Fate seemed so set against him as now. With his ankles tightly bound he would be helpless as a cripple, even if he could break away. Before he could hop ten paces, he would be shot.

The third blow of the whip sank through his coat and undershirt, breaking the flesh of his back over a bulging muscle. Clothing, skin and living tissue would be churned to a bloody, pain-racked froth if this continued. He did not doubt his ability to steel himself against the torment. But in this case, resistance would accomplish nothing.

As the fourth stroke fell, he let a groan burst from his lips. His body twisted, then sagged. "Stop—stop! Oh, God—I can't—"

His acting was superb, the whimpering complaint of a wretched, weak-willed man whose spirit had broken. Insensibly the two clutching his arms relaxed their hold. And in that instant the Agent's muscles, unmarred as yet by the scourging whip, contracted like released springs.

He flung his head sidewise. His right arm wrenched free, tumbling the man who held it off his feet. The arm swept outward, forward, clamped over the wrist of the man holding the gun. The Agent twisted, squeezed until bone grated on bone.

But as Agent "X" struggled to seize the gun, the guard's finger contracted, and a bullet passed screamingly close to "X's" chest. He wrenched his left arm free at the same instant, made a furious lunge, and tore the weapon from the other's fingers.

Swearing, cursing men flung themselves on top of "X" to pin him down, but he struck right and left with the gun muzzle, then gave a savage roll that took him clear of the cot.

Death hovered to the room. The odds were all against Agent

"X." He had the gun—but the tape was still across his eyes; the ropes bound his feet. Apparently his maneuver had been the reckless, futile stunt of a fear-crazed and desperate man. Actually it was based on calculation, logic and a carefully thought-out plan.

For with one swift sweep "X" tore the adhesive from his eyes. Then he held his breath, crouched tensely. The tape was gone—but its cruel pressure on his eyeballs over a period of time had made the retinas cast blurred and distorted images. He could see only that these men in the room with him were masked with some sort of black stuff that made them look now like ghoulish monsters. They were staring at him, coming toward him, and one seemed to be raising a gun.

The Agent fired a single shot quickly and heard a man cry out. He didn't often kill, but the memory of those crushed and mangled children in the zone of that first horrible robbery was still in his mind. The memory also of the lacerated body of the murdered Ellen Dowe. These men were fiends, human vultures, and what stayed his hand now was not mercy for their lives, but the knowledge that he could not shoot straight because of the state of his eyes—and a pressing need he had for at least one of the bullets in the gun. He snarled a fierce order.

"Back there—all of you! Against the wall!"

They did not know that he could barely see them. His one lucky shot had made its impression. Tensely the masked men moved backward toward the wall.

And, as they stood there, the Secret Agent suddenly did a strange thing. His gun left the masked figures. He bent like lightning, thrust its muzzle between his shoes, felt quickly with the fingers of his left hand, and then slammed a bullet through the ropes that held his ankle. The crashing lead, fired at close range, was quicker, more effective than any knife. Two ropes parted, and Agent "X" spread his feet and kicked the others off.

But his act, quick as it had been, had given his masked enemies a chance for a treacherous move. An arm flashed out, a finger jabbed forward, and there was a *click* in the room as every light went out. Some one had pressed a switch.

And the instant darkness fell the Agent heard stealthy movement. These men knew the room, he did not, and death was creeping upon him out of the dark. Instinct made him drop, fling himself sidewise, and as he did so pinpoints of flame stabbed the darkness, and a half dozen bullets crashed into the wall, close to where he had stood.

He raised the weapon in his own hands, fired twice and leaped away again. Another cry sounded. His aim at the points of fire had been true. But the next time he shot his gun clicked empty. He was unarmed in that room with killers creeping upon him.

HANDS stretched along the wall, the Agent felt for some possible means of escape. And suddenly the smooth knob of a door brushed against his fingers. The Agent yanked the door open, saw a glimmer of light. He didn't know, but perhaps this led to the passage to the street through which he had been carried. Then the next second he saw a narrow stairway.

But he had no choice now. He leaped toward the cavernlike mouth of the stairs, dropping to his knees as bullets whined about him. He flung the empty gun over his shoulder, heard it crash into the room, and ascending the stairs in long-legged strides, entered a dark hall. His flashlight, winked on for a moment, disclosed an old-fashioned hatrack, a pair of high front doors with curved Gothic tops. He turned the other way and saw draperies and barred windows beyond. Dusty, ancient furniture stood against the walls. The bandits had chosen an old house, obviously long closed and locked, for their hideout.

He knew there was no quick exit from this floor; knew also that his gas gun, strapped in a flat holster to his leg would not stop a crowd of armed men. As feet pounded up from below, "X" leaped to the stairs behind him, leading to the rooms above. He whipped out his gas gun, expecting to be challenged by more of the band upstairs.

But no challenge came. The rooms on the second floor were empty, their windows barred and shuttered. He knew this type of house. Sixty or seventy-five years old, it was a relic of the brownstone era. There should be an attic, with a wooden scuttle giving on the roof. He climbed quickly, leaped up a short, steep flight of stairs and found himself in the attic. Then he paused.

Sudden silence had descended on the house. No sound of footsteps was audible now. The whole place was as quiet as though the gang of torturers had vanished. "X" considered this unexpected development uneasily. Then, as he peered down over the railing of the stairs, he found a gruesome explanation. A faint draft of musty air came up. And it was tinged with something beside the odor of old walls and dusty furniture. Smoke, acridly pungent, drifted to his nostrils!

He leaned far over the deep stairwell and stared down. At the bottom, four stories below, there was a flickering gleam. Fire! As he watched, it fanned out, turning from red to orange, then to hot yellow flame. Mixed with the smoke funneling up was the scent of gasoline!

The Secret Agent's jaws clamped shut. He knew the first floor of the building would already be an impassable inferno. He could not go down. The attic had two rooms separated by a short hall. In this a wide-stepped ladder rose toward the roof. He climbed quickly, searched with tense fingers for the hooks in the wooden scuttle.

But he grew suddenly rigid, and felt a coldness at his heart. Not hooks, but huge padlocks held the scuttle down. Two of them, products of some locksmith of long ago, with thick rings stuck through strong hasps bolted to the beams.

It was an obstacle he hadn't anticipated. He carried tools—the gleaming chromium rods with slender ends and tiny pivotal extensions that had often been used to unravel the mysteries of modern locks. With these no door was barred to him. But these rusty, ancient padlocks—would he be able to open them in time?

CHAPTER VII

RED DEATH

THE SOUND OF the fire was mounting every instant into a fearful, smothered roar. The attic was insufferably hot. Sweat trickled down the Agent's neck and bathed his body.

The mechanism inside the old lock seemed rusted in a solid mass upon which his delicate tools made no impression. He tried another and another length of metal. He needed oil to free the rust-corroded pivots.

Desperately he thrust his hand into his pocket and brought out a small cigarette lighter. It was of silver, with pebbled leather sides, and had been a present from Betty Dale—the only girl in the world who knew the nature of his dangerous work. With feverish concentration, making every motion of his deft fingers count, "X" drew the woolen wick from the lighter, squeezed drops of the fluid into the old lock. Before taking up his tools again, he treated the second lock in the same way.

Then he adjusted his rod with pivotal extensions, one of his most ingenious chromium pieces. In response to its probing, he felt something give inside the old lock. One piece of metal moved, another.

Somewhere below, a falling balustrade blasted up heat and sparks. Clouds of soot swirled about "X's" head. The air was scorching. His eyes smarted painfully as he worked.

Slowly the rusted lock worked free. Pivots that had not moved for years creaked protestingly as he got the hang of the pins and slots inside. He found a spot that gave, pressed at an angle—and the curved hasp of the padlock opened.

He drew it out of the staple, dropped it to the floor, and began on the second lock. This should be easier, now that he knew its secret.

But his race with death was getting close. A tongue of flame licked up the attic stairs. Far below in the fiery maw of the old building there was a thundering, like the rumble of an earthquake. The ladder squeaked under his feet as the floor beneath it slanted. In another few seconds he would drop into that inferno of raging flames.

Hardly able to see because of the smoke pouring into the room, "X" opened the second lock. He flung it from him like some poisonous thing, climbed a step higher and heaved up on the scuttle above. Paint broke loose, the scuttle rose, seemed to lift out of his hands as heat exploded it outward. The fire below gave a deep-throated, warning roar. Imprisoned heat shot skyward. Sparks and burning embers whirled past Agent "X" as he sprang onto the roof.

He could feel the tar covered roofing sag under him where supports had given way. It was blistering hot, the tar boiling up in black, sticky, smoking masses.

He leaped to the top of an adjacent house. As he did so the roof over which he had come sagged crazily, one corner fell in with a rumbling crash, and flames volcanoed upward.

The Agent was safe, safe from the death his captors had planned. For he sensed their double motive in firing the house. They wanted to destroy all clues; and they wanted his life as well.

He ran across two adjoining rooftops, found a fire escape snaking down an empty building, and made his way along it to a back yard. The street was cluttered with the hurtling red forms of fire engines. The air was lurid with the wail of sirens and the shrill clang of bells.

But Agent "X" did not linger. He knew the bandits might have a watcher posted. And he wanted them to believe he had been consumed in the flames as they had planned. Let them think Hearndon was gone forever.

In a taxi, he hurried to one of his hideouts. Here he changed his disguise to that of Martin, replaced his sooty clothing with a fresh gray suit, and went directly to the raided bank.

Traffic was moving through the streets again, but there was a police line around the bank itself. Throngs surged about it, jostled and kept back by police. The Agent's eyes darted on all sides. He saw many excited newspaper men, men from the newsreel syndicates and press photographers, then his gaze wandered to a building opposite the bank.

THERE were small shops along the street floor of this, apartments above. Behind a "vacant" sign in one of the apartment windows Agent "X" glimpsed a familiar face. Instantly he crossed the street and entered the building. Tenants stood in the open door. He brushed by them unnoticed, climbed the stairs.

In an empty third-floor front apartment Jim Hobart was waiting, his movie camera with him. He had used a set of skeleton keys with which "X" had long ago provided him, and had come here before the falling of the fearful dark. But he shook his head when he saw the man he knew as Martin. His face was pale, his voice husky.

"I did what you said, boss—cranked away. But it got dark, so dark I couldn't see my own hand. And I'm afraid—"

"Let's have the films." There was tense excitement in the Agent's tone. He took the metal drum of celluloid that Jim Hobart handed him, thrust it under his coat, said: "Take care of the camera, Jim," and was off.

He slipped through the excited crowd around the bank, went to his coupé again. In fifteen minutes he was closeted in a dark room in one of his hideouts. There was elaborate equipment before him. Reels for winding movie film. Trays of chemicals, developer, fixative. The precious drum that Hobart had given him was being slowly unwound, run through its acid baths, for "X" in this small compact chamber could turn out work as finished as that of the laboratories of any movie studio.

For nearly three hours he worked. Then he took, from the reel of a special dryer, a printed, transposed celluloid of the film Hobart had made. He went to a larger room outside the dark chamber, removed a small movie projector from a box and put the film in it. A six-foot screen was on the opposite wall. With tense fingers, knowing already that Hobart's film, taken in utter darkness had picture impressions on it, he focused his projector on the screen and switched on the electric motor that turned it.

Then the Agent leaned forward in enthralled interest. For Hobart had begun to crank his camera just as the darkness had started to descend. And there on the silver screen before "X's" fascinated eyes, tiny, weirdly helmeted figures were visible. He stopped the projector once to look at a shot which plainly showed a helmeted head.

Mad crowds of terrified people showed in the street. "X" saw the black car that the raiders came in, saw something else that made his eyes widen. This was a small electric truck that looked like one from the city's lighting company, and which had parked along the curb not far from the bank. The tiny line of a black cable led from the truck's end to an open manhole. Then, as the amazing scenes of the raid unwound on the screen, "X" saw the bandits' black car drive off, after small helmeted figures had carried sacks of loot to it.

More interesting still, he saw the figures of two men in workman's clothes descend unhurriedly into the manhole; remove the black cable and coil it into the truck. While the whole block was held in icy terror, while a sinister raid was in progress, these men, tapping the city's electric current, could work calmly. There was only one explanation of that. They were part of the raiding gang, and that light truck housed the strange mechanism which had made the darkness.

But what of the darkness itself? Here on the screen was proof of Thaddeus Penny's amazing statement, proof that the sun had been shining, did shine, while that darkness fell. The movie camera's lens had not been hampered by it. The sensitive film, impressionable to light, had functioned normally. Only human eyes had been affected, blinded. Only they could not see. And Agent "X" had uncovered a riddle that seemed too deep to explain.

CHAPTER VIII

THE HOUSE OF MENACE

HOURS LATER, AGENT "X" was moving stealthily across the velvet smoothness of a wide lawn. Ahead of him loomed an ornate, old-fashioned mansion set amid thick clumps of shrubbery and tall, leafless trees. Behind him was the high brick wall which he had scaled a moment before.

It was night, starless and black. He was on the property of Roswell Sully, famous utilities man and admirer of Vivian de Graf. For over an hour he had followed her, and she had finally led him here.

There was grim purpose in the Agent's eyes. Even this clever, provocative woman could not escape justice if she were in league with the criminals. Innocent Ellen Dowe had met an unthinkable fate. Pain had stolen her young life away by inches as she lay helpless and writhing under the sadistic lash of a human fiend. Her death and the deaths of those children must be avenged.

Agent "X," in his daring battles against crime, had met other women, as beautiful as Vivian de Graf, whose charm had been only a cloak for untold evil; women who used their wit and beauty as bait to gain some unholy end. Vivian might be such a woman. He didn't know, but he was going to find out. And besides his own direct suspicion, based on the episode in the bank, there were certain facts against her.

She was the wife of brilliant Emil de Graf, professor of science at the university. But she preferred the company of other men. For years Roswell Sully had danced attendance upon her. Unescorted by her husband, she had often been a guest at the unwholesomely gay parties for which Sully was notorious. Her wit and beauty had made her a sought-after favorite with the set of careless ne'er-do-wells who were Sully's intimates.

Then, with the stock crash of '29, Sully's utilities empire had collapsed in chaos, dragging thousands of investors down with it. And Vivian de Graf had aided the former wizard of high finance in the secluded life forced upon him by the debacle. She had acted for him as go-between in financial matters—and "X" knew for a fact that she received handsome commissions on every deal he managed to put through with her help.

Possibly some business of Sully's explained her presence at the Guardian Bank at the moment when it was raided. Possibly Sully was responsible for the presence of Norman Coe, too. For Coe had helped expose Sully after the big crash, and had worked tirelessly to have him prosecuted for the ruin he had caused. These things the Agent knew. But the woman herself was still an enigma—an exotic, mysterious personality.

The car she had come in, a luxurious phaeton, was parked outside the gates. Sully would allow no vehicle within his grounds. The old carriage entrance was kept closed and locked. Rain or shine, visitors were forced to walk up the long drive. Coal and provisions came the same way. Frequent harsh threats made against Roswell Sully by the investors he had mulcted had made him wary. His past haunted him always like a grim specter, even though he had salvaged enough for himself to live on in luxury. He had been called the most hated man in America.

Agent "X" climbed the wall and dropped silently into the forbidden grounds. With the bleak winter wind stirring the branches of the trees overhead, he crept forward. His senses were alert. It was rumored that Sully kept guards.

"X" was disguised as a young, nattily dressed man; not Martin, but another personality for which he had chosen the cognomen of "Sid Granville." Under one arm he carried a newspaperman's camera with focal plane shutter and high-speed lens. If caught, he was prepared to play his bluff to the limit. Vivian de Graf must not be made suspicious—and she would only be amused at the predicament of a young reporter, eager for a scoop. He would admit that he had followed her in the hope of getting a good news story, and a flashlight picture for his sheet. The news value of her presence at the raided bank would be his excuse.

But suddenly the Agent paused and listened. He had heard an ominous sound in the darkness ahead—a dog's soft growl. He tensed, standing close to the fragrant blackness of an ornamental spruce.

ACROSS the lawn an electric lantern flashed, and sent its sharp white beam straight toward "X" as its bearer came forward through the trees. The Agent darted to the left, moving with swift strides. He watched with relief as the light continued in the direction of the wall. But an instant later he heard a rustle in the dry grass behind him, and whirled to see phosphorescent eyes gleaming.

He crouched and waited as the dogs came toward him. There were at least four. They did not bark again. Trained watchdogs, they had been taught not to yelp at everything they saw. They would ring their quarry first, then give warning.

He heard the pad of feet, then saw their silhouettes against a street light shining over the wall. They were huge police dogs, ears alertly pricked, hackles stiff. Soon they would give tongue, or attack with flashing fangs.

But the Agent didn't even feel for the only weapon he carried—his gas gun. Instead, he sent a low whistle into the night. It was the strange, weirdly melodious whistle of Secret Agent "X," as eerie as the note of some wild thing.

The dogs stood still as though frozen. Then they approached him slowly, and he spoke to them with low, soothing words, holding out his hand. For a tense moment they held back, fangs bared and legs stiff. Then with a low whine the leader went forward. Agent "X" stroked the animal's muzzle and at that sign of friendship, the others came close, too. The watchdogs set to guard Sully had become "X's" friends.[4]

An ironic smile twitched the Agent's lips as he moved on toward the house. He was approaching with an escort, now. He could hear the man by the wall whistling, baffled by the disappearance of his dogs. But the great beasts preferred the company of their new-found friend to that of their master.

"X" SENT them away with a low-whispered command when he came close to the mansion. He could risk no sound from them, to interfere with the daring entrée he had planned.

As he stepped near the house, his fingers felt for the ingenious chromium tools and master keys hidden cunningly in secret pock-

---

4 AUTHOR'S NOTE: *Often before, the Secret Agent's strange, almost hypnotic, power over animals has been noted. Psychology plays some part in this. Animals respect those who show no fear; and "X," with the Grim Reaper ever at his elbow, is fearless of animals as well as human beasts.*

ets of his suit. Choosing an unlighted sun-porch at the building's side, he had the door open in less than a minute and was tiptoeing across the porch in his rubber-soled shoes.

Before entering the door into the house itself, he drew a case strapped close against his thigh an instrument no larger than the smallest vest pocket camera. It looked so much like a camera that it would deceive anyone. But when he opened it, no lens or bellows showed. There was a small rubber disc and a coil of flexible cable inside instead.

Courtney

He pressed the disc to the outside of the door, put the body of the instrument to his ear, and fingered what appeared to be a film wind. This was a delicate rheostat control. There was no film inside the thing, but small round batteries which seemed to correspond. In the Agent's hand was the most compact and powerful sound amplifier in existence, a mechanism which he had worked out himself.

Carefully adjusting the rheostat control, he listened to various noises far in the interior of the big house. Somewhere footsteps sounded, but they were several rooms away. Voices came to him—but the thicknesses of intervening walls made the words too indistinct even for the instrument in his hands to clarify.

Convinced that no one was behind the door, he opened it quickly, entered, and found himself in a large music room. A grand piano stood against one wall. The Agent tiptoed toward it, blinked on his small light. Faint dust on the keys showed that the piano had not been used for months. This room, eloquent of the big parties Sully had indulged in in bygone days, was empty now. He had made a wise choice in entering it.

The Agent crossed it swiftly. Beyond, through heavy portieres, he came to a small reception room with a thick, soft carpet underfoot. There was a door at the end of this and a faint spot of light gleamed through the keyhole. Another door led to a wide hall, where he saw the faint glow of a shaded light. He moved toward this, then stopped abruptly. A board somewhere under the heavy carpet had squeaked under his stealthy tread.

The sound was faint, mouse-like, yet a shadow moved instantly in the hall. Agent "X" could see huge shoulders and a giant head thrown in black silhouette on the opposite wall. The shadow moved, changed size as the man behind it approached slowly.

Sucking breath between his teeth, the Agent backed into the shadows of the reception room. He crouched behind a chair and waited.

The shadow moved to the door, and the man was revealed in the subdued light behind him. Big, heavy-set, he had the flattened features of an ape. His head was bent forward on a thick, bull neck. Something in his fingers gleamed dully. An automatic—proving that this was one of Roswell Sully's paid guards. The financier had taken a tip from the racketeers he resembled, had hired paid gunmen to protect him.

Agent "X" drew his gas gun from his pocket, but hesitated. He dared not use it now. The faint chemical smell of the gas might drift through the house and attract attention. It might arouse the suspicion of whoever was in the room behind the lighted keyhole. No, he could not use the gas gun, though it was his only weapon. As he waited, "X" heard voices raised in the room beyond. It made him tingle with excitement. He felt a stab of annoyance at this interruption.

The apelike gunman came through the door and moved stealthily toward a wall switch, obviously intending to flood the room with light. And that would not do! As the man's fingers reached for the switch, "X" sprang.

He made two coordinated movements. He wrenched the gun from the giant's hand and at the same moment clapped a palm over the mouth that parted to let out a bellow of surprise. Then, before the disarmed guard could begin a hand-to-hand struggle which might result in noise and the upset of all his carefully laid plans, Agent "X" doubled up his knuckles and delivered a famous jiu-jitsu blow—the deft thrust directly under the heart, as taught by Tatsuo Shima, instructor to the bodyguards of His Imperial Highness Hirohito in Tokyo. A man could be killed by that blow, or merely knocked insensible, and Agent "X" was a master of the lighter, stunning thrust.

The big guard went as limp as though a bullet had crashed into his brain, and "X" lowered his unconscious body to the carpet.

No noise had disturbed the quiet of the room, and the way was clear. Agent "X" tiptoed on toward that door from behind which came the sound of voices, one of which was harshly raised.

CHAPTER IX

WOMAN OF MYSTERY

THE LOUD VOICE was a man's, the other a woman's, and in the latter the Agent recognized the drawling, cultured accents of Vivian de Graf.

He tiptoed closer, found the door into the room slightly ajar, and cautiously widened the opening, bringing into his line of vision the couple at the far end of the room.

Vivian de Graf, sumptuously clad in furs, was seated in a deep, brocaded chair, her slim legs crossed, gloved hands toying with a jade cigarette holder. She looked utterly bored.

Roswell Sully stood before her. His face, with its clipped and bristling mustache, was red beneath its thatch of white hair. Anger showed in every line of his dapper figure. A big diamond on one well-manicured hand flashed as he gesticulated.

"Vivian—I can't stand it!" he was saying thickly. "All afternoon I've been waiting, counting the minutes, expecting that you would keep your promise to stay and dine with me. Now you say you can give me only half an hour. Really, I—"

Vivian shrugged, sniffing delicately at the spotted orchid pinned to her coat. She spoke languidly: "Do you expect me to dance attendance on you all the time, Roswell?"

"All the time!" Sully's voice rose jaggedly. "All the time—when you've only let me see you twice this week. To discuss business matters!"

Vivian de Graf fumbled in her bag, shrugged again. "A cigarette please, Roswell. I seem to have run out."

Sully ignored her request. "You forget," he went on furiously, "all I've done for you. The money you've made through me, the prestige my name has given you—the people you've met! What would you be without me? Nothing! And yet you—"

A sigh fell from Vivian de Graf's lips. Without replying, she rose languorously and crossed with swaying hips to a table where she helped herself to a cigarette from a red lacquer box.

Emil de Graf

Sully stared at her insolently turned back. "By God, Vivian," he began passionately, "if you're playing around with some other man—If you leave me after all I've done for you, I'll—I'll—"

She turned slowly, touching a match to her cigarette. Her tapering fingers were steady. Her soft laughter was faintly derisive as she let smoke trickle from her nostrils.

"What?" The drawled word was a challenge. "What will you do, Roswell?"

"Kill you!" Sully shrieked. "Kill you—even if I go to the chair for it. Kill you—and tell the world what you are. A damn, calculating gold-digger!"

Vivian de Graf leaned against the table, and laughed in his face. "Kill me! You? Why—you haven't that much nerve left! You're afraid—afraid to leave this house. Even to show your face in the streets."

Sully stepped close to her, his fingers raised and tensed as though he would clench them about the woman's white throat; but his hands were shaking like withered leaves in a wind.

Vivian de Graf laughed again, but the amusement had left her voice. "Don't be a fool! And don't touch me! It's you who are in debt to me. I'm a young woman and people say I'm beautiful. What have you to give me? You're getting old, Roswell—old—old! If you must know, you bore me, and—I have other friends."

Her words seemed to stun Sully. He stood swaying on his feet, staring at her. His clenched hands fell laxly at his sides.

Vivian de Graf ground out her cigarette, gathered her furs about her.

"Well, shall we say good-by?" She moved toward the door.

At that, a change came over Sully's face. The red flush of anger faded, leaving it dead white. "Vivian—Vivian, for God's sake don't leave me like this! Forgive me for speaking as I did. I'm just an old fool. But I'm insane about you—" With frightened, abject remorse,

Roswell Sully dropped suddenly to his knees, caught the hem of her dress, and kissed it.

Vivian twitched sharply away. "Don't be dramatic, Sully," she said scornfully. "It makes you ridiculous. And besides, it's so—tiresome." She walked away toward the door.

"X" QUICKLY left his observation post and slipped out of the house as he had entered it. He heard Sully's voice still pleading as the front door opened. But Vivian de Graf went out and down the drive; her head arrogantly high.

"X" crossed the lawn to the wall, scaled it as he had before, and crouched in the shadows. Apparently, Vivian de Graf had a key to the gate, for it opened and closed silently, and she appeared in the street. There was the click of high heels as she walked toward her car.

Agent "X" edged nearer, silent as a shadow. He was debating whether to speak to the woman now, or follow her, when he drew in a sudden sharp breath. For some one else was watching Vivian de Graf.

Across the street another shadow had detached itself from the hedge bordering an estate opposite Sully's. It moved cautiously along the walk, then started across the street toward the car. There was a furtive tenseness in the man's movements. And something glittered in his hand.

Just as Vivian opened the door of her car, and was bending to climb in, the man sprang toward her. She turned her head and a startled, terrified cry came from her lips. She crouched as though she were facing a wild beast. The man's arm drew back.

Agent "X" leaped forward out of the shadows like a hurtling catapult. His clenched fist struck at the thing gleaming in the man's raised hand, sent it shattering to the street.

Vivian de Graf swayed against "X," and while he steadied her the man ducked around the car like a startled rat and fled. The woman straightened then, and "X" sprang in pursuit of her attacker. The man had disappeared through the hedge across the street. When "X" pushed through, his quarry had lost himself in the dark maze of trees covering a wide lawn. The Agent knew there would be no use in further pursuit.

He went back to Vivian de Graf. Something had splashed onto his wrist from the thing in the man's hand, and it burned like a spark of fire. He reached down to rub it off on a strip of grass by the curb, and his nostrils tingled with an acrid smell that rose from the sidewalk.

Vivian de Graf had regained her poise. Her dark eyes met his calmly. "Who are you?"

The Agent tapped his camera, smiled. "Just a newshound who happened to be passing. And it's lucky I was!"

The woman poked with her toe at a jumble of broken glass on the sidewalk.

"What is that?"

"That," said "X" gravely, "is acid. Somebody wanted to mar your beauty, I'm afraid."

"Well—" her voice was cool, "you saved me from a nasty situation, anyway, and I want to thank you."

"Aren't you going to report this to the police? Do you know who that man was?"

Vivian de Graf's laugh was mirthless and harsh. "An old—friend, I think. Drunk, probably."

"Or just playful," the Agent said sarcastically. She glanced at him sharply. His smile was disarming. He seemed to be merely a guileless young newspaperman. But the woman's next words were tinged with suspicion.

"It occurs to me that it was rather odd—your being here just at the right moment."

"X" THOUGHT quickly. This woman was shrewd. A display of frankness would be safest for him. He smiled again, showing even white teeth.

"Not as odd as you think, Mrs. de Graf, since I've been trailing you all afternoon."

Dark eyes and arched brows questioned him.

"It's that robbery at the bank," he said. "You were there. I want your story of the thing—and a picture. It'll get me in solid with the old man. How about it?"

His eyes bored into hers, trying to discover whether or not he had convinced her. But her eyes were inscrutable as she smiled and gestured toward her car.

"One good turn deserves another, I suppose," she said lightly. "But we can't stand here in the cold and talk. Hop in."

There was a thin smile on the Agent's lips as the phaeton purred downtown. Nothing could have pleased him more than this. He was alone with his suspect, in a position to study her closely. Already he had proof that she was a woman of startling poise and stamina. A woman cool-headed and callous enough to cast in her lot with criminals.

"Don't forget," he said eagerly, "that I want your picture. Society beauty tells story of bank holdup. That's feature stuff. The crime has got the whole police force gaga. It's a mystery, it doesn't make sense—so it's hot news."

"But you, a bright young reporter, will solve the mystery of course."

Her smile challenged him, mockery gleamed in her eyes. He was careful to stick to his role.

"I wouldn't say that, Mrs. de Graf. It's got me stumped, I'll admit. But I'm going to take a whack at it." He paused a moment. "You were there," he added. "Haven't you got some theory?"

She nodded. "Personally, I suspect that man Hearndon, who came into Banton's office just before the raid."

"I don't know," said the Agent. "The cops are looking for Hearndon—and Washington says there isn't any such name on the Department of Justice list. He was a phony, all right, and yet—"

Grim amusement twitched the Agent's lips in the semidarkness. What would Vivian de Graf do if she knew that "Hearndon" was sitting close beside her?

"There's absolutely no doubt," she said positively, "that Hearndon, whatever he was, acted as an advance scout for the gang. His coming was the signal for the raid to begin. That's what I told the police when they questioned me."

"But Hearndon wanted the bank closed! How would that have helped the crooks?"

The woman laughed softly. "Hearndon knew there wasn't time to close the bank. That was only a stall. There are clever men behind this thing!"

THE phaeton sped across the city and entered a mews. It was close to the edge of a park, in an ultra-smart residential section liked by those who leaned toward the Bohemian. Wealthy actresses, painters and musicians had studios here.

Vivian de Graf stopped her car before a two-story building of pink stucco. It comprised two apartments, each with its private entrance. She had chosen a setting typical of a woman whose private life would not stand close inspection. An ideal residence, too, "X" thought, for a person who wished freedom to come and go unnoticed at any hour of the day or night.

With her own key, Vivian de Graf opened the door and showed "X" into a large, exotically furnished drawing room. Two blue vases filled with spotted yellow orchids caught the Agent's quick eye instantly, one on top of a piano, another on an antique table. They added the final touch of the bizarre to this exotic and very expensively furnished room.

"You'll have something to drink," Vivian de Graf murmured as she slipped the soft mink cloak from her shoulders. "Some sherry, perhaps?" Her slim hand reached for a cut-glass decanter.

The Agent nodded. "Thanks."

His eyes were alert. Something in the room seemed to hint at the crouching shadow of evil. The still draperies were too luxurious, the furnishings too expensive, this woman a bit too poised and casual. And those dozens of spotted orchids, which must be worth a small fortune, seemed the symbols of an unwholesome mystery.

He drew the nearest vase toward him and examined the heavy blossoms, with the eye of a connoisseur. He had never seen blooms like these before. He was familiar with most of the thousands of orchid species scattered throughout the world. He had thought all those in cultivation were known to him.

But these eluded classification. They reminded him of the Queen Cattleya orchids, yet were larger, deeper in their saffron tint. They bore some resemblance to *Cyripedium Argus*.[5]

His eyes switched abruptly from the flowers to Vivian de Graf's white hands. Almost unconsciously he had detected a minute but incongruous movement she had made. In pouring his glass of sherry she had let something fall into the wine—a few drops of colorless liquid from a ring. She had put either dope or poison into his drink!

---

5 AUTHOR'S NOTE: *Botany and toxicology are closely allied, and Secret Agent "X" had delved into both in his criminological studies. The poisons that come from plants—belladona, aconite, stramonium, nux vomica, and a hundred others—are familiar to him, since they have been used often as instruments of death by cunning murderers. His knowledge of the orchid family was an indirect result of these botanical studies.*

CHAPTER X

COUNTERPLAY

NO SLIGHTEST TREMOR of uneasiness showed in the Secret Agent's manner. He was, in fact, elated at this development. Here was final proof that Vivian de Graf was a dangerous, unscrupulous woman. Her act was to him a tacit admission of her guilt. And in it he saw a great opportunity to make her betray herself further.

Doctored liquor was an old story to Secret Agent "X." Once, long ago, in an espionage assignment against one of Europe's most famous spies, such a trick had caught him unawares. Ever after that experience he had been on the lookout for a possible repetition of it, and had taken simple but adroit precautions to checkmate it without rousing suspicion.

Vivian de Graf was watching him through drooping lids. Her eyes were brightly alert behind them. Her white teeth showed in a flashing smile. Her graceful, supple figure was relaxed in her chair.

Before drinking his wine, "X" offered her a cigarette which she accepted. He struck a flame on the lighter Betty Dale had given him and which had served him so well in the burning house, touched it to Vivian de Graf's cigarette and to his own, then returned the lighter to his pocket.

When his hand came out-again, something came with it—a small syringe of pliant rubber, like an old-fashioned camera bulb. To it was attached a tiny curved tube. "X" held the syringe cupped in his right palm, the third and fourth fingers pressed against it, while his second finger hid the tube.

Lifting the sherry glass in thumb and forefinger, he raised it to his lips. Then, as he tipped it slightly as though sipping, he let the tube's end drop into it, releasing his two fingers on the syringe. The bulb at once began to fill. As the Agent tipped his head and the glass back farther, the sherry disappeared directly before Vivian de Graf's eyes.

No one, save a person well versed in stage magic and sleight-of-hand, could have conceived that the wine had gone anywhere except into the Agent's mouth. "X" had, in fact, learned the trick from a famous vaudeville magician.

He set the glass down, let his right hand fall to his side under the table, thrust the syringe back into his pocket and gave a twist to the tube which sealed it.

Vivian de Graf was smiling. "Now," she said, "what about that picture you wanted—or were there some other questions you'd like to ask to round out your story?"

"Let's see." The Agent took out notebook and pencil. He made several notations, seeming absorbed in his work. He was conscious that Vivian de Graf was observing him, conscious of a new watchfulness in the woman's eyes. There was a catlike quality in it that was definitely sinister.

This was a tense moment for the Agent. Perhaps some devilish, quick-acting poison had been dropped into his glass. Perhaps it had been only a drug. He did not know. He could only stage an act, and hope it would be convincing.

At the end of a few seconds he looked up from his notes, passed a slow hand across his forehead and blinked confusedly. "If you don't mind repeating a few things," he said. "I seem to have forgotten. Don't know what's the matter with my memory. This man Hearndon—"

He let his speech trail off, laughed as though in embarrassment. "Here—let's see." He made a few ineffectual dabs at his pad. He appeared to study them, but his head sank lower and lower. "Hearndon," he muttered, "Hearn—"

His body swayed in the chair. He made a feeble, sleepy clutch at the edge of the table, slumping sidewise to the carpet. He lifted himself once feebly, then fell back and lay inert, every muscle lax.

His eyes were closed, his body limp, but his pulses were hammering. There was a chance he hadn't manifested quite the right symptoms, that the woman's suspicions had been aroused. Her silence made a breath-taking moment of suspense. She made no sound, said nothing for several seconds.

Then she rose and bent over him. Self-control was difficult for the Agent at that moment, the temptation to open his eyes at least a slit, almost overpowering. For all he knew, Vivian de Graf might be planning to jab a knife into him. But a moment later she moved away across the carpeted floor.

SHE picked up a telephone and dialed a number. Agent "X" listened intently. His ruse had worked. Vivian de Graf thought him unconscious or dead, and her next move should betray her further.

Her voice came to him. "Lorenzo—this is Vivian. Please drop over, at once! There's something that may be rather important."

Lorenzo! The Agent's heart beat fast. Through his act of appearing to swallow the drug it seemed he was about to meet some one else closely connected with the criminal gang. Vivian de Graf's whole manner during the last hour had served to convince him that his first suspicion of her had been right.

He lay quietly, apparently in the depths of dreamless unconsciousness, when the woman returned to her seat. She hummed a few bars of a popular song with astounding casualness. She had jilted a wealthy lover of years' standing, she had had acid thrown in her face, she had given another man drugged wine—yet she could sing! Here was a woman of the temperament and caliber of the Borgias.

She went into an adjoining room, leaving the door open. "X" could hear the soft rustle of feminine garments. Then she returned, settled herself in a chair and idly flipped the pages of a magazine. Shortly afterward a buzzer sounded, two short notes, a long, and another short.

Vivian de Graf crossed quickly to the door, opened it and said: "Come in, Lorenzo."

Agent "X" heard a man's tread. He slitted one eye and stared toward the door in time to see a man enter. He was about thirty, smooth-shaven, suave, with sleek black hair. But his features bore the lines and blotches of dissipation, making him look older.

He started at sight of "X's" body, then gave a lop-sided smile. The door closed and Vivian de Graf said casually, "Just a friend who dropped in, Lorenzo. He's had one drink too many. You see the result."

"Up to your old tricks, Vivian," said the man called Lorenzo. "Just what does it mean?"

"Never mind now!" There was a note of authority in Vivian's voice, as though she were accustomed to getting her way with men. "Take him out of here at once—and when he has recovered, it might be well to question him. He was very helpful, tonight—

overly solicitous of my welfare. And when people get that way I'm always—well, suspicious!"

The young man with the gleaming black hair laughed again. "Aren't you going to offer me a drink, too, Vivian?" His tone was caressing.

"This is not a social visit," the woman answered icily. "Quick—get him out of here. Some one might come!"

LORENZO approached "X," placed hands upon his shoulders and began shaking roughly. This gave the Agent his cue. He was not supposed to be poisoned, only drugged—and evidently, with some drug from which he could be aroused.

He sighed, stirred faintly, letting his head flop as Lorenzo shook him, manifesting the sluggishness of a man in a chloral hydrate coma. Lorenzo lifted him to his feet, and Agent "X" shuffled feebly, moving like a sleep-walker.

Vivian flung the door wide and Lorenzo marched his charge out to a waiting car. Agent "X" stumbled, almost fell, letting one knee strike realistically against the car's door. Lorenzo bundled him in, slammed the door after him, and went round to the driver's seat.

Gears clicked, the car purred away, with Lorenzo driving carelessly and Agent "X" slumped in the seat, breathing heavily. But his eyes were open now. If Lorenzo had turned to scrutinize him in the darkness he would have beheld not a stupefied man, but one whose gaze was brightly, speculatively alert.

The car turned out of an avenue, into a street where the lights were far apart and shadows lay heavily. "X's" right hand began creeping toward a secret pocket in his suit. He was reaching for the compact gas gun that could knock a man out within a radius of twenty feet—one of the Agent's most useful, non-lethal weapons.

But just then a car came out of a side street, and as it passed the interior of Lorenzo's car was brightly illuminated. In that instant the man detected the change in "X's" attitude. He gave a stifled exclamation, applied the brakes, and whirled toward "X." One hand clamped over "X's" arm, the other doubled into a fist to drive a blow into the Agent's face.

Rubber squealed beneath the car. The vehicle lurched dangerously, threatened to plunge across the sidewalk into a fence. Even at that moment Agent "X" had presence of mind enough to twist the wheel, while he warded off Lorenzo's blow with a deft twist of his head and a countering left. The car came to a stop, slewed around, and as it stood crazily across the curb in the shadows, a short, fierce struggle was waged within it.

Lorenzo proved himself a fierce fighter. He was angry, frightened, and he fought with the ferocity of a cornered animal, using every savage trick he knew. He tried to twist over and ram a knee into the Agent's groin. He gave the Agent no time to pull the gas gun from his pocket. But neither could he draw his own automatic which made a bulge under his armpit. It was a battle of wrenching hands and knotted fists.

Once again, "X" resorted to a Jiu-jutsu blow. Any moment the queer position of the car and the struggling figures in it might attract attention. A patrol police cruiser might come along. Agent "X" could afford to take no chances with his prize.

His knuckles struck Lorenzo on the side of the neck. The man's head jerked up spasmodically, his hands clawed frantically at his throat, his tongue protruded. For a moment he was like a man choking. The blow the Agent had given him was the well-known strangling blow, which temporarily cuts off air in the windpipe.

It gave the Agent time to do what he wanted. He drew his gas pistol from his pocket, took a deep breath himself, and then calmly fired full into Lorenzo's face.

The man's body slumped limply, and Agent "X" quickly cranked down the windows of the car, letting a draft blow through. He held his breath for nearly two minutes. By that time the gas inside the car had dissipated into a mere chemical odor.

He climbed out, pulled Lorenzo's body from under the wheel, shoved it where his own had been, and took the wheel himself.

Agent "X" was now in complete command of the situation, and with his unconscious burden, in a confiscated car, he drove swiftly away into the night.

CHAPTER XI

CLUES TO DANGER

THE AGENT DROVE down a wide avenue, twisted through a maze of streets, turned into the driveway of an old suburban house. The houses on both sides were shuttered and vacant. Under an assumed name Agent "X" had rented this place as a convenient hideout. It had certain special qualifications.

He got out, opened the garage door, and drove in, closing the door after him. At the side of the garage was a doorway leading directly to the house. This was what made it useful to the Agent. Several times in the past he had carried unconscious bodies through that passageway, as he now carried Lorenzo.

Depositing the man on a couch in a room with drawn shutters, Agent "X" clicked on an overhead light. He went quickly through the man's pockets, found a wallet with an identification card, and nodded to himself. His own encyclopedic memory supplied the details the card lacked.

The man before him was Lorenzo Courtney, black sheep son of a once wealthy family. There had been a time when a Courtney had sat on the board of every bank in the city. The family had died off gradually, leaving only Lorenzo, the spoiled and pampered darling of a doting widowed mother. He had joined a banking firm like the other members of his family before him; but the bank had been one of the first to collapse in the depression. Courtney, like old Roswell Sully, had been disgraced in the public eye.

Leaving his captive on the couch, Agent "X" drew elaborate equipment from a cabinet. This included special lights, photographic apparatus, a sound-recording mechanism and a fingerprint set. He set the articles up one by one, ranged around Courtney, prepared to make a more complete study of the man than he would undergo even at police headquarters. He was going to force Court-

A startled, terrified cry came from Vivian de Graf's lips.

ney to talk. The private third degree through which he was about to put him would bring out whatever the man knew about the criminal band. Ruthless, unconventional measures were justified in the face of such horror as had occurred outside the looted banks.

He forced liquid stimulant between Courtney's lips to offset the effects of the gas. When Courtney stirred, the Agent propped him in a chair, facing the battery of lights. Then he turned on the silent mechanism of his phonographic device. A stylus would make a permanent record of Lorenzo Courtney's voice.

Courtney opened his eyes at length. He was confused for a full minute. Then his gaze focused on the stern face before him, and he gave a visible start. A curse came from his lips. He tensed as though to leap from the chair, but the Agent stopped him with a sentence.

"Stay where you are, Courtney!"

The voice of the Agent had a compelling ring, and Courtney seemed to freeze. Then his eyes became combative. But he didn't move, not with the odd, magnetic gaze of the Secret Agent fixed upon him, not in this room which seemed to speak of mystery and power.

"Who are you?" he asked harshly. "Why did you bring me here? What do you want of me?"

A laugh devoid of humor sounded in the room—the harsh laugh of Secret Agent "X". Then he said: "A half hour of your time, Courtney, and the answers to the questions I shall ask."

Courtney's eyelids narrowed. He was fully awake now. "So," he said. "Vivian de Graf had a right to be suspicious of you. You are a detective?"

Agent "X's" reply was stern. "I'm the one who will ask questions. You are to do the answering."

Courtney's glance flashed around the room. He saw that the Agent held no gun on him, yet he appeared to realize that he couldn't escape. His voice was hoarse when he spoke again.

"This isn't police headquarters," he said. "You are not—" He didn't finish the sentence. He let his voice trail off. His belligerence slowly vanished. And his face became mottled with the pallor of fear, while into his eyes crept a look of awe. "You—" he stammered. "You—"

The Agent smiled with thin lips. "Quiet, Courtney! Listen to what I have to say."

A cry burst abruptly from Courtney's lips; a cry of despair and terror. "I understand," he cried. "I understand! You are the man they call—Secret Agent 'X'!"

THERE was tense silence in the room. The Agent didn't reply, and Courtney took his silence for assent. The banker's hand darted abruptly to his breast pocket. Two fingers disappeared, and came out clutching a white capsule no larger than a bean.

"X" leaped forward, but not quite soon enough. For Courtney had thrust the white object into his mouth. He had clenched his teeth over it, swallowed—and he broke suddenly into a peal of wild laughter.

For an instant Agent "X" stared at the man. Then he sprang toward a small medicine cabinet containing antidotal drugs. He knew what Lorenzo Courtney had done, knew that the capsule must have contained poison. But when he turned with a bottle in his hand, he saw he was too late.

For there were beads of perspiration on Courtney's forehead already, and his skin was turning gray. From his open lips came the pungent smell of bitter almonds, an odor Agent "X" had sniffed before. Courtney had swallowed deadly cyanide, had taken his own life, and nothing any man could do now could stop the inroad of that terrible poison, already saturating his system.

His breath came in labored gasps, his hideous laughter rang out again, and there was an expression of malicious triumph in his eyes as he stared at "X."

"You'll never—know!" he suddenly screamed. "You'll never—know—now—"

His head fell sidewise. He jerked off the couch, twitched on the floor in racking spasms, then lay still. When Agent "X" stooped over him to feel his pulse, there was no flutter beneath his fingers. The man was dead.

Bitter disappointment made the Agent's eyes bleakly grim. He had felt certain this man was a member of the bandit gang. Now Courtney's lips were sealed forever. Now no third degree could sweat secrets from them.

Yet the Agent did not give up hope. Something of value might be salvaged from the wreck of his plans. He went quickly to work. Time—that was the big factor now. Time—before the makers of darkness had worked still more havoc in the city, before others met such a fate as Ellen Dowe.

Already Lorenzo Courtney's features were changing perceptibly, showing the first masklike aspects of death. The Agent, moving tensely, propped the dead man up with pillows, focused the powerful mercury vapor light upon him. He set up his camera, thrust in a holder of achromatic plates, took pictures of Courtney's features from many angles. Then he made a series of careful measurements and fingerprints, piled them and the plates away to be developed as soon as he had time. He thrust Courtney out of sight in a coffinlike compartment under the couch, changed his disguise to that of A. J. Martin, and quickly left the hideout.

Back in Martin's office, "X" sent grim orders over the telephone to Hobart. Other orders clicked over the air in the special code signal that would reach Harry Bates.

"Drop present work. Rush through secret investigation of Lorenzo Courtney, ex-banker. Get information concerning friends, clubs, personal habits. Rush this to me!"

He sat for a moment in intense concentration, then with a decisive motion picked up a volume of "Who's Who" from his desk. He flipped it open, turned to the "D's," scanned the columns, and stopped at "De Graf, Emil." The paragraph beneath this name read:

> Physicist. Born Milwaukee, 1892. Student, Randall Scientific Foundation, 1910. Graduate University of Munich, 1914. Awarded Hopkinson Prize 1919 for bombardment of lithium with atomic hearts of hydrogen. Author: "Spectroscopy and the Variable Stars"; "Man's Dependence Upon Matter." Professor of Physics at City University.

A city directory passed next through the Agent's hands. Once again he found the name de Graf, then left his office quickly and sped across town in his car.

FOR the moment he was not concerned with the beautiful Vivian de Graf. It was her scholarly husband whom he sought, the man who spent his time in classroom and laboratory, experimenting with the mysteries of the universe, while his wife experimented with human emotions.

There was a compelling double motive behind the Agent's desire to talk to Emil de Graf. In the first place, the man was Vivian de Graf's husband. In addition to that, he was a brilliant and original worker in experimental science. He must have some theory concerning such a phenomenon as this weird darkness which had been used as a cloak for crime.

The Agent's mouth was grim. He felt he was working in a darkness almost as impenetrable as that which the raiders so mysteriously created. Never had he encountered any crime quite so baffling.

Two things he must find out, before he could combat it. One, the identity of the men who operated behind the weird darkness; the other, how that darkness was created. He knew now from Thaddeus Penny's statements and from the pictures Hobart had made, that the sun shone even while the darkness fell—two inconsistent happenings which nevertheless formed a theory in the Agent's mind.

The address given in the directory proved to be an ancient, brownstone house—a very different residence from the pink stucco apartment which Vivian de Graf maintained separately.

A slatternly servant on squeaking shoes let the Agent into a hall that smelled of dust and mothballs. She bade him wait, squeaked off into the rear of the house and returned in two minutes.

"The professor will see you. This way if you please."

The rear room, converted into a laboratory, where de Graf worked, was as modern as the rest of the house was ancient. Gleaming scientific instruments stood about. Shelves of books on mathematics, chemistry, astronomy and physics lined the walls. A man with a thin face and stooped shoulders came forward, peering at "X". He had faded blue eyes, a vaguely sweet smile. He extended a dry, cold hand, said:

"Yes. What can I do for you? I didn't catch the name?"

Agent "X" studied the man for a second. It was hard to picture the dazzling Vivian de Graf married to such a person. One of nature's little jokes that these two had been thrown together—the withered student and the gorgeous butterfly. The Agent handed his card, bearing the name A. J. Martin, to de Graf.

"From the press," he said. "I wanted to ask you a few questions about a thing which vitally concerns the public at the moment."

Emil de Graf made a weary, harried gesture. "I'm sorry—please! I never like to give out statements of my experiments except to authenticated scientific journals. No offense meant, but the newspapers have a way of misquoting, you know. Most embarrassing."

The Secret Agent interrupted. "This is not about your work. Perhaps you don't read the papers, but you must have heard of a bank robbery that took place today under odd circumstances—after the coming of darkness."

"Darkness," echoed de Graf. "Of course. I heard some of my students talking about it. But really, I'm not interested in crime."

The Agent was watching the professor intently. De Grafs eyes were vague, expressionless. No sign of emotion was betrayed in the thin face.

"You're a scientist," "X" said. "Have you no theories as to how such darkness might be created? A statement from you would be interesting."

De Graf laughed wearily. "Interesting perhaps to a thrill-seeking public. But hardly to scientific men, for I have made no study of this darkness you speak of. I don't—"

The Agent cut him short again, a frown of annoyance on his

face. De Graf's attitude was irritating. "Since your own wife was at the scene of the crime I thought perhaps—" the Agent began.

DE GRAF chuckled. "Vivian, of course! A woman with very modern ideas, but still a child at heart. Full of zest, always getting herself into predicaments. We understand each other perfectly, she and I."

"Then you have no statement to make about this darkness?"

De Graf waved his hand. "My dear fellow, if I had any, you as a layman would hardly understand it! But, as I said, I have no interest—"

The Agent saw the uselessness of talking to the man. He thanked him and left.

But as he drove away, "X" found a vague suspicion gnawing at his mind. De Graf had been almost too offhand. Even though he were a man lost in a world of experiment and theory, it seemed incredible that any scientist could feel such utter lack of interest in a phenomenon so directly allied to his own field.

The Agent had sensed strong undercurrents in the man's personality. De Graf was the suppressed type, of course, one whose brain had driven human emotion into the background. But emotion was there, lurking. And there was no saying into what strange channels it might be diverted. The Agent decided to order Hobart to have a man keep track of the scientist's comings and goings.

Two hours later "X" had received reports on Lorenzo Courtney from both his investigating groups. These reports were not as complete as he would have liked. Yet they contained much valuable information. It would take days or weeks to unearth all the details of Courtney's life.

The whole matter of the dead man's connection with a crashed bank was there. Hobart had sent him a newspaper clipping including a statement made by Norman Coe, head of the Citizens Banking Committee, giving the details which had caused Courtney's indictment before a grand jury.

This statement proved conclusively that even at that period of his life Courtney had gone in for unethical practices. He had taken part in the misappropriation of depositors' money. He was on his way to becoming a criminal then.

And the reports from his two investigating groups had given "X" a list of Courtney's friends, of the clubs he frequented, the restaurants he patronized, the names of his tailor, his barber, his doctor. Bates and Hobart had done good work. Until a counter order from

"X" stopped them they would go on collecting data until a clear picture of the man had been constructed.

But "X" could not wait longer. Every hour that passed complicated the difficulties of the situation. Courtney was dead, and those interested in his welfare might wonder where he had disappeared, grow suspicious. That must not happen.

Eyes staring into the dark streets before him, hands clutching the wheel of his car. Agent "X" drove back to the secret hideout where Courtney's body lay. He had a plan in mind—a scheme that no other investigator of crime would have thought of, much less undertaken. This was to create a disguise more daring, one fraught with greater possibilities of danger, than any he had attempted in his whole career—the disguise of Lorenzo Courtney.

CHAPTER XII

SECRET ORDERS

IN THE SECLUSION of his hideout he set feverishly to work. A small electric clock on a shelf marked off the seconds, warning "X" that the thing he planned was dependent more than anything else on time. The impersonation he was about to make was not like the stock disguises he had used many times before.[6]

To create this disguise, all his artistry, all the amazing scientific skill of the Man of a Thousand Faces, was required. Lorenzo Courtney's features had changed completely now. *Rigor mortis* had set in. The face of the sleekly groomed ex-banker had the masklike rigidity, the pinched nostrils, the sunken cheeks of death. The strong mineral poison he had taken had added a horrible grayish hue to his face. Courtney could not now be used as a pattern for disguise.

The Agent quickly developed the plates he had made, set them with special fixative, dried them in a fan dryer, and made quick prints.[7]

Then, after removing Courtney's outer clothing, he put the body back into the recess under the couch. In creating this disguise he preferred to make use of his prints and measurements, and his own graphic impressions of the man in life.

---

6 *AUTHOR'S NOTE: In the creation of these, Agent "X" has disciplined himself to conserve time and movement, so that one or two of his stock disguises can even be built up in total darkness, by the sense of touch alone. Like a musician who practices pieces till he can play them without notes, the Secret Agent has memorized a repertoire of disguises.*

7 *AUTHOR'S NOTE: The Secret Agent's photographic equipment and his knowledge of the photographer's art are as complete as his apparatus and data in radio. He employs and has employed many types of camera, from the tiniest watch camera, used for taking secret snapshots, to cumbersome motion picture units. And in his special dark rooms he makes use of the most advanced methods of developing and printing. It is necessary for him to do his own work in this line, since he could not risk his secrets in any commercial studio.*

While his long fingers worked their magic, he turned on the phonographic record of Courtney's last speech.

Then his own lips moved. He was imitating the sound of Courtney's voice, the suave English accent that the banker had affected.

He imitated the man's features on his own face, slipped a black toupee over his own brown hair, carefully combed the artificial locks until they duplicated the lustrous blackness that had crowned Courtney's head.

For seconds after the disguise seemed complete, he worked on, adding the deft touches that distinguished his masterly impersonations from the crude attempts of other investigators. The tiny lines, the moles, the slight skin blemishes that made the disguise perfect.

When he arose and donned Courtney's clothing, the effect was weirdly startling. The dead man seemed to have come to life in the room. Fate had played into "X's" hands to the extent of making Courtney as tall and broad-shouldered as himself. The only point in this strange case where Fate had chosen to be kind, and that kindness might lead the Agent to his death.

For his data concerning Courtney was still incomplete. Never had he undertaken an impersonation upon which so much depended, armed with less information about the man he was impersonating. The outward perfection of his disguise was the one thing he could depend on. For the rest, he must trust to his wits.

Among the facts Jim Hobart had sent him were the two addresses Lorenzo Courtney maintained. One, the old-fashioned brick mansion on a fashionable avenue where his mother reigned like a dowager empress; the other, Courtney's bachelor apartment.

"X" had quietly confiscated the contents of Courtney's pockets. A wallet, containing a roll of bills and an uncashed allowance check from his mother. Cards to several exclusive clubs. A ring with more than a dozen keys on it.

"X" LEFT his hideout, carefully keeping to the shadows and cutting across two vacant lots till he reached another street. Here he walked several blocks before summoning a taxi. The address he gave the driver was that of Courtney's apartment.

The place, when he reached it, was very much as "X" had visioned it—a flamboyant suite of chambers in an ultra-smart building. A dizzy blonde at the telephone desk nodded at him. There was a flash in her eyes and a knowing moue of her red lips that seemed to speak of intimate acquaintance. The Agent returned her smile with a wink. He said: "Good evening," to the elevator boy, and ascended to Courtney's floor.

The shape of the keyhole told "X" which key on Courtney's ring would fit the lock. He opened the door, entered, and listened a moment to see if there were anyone about. Courtney might have a servant. But none appeared. And "X" saw a moment later that the kitchenette and serving pantry showed lack of use.

He became tensely active at once. The hungry gleam of the quest was in his eyes. A small secretary with locked drawers stood at one side of the living room near a luxurious davenport. The Agent opened this quickly and searched it, but found nothing save many letters addressed in various types of feminine hand-writing.

He cast these impatiently aside. He wasn't interested in Courtney's *affaires de coeur*. What he wanted was some clue to the man's criminal activities.

He began a quick, deft search of the whole apartment. This was routine work for a man who had been associated with criminals and their ways for years. Systematically, thoroughly, he went over the room, examining the walls first, tapping them for hidden compartments, lifting rugs, scrutinizing furniture.

His search was half completed when he came to a handsome antique straight-backed chair covered in rich tapestry. An irregularity in this caught his eye—a tiny roughness on one leg, below and behind the seat. He turned the chair around and found a corresponding rough spot on the other side. The varnished finish did not quite match. With his knife blade, "X" probed, and the varnish came loose to reveal a circle of plastic wood.

He turned the chair over. Its bottom had nothing to attract attention—ordinary black cloth covered the webbing over the springs. But his fingers felt along it, and encountered an unnatural piece of metal. He pressed it. Something clicked. He turned the chair upright again, pushed up on the seat, and gave an exclamation of satisfaction. The seat, he found, was held by pivots hidden beneath the plastic wood, and formed the top of a small box, in which lay several objects.

One of these held the Agent's fascinated gaze. It lay there like a coiled snake about to spring—a rawhide whip of pliant leather. The end of it was divided into three small lashes, each tipped with steel like one of the old-time cat-o'-nine-tails. And there were brownish smears on one of the tips. Dried human blood.

Here was one of the terrible whips that had been used on men and women as though they had been cattle. Here was concrete proof that Courtney had been a member of the band.

The Agent thrust the whip aside and drew out what lay beneath it, his eyes glittering with excitement. For he now held in his hand a mask of black cloth. But a quick examination of it brought disappointment and a puzzled look to the Agent's eager eyes. There was nothing covering the eyeholes, no goggles like those he had felt on the man he had fought in the bank, and seen so graphically in the shots of Hobart's film. This mask was of plain black silk.

TWO GUNS, a small blackjack, and a compact set of burglar tools completed the contents of the box. Courtney's hidden equipment alone was enough to convict a man of felony.

Then the sharp ringing of the telephone interrupted "X's" search. He answered it instantly, using Courtney's suave voice. It was a girl, one of Courtney's "big moments," judging from her petulant complaints. When was he going to see her? Why had he neglected her? Why hadn't he answered her letters?

Playing the role of Courtney, "X" stalled. Business matters had kept him occupied. He had been called out of town suddenly. He had not forgotten her. He finally stilled the girl's syrupy gushings and hung up.

He continued his search of the apartment, overlooking no possible hiding place, until he had convinced himself that he had found Courtney's only secret cache. The man evidently did not possess one of the mysterious helmets which enabled the members of the bandit gang to see in the darkness. And this puzzled Agent "X."

He closed the secret box in the chair, paced the apartment for a time. Two courses were now open. He could wait here till something of importance reached him, some clue to Courtney's activities; or he could move as Courtney through the clubs and restaurants where the young banker had been an habitué. The first plan seemed more logical. This was Courtney's private retreat. He would receive important messages here, surely. But the inactivity of waiting tore at the Agent's nerves.

In a fever of impatience he continued his pacing of the room. Three more calls came, all from women. "X" listened to each intently, weighing every word spoken in the hope that there would be some inkling of Courtney's connection with the gang. There was not; and Agent "X" began to wonder if he had pursued the right course.

Frequently in his life great issues had depended on guesswork, hunches. More than once the uncanny correctness of his hunches had brought him success. Now, his instinct told him that sooner or later information of value would reach him at this apartment. But his senses cried out for action; his imagination painted ghastly pictures of what might be taking place outside, even at this moment.

At eleven o'clock, after he had been tempted a dozen times to leave the place, the telephone in Courtney's apartment rang for the fifth time since his entrance. And now it was no feminine voice that greeted him.

His fingers tensed over the receiver as a slightly muffled man's voice sounded. Agent "X" got the impression that the person was talking through a cloth, to disguise his speech. "X" crouched eagerly over the instrument.

"Courtney?" the voice said.

"Yes—Courtney speaking," the Agent replied.

A slight pause. Then a muffled voice made a sudden, clipped statement in a tone of dry authority. A statement that brought a thrill to the Secret Agent's taut nerves.

"We meet at twelve. I shall expect you, Lorenzo Courtney."

CHAPTER XIII

MURDERER'S HIDEOUT

NO OTHER WORD was spoken. The muffled voice was silent. The receiver clicked up. But Agent "X," turning in taut excitement from the phone, no longer wondered if his decision to remain in Courtney's apartment had been wise. He *knew* it had been, for there was every reason to believe that the man to whom he had just listened was the leader of the devil-dark gang.

Yet the message had been too brief to be satisfactory. Members of the band who used scourging, torturing whips to clear the way for their criminal activities were meeting at midnight. But where?

"X" was aware suddenly of his perilous lack of information concerning Courtney; aware of the difficulties the man's self-inflicted death had thrown in his way. Courtney's hideously mocking laughter seemed to ring in his ears. Courtney's dying words echoed in his mind. "You will never know—now—"

Agent "X" walked to the secretary in Courtney's apartment, sat down for a moment and studied the itemized reports that Bates and Hobart had rushed to him. The list of young Courtney's friends held his attention.

Certain characteristics of the devil-dark criminals were known to "X" now. They were not ordinary underworld characters. They did not haunt the murky byways of crookdom. That was why neither Bates, nor Hobart, nor the police had been able to pick up details concerning them. And Thaddeus Penny had corroborated "X's" own impression that the mysterious raiders were men of education, even culture.

"X" had a theory to explain this. Lorenzo Courtney had been living proof of his theory. Educated, well-bred men did not go in for crime generally unless other customary fields of activity were closed to them. Courtney had been a failure in banking. He had

73

left his profession in disgrace, with the threat of a prison sentence hanging like a shadow over his life. He had been greedy, ambitious, vain at heart. Failure, disgrace, had brought out the innate criminal instincts that lurk in many men. The same forces would bring out those characteristics in others.

And on the list of Courtney's friends which Hobart had given him was one which a card in Courtney's wallet also showed. This was a man named Chauncey Doeg, a man who, according to Hobart's data, had even served a two-year sentence for defrauding the mails in connection with the advertising of a certain bond issue. Doeg, like Courtney, had been a member of the younger sporting set, a polo player, yachtsman, and society gallant, much sought after by the mothers of debutantes, until disgrace had clouded his life.

Disgrace, obscurity, would be bitter pills for such a man to swallow; for the most intolerable poverty of all to bear is the poverty of those who have once possessed regal luxury.

Secret Agent "X" struck the secretary sharply with a clenched fist. His eyes were gleaming with the quest again. His logical brain had unearthed the possible hidden seeds of crime. He had made his decision—and was ready once more to gamble. But before he left Courtney's apartment he did an odd thing for Agent "X." He went to a glass decanter, poured himself a drink of whiskey and tossed it off. This was not because he needed stimulant. It was to make his disguise of the wastrel Courtney even more complete, by adding the odor of liquor on his breath. Twenty minutes later a car slowed and stopped at the corner of a block of shabby apartments. Agent "X," still disguised as Courtney, was behind the wheel. He got out, sauntered halfway down the block, and merged suddenly with the black shadows at the mouth of a tradesmen's entry. Here, with a view of the buildings on the street's opposite side, he waited. One of those buildings held the apartment of Chauncey Doeg. And "X" had taken pains to learn that the banker was at home. He had asked Betty Dale, the one girl in the city who knew the true nature of his daring work, to call Doeg's number. She had been instructed by the Agent to ask for "Charles Doeg," then apologize timidly for calling the wrong party. She had reported to "X" that Chauncey Doeg was home.

"X" WAITED now with a feeling of impatience, a feeling of uncertainty that he had to fight down, akin to the same emotion he had had in Courtney's apartment. Yet now it was even worse. For he had definite information that there was a secret meeting tonight. And, if his surmise concerning Doeg was wrong, the knowledge that the meeting had passed without his attendance would be intolerably bitter.

Yet all the facts pointed toward the verification of the Agent's theory. These shabby apartments where Doeg dwelt proved that the once prosperous banker had come down in the world. He had had no doting and wealthy mother like Courtney to give him an allowance. If Courtney had been tempted into crime, how much greater must the temptation of Doeg be? And "X," in his conversation with Betty Dale, had made quick check-up on the man. She was in a position to know, and she had given him certain facts.[8]

Doeg's character had changed since his stay in prison. He had become silent, irritable, appearing only in fashionable circles, and then to attend the wedding of a boyhood friend. For the rest he kept to himself, brooding apparently over his grievances.

But minutes ticked by, and the Agent's uneasiness grew. He looked at his watch. Eleven thirty, and still no sign of Chauncey Doeg.

It wasn't till twenty minutes of twelve that a heavy-set figure appeared in the vestibule of the apartment opposite. A shabby coat of a once modish and expensive cut fitted powerful shoulders. Above a white silk scarf a brutally aggressive chin showed, framing the thick lips of a sullen mouth. "X" recognized Chauncey Doeg from the minute description Betty Dale had given him.

The young ex-banker peered up and down the block for a moment. Then he stepped imperiously to the curb and summoned a passing taxi.

"X" left his hideout as soon as the taxi's tail-light was a disappearing red eye dawn the street. He walked swift strides to his own coupé, made a U-turn and followed the cab, careful not to get too close.

Once, to avert any possible suspicion in Doeg's mind that he was being followed, "X" took a chance, speeded up and plunged into a right-angle street. Then he swerved around a corner, raced along a parallel block and came back in on the route that Doeg's taxi was following.

---

8 AUTHOR'S NOTE: *Betty Dale has a job as reporter on the* Herald. *She has often been assigned to "society events" and has a wide acquaintance with wealthy, influential people. Many times her keen memory and clear powers of observation have aided the Agent.*

When "X" saw Doeg's taxi draw to the curb he was a good two blocks behind. He immediately plunged into a side street, parked out of sight and reappeared on foot. Doeg must not see him. He would certainly think it odd that his friend, Lorenzo Courtney, was shadowing him.

So skillful had the Agent's maneuvers been that Doeg was unaware that he was under surveillance. He moved with a lumbering, bearlike stride on along the street, in the same direction that the taxi had been following. At the next corner he turned left, walked two blocks till he came to a section of small shops and old-fashioned brick dwellings, and paused before a cast-iron fence.

Now for the first time he manifested furtive caution. "X" had ducked out of sight in an areaway. From the shadows of this he saw Doeg survey the street in all directions. Then Doeg ran quickly up the front steps of a shuttered house and plunged a key into a lock. An instant later he disappeared from sight.

The Agent waited a full minute. He looked at his watch again. It was now eight minutes of twelve. He came from his hiding place, moved almost invisibly in the shadows, walked around a full block and approached the house which Doeg had entered from the other direction.

Ascending the steps briskly as Doeg had done he made a quick examination of the lock. He had his special chromium tools with him, was prepared to use them if necessary, but he saw at once that an odd-shaped key on Lorenzo Courtney's ring fitted this door.

In a moment he had opened it and was inside the mysterious house. No slightest sound reached his ears. He waited a moment, then drew his cameralike sound-amplifying mechanism out. To be caught with that in his hand would be to attract certain suspicion and attack if he were seen. But a blundering examination of the building would be equally as bad.

He pressed the disc-shaped microphone to the wall, heard a faint sound and, kneeling, shifted it to the floor. Now footsteps reached his ears plainly. They moved for some time as he listened, grew fainter and fainter, as though they were traversing a corridor or passage. They were obviously on a lower level than himself.

THE AGENT moved down a rear stairway to the basement floor of the house. He was now in a room similar to that of the house where he had almost burned to death.

He pressed his microphone to the floor again, heard the footsteps on a still lower level. His eyes widened. He strode at once to a cellar door, which the shifting beam of his flashlight revealed.

He didn't need his microphone to guide him now. The dust of these cellar stairs had been disturbed. So had the dust on the cellar floor of this supposedly empty house. Many footprints were visible to the sharp, highly trained eyes of the Secret Agent. Many footprints all leading in the same direction. He followed them across the chamber till they ended close to a seemingly blank wall.

But there were cracks in the plaster before him, and a spot at his feet showed a jumble of ancient iron pipes where the house water connected with the city's main. There was a shut-off here with a bent handle.

The Agent pressed against the wall ahead of him. It appeared to be rigidly solid. Here was an incomprehensive mystery, a point which might have stopped him—if he had not listened to those retreating footsteps through the earpiece of his sensitive amplifier. But men did not walk through solid walls.

He looked for hidden keyholes, found none. Then made a careful examination of the pipes, till he came to the apparent cut-off. Tentatively he turned this, half expecting to hear the swish and gurgle of water in ancient, rusty pipes. None came, but there was a distinct metallic *click,* and the solid appearing wall before him seemed suddenly to shiver.

The Agent pressed it again, and now a section of the wall turned on a pivot disclosing a jagged, lopsided doorway, cleverly following the haphazard line of the cracks. The cut-off had been contrived into a simple but effective lock.

The Agent closed the strange door behind him as Doeg must have done, walked on across another cellar room. This time the footprints visible to the Agent's trained eyes led to a coal bin and disappeared. He plunged through the narrow door of the bin, and saw at once that the square piece of boarding at one corner must be the top of a trapdoor. There was no other possible exit from the coal bin except the window to the street chute, and that was thick with dust.

His questing fingers found a keyhole at the side of the boarding, which another key on Courtney's ring fitted. He thrust it in, lifted the board cover, and descended a flight of steps. The weight of the cover surprised him till he looked up and saw that it was sheathed on the inside with heavy armor plate.

At the bottom of the steps he found himself in the passage

along which Chauncey Doeg's feet had echoed. His pulses were hammering with excitement. He had seemingly entered a bizarre and fantastic world of secret crime beneath the city's peaceful life. And these precautions, the hidden doors, the subway-like passages, spoke of infinite power and cunning. The sides of the small passage he was in, hewn from the clay soil beneath the houses, were not fresh. They were at least a month or two old, proving that the brain or brains behind the devil-dark band had plotted crime long in advance of the actual commission.

But the Agent did not pause. Somewhere ahead of him he knew a password would be demanded of him surely—one that he did not know. But his quick brain had devised a daring answer, and he was glad that he had the smell of Courtney's whiskey on his breath.

The passage curved beneath the ground, till Agent "X" in his excitement lost all sense of direction. The evident premeditation of the thing appalled him. What chance had society against such cunning, ruthless criminals armed with such a weapon as the strange darkness? The average evil-doer would consider a catacomb like this a rare feat. It was only a secondary precaution of the devil-dark gang.

At last the long curving passage ended in another stone wall with a steel door set in it. Here was no lock, no opening, except a narrow slit in the door's center, now closed on the inside with a plate of metal, and a small signal button beside the frame.

No password had been demanded of the Agent as yet, but here was a barrier just as dangerous. In such a criminal group, each member surely would have his own signal, and "X" did not know Lorenzo Courtney's password.

Yet he did not stand in uncertainty even for a moment. It was the Secret Agent's way to act quickly, play hunches, flirt with Death itself. Firmly with no tremor in it, his finger pressed the circular eye in the button's center and stayed there.

CHAPTER XIV

BLUFFING DEATH

FOR A FULL second he held the button down, then removed his finger and fished in his pocket for a cigarette. If any bell had sounded inside he had not heard it, and he couldn't risk the use of his amplifier now. His own flash beam had revealed a small electric bulb in the roof of the passageway's end. Any instant that slit in the center of the door might open, and if it did, and he had his amplifier, he would be caught red-handed.

The cigarette he lighted wasn't in answer to a nervous craving for nicotine. Neither was it an act of bravado. It was done deliberately to create a certain impression which he wished to give. The cigarette was one of Courtney's own, cork-tipped, expensive. The Agent let it hang loosely from his lips, swayed on his toes, and hummed beneath his breath as he waited.

Almost a minute passed, and then the bulb over his head and the slit before him glimmered at the same instant. One slid back. The other lighted up with a startling click. But the Agent did not jump.

Still swaying on his toes, his cigarette lax in his mouth, Agent "X" faced the mysterious slit and smiled. He smiled—perhaps into the very face of Death.

For there was no further sound from the opened slit, no visible sign of life or movement. The chamber behind it was obviously black. The light overhead had been so arranged as not to fall into it. Yet "X" knew for a certainty that a human eye was there, an eye hidden, yet scrutinizing him with grim intensity. He sensed with intuitive awareness that he was not approved of.

At least another ten seconds passed, then a sepulchral voice spoke:

"Lorenzo Courtney!"

"Right!" The Agent put the same aplomb into his answer as was expressed by his teetering attitude, and the drooping cigarette. He squinted one eye to shut curling smoke out, said: "What's the idea of keeping a fellow waiting?"

There had been a sinister harshness in the words of the unseen watcher; the harshness of the same voice that "X" remembered hearing in Craig Banton's office during the fall of the uncanny dark. His one answer was like an insult, or a defiance hurled into the teeth of doom. But it brought the retort he had expected.

"Lorenzo Courtney, why did you not give the signal?"

The Agent's coolness in the face of this demand was incredible—as fine a bit of acting as he had ever done in his life. He shifted his cigarette, removed it lazily from his mouth, flicked ashes to the floor of the passage.

"You won't believe it, old man! But—the fact is—I've forgotten it!"

The Agent gave an amused titter, and drew a hand across his mouth. His accent had perfectly duplicated the British twang of Lorenzo Courtney. He continued the same suave tones, adding a slight thickness.

"Sorry! You'll be wanting to use your damned whips on me next. But I was called to the club this evening for a few cocktails—and—" The Agent tittered again. "Frankly this mumbo-jumbo gets on my nerves at times. You ought to thank me for finding my way in."

A single word came from behind the metal door: "Fool!"

A second passed, while the Agent still waited, hiding the breathless uneasiness he felt. He had thrown one of the strangest and most daringly simple bluffs of his life. Told a member of a hideously vicious gang that he had forgotten a signal which he had never known. Would it, could it possibly work? The Secret Agent had rolled his dice again.

And it appeared that he had won, for abruptly the door moved back. An arm reached out, yanked him angrily inside. A harsh voice spoke in his ear.

"Once perhaps you can get away with this, Courtney. But the Chairman would never allow it a second time. That would mean death! You took the pledge like the rest of us. You are under oath! I shall be forced to tell the Chairman of your conduct."

The "Chairman." Agent "X's" thoughts raced. A moment later he almost started in spite of his iron self-control. For lights blazed above his head. He got a glimpse of his surroundings, and saw that he was in no damp passage or dusty cellar now. He was in a small corridor lined with white marble tiling, and at either end a neat door showed.

THE man standing before him, the man who had questioned him and let him in, was glaring at him now. Glaring through the eyeholes of a silk mask such as "X" had found in the chair in Courtney's apartment and now carried in his pocket. The mask hid the man's entire face. But a thrill passed through the Agent. For in that angular frame, that horselike head with its high, narrow forehead, those hunched shoulders, "X" believed he recognized another member of a now defunct banking firm, one Victor Blass, who had had a serious run-in with both the State insurance department and Norman Coe over the legality of guaranteed second mortgages on worthless property. Blass had been a wily scoundrel who had escaped the law. And now apparently he had joined forces with outright criminals. More than that, he was apparently in second command to the mysterious Chairman himself.

The Agent's excited speculation made him appear to be in a daze.

"Put on your mask, fool!" said Blass. "You shouldn't have come in without it any more than you should have forgotten the signal. Hurry! The others are ready. It is nearly time for the Chairman to come."

"X" quickly adjusted the black silk mask of Lorenzo Courtney's over his head, and Blass gave him a shove toward the door at the farthest end of the corridor.

Agent "X" opened the door and walked into a room that amazed him even more than the marbled entryway had done. For here was a carpeted chamber, with a polished desk, upholstered chairs and ornate electrical fixtures in it. The chairs were ranged around the floor, all facing in one direction, and ten men sat in them.

The group of black-shrouded faces under the glaring lights was weirdly incongruous. Their silence and preoccupied attitudes were strangely sinister. A few turned to stare at "X" as he took his place in a vacant chair. The rest held their gaze straight ahead. At the very end of the room a fine meshed, metal grille rose from floor to ceiling. Behind this was a single chair with a desk beside it. It was toward this desk and chair that the masked men were looking.

Agent "X" waited for the mysterious Chairman to arrive. His pulses were throbbing. It was obvious that this night he was going to see the body at least of the sinister being whose brains were responsible for the activities of the devil-dark gang. The man's face would be hidden, but his movements, his mannerisms, might give the Agent some clue to his identity.

As the seconds passed "X" glanced at some of the still figures about him. He thought he recognized the bullet-headed, heavy-set form of Chauncey Doeg, the man he had followed here. Doeg, like the others, was awaiting the arrival of the Chairman.

Then abruptly Agent "X" tensed in his chair. The fingers of his right hand pressed involuntarily against its wooden edge. For a change seemed to have come over the room. The bulbs overhead seemed suddenly dimmer. There was an odd humming sound in the air that brought back vivid memories. Light moved before his eyes for a moment. He seemed to hear the terrified shrieks and curses of frenzied men and women in his ears.

THE lights grew dimmer, dimmer. The masked figures around him took on the appearance of weirdly, distorted ghouls, of beings from some unthinkable nightmare. Then they disappeared entirely, and blackness, utter and complete, enveloped the strange room.

"X" was not deluded. He knew that the lights above him had not gone out. He knew that it would be useless to wink his own flashlight on. For this was the same uncanny darkness that had descended on the bank; the same under which innocent people had been scourged brutally with whips that they might not interfere with the looting of the vault.

There were no cries or gasps around "X" now. The masked men evidently expected this to happen, were prepared. There was stillness in the room, until a slight, metallic scrape sounded from behind the grille. Then the faint scrape of a chair, then a voice.

"Greetings! I see you are all here! The meeting is about to begin."

Agent "X" knew that voice. Its muffled, disguised tones had spoken to him over the telephone in Courtney's apartment, given him his instructions to come. But it was distorted beyond recognition of the man from whose lips it came. And its words seemed a mockery of his purpose in coming. For it had said: "I see you are all here."

That meant one thing. This man, this sinister Chairman, whose arrival had been awaited so tensely, wore a mask unlike the others in that room—a mask such as all the raiders on the bank had worn, and which enabled him to see his board of directors now. It meant, beyond a shadow of doubt in the Agent's mind, that the directors did not know the identity of the Chairman who guided them.

The muffled voice of the unseen man behind the grille continued.

"Today, gentlemen, we have witnessed the complete success of our plans. The method, given a preliminary test a week ago, and which I outlined to you all last night, has proven itself more than adequate. You have read the papers this afternoon. You have seen how our little venture baffled the public and the police. I say 'little,' because what we did today is as nothing compared to what we shall do.

"Already our investment has paid a hundred per cent profit. There were two million in cash and negotiable securities in the Guardian Bank. Each of you shall receive his share. Dollar for dollar for the time spent, this is greater profit than any of you ever made in the heyday of your public careers. But the future, not the present, is what we must look to. The future, when we shall all be multimillionaires—able to do what we want, buy what we want—and wield the power that is the rightful heritage of brainy men."

There was a gloating, confident note in the muffled voice. The hidden Chairman of this unholy meeting of criminals was talking as though he were at the head of some successful and legitimate enterprise. But brutal harshness crept into his tone as he continued.

"Discipline! As I said to you last night, that is the backbone of our organized power. We must have discipline if we are to get the maximum return from our investment. And because I realize the necessity of this perhaps more than any of you, I have given certain commands that some of you may think harsh. I have said that punishment even to death, awaits any man among you who does not submit to the majority will. I have ordered each of you to check up on the conduct of his neighbor, for in spite of the masks you now wear, most of you are known to one another. That none of you know who I am is an asset to you all, for in it lies unity and power. If it becomes necessary to impose a death sentence on one of you, I personally shall take pains to see that it is carried out."

Chorused growls of approval greeted these sinister words. Then a harshly bitter voice spoke in the darkness a few chairs away from Agent "X."

"Death!" the voice said savagely. "Shouldn't we, Mr. Chairman, extend that penalty beyond our own membership to those who are and have been our enemies? There are several persons I have in mind; but one especially who exposed and helped to ruin many of us during our banking days. I refer to Norman Coe with his prying citizens committee behind him. Because of his officious meddling into my affairs I even served a prison sentence.

THE Agent guessed then that this was Chauncey Doeg speaking, still bitter that the law, through Coe's efforts, had punished him for his shady financial dealings. The voice of the Chairman gave answer.

"You are right, my friend. There are many enemies we must and shall settle with in time. But at the moment personal revenge must wait on more important matters. And meanwhile, gentlemen, for minor breaches of discipline within your own ranks, you have the whips! The whips! You saw how well they worked on the people in the bank today. You saw how the girl we were forced to interrogate before the raid, even though she was stubborn to the point of sheer stupidity, eventually submitted under the lash.

"And I do not doubt that your whips will be sufficient to enforce discipline among you under all normal circumstances. In case the whipping of a member becomes necessary, I have worked out a plan which will remove the element of ill-feeling. I shall provide eleven of you with the helmets you wore today, while the member to be punished will wear only such a mask as you have on. He will not know who among you is whipping him.

"And now we come to our immediate future. I have looked over the field, gathered data for our next venture. There were several promising possibilities. It was merely a matter of selection. That I have made. We have successfully looted two banks. We have proved that our method has no limits. To show that we can operate with equal success over a larger area I have chosen a department store this time. That of S. Carleton & Co."

The Agent's body tensed. A chill of horror crept up his spine. This criminal, this unseen Chairman, was deliberately, calmly, plotting a crime which, if carried out unimpeded, might bring death and injury to thousands. For the fearful, blinding darkness would cause a worse panic in the big store than it had outside the bank. Yet the Chairman's voice continued:

"To insure that the cashier's safe will not be empty we shall change our time from noon to four o'clock. The date is tomorrow. We shall meet and the helmets will be distributed among you in the same manner as they were today. And now, gentlemen, are there any more suggestions you wish to make, or breaks of discipline to be reported?"

A few seconds of silence followed in the uncanny gloom of the room; then a chair creaked and the voice of Victor Blass sounded. It was low, nervous, as though the man were half afraid to speak, yet more afraid not to.

"I have a report to make, Mr. Chairman," he said. "It is my duty to complain against a member. I have taken the pledge like the others, and you have seen fit to make me responsible for their conduct. Therefore I must speak."

"These explanations are unnecessary," said the cold voice behind the grille. "Who is the member you wish to complain of?"

"Lorenzo Courtney, Mr. Chairman."

CHAPTER XV

A SENTENCE IMPOSED

THE SECRET AGENT sat rigid and waiting in his chair. The harshly precise voice of the invisible leader behind the grille droned on:

"Lorenzo Courtney! Before I hear the charge against you there is a certain matter I must ask you to report on. Earlier this evening you were commissioned by a friend of our organization to take charge of and question one suspected of being a possible dangerous enemy. I refer to the newspaper man, Sid Granville. What have you to say about this?"

Prickles of tension coursed up the Secret Agent's spine. He could almost feel those unseen eyes back of the metal grille boring into his own. A faint rustle of clothing and creak of chairs in the gloom around him, told that the other members of the meeting were straining to hear his answer. And on that answer might depend the success or failure of his desperate, daring step in coming here. He rolled his shoulders, shrugged, and kept his voice nonchalant.

"I did my best, Mr. Chairman, but the man wouldn't wake up. Mrs.—er—our friend gave him too strong a drink. I had to leave for this meeting before his answers made sense."

"So—and where is this man now?"

"At my apartment. I'm still holding him."

"You have taken every precaution, of course, to see that he does not escape?"

The Secret Agent let a moment pass before he answered. Then, with deliberate craft, he put a quaver of uncertainty into his voice. "Yes, sir—I think—that is, I'm sure he is safe."

Victor Blass spoke with sudden excitement. "Pardon me, Mr. Chairman, but you should know before this goes farther that

Lorenzo Courtney was drunk when he arrived tonight."

"Drunk!" The word came out of the darkness explosively. "You mean he came to this meeting drunk?"

"Yes." There was hesitancy in Blass's voice now. "And if I hadn't known him—hadn't recognized him at once—I wouldn't have admitted him. He couldn't remember his signal, sir, and he had neglected to put on his mask."

A stifled curse sounded behind the grille. A momentary silence followed it. Then the Chairman spoke as calmly, as precisely as before; but with a touch of sardonic mockery in his tone.

"Courtney is at fault—wholly and unquestionably. Men engaged in such an enterprise as ours cannot, must not, touch liquor. But shall we say, Victor Blass, that your own conduct has been entirely wise and praiseworthy—a perfect model for the other members to follow?"

A gasp sounded from the direction of a chair in the rear of the seated group. The relentless voice of the Chairman, continued:

"You had your orders not to let any member into this meeting until he gave his signal. Do orders mean nothing to you?"

Stark terror, proving the power that this leader had over his men, trembled in Blass's reply. The brutal confidence he had displayed during the bank raid was gone.

"I—I was afraid to turn him away in his condition. I weighed the factors—and reached a decision to meet the emergency. I—appeal to you, Mr. Chairman."

The Chairman's laugh held no mirth, no mercy. "I shall give the matter thought, and meanwhile—"

"Meanwhile, Mr. Chairman, if Courtney was responsible for a prisoner, something ought to be done. He is in no state—"

"I am coming to that, Blass! Two of you, Doeg and LaFarge, will accompany Courtney back to his apartment at once. If Granville is still there, Courtney will be punished for his misconduct with a whipping only. If Granville isn't there—I shall consider that Courtney has committed a major breach of discipline and is of no further use to this organization. In that case—I shall decree his death!"

There was another silence in the room, during which there came again the scrape of a chair and a faint click. Then, weirdly, mysteriously, the chamber began to grow light. The masked faces of the men around "X" appeared slowly as out of a haze.

Instantly his eyes swiveled toward the grille at the end of the room. But the chair was empty now. The sinister Chairman had withdrawn. There was some doorway close to that desk through which he had passed. It was he who controlled the falling and rising of the darkness.

TWO masked figures in the group arose at once: Doeg and La-Farge, the members delegated to go with "X" to Courtney's apartment. "X" stood up also, walked toward the door into the corridor through which he had come. Victor Blass opened the metal door with its slitted peephole, letting them into the outer passage. The two who were now "X's" guards removed their masks, and he did likewise.

They stared at him with open hostility, pushed him roughly ahead of them along the passage, and Chauncey Doeg, Courtney's supposed friend, spoke:

"You've been a damn fool, Lorenzo! You deserve anything you get! Your conduct reflects on us all. From now on you'd better watch your step. Understand? If you don't—we know what the Chairman would expect!"

Doeg flipped open his coat, exposing the black butt of an automatic worn in an armpit holster. The other man, LaFarge, laughed mirthlessly and nodded. "X" knew that these two wouldn't hesitate to shoot him. The disapproval of the Chairman, the sentence of a brutal beating already imposed upon him, gave them little respect for his life. Their own selfish interests swept friendship aside. There could be no loyalty among criminals, except that inspired by fear.

But the Agent did not intend to let these two men accompany him to Courtney's apartment. The mythical Sid Granville wasn't there. Ironically, the man who had impersonated Granville was now before them and they didn't know it.

"X" wasn't interested in either Doeg or LaFarge now. They were only cogs in the amazing crime organization that the mysterious Chairman had built up. Even Blass had proved himself to be a mere subordinate. The Chairman shared his secrets with no one. Unseen, unknown, he controlled the darkness and gave out the helmets which offset it. It was he who was the guiding genius of the devil-dark group. And his sinister orders would start the pillaging of S. Carleton & Company's great store tomorrow.

The Agent moved like lightning, just as they reached the shadows surrounding the spot where LaFarge had parked his car. Before Doeg was able to draw his automatic, the Agent's fist cracked sharply against his chin. The Agent whirled, struck again, and the second blow, with the impact of a trained boxer's behind it, connected with LaFarge's jaw.

Both men dropped senseless to the pavement while Secret Agent "X" turned and sped away. He ran two blocks, turned a corner, and leaped into his own parked coupé. In a moment he was speeding off into the darkness.

TEN minutes later Agent "X" turned into the mouth of the mews where Vivian de Graf dwelt. The pink stucco building which housed her ground-floor apartment was in the center of the block. A faint light seeped around the edges of drawn shades. In spite of the late hour the woman was still up.

The Agent, still in the guise of Courtney, pressed the bell button.

None of his inward excitement showed on his disguised face as he waited for his ring to be answered. The smell of Courtney's whiskey was still on his breath. He had paused a few moments before entering the mews to bring his impersonator's art into play. He had added a few deft touches of discoloration to the plastic material on his face. His lips were paler. There were circles under his eyes. The eyes themselves were bloodshot.[9]

He teetered unsteadily and let his lids and his lips droop in an unpleasant smile as the door before him opened.

Vivian de Graf, clad in a becoming pair of blue lounging pajamas, stood in the threshold. Highlights gleamed on her dark hair and on the clinging silk that covered her. They emphasized the pliant grace of her figure. Her complexion was freshly made up as though she expected a guest. Her scarlet lips were startlingly defined, her eyelashes heavy with mascara. Never had she looked more alluring—never more exotically beautiful.

But her features froze as she saw the man who came as Courtney. She did not move aside. Her voice was hard.

"What is it, Lorenzo? What do you want—coming here at this hour?"

---

9 AUTHOR'S NOTE: *No trouble is too great for the Agent to take in building up the realism of a disguise. He has on past occasions used a preparation of belladonna to make his eyes appear larger by increasing the size of the pupils. In this case, to make the whites temporarily bloodshot, he touched them with powdered alum, enduring the resulting smarting to achieve the desired effect.*

The Agent gave a tipsy salute. He leered at her knowingly. "Jus' wanna have a li'l' talk with you, Vivian. Jus' a li'l' talk."

"You've been drinking," she said scornfully. "I can't see you now."

She tried to shut the door in his face; but Agent "X" thrust out his foot.

"Bad girl, Vivian! Treat a frien' like that!"

He pushed her aside, swaggered into the apartment where the faint, but all-pervading scent of the saffron orchids lay. Vivian de Graf was beside him instantly, panting in anger, her chin outthrust. Her beauty now was like the sinister grace of a lioness about to spring, with rending claws hidden beneath sleek fur.

"Get out!" she cried huskily. "You—drunken fool! What makes you imagine I want to see you?"

"Nobody—said—you—did," the Agent replied slowly. "But—I wanna see you." He took off his hat, dropped it into a chair, fingered for a cigarette. Vivian de Graf eyed him keenly. A sudden look of uneasiness crept into her gaze.

"How long have you been like this? What did you do with Granville? Where is he now?"

The Agent held up a protesting hand. "Not—so many questions at once, Vivian, m'dear! One at a time, please."

"Where is Granville now?"

Agent "X" lighted his cigarette, let smoke dribble from his lips before he answered. Eyes half closed, drunken appearing, he watched her growing uneasiness.

"That," he said haltingly, "is what I wanna talk to you about. He—got away."

Anger became fury in the woman's face. Her hands clenched at her sides as she stepped close. Her sleekly clad body was taut in every rippling muscle.

"Fool! Fool!" she said again. "I asked you to be careful! I thought I could trust you—that much!"

"Sorry," said the Agent. "But I'm the one you wanna worry about. I'm in bed with the boss—an' you—gotta help me!"

"Exactly what do you mean?"

"X" gave a humorless laugh. He waved a finger close to her face. "There was a meeting tonight, an' the boss wanted to know what I'd found out about Granville. I stalled. I couldn't tell him the bird had flown. I said he was at my apartment. Then the Chairman, the boss, sent two fellows back with me to find him. The boss said that if Granville wasn't there—I'd—be killed. So I shook them—and came here."

THE woman's expression showed that she understood all he had said. "Well—what do you expect me to do?" she asked.

Agent "X" drew himself up with the exaggerated dignity of a drunken man. He stared at her solemnly, accusingly. "You got me into this! You—wished that bird on me! Now—you gotta make it right with the boss. You know him!"

She didn't deny it. She gave a scornful laugh. "It's your own funeral. If you hadn't got drunk—"

The telephone sounded suddenly, and Vivian de Graf turned. The first flare-up of her anger had passed. She was poised now, coldly scornful. "X" watched her lift the receiver. Saw her listen and glance his way. He couldn't hear the voice that spoke at the other end of the wire; but the meaning of her answer was plain.

"He's here now. You'd better have them come—at once!"

There was a note of cruelty in her speech. She clicked up the receiver and faced him, smiling thinly with red lips.

"It's too bad, Lorenzo! You might have gone far—if you hadn't been a fool!"

The Agent let panic come into his voice. "You told him I was here! You—They'll kill me!"

Vivian de Graf threw back her head and laughed, white teeth gleaming, supple body relaxed. The thought of his death seemed to amuse her.

"You will get only what you deserve," she said.

The Agent's manner changed as though fear had cleared the fumes from his befuddled brain. He drew his face into a scowl; clenched his fist. "No—I won't wait to be murdered. And—you'll be sorry for this!"

She did just what he expected then. Her white hand streaked to a drawer in the table at her side. It came out clutching a gun which she centered on his vest.

"Stand still, Lorenzo, or I shall save them the trouble of killing you—by doing it myself."

Her steady hand, her merciless eyes showed that she meant it. A cruel smile still curved her red lips.

She was standing on a rug. The other end of it was close to the

Agent's feet. There was polished flooring beneath. Suddenly his heel moved forward and jerked back on the fabric. It was done so quickly, so deftly, that Vivian de Graf made a clutch at the table to save herself from falling. In that instant, before she could swing the gun muzzle toward him again. Agent "X" leaped forward and disarmed her.

Furious, white-faced, she stood before him as the Agent centered the weapon on her heart. He was still playing the part of Lorenzo Courtney, but in another, more masterful role.

"Now," he said, "call the boss! Tell him that if he sends anyone to get me—you'll die first."

Tense seconds went by while the woman weighed his words. He had no intention of making good his threat; but she didn't know it. It was made only to force her to reveal the mysterious Chairman's telephone number. Vivian de Graf shrugged and said in a flat voice:

"You win, Lorenzo. You are smarter than I thought."

She turned toward the phone, reached out resignedly to pick it up, and as she did so Agent "X" caught his breath. For a change was suddenly apparent in the room. The walls were growing darker, the electric bulbs overhead dimmer, and there was a buzzing sound in the Agent's brain, while streaks of light danced before his eyes.

Vivian de Graf's white face was becoming blurred. He saw her drop her hand from the phone, saw her turn toward him, but he couldn't see her features clearly enough to get her expression. Yet he knew what was happening, knew that the weird, blinding blackness of the devil-dark gang was descending in the room.

CHAPTER XVI

DEATH IN THE DARK

THE SECRET AGENT stood frozen. He wasn't afraid. He was amazed. This upset all his plans. It baffled him utterly. He crouched and moved crabwise toward the wall. He fumbled along it toward the door, listened for steps in the street outside. The room was completely black now. There was no sound from Vivian de Graf. He couldn't even hear her breathing. He put his hand on the doorknob to turn it, knowing there might be men with guns waiting outside. But he was ready to take a chance.

Then he heard a noise which came from directly opposite across the big room. There were French windows there. His roving eyes had noticed them earlier. The noise sounded like one of the windows being pushed open by a stealthy hand. The killers were evidently coming to get him that way. They had the front guarded, the place surrounded, and all ways of escape cut off.

But his reasoning was upset the next instant. For Vivian de Graf spoke in the darkness, mortal terror seeming to constrict her throat.

"Who's there? Who is it? Oh, my God—"

The person by the window didn't answer with words. His reply was more abrupt, more terrible than any speech could have been. It was a shot in the utter gloom of the room, a shot that seemed to find a mark, for Vivian de Graf gave a piercing, pain-racked cry.

The Secret Agent waited aghast, trying to make sense out of this seemingly senseless thing. He heard the woman's cry repeated, heard it choke in her throat as though Death's fingers were already pressing there, heard the table go over as though she had clutched at it. Then came the unmistakable thud of a falling body. Even the rug could not muffle it entirely. It only made the sound more gruesome—like rock being thrown on a coffin lid.

The thud was followed by a moment's silence. Agent "X" thought the unseen assassin was taking aim at him. But instead there came a frenzied curse in the darkness and the crash of a falling vase. It was not accidental, for swift footsteps moved across the floor, then another vase was shattered, and still another.

A madman seemed to have entered the chamber under cover of that blinding dark. He appeared to be preoccupied in some inexplicable work of destruction all his own. For "X" could hear him crushing the pieces of broken pottery underfoot, stamping among them, breathing in great gasps.

Every muscle tense, the Agent suddenly leaped forward. He could learn nothing by crouching in the dark. His curiosity was aroused to the point of risking death.

A man snarled. "X's" plunging body struck yielding flesh. Something crashed against his shoulder, and a second shot sounded deafeningly in his ear. But no bullet struck him, and his fingers closed over a human arm.

He dug in, swung his left arm around the man he had gripped, and knocked the mysterious visitor off his feet. In a tumbling, crashing heap, they went down together among the pieces of splintered vase.

Deliberately then the Agent reached forward to feel the man's head, expecting to encounter one of the round helmets such as he had touched in the bank. But this man, though he could obviously see in the dark, was not wearing the same sort of helmet. His was softer, more wrinkled, fitted with a cord around his thin neck. The Agent tried to tear it loose, and the man seemed to go insane.

He was bony, lean almost to the point of emaciation, but possessed with the superhuman strength that some inward fire of emotion gave him. He fought like a madman, biting, clawing, kicking.

The Agent drove a knuckled fist against his jaw; but the pliable helmet deadened the blow. The other's head snapped back, but he did not pass out. And, able to see, when "X" couldn't, he succeeded in bringing the muzzle of his gun down on the Agent's wrist with paralyzing force. "X" felt his fingers loosening, felt the muscles of his arm where the blow had fallen going limp. He levered his other arm forward, grabbed the gun, and jerked it free. But as he did so, the lean man rolled away across the floor.

"X" heard the window grate again. He swung the gun toward it, started to pump the trigger, but held his fire. His quick mind was already checking over impressions. Something had clicked in his memory.

THE window slammed back as a man leaped out. A shoe scraped against stone in the darkness outside, no blacker than that in the room. But in another moment, as "X" picked his way gingerly over the floor, nursing his bruised arm, lightness began to come. Not through the window, but from the bulbs overhead. The darkness was lifting again, as mysteriously as it had fallen—and it lifted on a room of death.

For Vivian de Graf lay sprawled on the rug by the overturned table. Crimson was spread over her blue pajama coat; crimson, just under the heart, darkening the glisten of the silken fabric.

The Agent crossed to her in one swift stride. He bent down and pressed his fingers on her outflung wrist. But there was no pulse flutter. That single shot, fired in the dark, had done its work well. Vivian de Graf was dead. Even so, she was beautiful, red lips a splash of color across the whiteness of her face, eyes closed as if in sleep.

But the Agent did not pause to stare. Hers was not the only beauty that had been stricken in that room. The frenzied slayer's passion had not stopped at taking human life. Among the splintered pieces of pottery lay the stems and petals of a score of saffron orchids. The Agent's eyes darted along the floor. Three vases filled with the flowers had been smashed. The spotted blossoms had been trampled on, their destruction as deliberate as the woman's death, and done in the same murderous fury.

A single orchid, kicked accidentally under a chair, had escaped. The Agent picked it up, stared curiously. The poisonously spotted petals curled like living things. The flower's dark center seemed an accusing eye.

He took an envelope from his pocket, dropped the flower in and slipped it in his coat. Then he glanced at the woman again, and noticed for the first time that the rug at her feet had been kicked away by her silken leg as she fell. Under the rug's edge, close to the table, was a small metallic plate set just above the level of the floor. Some sort of electric switch—and the Agent's eyes narrowed instantly.

He strode to it, placed his foot on the thing tentatively, and pressed down. Almost at once the lights above his head grew dimmer, and there was that strange buzzing in his ears. He took his foot off and the sensation stopped. He understood now. This was how the darkness had been made.

There was a hidden mechanism to produce it somewhere in the room. Wires led from it to this floor switch. Vivian de Graf had tricked him when she pretended to reach for the phone. She had stepped on the switch beneath the rug, started the mechanism in motion. The shot that found her heart and made her fall, had released her weight from the plate and automatically turned the mechanism off.

Agent "X" began a hurried search for the thing that could bring darkness blacker than night to human eyes. It would be hidden, but it must be somewhere in this chamber. He bent above the floor switch again, intent on seeing which way the wires beneath it led.

But abruptly his search ceased. For a car whined in the night outside and came to a purring halt. Then voices muttered and footsteps sounded close to the vestibule door. The bell of Vivian de Graf's apartment made a silver tinkle in the kitchenette, a moment passed, and a key grated in the lock.

The Agent leaped from his kneeling position over the switch. He must not be found here, whether by bandit members or police. There was much to be done, a fresh lead he believed he could follow, a new line of action to pursue. He flung toward the window soundlessly on his rubber-soled shoes. He opened a side of the casement with quick care, stepped through into the darkness of a court as the unseen assassin had done. A moment more and the shadows of the night had swallowed him completely.

HE emerged from shadow fifteen minutes later to cross the rear yard of an ancient brownstone house. He had climbed fences, come through other yards to get here. Light from a single large window in the house before him cast dim illumination on the stone flagging at his feet. The Agent looked like a flitting ghost as he moved forward. He was still disguised, as Lorenzo Courtney. His eyes were raised to the window above. There was a look of intense concentration on his face.

For a man's head moved across the window, turned and moved again. Some one was pacing restlessly in the lighted room, some one who could not keep still, though the hour was late and the rest of the house was dark.

The Agent slipped through an alley at the building's side. He passed into the quiet street. Here he turned and silently mounted a flight of steps. There was a door before him and a bell button to press, but he did not touch the latter. His set of oddly shaped chromium tools came out. Under the pencil-thin beam of a tiny electric flash he probed in the keyhole.

So quickly and silently that the pacing man was unaware. Agent "X" entered the hallway of the house. He moved directly toward the rear, toward that single lighted room. His eyes were gleaming, his whole body was alert, and in his right hand was the gun he had taken from the mysterious killer who had come to Vivian de Graf's. But as he pushed the door before him softly open, he held the weapon behind him.

The man in the room was thin, stoop-shouldered, with the look of a scholar about him. His gaunt face had a sickly, ghastly pallor. When he saw what appeared to be Lorenzo Courtney standing specterlike in the door he gasped and crouched back.

A thin smile curved the Agent's lips. He was watching the other's actions intently. And he had learned from them what he wanted to know. "I see that you recognize me, de Graf!"

The man who had been pacing the lighted laboratory in the old-fashioned house, leaned against a chair and passed a shaking hand across his face. He looked ten years older than when the Agent had last seen him. He raised haggard eyes, stared at the Agent dully.

"I don't know what you mean," he said. "I don't know who you are. Get out of here—before I call the police."

The Agent's answer came relentlessly. "Emil de Graf, you're lying. I recognized you when we fought—even though I couldn't see you! And this is your gun."

He thrust the weapon into sight, saw the scientist start guiltily.

"It's the gun you killed your wife with. You are a murderer, de Graf—the murderer of your own wife!"

The face of de Graf had become grayer still. He was swaying on his feet, staring dazedly at his accuser, and Agent "X" continued:

"I know your motive. You were jealous, de Graf—insanely jealous. Behind that pretended calm of yours, behind that tolerance you professed, you were angry at your wife's interest in other men. That's why you killed her!"

Emil de Graf clenched his fists. "I should have killed you, too, fool that I was!" he cried. Then added hoarsely: "For God's sake who are you? What do you want?"

The Agent's answer was to walk slowly forward, the gun pointed at de Graf. His stare had the inexorable quality of Fate itself.

"Then you admit it," he said quietly. "You admit you killed your wife!"

The scientist cringed, backed away. "No! No!" he gasped. "I admit nothing. You can't have me arrested. They can't send me to the chair. There's no proof—" He broke off, breathing heavily, and stood as though transfixed by the Agent's level, accusing stare.

"You are a scientist, de Graf," "X" said quietly. "You know that, given certain facts, you can discover the truth about natural phenomena. It is the same for human actions. I know that you were jealous of your wife. I know you tried once to throw acid in her face, so that other men would not find her beautiful. I know that when your attempt to mar her beauty failed, you became desperate to the point of madness. Can you deny that?" The Agent stepped closer to de Graf. "I know that you came to Vivian de Graf's apartment an hour ago. I fought with you in the darkness. Your wife lies dead in that room now, shot through the heart. Here is the gun from which the shot was fired. Your gun, de Graf! You killed your wife!"

Clammy moisture beaded de Graf's forehead. His shoulders drooped. He seemed on the verge of collapse as he nodded slowly, unable to face the Agent's accusing eyes.

"Yes—" he said dully. "Yes—I shot her, as you say." The smoldering fires of passion flamed in his eyes. "But she gave me cause! She has tricked me, humiliated me, hurt my pride for years. She was a poor girl when I married her. She looked up to me as a great scientific worker. I took her out of the impoverished life she had known. We traveled, met interesting people. Then she got a taste for luxury. Men flattered her. It went to her head. She forgot all I'd done for her, forgot the vows she'd made. She called it being modern. When I objected she threatened to leave me. To keep her, I had to agree to her ways. She dragged my name through the public press, created scandals. She even took up with—a criminal."

The Agent's eyes flashed. He leaned forward. "This criminal, de Graf, who was he?"

"I don't know his name. But she dared brag to me—boasted that she'd grown tired of Roswell Sully, and had found some one who suited her better. A criminal who, she said, was a greater scientist than I. She was a child about such things. I didn't believe her until I visited her one night at her apartment, and she turned the darkness on me from a mechanism this man had given her. She laughed at me under cover of it, and said she was afraid of me no longer—and would leave me for good—" He broke off, trembling.

"And so you set to work to find out what the darkness was," Secret Agent "X" prompted, "and made a helmet to combat it. You learned that it wasn't darkness at all, but a force that blinded human eyes."

"Yes," the scientist nodded eagerly. "I had to show her I was as good a man as that lover of hers—even though I couldn't shower her with orchids. And I—I—"

"You succeeded—and you killed her."

De Graf nodded. "Yes, I succeeded, and now that you know the truth you're going to turn me over to the law. You are a detective, of course."

The Agent shook his head. "No. Hunting criminals is my work—just as yours is science. But I'm not interested in crimes such as yours—crimes of passion."

"Then why did you come here?" de Graf snarled. "What do you want?"

"Only one thing," the Agent said sternly. "The helmet—the one you used tonight. Give me that and the law shall never hear from my lips that you are the murderer of your wife."

CHAPTER XVII

THE NIGHT'S NEMESIS

THE FOLLOWING AFTERNOON Secret Agent "X" stood near the marble and chromium main entrance of S. Carleton & Company. Shabby clothing covered the powerful, athletic lines of his body. Nondescript features disguised his face. His manner was dejected. The fiery alertness of his eyes was hidden by the wilted brim of an ancient felt hat.

He attracted little attention from the throngs surging in and out of the city's largest department store. Once an old lady, touched by his appearance of abject want, slipped a dime into his ungloved hand. The Agent, living up to his role of down-and-outer, acted humbly grateful as he pocketed the coin.

Inside the big store, three thousand shoppers, unaware that the hideous shadow of crime hovered just above their heads, crowded through the aisles, pushed into packed elevators, stood impatiently on escalators, jostled, talked and laughed. Scores of detectives, pretending to be shoppers also, mingled with them. These were picked men of the headquarters division, warned into utmost caution by strange orders they had received, and keeping their guns, blackjacks and bracelets carefully out of sight.

They had arrived from two o'clock on, singly and in pairs, converging on the store from many directions, entering unobtrusively through a dozen different entrances. And the Agent had smiled in grim satisfaction as he watched them come.

No one of the passing detectives gave his drooping, shabbily clad figure a second glance. They took him for what he appeared to be—merely a dejected member of the city's army of unemployed. Yet it was he who was responsible for their coming there. It was he who had telephoned a startling message to the commissioner earlier in the day, giving the police head explicit directions.

Agent "X" had refused to tell his name. But his voice had carried the ring of absolute assurance, and he had made the police commissioner an amazing promise—so amazing, in fact, that though the commissioner was skeptical he dared not ignore what his nameless informant had said. And the steady but cautious arrival of detectives on the premises of S. Carleton & Company proved that he had acted at once.

As Agent "X" stood in front of the store, a newspaper dropped by a careless shopper, slid by his feet. The Agent picked it up like a down-and-outer, grateful for any small favor that circumstance bestowed.

Lurid headlines screamed the news: "Society Beauty Murdered." A picture of Vivian de Graf stared arrogantly from the page. The words beneath described the finding of her body in her exclusive mews apartment. They stated also that her husband, Emil de Graf, distinguished professor of physics at City University, had been found murdered in the brownstone house where he lived in another part of the city.

This did not surprise the Agent; though he read the story with interest. He had promised not to mention de Graf's crime to the law, and he had kept his word. But the criminals with whom Vivian de Graf had cast her lot had taken swift vengeance, guessing apparently, just as "X" had, who her slayer was.

He turned the page over, saw one more news item which held his attention for a moment. This told of the finding of Lorenzo Courtney's body on a park bench early that morning. A patrolling cop had made the discovery. Letters and a wallet in the dead man's pocket had led to speedy identification. Financial worries were supposed to be the cause of the suicide.

The real motive was known only to Secret Agent "X," the man responsible for the placing of the body on the bench in the dead of night. For that had been his answer to the unknown Chairman of the criminal group—an answer that would lull suspicion. And only he, outside of the criminals themselves, knew how closely these three events—the murders of Vivian and Emil de Graf and the suicide of Courtney—connected.

He dropped the paper, strolled to a corner of the big store where he could see in both directions. Casual as his manner seemed, excitement pulsed through his tautly alert body. The zero hour of four was almost at hand.

Down the block, a small electric truck with the name of the city lighting company on its sides rattled into view. It stopped beside the curb and a man in overalls emerged, carrying a pair of large, heavy pliers. He looked like a workman. Another man in overalls followed him, a coil of black wire slung over his arm. They lifted a manhole cover and descended below street level.

A minute or two passed, and both reappeared, drawing the length of wire from the hole in the street back to the parked truck.

The thing seemed commonplace. No one passing gave it a second glance. But the grim light of battle sprang into the Secret Agent's eyes. Collar turned up, blowing on his hands like a bum trying to keep warm, he shuffled nearer the workmen and their truck.

From the corner of his eye he saw two other cars draw up on the same block. There was an air of casualness about the young men within them. They didn't get out at once, but lighted cigarettes and shuffled through the pages of small books like salesmen going over territory lists.

THE Secret Agent looked quickly across the street toward a window where a clock giving U. S. Naval Observatory time was visible. He watched the minute hand crawl around its arc till it touched the exact hour of four. Then he glanced back at the parked truck again. One of the men, as the Agent stared, disappeared inside.

A moment passed, and the Agent stiffened. A sharp tingle shot along his nerves. It was getting dark now. A cloud seemed to have passed over the sun, a gloom like twilight was settling down. And in the Agent's head was the strange buzzing that foretold the coming of synthetic night.

Grimly, tensely, he stepped into a doorway out of sight and drew a piece of rubberized fabric from a pocket. It was the helmet mask de Graf had given him the night before, the mask that represented hours of patient, secret research on the part of the murdered physicist.

The Agent knew now, had known for many hours, since the unfailing eye of Hobart's movie camera had made its record, that the darkness had no external existence, but was in the eyes of human beings alone. It was a force, a ray probably, that temporarily paralyzed the optic nerve. No wonder that the darkness seemed more complete than any night. No wonder that criminals could work beneath it with impunity—criminals equipped with insulating helmets which made their own eyes impervious to the ray.

There was sweat on the Agent's forehead as he adjusted the strange mask over his head. A great crime was about to take place—

and the safety of thousands depended on him alone. The police were coming. Detectives were already in the store; but police and detectives would be helpless against the blinding dark. They would flounder as futilely as they had on other occasions when it had fallen. Whips would be plied by the raiders, men and women would stampede, horror would be repeated perhaps.

Yet to trap the criminals red-handed, to expose them for the fiends they were, "X" had been forced to wait until the darkness fell before he acted, forced to let the first fearful horror of the thing descend.

The mask of de Graf, fashioned of gum rubber impregnated with lead sulphide and the rare metal, thorium, had goggles of pressed mica and glass. It was almost a perfect insulator. Already the buzzing in the Agent's brain had diminished, as the action of the invisible, nerve-paralyzing rays was lessened. The lights before his eyes had ceased to dance. The twilight grew brighter.

But pandemonium had arisen in the street, and the scene he saw before him was like a glimpse into some unearthly hell—a nightmare of horror that the Secret Agent was never to forget. On all sides people were floundering, pushing against each other. Their eyes, though blinded by the devilish ray, were wide with terror. The hoarse cries of men mingled with the piercing screams of women in a shrill tumult. Hysteria quivered like jagged lightning through the crowds.

The Agent turned his helmeted head toward the electric truck. The two workmen were carrying on their task quite calmly in the midst of mad confusion. How they could do this was plainly evident to "X" now. They, too, had helmets on their heads—helmets which proved their guilt as members of the devil-dark gang.

"X" SAW other helmeted figures slip from the two cars that had so quietly parked. Whips and canvas sacks were in these men's hands. They pushed their way through the staggering, milling crowds toward the department store's front. They entered as the Agent watched. He knew that others were entering through other doors that he could not see; knew that the raiders were gathering to do their work of looting. In a moment more, when the dark had so frightened the crowds inside that panic swept among them, those cruel, metal-tipped whips would begin to descend.

A second longer the Agent crouched in the doorway, looking both ways along the street. He hoped somewhere to see the directing genius of all this, the mysterious Chairman whose identity he did not know. But if he was here he was well hidden—hidden even from the Agent's searching gaze.

Glancing back at the truck again, he saw one of the workmen strike out with a whip. A man and a girl had stumbled over the cable on the pavement, and were being lashed out of the way.

The whip curled around the girl's body like a snake, its metal tip tearing at her dress. The workman drew it back, lashed again, ripping the clothing in great jagged seams, baring the white skin beneath. The girl screamed wildly, and ran headlong from the vicinity of the truck. The young man with her tried to follow, but stumbled against the vehicle instead, and a shower of stinging strokes sent him cowering back.

With breath hissing between clenched teeth, with fury lying hot against his heart, the Secret Agent fought his way through the seething mass of humanity about him. It was time for him to strike, time for him to make good his promise to the police.

People flung themselves against him, clawed at him blindly as he circled and made for the truck. He slipped like a ghost in that black gloom through crowds now almost mad with fear.

Feeling themselves secure, not knowing that anyone had guessed their secret, the men by the truck did not see the weirdly helmeted form until "X" was within twenty feet of them.

A startled cry came from behind one of the helmeted heads then. The man shouted something to his companion above the uproar. Both men stared. Then suddenly they dropped their whips, and automatics gleamed dully in their straining hands. Like weird monsters they crouched to fire.

Only rarely did the Secret Agent carry deadly weapons. But against this hideous band of whip-torturers who had killed women and robbed innocent children of their lives he had come armed. The weapon in his hand spoke quickly now. With the gun held close against his hip, not even taking aim along the sights, he fired twice, at the same instant that the others shot.

Bullets whistled close by his head, slapped against a building behind him. But the Agent had ducked the moment after he fired, and his own shots had found their mark. One of the helmeted men cried out and pitched forward. His hands dropped at his sides. Like a puppet with suddenly severed strings he collapsed. The other man staggered, his gun clattering to the street. He was not mortally hit like his companion, for he plunged to the back of the truck, his hand flew forward to a hidden switch, and an instant later a blast of blue and orange flame came from the truck's interior.

The wounded man leaped back from the vehicle with a cry of pain. His plunging body struck the Agent. Both went down, and scorching heat funneled out from the burning truck, singeing their clothes. The wounded man groaned and went limp.

Agent "X" dropped his gun and pulled the man away from the hungry heat of the fire. For a moment he went dangerously close himself, trying to get a look inside the truck, and glimpse the mysterious mechanism. But it was hopeless. Some violently inflammable substance had obviously been planted to make the complete destruction of the mechanism possible in case of emergency. White-hot flames hissed and interlaced, as though a hundred blow torches had been fired at once. Glass tubes were popping in a series of miniature explosions. Lead connections were melting away. Metal was fusing into a bubbling, shapeless mass.

THE Agent backed away from the mystery truck and looked around the street. A change was already beginning to make itself apparent in those about him. The excited, terrified milling of the crowd was beginning to cease. Suddenly a man screamed and pointed toward the fire. There was a note of hysterical joy in his voice.

"Light! Light!" he shouted. "Light again—thank God!"

The fierce white-hot glare of the inflammable material planted in the car had broken through the blinding darkness of the Stygian night. Did that mean—As though in answer to the Agent's unfinished thought others around began to shout:

"The sun! The sun is coming out again!"

With a grim smile on his lips, the Agent tore his helmet off and stuffed it in his pocket. It was true! His own eyes, unaffected previously by the strange rays, could see perfectly now without the glass goggles. The rays were no longer radiating. The mechanism in the truck had been put out of commission by the fire. The crowds in the street were slowly regaining their normal sight as temporarily paralyzed optic nerves began again to function.

And it was the Agent, by his swift attack, who had forced the raiders to destroy their own dark-producing device. The burning had been done, of course, as part of a prearranged plan, thought out by the Chairman, to prevent the secret of the blinding rays from falling into the hands of the law. Normally, before the effect of the rays wore off, the raiders would have time to escape—as they had done on two previous occasions. But here again the Secret Agent's action had changed things.

For the helmeted raiders were now in the big store of S. Carleton & Company, detectives guarded every exit, and neither of the two men in charge of the truck had been able to warn their companions what had happened.

Agent "X" turned and made his way quickly to the store. By the action of the people around them, the raiders had now learned that something was radically wrong with their plans. But for them it was too late. Their lashing, metal-tipped whips could beat blinding humans into cowering fear, but they were of little use against grim detectives, armed, and already partially able to see. The Agent watched the scene tensely. He had done his work well, given the guardians of the law more than an even break—and they were making good use of it.

When two of the helmeted raiders discarded their whips, drew guns and started to fire, they were met with a volley of bullets. But a fierce fight was raging by another exit. Four of the raiders had concentrated their frenzied attack to escape here. Two were grabbed by wounded detectives and made prisoners. Two others managed to break through.

Grimly the Secret Agent crouched with his gun in hand again. He fired as the helmeted running figures appeared, sent bullets smashing into the bandits' legs, and saw them sprawl cursing and screaming to the sidewalk.

Inside the store, the terrific battle had been won. A dozen detectives lay dead and wounded on the main floor. Victims of the first slashing onslaught of the terrible whips cowered in whimpering terror against the walls and counters. But the raiders—those still alive—were in the hands of the police, guns pressed against their sides, steel handcuffs clamped over wrists.

Not a single member of the raiding gang had escaped. They had been caught red-handed with all their hideous paraphernalia—their cruel scourging whips tarnished with the blood of a hundred victims, their guns, canvas sacks to hold the loot, and their strange helmets.

Detectives, coldly angry at the death of some of their comrades, were jerking the helmets off the heads of their prisoners, smashing down with blackjacks and gun muzzles when open rebellion flared. And the raiders were a bruised and vicious group when their faces were finally bared to the gaping crowds. The Agent recognized a few; Doeg, LaFarge and Blass among them. The others were obviously men of education also; ruined bankers and financiers, unable to stand the gaff of failure, and slyly engaged in desperate crime.

Agent "X," the man who had engineered this tremendous victory for the law, the man in down-and-outer's clothes, stood on the sidelines and watched.

He was at the curb when the members of the devil-dark gang were shoved into Black Marias. Later, in the disguise of A. J. Martin, he went to police headquarters, and was there when the commissioner himself made a statement to the press. The police, the commissioner said, were satisfied. The most fiendishly vicious group of criminals in the city's history had been rounded up. True, the mechanism by which they created their blinding darkness had been destroyed by fire, its hideous secret kept a mystery, and millions in loot from previous raids were still to be salvaged. But the commissioner was confident that information leading to the recovery of the money could be sweated out of the prisoners. He was confident that not one man of the group had escaped; confident that the menace of the strange darkness would never fall on any city again.

In half-uttered confessions, several of the raiders had indicated that Vivian de Graf had been connected with the band before her death. It was the commissioner's private belief, he stated, that her murdered husband might have been the originator of the darkness, since it was known that he was a profound worker in science. The commissioner's smile was complacent as he assured the gentlemen from the press that the whole mystery of how such a group came to organize would be unraveled as soon as his prisoners had confessed.

All this the Secret Agent heard, and a smile twitched at the corners of his lips also; but it was humorless, sardonic. The police commissioner and the whole police department might be satisfied. He was not! And he never would be satisfied, or consider the case closed, until the unknown man behind it all, the mysterious Chairman, who had given the orders at the meeting that others carried out, had been exposed and caught.

CHAPTER XVIII

BLOSSOMING CLUES

MONTHS AFTER THE capture and imprisonment of the devil-dark gang, Secret Agent "X" moved through the exhibition rooms of a flower show in a large mid-western city. He was in the disguise of a white-haired, benign looking old man now. There was a silver-headed cane in his hand which seemed a necessary re-enforcement to his faltering steps. Under his left arm was a portfolio containing notes on flowers and copies of horticultural journals.

On both sides of the corridor through which he walked, flowers were banked in a riotous profusion of color. Roses, chrysanthemums, carnations, dahlias, geraniums—all the well-known garden blooms, together with fuchsias, gardenias, and other delicate hot-house blossoms.

The humid air of the big building was heavy with their scent. Flower lovers and horticulturists of all sorts and ages strolled close by. Pretty girls at gaily decorated booths passed out advertising pamphlets, and free sample bouquets. A red-lipped, coquettish miss beckoned to the Agent and laughed up into his face as she drew a red carnation through his buttonhole. He smilingly submitted, then moved on toward the west end of the room where an elaborate arch of blue silk, stretched on a wire framework, had the word "Orchids" emblazoned across it in letters formed of the flowers themselves.

In a moment he was in a chamber filled with thousands of the strangely shaped plants, rarest and most expensive of cultivated blooms. Many looked like bright-colored insects; like butterflies and moths poised for flight. Most of these the Agent, a student of many sciences, knew by name. There were the *Habenaria*, the *Spiranthes* and the *Oncidium* types.

He paused at last before a group of blossoms yellow as saffron and marked with the startling spots of a leopard's coat or some poisonous reptile's skin. The flowers were beautiful and exotic; but somehow unwholesome, as though nature had been tortured and tormented for their cultivation. There were no other blooms like them in the whole building.

The eyes of the Secret Agent gleamed as they fastened on these blooms. A faint, humorless smile curved his lips. He seemed a gentle old man bending forward to study the loveliness of rare flowers.

Those who saw him did not guess that the benign and aged face masked the features of the most masterly crime hunter in existence. They did not know that he was on the trail of a criminal at this very moment; that, having sworn never to give up till he had his man, he had waited months to track down and capture one of the most elusive criminals he had ever encountered in his whole career. They did not know that in his pocket at the moment was a telegram in code, written by one of his own trained operatives, which concerned those saffron flowers before him.

Weeks before, the Secret Agent had instructed paid operatives in a score of cities where horticultural exhibitions were scheduled, to get in touch with him if this special variety of saffron orchid appeared. He had equipped these operatives with a detailed colored plate of the flower itself, made from the single blossom he had picked up on the floor of Vivian de Graf's apartment. For "X" believed that the admirer who sent those orchids to the society beauty was the unknown Chairman of the devil-dark group—the man who had not been caught in the police round-up.

He straightened slowly from before the orchid exhibit, turned his smiling face toward a winsome girl attendant, and beckoned to her.

"These flowers," he said, "are most beautiful. I would like to learn more about them. Would it be too great an inconvenience to give me their owner's name and address?"

His voice was smooth, gentle, the soft voice of a polite old man. The girl looked at the number of the exhibit, consulted her register, and wrote a name and address on a slip of paper.

"You'll find the man who grew them at this address," she said. "But the flowers are not for sale and neither are the plants. They are here as competitive entries only."

The Secret Agent thanked her and looked at the paper in his hand. It said: "D. H. Brownell, 36 Rose Hill Road." Slowly, with the wistful smile still on his face, the Secret Agent moved toward the exhibition's exit, sniffing from time to time at the spicy fragrance of the carnation in his buttonhole.

He was panting, forty-five minutes later, as he climbed the gentle slope of Rose Hill Road. This was in a wealthy suburban section of the city where the horticultural exhibition had been held. Huge estates with green lawns spreading before them lined the well-kept street. Shade trees arched overhead. The feathery green of spring foliage showed in their interlaced branches. The air here, too, was sweet with the scent of flowers. Crime seemed as remote as some distant star. Yet it was crime's black trail that had brought Agent "X" away from his usual haunts, brought him on a mission as strange as any he had ever embarked upon.

HIS forward progress was interspersed with frequent halts beside some handy fence to catch his breath and fan himself with the fluttering leaves of a horticultural journal. He was playing the part of an old man well. His silver-headed cane tapping the sidewalk beside his shuffling feet, helped him at last to reach the house marked 36.

Here he rested again, mopping his forehead with a cambric handkerchief. Then he clicked open a gate and moved along a cement walk between rows of ornamental shrubs. The house before him was a large one. It and the grounds showed signs of lavish care and unstinted wealth.

A great dog came bounding toward him, barking furiously. The Agent paused with the timid uncertainty of an aged man and waved his cane at the animal, calling in a cracked voice for some one to check the beast's rushes.

In a moment a man appeared from the side of the house where he had been supervising the laying out of a new flower bed. That he was not a gardener was evident by his clothes. He was dressed in a stylish, white flannel suit. In contrast to the lightness of the cloth a jet-black beard covered the man's cheeks and chin and spread magnificently over the whole front of his coat. The rest of his face was ruddy, healthy with the glow of good food and wine and robust living. But there was in the depths of his eyes a certain furtive sharpness, a certain swift calculation, and he glanced suspiciously at his visitor and frowned.

"Here, Daniel!" he cried to the dog. "Stop it! Get back to your kennel!"

The dog flattened its ears, dropped its tail at once, and slunk away, rolling the whites of its eyes at its master, as though grim discipline had taught it to obey. The man turned ungraciously to the white-haired stranger.

"Well—what do you want?" he said.

Secret Agent "X" pushed his handkerchief into his pocket with a deliberately trembling hand. He leaned against his cane, panted for a second or two, then drew an ancient alligator skin wallet from his pocket. He adjusted steel-rimmed glasses on his nose, fumbled in his wallet prodigiously, and finally pulled forth a yellowed card. On this was printed: "Alfred Burpee, Editor Emeritus, *Flower Lovers' Quarterly*." With solemn dignity Secret Agent "X" handed the card to the frowning, bearded man before him.

"Mr. Brownell, I believe," he said. "It gives me pleasure to introduce myself, and it gives me pleasure also to meet a brother horticulturist of such distinctive taste as yourself." He waved a hand toward the carefully kept flower beds on all sides. "This is indeed a choice display of garden landscaping you have here. It is what I am in the habit of referring to in my articles as 'floral chromatization.' It is, however, what I should expect of a man whose exhibit is the talk of the flower show now being held."

The bearded man was rolling the stub of a cigar between his moist red lips. His gimlet eyes still bored into the face of the stranger who had introduced himself as Alfred Burpee. There was nothing on that face but guileless admiration and gentle interest. The Agent fumbled in his portfolio and drew out a copy of the *Flower Lovers' Quarterly*. He turned the pages eagerly.

"I still do articles for this, Mr. Brownell, though I am a bit too old to stand the exigencies of editorial work. I do articles—and it is my belief that you, if you would be so kind, could give me material for one of the best I have ever done. That you have unusual taste is evident. That you are a man of considerable talent I earnestly believe."

The bearded man flipped the pages of the magazine "Burpee" had given. The look of suspicion had begun to leave his eyes. His whole manner was growing relaxed. He cleared his throat importantly.

"You saw my orchid exhibit then?"

"I did. And I was so impressed with it that I asked the young lady attendant if I might pay my respects to the owner of such beautiful flowers. She was so kind as to give me your address. And here I am. I hope that you will find it possible to spare a few moments of your time."

"You want to do an article, eh?"

"Exactly—something with color photos if possible, and—"

A certain grimness came into Brownell's voice as he interrupted. "I'm sorry—no photos! I don't like people with cameras walking about—spoiling the flower beds."

"Then let us say just an article," the Agent said mildly. "Something that would be helpful to other horticulturists and give them an inkling of how you achieve your success."

THE bearded Brownell turned and beckoned for Agent "X" to follow. He strode off across the lawn, and "X" admonished him gently.

"Not too fast please—for an old man!"

Brownell showed his visitor many lavish displays of flowers. "X" saw a number of gardeners and their assistants at work. Brownell seemed to have little to do except spend his apparently unlimited resources caring for his estate. Huge greenhouses spread on a spacious lot behind the mansion. Brownell took Agent "X" through these, also. There were many handsome flowers here, many varieties of orchids even; but none of the saffron kind that had been shown at the exhibit. The Agent let wistfulness sound in his voice as he spoke.

"Beautiful! Beautiful!" he said, "but I see you do not keep the precious gold of your special plants in with the more common sorts. Or perhaps the flowers I saw at the show are all you have of that variety. In any case I want to congratulate you on raising some of the handsomest and most unique specimens of the orchid family it has ever been my privilege to behold."

Pride gleamed in the eyes of Brownell at the Secret Agent's flattery. He shrugged suddenly. "I did not intend to let any visitors here in on my secret. But after all, there's no reason why you, Mr. Burpee, shouldn't know. Come this way, please."

Agent "X" hid the thrill of excitement he felt. He had played his cards well, played on the vanity of a man to whom no other emotion except fear would appeal. For, that the man before him was vain of his yellow orchids, he had sensed months ago. Otherwise he would not have laid them at the feet of the woman he wished to impress.

Brownell led Agent "X" into the big house itself. It showed signs of recent expensive redecoration. The Agent's bearded host ushered him down a flight of winding stairs into a cellar room. A door showed at the end of this. Brownell opened it, motioned "X" to enter. He did so, and gasped at what he saw.

For here in this moist chamber, warmed even now by coils of steam pipes; here without any scrap of daylight or vent to the outside air, the prize saffron orchids grew, rearing their spotted yellow heads among jumbled piles of rock, on specially constructed concrete tables. They were everywhere "X" looked, sprouting amid rank green leaves, almost like some startling fungous growth. The plants seemed to be staring at him as though they had life of their own.

He put surprise into his voice, made his eyes widen.

"No sunlight! Good gracious, sir, you mean you raise these lovely flowers in this dark cellar chamber?"

The man who called himself Brownell smiled. "In a cellar chamber—yes. In the dark—no! Look!"

He gestured toward the ceiling where an intricate grillework of glass tubing showed. It seemed somewhat similar to slender Neon lighting tubes, but was arranged differently. No light was visible in them now. The light that revealed the bright flowers came from a big bulb Brownell had switched on when he opened the door.

"There is my sun," he said. "There is the light the orchids are grown in."

"Light!" echoed the Agent skeptically, in the tone of a puzzled old man. He adjusted his glasses again, peered up at the gleaming tubing as though to detect some illumination.

AGAIN the man called Brownell laughed in the depths of his wiry black beard. "You can't see it," he said. "It is invisible—beyond the range of the spectrum which human eyes can detect. Yet it is there—just as invisible and just as powerful as the ultra-violet rays which can blister the skin. That's where my orchids get their power to grow, and, because this light is never lacking, I've been able to create hybrids never produced before."

"It is incredible," said the Agent softly. "You've been experimenting with these flowers for years I suppose?"

"Yes, ever since I was a very young man. And it took me a long time to develop this light. I'm proud of it. It's rather an accomplishment you must admit—and I'm glad I have the leisure to indulge my hobby."

"An exceedingly constructive hobby," murmured the Agent. "And a great deal of time and patience must have gone into it."

"More perhaps than you realize," said Brownell boastfully. "Very few men would have had the will power to persist. It took me months, even, to gage the right intensity of my ultra-ray light. A trifle too little and the flowers would grow pale and die! A bit too much, and it would literally burn them up. Do you feel anything odd in your head right now?"

The Agent nodded, smiled.

"A slight buzzing it seems. It is most remarkable—and how you can control such a thing is a mystery to me!"

"It would be," said Brownell superciliously. "But I'll give you an idea how it's done."

He led Agent "X" to the end of the cellar chamber where the saffron orchids grew, opened a door into still another room. No plants showed here. It was filled with complex electrical mechanism. There many small tubes, many elaborate coils of wire, dials and delicate rheostat controls. An electric motor in a dust-proof casing gave out a low, continuous hum.

The tubes in the outer chamber where the plants grew were all connected to one central outlet which went through the wall of this power room. There was a big graduated dial and a leverlike handle near the low-humming motor. It reminded "X" of a control in some great ocean liner.

"There is my light throttle," said Brownell. "With that I control the invisible candlepower in the next room and in here, too, for the light that those tubes generate can come right through stone walls, right through metal, glass, anything! I have an insulating substance in the outside walls and ceiling, or else, if I turned the lever too far every one in this house might—"

Brownell checked himself suddenly; frowned as though his enthusiasm had made him say a little more than he had meant. He added rather brusquely:

"This branch of my horticultural hobby won't interest you, Mr. Burpee."

The Secret Agent was smiling. The wrinkled contours of his disguised face were deceptively gentle. Never had he looked more benign; never more harmless.

"On the contrary, Mr. Brownell," he said. "I am most interested—fascinated, I might even add! For many months I have wondered how you raised those exquisite orchids."

"Many months! They have never been on exhibition before!"

"Never on public exhibition—but, you can see how rapt my interest in them has been!"

SLOWLY, while a gradual change came over Brownell's face, the Secret Agent reached in his pocket. He took out an envelope, took from it a withered flower; one whose yellow spotted petals nevertheless showed. With the flower he displayed a small color plate, made while the bloom was still fresh enough to reveal accurate tints. Brownell's bearded mouth gaped for a moment.

"Where—where did you get that?" he asked.

"In the apartment of a very lovely lady," said "X" softly. "In the apartment of Vivian de Graf! It was one of the last of the flowers you sent her—before an assassin's bullet struck her down. Too bad that your gallant attentions so aroused the jealousy of her devoted husband!"

Brownell made a sound in his throat like a curse. Suddenly, furiously he struck the dried flower and color plate from "X's" fingers. He stepped back, stood with feet apart, glaring and panting at his white-haired visitor. The change that had come over his face above the beard was startling. It was furious, contorted in its anger, eyes glittering slits, veins standing out on the sweating forehead. It was the face of a hideous, sadistic criminal, the face of a man who, for all his esthetic love of flowers, had the instincts of a ruthless, predatory beast.

"So," he said. "Alfred Burpee. eh? The editor of a flower journal—interested in orchids—and in the light I raise them by!"

Suddenly Brownell threw back his head, opened a cavern of a mouth in his black beard, and gave vent to hideous laughter. He choked at the end of it, squeezed tears from his eyes. "Light!" he bellowed. "Light, eh!"

With a move so quick that the Agent could barely follow it, he thrust the lever attached to the big dial near the motor all the way to its end stop. The motor's low hum rose to an ear-splitting whine. Instantly the sensation of buzzing in the Agent's brain increased. Increased. Instantly the room began to grow dark, and the beaded, distorted features of the man before him began to fade, while Brownell's wildly evil laughter sounded mockingly. "Light! Light!" he screamed again. "Light—but you can't see in it!" The bearded criminal had geared up his mechanism, until the blinding darkness, a by-product of his experiments on plants, had descended as it had months ago over the terror-stricken crowds at the points where the raids had taken place.

But Agent "X" was not terror-stricken, not even surprised. As quickly as Brownell had increased the power of the strange mechanism, his own hand darted to his side pocket. He brought out the helmet mask of Emil de Graf, slapped it over his head, and brought the goggles before his eyes.

The invisible rays had not had time to paralyze his optic nerves. The helmet was instantly effective. He could see Brownell adjusting a gleaming helmet on his own head; hear the man bellowing again.

"Light! You'll get it this time so it will blind you like a mole—blind you so that you'll never see again as long as you live—if you live. You'll get so much light it will split your damned head wide open!"

Brownell gave a final tug to the helmet, reached under a shelf in the room, and drew forth one of the wicked, metal-tipped whips that the devil-dark gang had used.

With a thin smile on his lips behind the helmet he wore, Agent "X" gave the knob of his silver-headed cane a twist. The knob came off. He drew from the cane's hollow interior another long, snake-like whip.

BEFORE Brownell could use his own lash, before he could even turn to see that the man before him was helmeted like himself, Secret Agent "X" struck. His first blow knocked the whip from the other's hand, brought a screaming curse to Brownell's amazed lips. His second blow stopped the bearded man's forward lunge by laying a biting lash across his chest so stingingly that it almost cut the clothing above it.

Brownell instinctively cowered back as the blinded, stricken victims months ago had done. And Agent "X" plied the whip with the memory of those tortured victims' screams in mind. He plied it ruthlessly, plied it till Brownell had huddled back into the farthest corner of the room, till he was screaming for the Agent to stop, till his coat showed long rents where the metal tips had struck.

Then Agent "X" stepped forward and snatched the helmet from the man's head. Brownell screamed even more fearfully now.

"The light! The light!" he cried. "It will blind me! Blind me! Turn off the lever for God's sake!"

Agent "X" stepped forward and put the lever back to the position it had been in when he entered the room. Then he stood over the cowering Brownell with the whip still in his hand. Words, harshly uttered, grated between clenched teeth. The mild old man, "Burpee," had become a living, human scourge, a champion of justice.

"Your criminal plot was a clever one," he said. "It seemed foolproof, and it might have been—except for certain things. Your pose as a public defender gave you unusual opportunities to smell out men with criminal instincts and hound them, ruin them, till they were fit material for your plans. And none of them guessed that the man they hated so was actually their leader. None of them knew that the unseen Chairman who directed their activities was actually—Norman Coe!"

The Agent laughed mirthlessly, staring at the bearded, abject man in the corner. "Norman Coe, head of the Citizens Banking Committee, champion of depositors' rights!"

"X" opened his portfolio, drew out a tablet and a pencil, thrust them into Coe's hands. The darkness was lifting now. Coe would soon be able to see again even without his mask.

"Write," said "X" sternly. "Tell exactly how you tricked your own criminal allies as well as the public. Tell how you discovered the blinding ray in your experiments with flowers; how you thought of it as a cover for desperate crime. Tell how you hid the stolen money for a time in one of the closed banks where your Directors' Room was; and how you retired from your position on the committee after a time, and supposedly left the country for a visit to England.

"Tell how you changed your name to Brownell and planned to spend your stolen millions in luxurious retirement. Tell how your colossal vanity wouldn't let you resist the temptation to exhibit your prize flowers. Tell everything, Coe, down to the last detail, and sign it! Or, as surely as I stand here, I'll turn the light lever over again and blind you, and then whip the life out of you as your fiends did the life of Ellen Dowe!"

Under this terrible threat the trembling hand of Norman Coe wrote. Behind his black beard which had seemed an adequate disguise his bloodless face twitched.

When he had finished at last, Agent "X" pocketed the signed confession and suddenly fired his gas gun full in Coe's face, knocking him unconscious for many minutes to come. He spent a few moments examining the light producing mechanism, then left the underground chamber as he had come. As he passed through the room where the orchids were, he stopped and gasped abruptly. Every poisonous saffron bloom lay wilted and dead, killed by the increased rays that Coe's frenzy of rage had loosed for a time. The Agent shrugged, moved on out of the cellar chamber and up into the house.

The incurious gardeners at work outside glanced up, and saw only an old, white-haired man shuffling by again. The Agent walked down the hill as he had come. A faint melodious whistle like the strange call of some wild bird floated after him. It was the eerily unique whistle of Secret Agent "X," and it indicated now that a baffling and unique case was finally finished.

Within twenty minutes after "X" had left the home of "Brownell," the police head of the city where the yellow orchids had been exhibited, received Coe's signed confession along with mysterious but precise details concerning the man at 36 Rose Hill Road and the light-producing mechanism in the cellar room. The police head was an intelligent man who kept abreast of the country's news events. With an inspector and a dozen picked detectives he went at once to round up a criminal whose capture he knew would be a nationwide sensation, a criminal whose extraordinary cunning had taken the skill of a master crime hunter to match.

BOOK XIV

TALONS OF TERROR

In ten days there were ten murders. Bestial terror talons ripped the heart and soul from a city—as they ripped life from its civic monarchs. And in the funeral wake of these awesome claws lay the dried, bloodless husks of what once were men. The Grim Reaper stalked the city with a handful of horror. Alone, bucking this mad march to the grave, was Secret Agent "X"—the Man of a Thousand Faces. Countless times had "X" manhunted murderers. But never before had his trail carried him up a corpse-runged ladder of human husks.

CHAPTER I

DRINKERS OF BLOOD

THE MORNING SUNLIGHT that slanted down across the austere town residence of Lewis Forman, the millionaire railroad magnate, made a striking contrast to the gloomy, half-terrified countenances of the servants who were huddled together in the sitting room.

Police were bustling within and without the palatial mansion. Several police cars sat at the curb. A uniformed officer was on guard at the door.

The broad-shouldered, dynamic man who swung from the taxicab cast a keen, quizzical look at the cars. His hawkish eyes caught the license number of the headquarters sedan immediately before the entrance. He looked up toward the officer on guard, said: "That's Inspector Burks' car, isn't it?'"

The patrolman frowned. "What's it to you, mister?"

The broad-shouldered man mounted the four steps to the entrance, displayed a press card. "The name is Martin," he said. "Associated Press. Burks is a friend of mine."

The cop thumbed toward the door. "You can go up. The inspector is on the second floor—in the bedroom."

Mr. Martin of the Associated Press nodded, and entered. Down the long hall on the ground floor he caught a glimpse of the sitting room through the open door; saw the servants grouped together in a dazed huddle, with a plainclothes man standing guard. Then he proceeded upstairs.

At the top of the stairs another uniformed officer was on guard. When Martin flashed his press card, he was permitted to enter the bedroom at the end of the hall. Here he found several other newspapermen, police photographers, fingerprint men, and a precinct lieutenant. There was also Inspector Burks who nodded sourly

from his position near the bed. Martin returned the nod, glanced toward the bed. The medical examiner's back barred his vision.

Martin approached, looked over the shoulder of the medical man. The body that lay there was that of Lewis Forman, the master of the house. But he was almost unrecognizable. The bed itself was a welter of blood. Forman's throat was a gaping, raw wound. Though Forman had been a physically big man in life, his body was now shrunken to a mummy-like husk. For the blood had been drained from it as though by a pump.

The skin lay against his ribs, showing the outline of every bone, as if he were a skeleton wrapped in some transparent material. His eyes were wide open, with the pupils turned upward. His cheeks were two gaunt hollows, and the skin lay in folds against his cheekbones.

Mr. Martin studied that body for a long time. He tore his eyes away from it as Burks stepped to his side, whispered bitterly: "Well,

The masked monster leaped to its feet, hurled itself at "X," disregarding the threat of the police.

there's another story you can flash over the wire. Lewis Forman, the biggest railroad man in the country—killed by some wild beast. The same as the others that have died in the past nine days. I suppose your rags will be panning the department again."

Martin turned, studied the harassed, drawn countenance of the police inspector. "The papers know you're doing the best you can, inspector. It's just that they have to have something to write about." He jerked his head toward the bed. "No clues to who did it?"

"*Who?*" Burks growled. "You mean *what!* There must be some beasts of prey loose here in the city. And they seem to pick the biggest men in town. They come at night, make their kill, drink their victims' blood, and steal away without leaving a trace. I tell you, I almost begin to think they're supernatural!"

Martin shrugged, remained silent.

IN a moment the medical examiner arose from the body, wiping his hands upon a towel. He heaved a deep sigh, brushed the back of his hand across his forehead, wiping off the beads of sweat that had gathered there. "Whew!" he exclaimed. "That was nasty work."

Burks demanded eagerly: "When did he die, doc?"

"He's been dead at least ten hours," the doctor diagnosed. "That makes the time of his murder somewhere before midnight."

Burks nodded somberly. "I thought so. Nobody died yesterday, and we were beginning to hope that it was the end of these daily murders. But here it is on schedule again."

The other newspapermen in the room were busy making notes. But Martin of the Associated Press was not bothering with paper or pencil. His gaze rested upon a tall, cadaverous looking man in a dressing gown who was standing at the other end of the room, puffing furiously at a cigarette.

This man noted Mr. Martin's glance, and returned it with a scowl. His eyes shifted away, strayed to the corpse on the bed, and he shuddered violently.

Martin said to him: "You're Stanton?"

The tall man nodded. "That's right. How did you know?"

"In my business," Martin told him, "we always remember faces. You're Oscar Stanton, the man who cornered Peerless Locomotive three years ago. Everybody knows you. They call you 'the man who beat Wall Street.'"

Stanton seemed to like that. He was obviously flattered that a newspaper man should remember him.

Inspector Burks shifted impatiently. "Never mind that stuff now, Martin. We've got to get down to business." He swung about, beckoned to a detective sergeant who stood near the door. "Reilly, get on the phone. Tell the commissioner I want the reserves out. We're going to patrol every street in the city, and see if these wild beasts can get anybody else tomorrow!" His ordinarily florid face became suffused with an even deeper glow. "You'd think this was the African jungle instead of a big city in a civilized country. I swear to you they won't get away with another murder!"

He turned to Stanton, who was lighting a second cigarette from the butt of the first with hands that shook slightly. "You say you were sleeping in the room next to this one, Mr. Stanton?"

The Wall Street speculator finished lighting his cigarette, ground out the butt of the old one on the floor under his heel, and nodded.

"I was visiting overnight with Forman. I don't understand how any sort of beast could have got into this house. I saw the butler lock up. It would take a pretty clever burglar to get in. And yet this—whatever it was—entered, killed Forman, and got away without making the slightest sound to attract anybody in the household."

Burks asked slowly: "How come you happened to be staying here overnight, Mr. Stanton, when you live in the city yourself?"

Stanton flushed, glared irately at the inspector. "Do you mean to suggest—"

Burks' bulldog jaw protruded at an obstinate angle. "I don't mean to suggest anything, Mr. Stanton. This is murder. I just want to get at the facts. Don't you want to help us corner these wild beasts? For all you know, they might claw your throat next. Suppose they had gone into your room instead of into Forman's? You've got to cooperate with me!"

"All right," Stanton yielded sullenly. "I was here on a business deal with Forman. We hadn't finished our discussion last night, and we decided to close it over the breakfast table this morning. That's why I remained overnight."

"What was the nature of this deal?" Burks demanded.

"Just a little stock transaction. We were going to pool our stock purchases."

WHILE Burks had been questioning Stanton, Mr. Martin had been kneeling beside the bed, examining a series of peculiar red marks upon the floor. Burks noticed what he was doing, suddenly desisted from questioning Stanton, and knelt beside him.

The marks which Martin was studying appeared at intervals on the floor along the bed in series of four. They were bloody marks, as if made by something that had been trailing Forman's blood along the rug.

"Have you seen these yet?" Martin asked the inspector.

Burks shook his head. "I hadn't paid any attention to them. But now—God! They look like the mark of an animal's paw!"

"They might be that," Martin said speculatively.

"Sure they are!" Burks exploded. "The damn thing ripped open Forman's throat, feasted on his blood, and then just turned and walked out of here!"

Martin said slowly, "Maybe. But it would be a funny kind of beast. You notice that these marks are all in a row along the bed here. If it was an animal that walked out, there would be two rows—unless it was a one-legged animal."

Burks got up from his knees, pushed Martin away. "Stand clear of it, Martin. I want to get clear photographs of these things." He snapped a curt demand to one of his assistants: "Get Roth back here before he leaves."

He saw Martin buttoning up his coat, asked: "Where you going? What's your hurry? Don't you want to stay while I talk to Mr. Stanton here and the servants?"

Martin shook his head. "I'd like to, but I have other business to attend to. Thanks for your courtesy, inspector. Any time I can do anything for you—"

He left the room after casting one more quizzical glance at Oscar Stanton, the stock speculator, who was watching him with a puzzled frown.

When Martin had gone, Stanton walked around the bed close to Burks, said: "That's funny—a newspaperman leaving before he gets the full story."

Burks shrugged. "I've known that guy a long time. You never can tell what he's liable to do. He's got a soft job, too—stays away for months at a time, and then shows up without any explanation." Burks sighed. "Well, let's forget about him. We got plenty on our hands."

INSPECTOR BURKS and Oscar Stanton would have been highly interested in Mr. Martin's subsequent movements. For Mr. Martin's next stop was not at any telegraph office or telephone, nor at any newspaper office. It was at a small inconspicuous looking apartment house on the upper west side.

Here he admitted himself to an apartment on the fourth floor, and stepped into a small cubby hole where a man lay upon a couch, apparently asleep.

Martin stood there, staring down at this man. The sleeper's features were familiar to thousands of people throughout the country. For they were the features of Victor Randall, the president of the Union Trust Company, and chairman of the board of dozens of financial enterprises whose assets ran into billions. Randall was not asleep. He was unconscious, under the influence of an anesthetizing drug.

Mr. Martin now proceeded to do a peculiar thing. He seated himself before a small dressing table. From a drawer in the table he took strange objects. They were jars of some sort of cream, small plates made of metal, and little vials of pigment.

Then, looking in the mirror, he raised long, graceful fingers to his face, began to manipulate them swiftly, capably. And a strange thing happened. For almost as if by magic, the features of Mr. Martin began to disappear. Now it became apparent that those features did not constitute Mr. Martin's true face. They were the product of an artistic application of plastic material, pigment, nose and face plates, in conjunction with a cunningly contrived wig. In only a few minutes, Mr. Martin was no more. For a short while there was revealed the true countenance of the man who sat before that dressing table.

John Lacey

It was the face of a strong willed, keenly intelligent young man, with deep-set eyes that reflected a strange sort of power. Those finely chiseled, almost eaglelike features had never been beheld by any man now living. For they constituted the true countenance of that strange man who moved in strange, inexplicable ways—Secret Agent "X."

Secret Agent "X" had interested himself in these strange murders of prominent men. And, under the very nose of Inspector Burks, he had gone to investigate this last murder—the death of Lewis Forman.

If Inspector Burks had known that the man with whom he had talked so casually a few minutes ago was Secret Agent "X", he would not have hesitated to shoot him without a moment's warning. For Inspector Burks, as well as the entire police department, considered this man of a thousand faces to be a public enemy of the first magnitude.

However, there were things which Burks and the rest of the police department did not know. For instance, they did not know that Secret Agent "X" operated on written authority from the highest power in the land to act in any way that he thought fit for the purpose of combating crime. Throughout the nation the officers of the law were pledged to shoot Secret Agent "X" on sight. Yet they did not realize that he was the most powerful ally which they had in their constant warfare against the forces of evil.[10]

The identity of A. J. Martin, the Associated Press man, was only one of many personalities which Secret Agent "X" found expedient to assume in his battle with criminals. Now, the disguise of Martin had served its purpose, and he was assuming another disguise—one which called for even greater artistry, for consummate acting ability.

His fingers manipulated the material on the table, and slowly, in the mirror, there grew another face—a replica of the man who was lying unconscious upon the couch. After ten minutes he arose from the table, glanced down at the face of Victor Randall, then back at his own reflection in the mirror, and nodded in satisfaction. No one, looking at both men, could have told which was which.

Now the Agent took a small mask from his pocket, placed it over his face. Then he went into the next room, returned in a few moments with two hypodermic syringes. One of these he placed upon the table, the other he injected into the arm of the sleeping man. Shortly, Randall began to stir, and opened his eyes.

The Agent fastened each of Randall's wrists to a rung attached to the metal frame of the couch, so that his guest was helpless

---

10 AUTHOR'S NOTE: *The readers of these novels will already have recognized the dynamic A. J. Martin as being in reality, none other than the man of mystery who hides his identity under the name of Secret Agent "X." Under that name, which is a symbol of the unknown quantity, Secret Agent "X" has made himself the scourge of evil. Hated by the underworld, hunted by the police, he has nevertheless, by means of his marvelous abilities, been the means of saving the lives and preserving the happiness of thousands of men and women throughout the country. His supreme devotion to the task which he has assigned to himself will be the more appreciated when it is understood that a man with abilities such as the Agent possesses could earn for himself a livelihood in almost any walk of life without endangering his safety at every moment of the day and night. But these are the ways in which Secret Agent "X" has chosen. Many readers have written, begging for more information about the Agent. The author is sorry he cannot accommodate them. The author knows all too little about the Agent himself. However, the author does know that Secret Agent "X" saw active service during the war, was wounded in action and later entered the Intelligence Service. He so distinguished himself there, that a high government official recognized his abilities and resources after the war by making him a remarkable proposition. He was made a free-lance agent, commissioned to act upon his own, with carte blanche; and to take whatever steps he deemed necessary in order to combat crime wherever it appeared in the nation. Such a commission was unprecedented in history; but it was fully warranted by the wave of lawlessness and crime that was sweeping the country. This strange man very soon proved that he was entirely worthy of the trust that had been placed in him. He became known as Secret Agent "X," and it was guaranteed that his anonymity would always be preserved. He has never betrayed that trust, no matter what personal sacrifice his duty entailed.*

to move. When Randall's eyes opened, he shuddered at the masked face bending over him. The Agent said in a low, soothing voice: "Do not be alarmed, Mr. Randall. I mean you no harm."

Oscar Stanton

RANDALL continued to stare up at him, slowly collecting his senses. Then he said hoarsely: "Who are you? How did I get here?"

"That is beside the point, Mr. Randall. Some day perhaps you will have the explanation of that. Now, there is much at stake, and very little time. You must answer my questions—quickly."

Randall's mouth set in a stubborn line. "I will answer nothing. I demand that you release me at once!"

The Agent's voice was impatient. "Mr. Randall, you are a wealthy, powerful man. But you are a fool. Your life is in danger, and I am the only man who can help you."

Randall's face paled. "How—how do you know that my life is in danger?"

"I know many things. I know that you received a call from Commissioner Foster. I know that you have been seeking protection from a detective agency."

"Who—who are you!" Randall demanded.

"X" hesitated a moment. Only his eyes, burning, intense, were visible from behind his mask. Then he said: "I am going to tell you something, Randall—something that I have hoped I would not have to disclose. I am—Secret Agent 'X'."

Randall started perceptibly, fear showed in his face. "You—"

"You must believe me," the Agent went on swiftly, "when I tell you that I have only your interests at heart in doing this. Men have died—died in cruel fashion. You are in danger, too. Are you willing to take a chance—blindly, in order to be saved?"

"But—but—if you are Secret Agent 'X'—"

The Agent laughed bitterly. "I know what you are thinking—that perhaps it is I who is behind these murders. That is what Inspector Burks thinks, and what Commissioner Foster thinks. And I shall never be able to correct them." He shrugged. "But it doesn't matter.

Perhaps it is better that they should think that way .... Randall, will you believe me? Will you believe that I mean you no harm—that I am working in your interests?"

Randall stammered: "B-but how do I know t-that you are Secret Agent 'X'? There's been much talk about you. Many people defend you. But even if Secret Agent 'X' is not a criminal, even if he is on the side of the law, how do I know that you are he?"

Professor Langknecht

"I will prove it to you," the Agent told him. Slowly he raised his hand, removed the mask.

Randall watched him, fascinated, as the mask was drawn away. Then he uttered a hoarse cry. He was staring into his own countenance.

"My God!" He blinked his eyes, stared again. Then he said in an awed voice: "Everything they say about you must be true. They say you are a superman. And only a superman could disguise himself like that. Why—I could swear that I was looking at myself!"

THE Agent bent close, demanded tensely: "Will you trust me? Will you answer my questions?"

Randall sighed, still staring, and nodded. "Your voice—it compels me to trust you. What do you want?"

"You had a talk with Commissioner Foster today. What was it about?"

"The commissioner called me. I am to be at his office at six o'clock tonight. He said that my life is in danger; that it's about those wild-beast murders. He says he has information that I am scheduled to die!"

"I thought so," the Agent breathed. "Six o'clock, you say?"

"Yes. Six o'clock tonight. Foster told me that there were to be some others there. That's all I know."

"Is there anybody who hates you—" the Agent asked him—"who might have reason to wreak such a terrible vengeance upon you? You were quite friendly with some of the others who died. Did you know of anything in their lives that might account for their being marked for such gruesome deaths?"

Randall shook his head. "No—Wait! You've heard of Grover Wilkinson, of course?"

The Agent sodded. "The utilities man who was indicted, and escaped from the country. They brought him back, tried him, and he was convicted. But he got off with a two-year sentence. I don't recall that you had anything to do with that, Randall."

Lola Lollagi

The banker said vehemently: "I did, in a way. And so did many of the others who have died. You see, just before the crash of his utilities empire, he appealed to us for funds. He wanted a loan of eighty million dollars. We turned him down. He was very bitter after that, and it's been whispered that he's mentally deranged. In fact, you know that the reason he got off with such a light sentence was that his attorneys pleaded temporary insanity. Then after his release, he disappeared. Shortly after his disappearance—two of the witnesses who helped to convict him were murdered. There's been no trace of him since."

The Agent nodded speculatively, asked more questions. He probed shrewdly into Randall's private life, touched on matters that Randall never suspected that anyone but he himself was aware of.

Finally the Agent finished. He said: "Now, Mr. Randall, you must understand that what I am doing is for your own good. I am going to keep you here until I have removed the danger which threatens you. In the meantime, I shall go out in your place. If there is any danger, it will strike me instead of you.

"For the time being you must remain here, and I shall make you as comfortable as possible. I shall put you into a comfortable sleep, and when you awake, you will have forgotten this interview. It is the only way. No one must ever know that Secret Agent 'X' has been working on this case—not even you."

Before Randall could open his mouth to utter a protest, the Agent had picked up the hypodermic from the table, and drove the plunger home into the other's arm. Almost at once Randall's head dropped back upon the couch, his eyes closed, and he began to breathe regularly, stertorously.[11]

The Agent waited until he was sure that the drug had acted properly, then he released Randall's wrists, turned out the light, and left the apartment as quietly as he had entered.

---

11 AUTHOR'S NOTE: Secret Agent "X" having made a thorough study of coma producing and amnesia producing drugs has been able to blend these into a combination which is physically harmless to a man, yet which will cause him to lose all recollection of events immediately prior to the injection of this drug. In the various personalities which the agent uses, he has been able to gain access to the results of the latest research work of the most eminent scientists and psychologists. In his leisure time he has spent hours in experimentation and research. Sometime ago, the Agent came upon the base for the formula which he employed in the drug. Recognizing the tremendous value of such a drug in his work, he labored unsparingly until he evolved the successful formula. He has kept this formula an absolute secret, fearing its misuse if it were made public. But very often, in the guise of a certain well-known scientist whose name he has refused to disclose to me, he has administered this drug where it was found necessary for the welfare of some patients to absolutely forget some particular matter. An instance of this occurred recently, when a young woman witnessed the death by drowning of her fiancé in the sinking of an ocean liner. She became hysterical, and it was feared that she would lose her reason because of the dreadful image of her drowning fiancé which she did not seem to be able to get rid of. The Agent read of this in the paper, flew by plane to the rescue ship aboard which she had been taken. He administered a dose of his drug, and the young woman went into a deep coma from which she awoke the next day with her mind a merciful blank as to the occurrences of the preceding twenty-four hours. Her sanity was saved.

CHAPTER II

24 HOURS' IMMUNITY!

THE NEWSBOY'S FACE was excited, flushed. His armful of papers was dwindling fast; he was doing a rushing business. His thin treble of a voice was raised to its highest pitch as he displayed his wares. The paper read:

MAYOR APPEALS TO SECRET AGENT "X"!

**Read all about the mayor's letter.
Read about Murder Number 10!**

The lunch-hour crowds were buying his papers as fast as he could hand them out. And at every other spot in the city where newspapers were sold, the same thriving business was being done. The men and women who bought the papers scanned them avidly.

The little newsboy's last paper was bought by the tall man of dignified bearing who had descended from a taxicab at the corner. Anyone familiar with the features of the dominant figures of the financial district would have recognized this man of imposing mien as Victor Randall; and might have wondered that so important a figure as Randall should be traveling about the city unescorted. It would have astounded such a person even further to have learned that the true Victor Randall was a prisoner in an obscure section of the city, and that this impersonator was none other than Secret Agent "X".

"X" gave the boy a quarter, waved the change away, and spread the paper open. As thousands of others were doing at the very moment all about him, he read the blaring headlines thrown across the top of the front page:

LEWIS FORMAN MURDERED

Tenth victim in ten days

The tenth grisly murder to take place in this city within the past ten days was discovered early this morning. Lewis Forman was found by his housekeeper with the jugular vein ripped open and the blood drained from his body in the same fashion as the other victims of the inhuman monsters which are terrorizing the city.

Commissioner Foster and the entire police department are without a single clue as to the nature of this horror that has descended upon the city.

Since the day Blaine Prescott was killed in similar manner, exactly nine days ago, every available man in the police department has been patrolling the streets, searching every odd, out of the way place in the city, in an effort to locate the mysterious monsters which have been perpetrating these deeds.

Thus far, the situation has remained a bloody enigma, with all the forces of the law in a frantic scramble to break the mystery before more murders occur.

The slogan of these beasts seems to be—A murder a day!

The Agent ceased reading at that point, and his eyes swung to the column where a last-minute flash had been set in big eighteen-point type:

MAYOR STURGIS APPEALS TO SECRET AGENT "X"!

Below is a copy of an open letter to Secret Agent "X" released by Mayor Sturgis to all the newspapers in the country. The message will also be broadcast over a nationwide network at 5 P.M. tonight. The letter speaks for itself:

OFFICE OF THE MAYOR

To the Man who is known as Secret Agent "X":

Our city—in fact, the entire nation, is faced by a terror ghastlier than any which could be imagined. Each day one of our prominent men is done to death in grisly fashion, his blood removed for some inhuman purpose. All efforts to discover what band of beasts is perpetrating these horrors have been futile.

You, Mr. Secret Agent "X," have always been viewed as a super criminal. Many people, however, have other opinions about you. They seem to feel that you are on the side of the law.

As a last resort I am making this appeal to you. If you are not a criminal, if you are really on the side of the law, this is your oppor-

Behind him "X" could hear the hoarse cries of Commissioner Foster and others.

tunity to prove it. You admittedly have qualifications and abilities which are far above the average. If you wish to clear your reputation forever of any taint of criminality, come forward now and offer your services. I have instructed the entire police department that you are to be granted immunity for a period of twenty-four hours beginning at 6 P.M. tonight, Eastern Standard Time. From 6 P.M. tonight until 6 P.M. tomorrow, you may present yourself to me personally, to Police Commissioner Foster, or to Chief Inspector Burks at any time, at any place which you may designate. You may come in any disguise which you prefer to assume, and I will guarantee to you that no effort will be made to penetrate that disguise, to discover your true identity.

If you should thus volunteer your services, taking advantage of this immunity which is offered to you, we will lay before you all the facts of the case, and entrust its solution to you. I realise that this is an unprecedented move for an official of the city to make, but the situation is so desperate that it warrants it.

This is your opportunity, Secret Agent "X," to prove that you are no criminal, that you have the interests of law and justice at heart

Will you accept my challenge?

JOHN F. STURGIS, *Mayor.*

The Agent read this letter carefully. Then he gazed down the busy street over the shoulders of the hundreds of scurrying people, many of whom were reading the amazing letter of the mayor of the city to the person known as Secret Agent "X". His eyes had detected a young woman who was hurrying toward the corner. She was slim, blonde, with a creamy youthful complexion, and a look of fresh innocence that brought a spark of momentary admiration to his eyes.

THIS girl approached the corner more or less hesitantly, glanced at the Agent, and then approached him. "Mr. Randall?" she asked diffidently.

He nodded.

"I was told to meet you here," she went on, "by a—a friend. He suggested there was something you can tell me which I could use for my paper. My name is Betty Dale."[12]

"This friend," said "X", "What is his name, Miss Dale?"

She hesitated. "He—he wouldn't want me to mention it."

"Then perhaps I can name him. I see you have a newspaper."

He gently took the newspaper which she was carrying folded

---

[12] AUTHOR'S NOTE: *The name of Betty Dale is well known to the readers of these chronicles. The daughter of a police captain who was killed in the line of duty, she was left an orphan at an early age, and befriended by Secret Agent "X," who had been a friend of her father's. Through the good offices of the Man of a Thousand Faces, Betty secured a position as a reporter on the* Herald. *Because of her father's connection with the police department she was accorded unusual privileges as a reporter, and became invaluable to the paper. Through the years that followed she was especially happy when she was privileged to aid on some way the man who had befriended her in her hour of adversity. Often in the past he had called upon her for assistance, and she had been glad to render it—would have been glad to do far more than the few trivial things he requested of her, for she had grown to respect the strange man whose true face she had never been permitted to see—more than that, there had gradually dawned upon her the realization that she loved him. But she understood that love could be no part of the life of Secret Agent "X"—the man who had dedicated himself to the service of humanity, to the eradication of crime. She nurtured this love secretly and in silence, and was thrilled whenever she met him in any of the various disguises which he maintained. And, though she felt that her woman's instinct should always tell her when he was near, she never succeeded in penetrating one of his disguises. Not till he was ready to disclose himself to her did she ever know that she was talking to Secret Agent "X."*

under her arm, spread it open. "Is he by any chance the man to whom this letter was addressed?" His long, slender finger pointed to the open letter from the mayor to Secret Agent "X".

Betty Dale gave an involuntary start of surprise. Her eyes grew wide with consternation. "Why—no—of course not!"

He smiled, and his voice took on a different inflection—somehow it deepened, softened. He said: "You needn't worry, Betty. You are not giving me away."

Betty put a slim hand to her throat, stared at him in amazement. She exclaimed huskily: "You! Disguised as Victor Randall!" Her face lit up in a happy smile. "But—but why are you disguised as Randall? What has happened to Randall?"

He took her arm, led her down the street to a quiet restaurant. When they were seated and had ordered coffee, he explained: "These murders that are being committed—there is apparently no motive, no reason for them. The newspapers hint, as you know, that more men are to be killed and there are ugly rumors going around, about a mysterious band of blood-drinking beasts."

Betty Dale shuddered. "Yes. People are afraid to go out at night. And they're afraid to stay home, too. These beasts attack anywhere. No one would believe it possible—that wild jungle beasts should be roving through our city—"

"There is more to it than that, Betty," the Agent interrupted her gently. "The police are hysterical and in their frame of mind they are ready to believe anything. If I thought that this were merely a matter of wild beasts killing at random, I would not be working on it. It would then be a matter for a concentrated hunt, and nothing else. I am afraid, though, that there is something here that is far more evil—something that will test the powers of all of us to the utmost!"

Betty looked worried. "They're talking of other things, too. They say that perhaps Grover Wilkerson has something to do with it. You know, he's really insane—a paranoiac of the worst kind."

"X" nodded. "That is why I wanted to talk to you. At the *Herald* you have every opportunity of picking up all the rumors that are floating about the city. I want you to make a complete report on these rumors—no matter how silly they sound. Keep track of them carefully. Try, if possible, to ascertain their source. I will call you later in the day."

Betty asked: "Are you accepting the mayor's challenge?"

"X" gazed at her somberly. "Yes, Betty," he said slowly, "I am accepting the mayor's challenge."

She put her hand impulsively on his arm. "But you mustn't. You'll be walking into a trap!"

"What makes you think so?"

"Because," she hurried on eagerly, "the mayor is exceeding his authority in granting you immunity. You have been accused of murder!" Her hands trembled on his arm. "I know, of course, that you have always helped the law. I know that you are good and fine and brave. But the others—Commissioner Foster and Inspector Burks—they'll never believe you innocent. They'll never let you get out of headquarters!" Her voice rose slightly. She was controlling herself with an effort.

"Nevertheless," the Agent said firmly, "I shall be at headquarters at six o'clock." He took her hand from his arm, pressed it gently. "I have already thought of everything that you tell me, Betty, but I must take the chance—if it will help to prevent more men from having their throats ripped open, and the blood sucked from their bodies."

Betty sighed. She knew the futility of trying to swerve this man from the path indicated by his sense of duty. "What—what disguise will you assume?"

"I shall go as I am now—as Victor Randall. Randall is safe in one of my apartments, and I shall take his place. I will be there, but the mayor will not know it. I am going to accept the invitation—in my own way."

He smiled, nodded in kindly fashion. For a moment Betty thought that she detected a glow of warmth in the depths of his usually inscrutable eyes. But it faded as quickly as it had come. It was as if he had drawn a veil across his soul. Once more he was the cold, masterful, strange man without feeling or sentiment—a superb machine devoted to the destruction of crime.

He raised his hat, bowed. Then he turned and walked swiftly away.

Betty bit her lip to keep back the tears which were welling into her eyes. She watched him until he disappeared into the throng.

CHAPTER III

WRITTEN IN BLOOD

THAT EVENING, SECRET AGENT "X" descended from a cab, a block from headquarters. As he walked down the short remaining distance toward the main entrance of the imposing building within which were housed all the law enforcing agencies of the city, he noted that several squad cars were drawn up along the street, but that there were no officers in sight. He glanced at his wrist watch. It was 6 P. M.

Apparently the way had been left clear in case Secret Agent "X" should choose to come. On the opposite side of the street, he noted a small, shiny black sedan at the wheel of which was seated a gorgeously beautiful woman. She was parked a little distance from the street light, but the Agent's keen eyes noted her sharp, clearly cut profile, and the black bobbed hair which was combed back behind her ears under a smart little green hat. Hers was a dark, beautiful face, and the semi-darkness in which she sat added mystery and piquancy to her appearance.

The Agent did not slow his gait, but two things registered in his mind. One was the license number of the automobile which he would be able to recall to his mind effortlessly at any time in the future. The other was the identity of that woman. His memory for faces was one of the things that had contributed to making him a nemesis of criminals.

If he should see this woman again after a lapse of ten years, that peculiar faculty of his would at once call up to him a picture of her in the car in front of headquarters. And just so did the sight of her face now bring up to him a picture of several years back, when he had been in South America, in Asuncion.[13]

He had seen her there only for a few moments, in a night club where he had had an appointment with one of his operatives. This woman in the car had been dancing there—a paid performer on the stage. The Agent had never learned her name, had never heard anything about her. But that one flash had come back to his mind automatically as he saw her now in the car.

He filed the item away in the back of his mind. What was this beautiful Paraguayan dancer doing here in front of headquarters? Could she have any connection with the murders that had shocked the city for the last ten days?

Within the headquarters building the Agent was ushered in to Commissioner Foster's office.

Here was gathered a varied group of men. The commissioner had relinquished his chair behind the broad mahogany desk to the mayor of the city. Mayor Sturgis was a stocky, florid man with an immense capacity for work, and a highly developed sense of civic duty. His square-cut, honest countenance was now pinched in worried lines as he surveyed the gathering in the room.

"X" also inspected the other men present. He nodded to several of them, who returned his greetings solemnly. These men who were gathered here at the commissioner's invitation were among the most important men of the city.

SEATED directly opposite the mayor was Gilbert Patterson, the head of one of the largest private banking concerns in the country. Standing beside the banker was Norman Marsh, the internationally known archeologist and explorer, who had uncovered vast mines of knowledge about the early human races of the world, and had written scores of books upon ancient civilizations. In a corner behind Commissioner Foster, who was standing next to the mayor, sat a man whom "X" did not know personally, but whom he recog-

---

13 AUTHOR'S NOTE: *The work of Secret Agent "X" often called him to the far places of the earth. The particular occasion that had found him in Asuncion had been concerned with a criminal gang that was operating throughout South America. Events had taken place at that time which the Agent has always been rather reticent about. He has always changed the subject or skimmed over it lightly when mention of South America is made. The author feels that there is quite a story behind the experience, and hopes sometime to be able to extract from the Agent enough information to base a novel upon. However, the author entertains little hope for accomplishing this, for the subject seems to be linked up with very painful memories for Secret Agent "X."*

nized from photographs he had seen recently in the papers. This man was Professor Hugo Langknecht, the well-known young German scientist and psychiatrist, who had come to this country only recently after making a name for himself throughout Europe and South America.

Then there was John Lacey, who was reputed to own more real estate in the city than any other ten men combined. Frank Larkin, the publisher of a country-wide chain of newspapers, and Oscar Stanton, the stock speculator who had cornered the market a dozen times in the past ten years, made up the rest of the group.

"X" had met Stanton only that morning at the home of the murdered Lewis Forman, but Stanton did not know it. In the suave, cultured Victor Randall whom "X" was now impersonating, Stanton did not recognize the dynamic Associated Press man who had been snooping around the murdered Forman's bedroom that morning.

Mayor Sturgis nodded to "X", said curtly: "We've been waiting for you, Randall. I have an important announcement to make, and I wanted you all together."

"X" nodded, stood with his back against the wall, surveying the room. He found himself beside Norman Marsh, the explorer, who turned to him and said under his breath: "Sturgis seems to be all wrought up about something. I wonder what we have to do with it."

"X" shrugged. "Haven't got the faintest idea, Marsh."

Gilbert Patterson who was sitting just beyond Norman Marsh, looked up at them with a worried expression. "This is an awful waste of time—"

He was interrupted by Mayor Sturgis, who said shortly: "I won't waste your time any longer, gentlemen. I've called you here to make an announcement to you. Every one of you is vitally interested in that announcement. Of course, you've all read and shuddered at the terrible things that have happened in the past ten days. Only this morning a man whom we all knew—Lewis Forman—met the same fate. The autopsy shows that he was killed last night—before midnight. Everybody is guessing at what sort of monsters these are that steal about in the night and rip open men's throats, suck their bodies dry of blood."

Gilbert Patterson stirred uneasily in his seat, and cleared his throat. From his rosy, smoothly shaven cheeks, and his almost colorless eyes, one would not have guessed that he was the head of the largest private banking outfit in the country.

"Of course, Sturgis," he said irritably, "we read all about these murders. Lewis Forman was the federal coordinator for railroads. With him dead, all the plans which he has been building up to stabilize the railroad situation are swept away at a single blow. Some of the other men who died have been equally important. If this keeps up, the very structure of our nation will be threatened. But I don't understand what we can do about it. The job is yours, and Commissioner Foster's. Why have you called us here?"

"I'll tell you why," said Sturgis. He appeared to be tense now, his fists clenched so that his knuckles showed white against the green blotter on the commissioner's desk. "You men here—" his gaze swept from one to the other of them—"are of great importance in the economic life of the country. You, Patterson, have put your finger upon the crux of the problem. We believe that a systematic attempt is being made to wipe out our prominent men."

JOHN LACEY, who had been standing next to Patterson, now exclaimed vehemently: "But why do they do it in such a horrible way—why do they rip a man's throat—why do they suck him dry of blood!" His voice trembled slightly, and he struck one fat, flabby hand into the palm of the other. "You've got to stop it, Sturgis. You've got the whole police department to do it with. We'll contribute money, anything that will help to put a stop to it!" He suddenly relaxed, patted his soft paunch. His face was gray, and his double chin shook. "God! Some of my best friends were among those ten men. I can still see them lying there, just a skinful of bones—with the blood all drained out of them!"

"Gentlemen," the mayor's voice was dry, tight. "I know just how you feel. But we have no time for talk like this. There is something I must tell you. I have called you together, not to seek any financial assistance, but to give you a piece of news. It is not fair to keep the information from you any longer."

There was a dead silence in the room as the mayor hesitated. Then he went on grimly: "Lewis Forman is not to be the last to die. There is some being in this city, a man presumably, who calls himself by the name of Doctor Blood. He is the one who has caused the deaths of your friends—of my friends—by some inhuman means that we cannot fathom. He has compiled a list—a long list—of names of prominent men. And he promises death for every one of them." Mayor Sturgis' eyes swung around the room, came to rest upon Gilbert Patterson, the rosy-cheeked private banker. He raised a hand, pointed a shaking finger. "You, Patterson—are next on Doctor Blood's list!"

The plump, well-fed, immaculately dressed private banker sat rigid, gripped tightly the arms of his chair. He exclaimed falteringly: "You mean *I'm* going to be killed?"

Mayor Sturgis nodded. He picked up a folder from the desk, extracted from it a sheet of paper. He handled the paper gingerly, almost with revulsion.

"X's" eyes, fixed on that sheet, were the first to note the peculiarity about it. The mayor held it low, so that they could all see. And a slow gasp of horror rose in the room. For the sprawling, boldly shaped writing was in red—and the red was unmistakably blood.

"Yes, gentlemen," the mayor said in a choked voice, "this is written in blood—probably the blood of one of those ten men who have already died!"

He held the paper before him, glanced around the room, and said: "Let me read it to you." His voice was low, almost inaudible as he read the contents of that message.

My dear Commissioner Foster:

You will doubtless be relieved to learn that the unfortunate occurrences which have been taking place during the last ten days can be stopped—at a price. I am enclosing herewith a list which contains three hundred and sixty-five names. You will find that the first ten names are those of the men who have already died. The next three hundred and fifty-five will die just as surely, one every day for the balance of the year.

However, there is one way in which those three hundred and fifty-five men may avoid having their blood drained from them. Each of them may buy immunity for the modest sum of twenty-five thousand dollars. This money must be paid in cash by each individual on the day he is scheduled to die.

In order to prove to you that I can do what I say, I will cause number eleven on the list to be killed in the same fashion as the others today. It is too bad that number eleven must die, but it is necessary that I convince you that this letter is no fraud.

Please communicate my terms to the rest of the men on the list. They will be instructed how to arrange to make their payments.

Yours for a long life,

Doctor Blood.

There was a hushed silence in the room when the mayor had finished reading that remarkable letter. Even the mayor's face was drawn and haggard. He said in a sort of choked voice: "You must understand, gentlemen, that we are doing everything in our power to apprehend this criminal known as Doctor Blood. I am vitally interested—for a reason which you will soon understand."

Norman Marsh said speculatively: "This Doctor Blood of yours is certainly an ingenious man, Mr. Mayor. Say only fifty percent of the men on that list that he talks about should pay on the line—let's see, how much would that make?"

Mayor Sturgis frowned at him. "You may take this lightly, Mr. Marsh, but wait—" He took another sheet of paper from the folder on the desk. "Here is the list that Doctor Blood speaks of. You all know the names of the first ten—those who have already perished with their throats clawed open and their blood drained from them. I will now read you the list of the next seven."

HE had said the last very slowly, incisively. Suddenly a hushed silence fell over the room. Secret Agent "X" had been studying each of the men present. His eyes had especially sought the tall, lean, cadaverous figure of Oscar Stanton, the stock speculator, who sat across the room facing Gilbert Patterson. He turned his eyes now toward Mayor Sturgis. That official began slowly to read from the list. "Number eleven—Gilbert Patterson; number twelve—Norman Marsh; number thirteen—" he gulped, then said quickly—"number thirteen—John F. Sturgis."

There was a gasp from the assembled company. Gilbert Patterson's face had become a pasty white; Norman Marsh, who had been pacing up and down, had stopped suddenly at the mention of his own name. He started to speak, then stopped, clamping his jaws hard as the mayor went on.

"You see, gentlemen," the mayor said with an obvious effort to control his voice, "I am on this list with you—so you cannot question my interest in unmasking this fiendish Doctor Blood—for according to the list, Patterson here dies today. Marsh tomorrow. And I, on Thursday."

He sighed, bent his eyes to the list. "But let me finish reading. I think you all can get what follows."

Oscar Stanton, the lean, gaunt-faced stock broker, raised his head and caught "X" watching him. He lowered his eyes quickly, turned to the mayor. "Yes—it means we're all on the list. The only question is, what day are we scheduled to die. Hurry, man, read the rest of the numbers!"

Sturgis went on more speedily now. "Number fourteen—Hugo Langknecht; number fifteen—John Lacey; number sixteen—Oscar Stanton; number seventeen—Frank Larkin; number eighteen—" his eyes lifted from the paper, met those of Secret Agent "X"—"Victor Randall!"

When he had ceased reading, a buzz of excited comment arose among the doomed men.

Commissioner Foster exchanged glances with Inspector Burks across the desk at which the mayor was seated, and raised his hand. "Excuse me, everybody."

He waited until the buzz of talk had subsided, and then turned to the only other man who had remained silent during the entire conference—Professor Hugo Langknecht, the German psychiatrist.

"Professor Langknecht," the commissioner said, "You must not misunderstand me when I say that in a way I am glad you are among those mentioned on Doctor Blood's list. You are as vitally interested as we are in discovering Doctor Blood's true identity. As a psychiatrist you may be able to study this note and arrive at some idea of what sort of person this bloody executioner is. In your profession, you've had occasion to study many queer kinds of people. Is there any hope you can give us—such as indicating what kind of man we ought to look for in searching for this Doctor Blood—anything what might put us on the right track?"

Professor Langknecht was quite a young man, considering the international reputation which he had already established for himself. His thin sharp features, his high forehead, proclaimed him a scholar. His eyes seemed to be lively, black, constantly flashing behind the extra thick-leased spectacles which he wore. His thin lips were pursed thoughtfully as he seemed to be giving the question weighty consideration before answering. Then he finally spoke:

"There are many things that we must take into consideration here, commissioner. In our clinic in Vienna—" he stopped, waved his hand impatiently—"but you will not be interested in that. What you want is concrete conclusion. Well, we must first look at the curious way that these murders have been committed—the tearing open of the jugular vein, the draining of the blood." He spoke in a cold, precise voice. He was a typical scientist, treating the problem as if it were an abstract theory of mathematics, rather than one which might involve his own death.

"Who," he went on, "would be apt to do these things to a man? In Cambodia, in Indo-China and in some of the wilder portions of South America, there are, I understand, beasts which subsist upon human—"

He was interrupted by Norman Marsh who suddenly snapped his fingers. "Of course!" the archeologist exclaimed. "I remember, in 1914 in my expedition to Brazil—"

Professor Langknecht stopped him. "Yes, yes, Mr. Marsh. But you must not jump to conclusions. There are other creatures that drink human blood, too—creatures which the mind of man refuses to believe, but which have been thought to exist from the beginning of mankind. Vampires, ghouls—"

It was Oscar Stanton who stopped him. "Damn it!" he shouted. "Are you going to begin telling us fairy tales now! Here we are, slated to die. There's Patterson—he's marked for today. There's Marsh for tomorrow, Sturgis for Thursday, and the rest of us—Lacey, Larkin, myself, and Randall." He jerked his thumb at Secret Agent "X." "Randall is the luckiest of us. He has a week to live. And here you are telling us about vampires and ghouls."

HE swung on Commissioner Foster: "Why don't you arrange with this Doctor Blood for us to pay him? He seems to have chosen you as intermediary. All right, I'm ready to pay!"

Professor Langknecht wiped his forehead with a large, yellow-bordered handkerchief. He subsided into his seat, looking slightly bewildered at the sudden vehemence of Stanton.

Norman Marsh suddenly started to laugh.

The others looked at him open-mouthed.

Marsh stopped laughing as suddenly as he had begun, his lean, tanned face setting into grim, stubborn lines. "I don't know how you others feel about it, but Stanton is all wet. I think this Doctor Blood is mad. Why, it's impossible to kill one man every day for a year—especially when we know who's scheduled next. I've faced worse things than this Doctor Blood's wild beasts in my life, and I'll take a chance!"

Stanton glared at Marsh. "You wouldn't talk like that, Marsh, if you'd seen what I've seen. Lewis Forman was the last to die—and I was a guest in his house last night." He shuddered. "I'll never forget how he looked this morning. The bed was soaked with blood. His throat was torn—clawed, ripped horribly. And—and his body was drained dry of blood. He was nothing but skin and bones. And you want us all to take a chance on having that happen to us—when twenty-five thousand dollars would square it. We're all wealthy here, we can all afford it easily. Why tempt fate?" Stanton swung on Inspector Burks, whose face had been growing redder and redder every moment. "You, Burks. Why don't you get something done? Why don't you arrange for these payments? Why do you call us all here for these useless conferences? There's only one thing to do, that is, pay up."

Inspector Burks shrugged, turned away from Stanton in contempt. John Lacey, the real estate operator, number fourteen on the list, placed a soothing hand on Stanton's shoulder. "Don't take it so hard, Stanton," he soothed. "Burks may catch this Doctor Blood before it's our turn to pay. Patterson here is the one who really has to worry. He's due to get his today—and there's no way out for him!"

Patterson came out of his reverie. His hunted eyes sought Mayor Sturgis. "What—what steps are you taking to protect me?" he asked.

Commissioner Foster answered for the mayor. "We are going to give you a police guard or, if you prefer, it would be better for you to remain in headquarters—where you should be comparatively safe. You other gentlemen—and you too, your Honor—would be well advised to do likewise."

Stanton snorted. "You'd be doing much better if you arranged to get these payments started. You know damn well that nobody is safe—not even in headquarters. You haven't been able to get the faintest idea of how these murders were committed, or of who did them. You haven't even gotten a glimpse of these beasts of Doctor Blood's. And yet you want us to take a chance. After all, we're all important men in this town. None of us wants to die yet. Maybe Marsh doesn't care. He's risked his life so often that it's come to mean nothing to him. But most of us others here have families, have important interests. We want to live. As far as I'm concerned, I hereby state that I'm ready to pay—unless Commissioner Foster can show me anything concrete which he has done to protect us from this threat!"

The Agent maintained silence during all this time. He continued to study Oscar Stanton. Stanton was known as a plunger in the market—a bear raider of great daring, who had amassed a fortune by his ruthless tactics. It was interesting to note how a man, who could be so merciless as he had been to others, acted when his own life was threatened.

It was Mayor Sturgis who quieted him. The mayor raised a soothing hand, and said: "Gentlemen, as you may know from having read the evening paper, I have taken a step which I hope will be of help to us. I have issued a public letter to—"

"Yes, yes," Stanton shouted, "I know all about that. I saw the paper." He sneered. "Set a thief to catch a thief, huh! This Secret Agent 'X' is probably the one who's behind all these murders—and you call him in to help us! Is that the best you can do? Come on—think, man—your own life is in danger here as well as ours!"

"Excuse me, Mr. Stanton," Norman Marsh interrupted coldly. "I have studied the career of this strange man whom you call Secret Agent 'X' with great interest. It is my profound belief that this man is not a criminal. In view of the gravity of our present situation, I heartily approve of the step that Mayor Sturgis has taken."

Inspector Burks, who had been listening to Stanton's diatribe with beaming approval, now made a gesture of impatience. He took a long black cigar from his pocket, lit it, and puffed furiously. He growled: "Mayor Sturgis is the boss, of course, but I'd never have done anything like that if it was left up to me. Why, this Secret Agent 'X' is the slickest crook in the country—in the world for that matter. I ought to know. I've been up against him dozens of times. If you think he is going to walk in here because he's been offered immunity, you're mistaken. He's probably laughing up his sleeve at us all right now!"

And it was at that moment that the inter-office 'phone on the commissioner's desk rang.

Commissioner Foster picked up the phone, listened for a moment, then quickly covered the mouthpiece, stared at the others with excited eyes.

He glanced at Burks, then stooped and whispered in the ear of Mayor Sturgis.

The mayor's eyes opened wide with excitement, and he rose. His fists were clenched on the desk. There was a look of extreme satisfaction on his face.

"Gentlemen," he exclaimed, "I have to announce—that Secret Agent 'X' has accepted my invitation! He is waiting outside now!"

CHAPTER IV

DEATH FOR EIGHT!

FOR SEVERAL MOMENTS after the Mayor's startling announcement, the room was the scene of astounded comment and bustling excitement. Voices were raised, everyone tried to talk at once.

Inspector Burks exclaimed harshly: "We've got him now! We'll put him in a cell and keep him there. And I bet you these damn murders stop!"

The mayor turned upon Burks irritably. "You'll do nothing of the kind, inspector! I've given Secret Agent 'X' my word that he is to have twenty-four hours' immunity, and I meant every word of that. You will keep your hands off for twenty-four hours!"

Inspector Burks lowered his head sullenly. "All right. But the minute the twenty-four hours expires, I'm grabbing him!"

The Agent withdrew to a corner of the room where he could survey all the occupants, and made ready to view this visitor who had come impersonating him. The various occupants of the room were still raising their voices in loud discussion and protest. Only one other man in the room was silent now; that was Professor Langknecht, the psychiatrist. He sat quietly, with his knees crossed, but his small, lively black eyes behind those spectacles had been busy surveying each man in turn in the room, listening carefully to all their comments.

The medley of voices ceased as Mayor Sturgis, turning to Professor Langknecht, said: "What is your opinion, professor? Shall we enlist the services of Secret Agent 'X'?"

Langknecht stirred as from a reverie. "You should certainly talk to him, Mr. Mayor. In a situation such as this, we must turn to anything at all that holds a possibility of salvation." He added with an air of eagerness: "As a psychiatrist, I am myself extremely anxious to meet this person who calls himself Secret Agent 'X'."

"All right," the mayor exclaimed with a sudden air of decision. "We'll have him in."

He turned to the 'phone, but Oscar Stanton shouted: "Then I won't stay here! I'll have nothing to do with this business. It's bad enough that my life is in danger, and that I can't get help from the police department. But to have to place my life in the hands of a felon like this Secret Agent 'X' is unbearable. I'm going!" He turned and stamped out of the room stormily before anyone could stop him.

John Lacey said disgustedly: "Let him go. I'd rather he wasn't here anyway. Maybe we'll all be better off."

"What do you mean by that?" Commissioner Foster demanded.

Lacey shrugged. "What do we know about Stanton anyway? His partner, Lewis Forman, has just been murdered. And Stanton was his guest last night. Stanton was in the room right next door, yet he claims he didn't hear a thing." He took a step closer to the Mayor's desk, glared at Burks. "Have you investigated Stanton at all? *I've* had occasion to. Do you realize that the ten deaths that have already occurred have been deaths of men who are influential in some of the largest firms in the country? Do you realize that the stocks of those firms have gone down in the market? And do you know what's happening? Our friend, Oscar Stanton, has been buying, buying, buying; buying the stocks of those firms at bargain prices! If they go up again, he will have made himself a million dollars by the deaths of these men!"

SECRET AGENT "X," standing against the wall near the window, glanced out and saw Stanton in the street now walking rapidly away past the car in which sat the beautiful Paraguayan dancer. The Agent could see the car from his point of vantage at the window; he watched closely as Stanton passed, but detected no sign being exchanged between Stanton and the woman.

Everything that Lacey had said was already known to Secret Agent "X." Stanton had been under observation by the Agent's operatives for the last ten days. And the Agent knew that as soon as Stanton turned the corner he would once more be picked up by a shadow, and followed wherever he went. The Agent's eyes were troubled, though, as he glanced out of the window. He wished now that he had taken the time to phone to his headquarters and ordered that a couple of operatives be placed on this woman who was parked across the street, to shadow her. He could do nothing about it now though.

He saw Foster pick up the 'phone, instruct the man at the desk outside to send in the visitor.

In the few moments that elapsed now, a great hush fell upon the room.

Inspector Burks chewed on his cigar viciously. Commissioner Foster interlocked his hands in front of him, and was cracking the joints nervously. Mayor Sturgis was drumming rapidly on the desk. The other men in the room were shifting about in their chairs, or pacing up and down in the narrow confines. The Agent could understand just how they felt. This was a momentous time in their lives in more ways than one. Not only were they being threatened with a gruesome death by an unknown individual who termed himself Doctor Blood, but they were about to come face to face with a man whose name had almost become legendary in the annals of crime—Secret Agent "X"!

The Agent, trying to appear as inconspicuous as possible, began to make his own arrangements for the reception of the visitor. It was true that this man might be only a publicity seeker, and harmless. On the other hand, he might be an emissary of the dread Doctor Blood, in which case he must be captured at all costs. "X" felt that if he could have such a person alone in one of his retreats for several hours, he would be able to elicit from him enough information to lead him to Doctor Blood.

The Agent moved closer to the door, surreptitiously extracted his gas gun from his pocket and held it in his hand shielded from the others in the room by his body. It was ready for instant use. Now he waited tensely for the appearance of the person who was masquerading as Secret Agent "X."

The silence in the room was like a blanket of dark expectancy. So quiet was it that the ticking of the little clock upon Commissioner Foster's desk was clearly audible.

And then the door opened. All eyes turned toward the doorway.

CHAPTER V

MESSENGER OF DOOM

A SIGH THAT was almost like an exclamation of astonishment arose from those in the room.

The Agent noted out of the corner of his eye that Professor Langknecht was the only one in the room who was not staring at the visitor. On the contrary, the Professor had turned his face away and buried it in his large handkerchief.

It seemed that the Professor had suddenly developed a great interest in wiping his face clean. This was strangely at variance with the desire which he had expressed a few moments ago to meet the person who was calling in the role of Secret Agent "X."

The Agent's lips tightened in a grim line. Mentally, he noted the Professor's name as another to be investigated along with Oscar Stanton.

"X" swung his eyes back to the doorway.

Mayor Sturgis exclaimed hoarsely, "What—"

He got no farther. A slight, weird figure suddenly became visible in the corridor—but only for the space of a second. There was a short vision of a twisted, vicious countenance; then a small metal object came sailing into the room, and crashed against the commissioner's desk. It broke with a faint, tingling sound, and at once the room became flooded with a biting, acrid, blinding fog through which it was impossible to see.

Pandemonium was let loose in that room. "X," holding his breath, leaped toward the doorway. But just then the heavy body of some one in the room barged into him, throwing him off balance, sending him tripping backward. The door slammed while "X" was scrambling to his feet. He did not know whether the visitor who had thrown that gas bomb into the room had entered or had departed. The fumes of the gas were overpowering. In the impenetra-

A feminine voice behind him ordered, "Release him at once, and stay where you are!"

ble darkness, there were sounds of men retching, of men stumbling, pushing against each other.

"X" had recognized the nature of the chemical which had come from the exploded bomb at once, and he had taken a deep breath at the first sound of the explosion. Now he held his breath, although his eyes smarted excruciatingly.

Grover Wilkerson

From across the room, Patterson's voice was heard, raised in an unearthly shriek which suddenly ended in a terrible gurgling sound.

Some one shouted agonizingly: "The beasts—they've got Patterson!"

"X" dashed across the room toward the spot where Patterson had screamed. He thrust aside the milling bodies of panic-stricken men, pushed past them until his sense of space told him that he was at the spot where Patterson had been sitting. Since it was impossible to see, anyway, he closed his eyes, still holding his breath, and groped blindly on the floor. His hand encountered a bloody, revolting body. He touched a severed artery, and came away sopping wet from the spurting blood.

And then his hand found something else—a mouth, a pair of bloody, slavering jaws. Somebody—or something—was stooping over that bloody, gory body, drinking the fresh, spurting blood!

There was the disgusting, revolting, animal sound of a bestial throat gulping down the crimson fluid.

THE Agent reached out his right hand, which still held the gas pistol. He reversed the pistol, brought the butt down with all the force that he could command upon the head of that vicious creature. Still with his eyes closed, he reached down, hauled the suddenly inert body up over his shoulder. His congested lungs seemed to be tearing their way out through his throat, but he managed to stagger across the room with his burden. He did not make toward the door to the corridor, but went in the opposite direction. He had seen another door, just to the right of the commissioner's desk.

From previous experiences of his at headquarters,[14] he knew that this little side door would lead him through a narrow corridor toward the rear exit of headquarters.

The room was now filled with groans, shouts, cries of pain. Men were stumbling about, groaning, groping blindly. Others were hammering at the door to the corridor. Apparently the strange visitor had turned the key in the lock after slamming it. There was no egress that way.

"X," still with his burden, found the small door he was heading for, reached out and tore it open. He stepped through into the cool freshness of the outside corridor, took a deep breath of the comparatively clean air, and opened his eyes. He could see once more. He breathed two or three lungfuls of air before he was able to talk. Then he shouted: "This way, everybody—this way!"

He placed his burden upon the floor, stared down at it with narrowed eyes. This was no four-footed beast of prey. It was a man, a young man, whose countenance even now in repose was distorted into a vicious mask of lust. Blood flecked his lips. It was a human being—but it had torn a man's throat, and drunk his blood!

This was the opportunity which he had been laboring for all this time—an opportunity to question one of the tools of the person who had signed the note to Commissioner Foster—Doctor Blood.

"X" had had this very thing in mind when he acted with such swiftness back in the commissioner's room. This strange being with lust of a beast of prey was nevertheless a man. And a man could be made to talk—by methods which the Agent alone knew.

---

14 AUTHOR'S NOTE: Readers of previous chronicles of the exploits of Secret Agent "X" will recall that on several occasions the Agent invaded headquarters for the purposes of his own. Indeed, he had so often been an uninvited visitor there, that he is practically as familiar with the place as Inspector Burks or Commissioner Foster themselves. Perhaps the outstanding instance of the Agent's daring was evidenced in the adventure related in this periodical some time ago under the title of "Hand of Horror," wherein the Agent entered police headquarters, overpowered Inspector Burks, and changed places with that officer. His purpose at that time was to release a criminal whom it was essential that he interview in privacy. In order to accomplish this, the Agent disguised himself as Inspector Burks, and cooly ordered the prisoner brought to him. It had been quite noticeable that from the date of that event the attitude of Inspector Burks has been more uncompromising than ever in regards to Secret Agent "X." The Inspector has spared no effort to track down the Man of a Thousand Faces, and absolutely refuses to listen to any defense of Secret Agent "X." This is quite understandable, of course, for the inspector was deeply humiliated, and his pride hurt. "X's" purpose of course, was not to wound Burks' pride, but the inspector seems to have taken it as a personal affront. And he is not alone in this feeling, for Commissioner Foster has been similarly inconvenienced by the Agent in the past. Both these officials are the sworn enemies of Secret Agent "X."

He stooped quickly, lifted the unconscious burden over his shoulder, and made swiftly down the corridor.

Behind him he could hear the hoarse cries of Commissioner Foster, Norman Marsh, and Mayor Sturgis as they found the opened side door and urged the others to come out through it.

"X" hastened down the little corridor and emerged through a side door which let him out into Lafayette Street.

He carried his inert burden down the street, and stopped before a police squad car which was parked at the curb. There were no officers in it, in accordance with Mayor Sturgis' orders to leave the coast clear for the arrival of Secret Agent "X." The Agent thrust the young man into the car, went around to the other side and got in under the wheel. There were no keys in the lock, but the Agent drew from his pocket a ring of keys, selected one and inserted it in the ignition. He stepped on the starter, and the motor turned over.

In a moment they were off, had turned the corner, and were headed east. After driving two blocks, "X" headed north four blocks, and drew up before a garage in the middle of a sleazy tenement block.

The Agent left his unconscious captive in the squad car, and entered this garage. In a few moments he emerged, driving a small coupé. This was one of the many cars which he kept planted at strategic spots throughout the city in readiness for just such an emergency.[15]

The young man's unconscious body was a heavy, inert weight, but it took "X" only a few moments to transfer him to the coupé. He then drove away from there, leaving the squad car at the curb

---

15 AUTHOR'S NOTE: *The peculiar nature of the Agent's work makes it absolutely necessary that he use money unsparingly. When a crisis such as the present one develops, when the lives of men are threatened and when death and horror hang over a community like damp fogs of terror, Secret Agent "X" must act swiftly, surely, without thought of expense. At the beginning of his career this necessity was realized by the person in Washington from whom he derived his authority. For that purpose that person enlisted the cooperation of ten of the wealthiest men in the country. They subscribed an unlimited fund which was placed on deposit to the account of the Agent in the name of Elisha Pond at the First National Bank. No questions are asked of the Agent, no accounting is required. It is merely stipulated that he use these unlimited resources in any way that he may see fit to combat crime wherever it rears its ugly head. As he uses the funds they are systematically replenished. Thus the Agent has been able to equip himself with anything that might aid him in his work. He has at his command numerous cars, not only in any part of one city, but in many of the spots which he ordinarily uses as a center of operations. Very often his very ability to get a car when he needs one has been the means of saving not only his own life, but the lives of thousands of others.*

to be found by the police.

Eight blocks away, the Agent braked his car to a halt in a quiet block along the river front before a small two story building set in between two large, darkened warehouses which were closed for the night.

This little building was one of the many retreats which the Agent maintained throughout the city.[16]

Once more "X" maneuvered his unconscious guest out of the car, slung him over his shoulder and carried him into the darkened doorway of the little building, and up a short flight of narrow stairs.

If he waited outside for another minute or two, he would have seen the small sedan which turned into the block right after him. This sedan was driven by the dark, beautiful woman whom he had observed sitting in the parked car in front of police headquarters.

She had followed him all the way, had watched while he made the transfer at the garage, and then had continued to follow him to this retreat. Her face as she drove past the small building between the two warehouses was inscrutable. But her eyes darted from the parked coupé to the building.

She drove past as far as the corner, turned into the next street, and parked her car. Then she got out, crossed the street and stood in a darkened doorway, watching the house into which the Agent had led his captive. In the darkness, her face showed white and drawn, and her black eyes burned with an intense fire.

---

16 AUTHOR'S NOTE: *Just as in the matter of cars, Secret Agent "X" has provided himself with retreats throughout the country. In many cities, as well as in many of the smaller towns, one may find apartments which have been leased under various names, and whose owners apparently never use them. Generally, no questions are asked, for the Agent has seen to it that these retreats are located in such a way that their unoccupancy will occasion no comment. In many of these retreats he has duplicated material and weapons such as his gas gun, as well as complete paraphernalia for a quick change of disguises. As to the number of these apartments which "X" maintains, the author is unable even to make a wild guess. I once asked the Agent, in a moment of levity, how much his annual bill for rent is on his places. He only smiled and replied: "You'd hate to have to pay the income tax on it, Brant."*

CHAPTER VI

WHO IS DOCTOR BLOOD?

WITHIN THE HOUSE, the Agent was unaware of the woman who watched outside. He carried the unconscious man up the stairs, and into a room on the top floor. This room contained some strange appurtenances. Here, cunningly concealed, were emergency kits of make-up material, a complete assortment of clothes for changes of character, and various instruments and gadgets which the Agent found useful in his continuous battle against crime.

In other rooms of this house there was a completely equipped chemical laboratory, a filing system which catalogued the names of thousands of underworld characters, and a library of several hundred books. This was one of the Agent's main retreats—a place where he often retired to work on particularly baffling puzzles.

The Agent deposited his captive in an armchair, and went to the window. The street outside was deserted. He could not see the woman who had followed him for she had not stayed to watch, but had hurried around the corner to an all-night lunchroom up the middle of the next block, and was busy at that very moment making a telephone call.

She spoke long and earnestly into the telephone, her eyes alight with a strange fire. When she was through, she hurried out of the lunchroom and returned to her vigil across the street. But it was in that interval when she had been gone that the Agent had looked out of the window. Now he was busy with his captive.

That young man was just beginning to regain consciousness. He stirred, batted his eyes. "X" slipped a pair of handcuffs on his wrists; went through his clothes quickly. There was not even a scrap of paper to indicate his identity. There was a large bump on his head, and there were flecks of foam upon his lips. "X's" eyes were inscrutable as he observed these things. What strange kind of being was this, who tore open men's jugular veins, drank their blood?

The young man's eyes were open now, were regarding "X" with a strange sort of terror. It was unbelievable that this timid, harmless looking youth had leaped in to make his kill like a jungle beast.

The Agent demanded of him: "What is your name?"

The other hesitated a moment, then answered sullenly: "Laurento."

"Who sent you to headquarters to pose as Secret Agent 'X'?"

Laurento's voice was monotonous, as if he were making stereotyped answers to stereotyped questions. "Doctor Blood sent me." He said it as if that explained everything.

"Why did you kill Patterson?"

A slow smile spread over Laurento's countenance. His bloody lips made the smile a thing of horror. "That is a question which you must ask of Doctor Blood."

"X" asked him softly: "Where can I find this Doctor Blood?"

Laurento veiled his eyes, and his mouth assumed a stubborn set. "You will have to find that out for yourself." He twisted his head around, rubbed his nose against the lapel of his coat as if it itched. The action was entirely natural, such as any man might make while handcuffed.

The Agent continued patiently, disregarding the subtle appeal to remove the handcuffs. "You are not an American?"

Laurento shook his head. "No. But I've lived in this country for a long time."

"Look here," Secret Agent "X" urged. "You realize that you've just committed a terrible crime. You were under some sort of strange influence when you did it. Now you are more or less normal. This Doctor Blood has made a criminal—a murderer—of you. Why do you protect him? Tell me who he is!"

THE Agent suddenly stopped talking, extended a hand to support the young man. For Laurento's head had dropped upon his chest, his body sagged, and he would have fallen from the chair if the Agent had not caught him.

Laurento's breath was coming regularly, though a trifle slowly. He was falling into some sort of coma. His lips moved weakly, and "X" caught the words: "Doctor Blood will—take care—of everything."

The words died away into silence as the young man lost consciousness. His body became a dead weight on the Agent's supporting arm. The Agent betrayed no sign of exasperation at this sudden checkmate. But he could not figure by what method Laurento had been suddenly thrown into this coma. Though he had done extensive research work in chemistry and the allied sciences, he knew of no drug whose action was so delayed that it could be administered at one time so as to produce an effect like this at a later hour. He forced open Laurento's mouth, sniffed his breath. He perceived no betraying chemical odor.

But his hand on the young man's coat suddenly felt a peculiar wetness on the lapel. He bent closer to examine the cloth, and a peculiar odor assailed his nostrils. Laurento's coat lapel had been saturated with some sort of drug. And the Agent had breathed it.

A staggering thought flooded his brain. Laurento had lost consciousness within five minutes of brushing his nose against that coat lapel. The same thing would now happen to the Agent.

Already "X" could feel a strange sort of dizziness in the back of his head. Peculiar spots were beginning to dance before his eyes. There was no knowing how long this drug would keep him in that comatose condition.

Doctor Blood's plans had worked far better than even that ingenious criminal had anticipated; for now, within five minutes, the one man who might possibly be able to frustrate his fiendish plans would be impotent, lying as inert and helpless as Laurento now was.

But the Agent did not lose his wits as another man in that predicament might have. He crossed the room swiftly but without panic to the opposite wall. He placed his thumb at a certain spot in the molding and pressed hard. Instantly a small panel about three feet square opened downward like a tray. Set upon this panel, and held to it by suction cups were dozens of small vials of vari-colored liquids, together with a hypodermic syringe.

The Agent's knees were beginning to shake, sweat was breaking out upon his brow. He was feeling the powerful effect of the drug which he had inhaled—knew that it would overcome him within a matter of minutes. Even now he was keeping on his feet by a supreme exercise of will power.

Jaws pressed hard together, his whole body straining in every fibre to resist the drug, his fingers nevertheless moved swiftly as he filled the syringe from one of the vials. Then he stripped off his coat, did not wait to roll up his sleeve but tore it from wrist to shoulder. And without stopping to swab off his arm with antiseptic he quickly drove home the plunger of the hypodermic. The syringe contained a powerful dose of adrenalin. "X" did not know the nature of the drug which he had inhaled, but was hoping that the adrenalin, which served the same purpose with other coma producing drugs would counteract the effect of this one.

He replaced the hypodermic upon the tray, waited tensely for the results. His whole body was in a cold sweat now, the light was dimming before his eyes, and he experienced a queer watery weakness in his legs. He clenched his hands, pressed elbows against his sides, and forced himself to stand stiffly erect.

The blood raced through the arteries, carrying the adrenalin to his heart, which pumped it back through his entire body. If only the adrenalin could become operative before that deadly drug took full control of him. It was a battle of will against matter—the powerful will of a man who had schooled his body to obey every impulse of his mind. He must hold out now—for how long?

Slowly he began to sway on his feet. The room had begun to dance about him. The floor seemed to be tipping, the walls to be slanting. His eyes sought the window where he seemed to see gray shapes in the black of the night outside.

Still he stood there stiffly, defiantly, a man fighting against the elements. And then suddenly, the walls stopped slanting, the floor stopped tipping. He could feel his heart beating faster and faster, recovering from the strange lassitude which had gripped him. The spots began to clear from before his eyes, and he uttered a deep sigh—the only sign of the tremendous, almost unendurable strain under which he had labored for the last three or four minutes. He had won.

Weakly he crossed to the window, swung it open, and breathed in deep gulps of the fresh night air. Then he sought a chair, sat back in it, relaxing and closed his eyes. For the moment he gave no thought to Laurento who had slipped from the chair and now lay in a huddled heap on the floor.

The Agent's only thought now was to regain quickly the strength which had been melted from his body. It was five minutes before he managed to stand once more. He smiled grimly. Only a man of his tremendous recuperative powers could have regained his full strength in so short a time after such an ordeal.

CHAPTER VII

MEN OR BEASTS?

IT WAS A half hour later that a middle-aged inconspicuous sort of man stepped out into the street from the doorway of that little building between the two warehouses. This man in no way resembled the Victor Randall who had carried Laurento in only a little while before. He had bushy eyebrows, a broad nose, and dark hair which was beginning to gray at the temples.

Secret Agent "X" had assumed a new personality—that of Arvold Fearson, a disguise which he had used on occasions in the past. As Arvold Fearson, Secret Agent "X" was known to many people in the city, including the police officials, to be a private detective in the employ of the Hobart Detective Agency. The Hobart Agency was run by a redheaded young man, an ex-policeman who had been befriended by Secret Agent "X." Now the Agent made good use of Hobart's organization.[17]

As Arvold Fearson, there were many things which "X" had to

---

17 AUTHOR'S NOTE: Jim Hobart will no doubt be welcomed as an old friend by the regular readers of these chronicles. He was, it will be recalled, a young patrolman who had been discharged from the force in disgrace on a trumped-up charge. The Agent had known that Hobart was innocent of the charges that led to his dismissal, and had interested himself in the redheaded young man, whose loyalty he had occasion to prove time after time. It was in his role of A. J. Martin, the Associated Press man, that Secret Agent "X" finally offered to back Jim Hobart in forming his own private detective agency. This occurred after Hobart had been reinstated in the good graces of the police by reason of a clever act of "X's." Jim Hobart now operated his own agency, and received most of his business from Mr. A. J. Martin, though he found that the publicity he received in many of the cases which he helped the Agent on did him no harm in a business way, and he began to get many private clients from the outside. This was what the Agent had referred to when he told Randall that he knew that Randall had enlisted the services of a private detective agency. The banker, upon learning that his life was in danger, had communicated with Jim Hobart, and retained that young man's services. Jim had lost no time in notifying his benefactor, A. J. Martin, and it was thus that "X" learned that Randall's life was in danger.

do now. He had left Laurento upstairs, after having placed him on a bed, securely tied against the time when he should wake up from the coma. Now he looked up and down the street before entering his coupé.

But he did not see the woman who had followed him there. For she had left her post of vigil across the street only a few minutes before, after making another hurried telephone call.

The Agent drove west for several blocks, and pulled up in front of a drug store. He went inside and entered a telephone booth where he dialed a secret number which was known only to himself.

In a moment a precise, military voice spoke over the phone: "Bates talking."

Bates was the head of another organization controlled by the Agent, similar to the Hobart Agency except for one important difference—no one knew about it. For this organization the Agent had drafted men from all walks of life after investigating them thoroughly. The existence of Bates and his vast network of operatives was entirely unsuspected by the public, and the number which had just been dialed was one that was never used by anybody but Secret Agent "X."

The Agent said quickly: "Report on Oscar Stanton."

"Right, sir," Bates said. "Stanton left headquarters this morning in great excitement. He was followed to his home, where we have a dictograph installed. I have a transcript of everything he said at home. He made a number of telephone calls. They were to his brokers, instructing them to buy certain stock when they hit certain low prices. These instructions are the same as he has been giving for the last ten days, except that he added to the list of stocks that he wished to buy the common stock of the Pacific Bank, of which Mr. Gilbert Patterson was the head."

"Tell me quickly what happened at headquarters this morning," the Agent ordered.

"Why, sir, a man came to the commissioner's office claiming to be Secret Agent "X." He threw some sort of bomb into the room. And under cover of the smoke, Gilbert Patterson was murdered as Doctor Blood had promised. It seems that Commissioner Foster had called a conference of seven or eight of the leading citizens of the city. We can't get any definite information, but it is suspected that the commissioner had some sort of inkling that these men were the next to be murdered by the blood drinkers. We are sure of one thing—that Gilbert Patterson was slated for today, and that

Doctor Blood succeeded in murdering him. In some way they managed to admit the beasts into the commissioner's office. The man who threw the bomb escaped and carried off with him Mr. Victor Randall, who was also present at the conference. I have men out—"

"You need not work on that," the Agent interrupted him. "Mr. Randall is safe. There was another matter that I asked you to look into—this business of Grover Wilkerson. What have you got on that?"

"I don't know what put you on the track of Wilkerson, sir." There was admiration in Bates' voice. "But he certainly ties in with these murders. I have a short résumé here. Shall I read it to you over the wire?"

"Go ahead." The Agent inserted another nickel in the slot as the operator told him that his time was up, and he listened carefully while Bates read from the résumé in a clear precise voice.

"Grover Wilkerson, ex-millionaire, utilities magnate, recently convicted in Federal Court of fraud and embezzlement and sentenced to five years in jail. Subsequently declared insane and committed to the Ohio State Asylum for mental incompetents. He escaped from the asylum one month ago. Killed two men in the middle west who had testified against him at his trial. Left note threatening to 'get even' with everybody who contributed to his ruin. Has not yet been apprehended in spite of countrywide search for him. Our operatives report he was last seen on a train leaving New York, but disappeared at a small local station. Wilkerson is believed to be very dangerous. Inspector Burks has just released a statement to the press to the effect that he thinks it quite likely that Wilkerson is responsible for the ten murders which have occurred here in the city."

THE Agent marshaled the facts carefully in his mind. "Have you completed the arrangements in regard to Wilkerson as per my instructions?"

"Yes, sir. All arrangements are complete. I have called in all our operatives from the middle west who had at any time seen Wilkerson. They are scattered throughout the city here, canvassing homes, walking streets, on the watch for him. They are instructed if they should find him, to capture him without inflicting any injury unless they should be placed in physical danger."

"All right," the Agent told him. "In addition to the work you are now doing, I also wish you to begin a thorough investigation of a person by the name of Professor Hugo Langknecht, the German psychiatrist who is now visiting this country and whose help has been enlisted by the police to solve these murders.

"Find out if he has any friends, with whom he associates, what his interests are. Find out if he has ever been known to associate with a young man by the name of Laurento. Have you got that?"

"Yes, sir," Bates acknowledged. "Report on Professor Hugo Langknecht—with particular reference to a young man by the name of Laurento. Right, sir. I'll get right on it."

The Agent hung up, and immediately dialed another number, said: "Hello, *Herald?* May I speak to Miss Betty Dale?"

In a moment Betty was on the wire.

"X" said, using the same inflection of voice that he had employed when he met her on the street corner:

"Miss Dale? This is the person—"

"Yes—I know," her worried voice interrupted him. "I have got together most of the information that you wanted from me. I've been working downstairs in the morgue since I left you and have a list of all the news items which have appeared in the past six months about those ten men who were mur—"

"Never mind that," the Agent broke in. "I'll meet you later and you can give it to me. There is something I want you to get at once. This German psychiatrist. Professor Hugo Langknecht—where is he staying while here in the city?"

"That's easy. Can you hold the wire just a moment?"

"Yes."

In a short time Betty was back with the information. "He has rented an entire house on the outskirts of the city. It seems he's doing some scientific research work, and he has equipped a complete laboratory out there. Here's the address."

"X" repeated the number and the street after her. He did not need to write it down. His mind was a vast storehouse of accurately catalogued information from which he could extract any item that he had once learned. He thanked Betty, and hung up after telling her that he would see her later.

CHAPTER VIII

THE WOMAN FROM PARAGUAY

SPUYTEN DUYVIL ROAD lay off the main highway far to the north, in one of the loneliest portions of the city. Cold blasts of night wind blew in from the waterfront at the road's end. Darkness lay like a shroud of menace over the deserted street as the Agent parked his sedan opposite the two-story brick building which Professor Langknecht had rented for his stay in the city. Before getting out of the car, "X" noted that all the windows in the front of the house were provided with metal shutters, and that they were closed tight. No streak of light was permitted to show. The house lay gloomy, silent, a fitting edifice for this out of the way, forbidding street.

Secret Agent "X" crossed to the other side, approached the doorway of the building, which was level with the sidewalk. His rubbersoled shoes made no sound on the pavement; his car, which was equipped with a specially constructed motor, had not made the slightest sound as he drove up; yet he was sure that his arrival had been noted, that he was being observed from some point of vantage in the building.

He rang the bell, waited silently. There was no sound from within, but suddenly the heavy oak door was swung open. The hallway within was unlit, but the Agent was able to discern the heavy, brutish features of the oxlike man who stood just within. This man was clothed in a white coat, and wore rubber gloves. He peered at the Agent out of small, piglike eyes, and said: "Yes?"

"X" asked: "Is Professor Langknecht in?"

The big man surveyed him without speaking for a moment, then asked: "Your name?"

"X" produced a card which he handed over. "I am Arvold Fearson," he said. "I should like to speak with the Professor on a personal matter."

The other took the card, said gruffly: "Vait here. I see." He shut the door, left the Agent standing outside.

A few moments later, the door opened once more, but this time on a chain. Through the crack the Agent could see the white coat once more. The gruff voice spoke to him through the opening. "T'e professor iss not in."

The door began to close, but "X" put his foot in the crack. "Just a moment," he said. "I am sure the professor will manage to be in for me if you will give him this message. Tell him that I wish to talk with him about—Laurento."

The man uttered a startled gasp. Then after a pause said: "Vait."

Once more the door was closed. This time it took a little longer, while the Agent waited, his eyes scanning the shadows that surrounded the house. Finally the door opened, this time wide, without the chain.

The big man in the white coat and the rubber gloves stood aside in the hallway. "T'e Professor will see you," he announced.

"X" entered, and the door was closed behind him. If he had remained outside only a moment or two longer, he would have seen the sedan which turned into Spuyten Duyvil road and drove up to the house, parked behind his own coupé. He would have seen the tall, black-haired woman with the green hat who descended from the sedan and inspected his coupé; would have seen her turn cloudy eyes in the direction of the house, then cross the street. But the Agent was already within, and the white-coated one was saying: "Follow me upstairs. But do not touch the banister or the wall. It is dangerous."

The other preceded him up the stairs, and led toward a room at the front of the house where he rapped upon another door which was fully as strong as the one downstairs.

This one opened into a lighted room. Professor Langknecht himself stood there, arrayed in a white coat, but minus the rubber gloves. He stepped aside for "X" to enter, said to the attendant: "You may go, Hans."

The attendant bowed, closed the door from the outside. The Agent was left alone in the room with Professor Langknecht. The professor turned and stared at him out of eyes whose expression was hidden by the thick-lensed spectacles which he wore. He was holding the Agent's card in his hand. He glanced down at it, then up again, frowning.

"I do not know of you, Mr. Fearson. What is this matter that you wish to speak with me about?"

IN the single quick glance which he had cast over the room upon entering, the Agent had noted that it was equipped as a very comfortable office, with a small desk at the farther wall, a couch, several chairs, and a row of filing cabinets. The filing cabinets covered an entire wall, and seemed to be divided into sections about three feet wide. "X" now stood tensely facing the professor. "I think you already know why I am here. You must have recognized the name of Laurento, which I told your man to mention to you. Isn't that why you consented to see me?"

His keen eyes were studying the professor, watching for the slightest reaction, for some sign of betrayal of his innermost thoughts. But the professor's face was a mask, his eyes inscrutable behind those glasses. He said: "You speak in riddles, my friend. I know no one by the name of Laurento."

"Perhaps," said the Agent still watching him closely, "you know him by some other name. I will describe him for you. He is a young man, short of stature, not over twenty-five years old; thin features, dark-haired, mild mannered. But his mild mannered aspect is deceptive—for today you saw him hurl a gas bomb into Commissioner Foster's office, and afterward you saw Gilbert Patterson dead on the floor, with his throat ripped open!"

Langknecht still retained full control of himself. Only his face darkened a little, and his lips parted slightly, showing two rows of even white teeth. "I am still unaware of what you speak, my friend. You are very annoying, and I am busy. I shall have to ask you to leave at once. I know of no Laurento."

"Not even," the Agent persisted, "if I should tell you that I know where Laurento is now? Wouldn't you be interested in learning his whereabouts?"

For a long moment the professor stood rigid, staring at the Agent. Then a long sigh escaped through his teeth. "Who are you?" he asked.

The Agent was tense now, ready for action. He had deliberately goaded the other into a half admission. "You can see my name on that card. I am a private investigator. If you are interested in learning Laurento's whereabouts, perhaps we can talk business."

The professor pondered for a minute or two. Then he said very low: "Yes, perhaps we can do business—but not the way you think!"

His hand darted to his shoulder, inside the white coat where there was a bulge. It reappeared in a moment, with a flat automatic. The professor was snarling.

BUT "X" gave him no chance to use the gun. With a movement so fast that it was almost imperceptible, he stepped in, brought his left hand down, palm open, in a slashing blow which caught the professor's arm at a point between the elbow and the shoulder. This was an effective, paralyzing blow which the Agent had learned many years ago.[18] It was knowledge and skill such as this that often made an unarmed man the equal of one equipped with the most dangerous weapon.

The professor staggered backward; the automatic dropped to the floor from fingers rendered numb by that paralyzing blow.

With a furious cry, he hurled his entire weight at the Agent, bore him backward, gouging mercilessly at "X's" face. The Agent twisted his head to escape those clawing fingernails, sidestepped, bent a little to the right and twined his left arm around the other's waist. Then he pushed hard with his right shoulder, at the same time twisting the other's body around. The professor was thrown off balance and crashed to the floor. He started to struggle upward again, but the Agent knelt, twisted his arm in a hammerlock.

Sweat began to break out on the professor's forehead; his small eyes glared viciously up at the Agent through the thick convex lenses.

The Agent was breathing evenly. "I am sorry, professor—" He stopped short. For he felt something cold and hard boring into the

---

18 AUTHOR'S NOTE: *The Agent never employs lethal weapons, and since he often found himself in positions where it was inadvisable to use his gas gun, the Agent's knowledge of strange means of offense and defense often served him well. There is an unwritten chapter of "X's" life, immediately preceding the entrance of the United States into the World War, when he spent a considerable period of time in the East. It was there that he was initiated into the high mysteries of the Japanese art of jiu-jitsu which employs the principles of balance and leverage as against the rougher theories of force and strength. This art of jiu-jitsu is often used by western readers as more or less a matter of charlatanism. The reason for this is that the true mysteries of this scientific art of self-defense have not been made public to the western world. It was only through an arduous process of making himself "persona grata" with a Korean sect of fighting men that Secret Agent "X" was permitted to study in one of the secret schools of jiu-jitsu under a master renowned throughout the East. It was here that he was taught the inner secrets of the true science of self-defense, that he was made aware of the four thousand nerve centers that come to the surface of the human body and which will cause excruciating pain if struck. It was such a blow which disarmed Professor Langknecht.*

back of his neck.

A feminine voice behind him, low and desperate, ordered: "Release him at once, and stay where you are."

The Agent relaxed his grip on the professor's arm, permitting the other to roll away and scramble to his feet.

The professor said, panting: "You have come just in time, Lola. The man is made of steel!"

The Agent rose slowly to his feet with the gun still boring into the back of his neck. The professor hurried to a closet, came back with a length of wire.

"Put your hands behind your back," he commanded coldly. His thin lips were pressed tightly together, his eyes lancing hatred at the Agent.

"X" obeyed under the compulsion of the woman's gun, and the professor wound the wire about his wrists, and twisted it tight.

"Now," he said, "we can talk."

The pressure of the gun was relaxed, and the Agent turned slowly. For the first time he beheld the woman. It was the one he had seen in the sedan outside of headquarters; the one who had followed him to the apartment where he had taken Laurento. He bowed to her in courtly fashion, saying with a half-smile:

"My compliments, madam. You entered this room with the silence of an expert." His eyes strayed to the opposite wall where a section of the filing cabinet had been swung open on a pivot, revealing a passageway through which the woman had come.

The woman held her gun steady, still pointing at the Agent. Her expensive fur coat was open, revealing a nile green dress which set off the whiteness of her long, slender throat. Under the bright electric lights she was as beautiful, as mysteriously bewitching as she had been in the shadows of the sedan.

The professor wiped perspiration from his face, pointed to the Agent, saying: "He has just told me—that he knows where Laurento is!"

Lola exclaimed, "Wait, Hugo. Come here, Hugo. I have something to tell you. I, too, know where to find Laurento!"

Hugo backed away from the Agent to where the woman was standing. She turned to the professor and whispered in his ear so low that the Agent could not hear what she was saying. All the time, however, she kept her eyes glued to the Agent.

When she finished her whispered message, the professor exclaimed: "That is different, Lola. We will go at once then. Let us put this man in a safe place until we return."

He ran his hands over "X's" clothing, frisking him for weapons. The Agent's various implements were securely hidden, safe except from a thorough search, but the professor found the gas gun in "X's" holster under his coat, drew it forth. He apparently thought it was an ordinary revolver, for he threw it carelessly on his desk.

Then he seized the Agent by the arm once more, led him out into the hall to a small door. The Agent could see that the door to the room next to this was open, revealing a complete laboratory.

The professor took a heavy key from his pocket, opened the small door before which they were standing, and thrust the Agent in. Then he slammed the door, locked it.

"X" was now in complete darkness. He listened closely for any sound from the hallway, but could hear nothing—not even the receding footsteps of the professor and Lola. This told him that the door of the room into which he had just been locked was not only heavy, but also sound-proof. The Agent waited quietly until his eyes became accustomed to the darkness, and until he had become assured that there was no one else in this room with him.

He manipulated his wrists against the wire which bound them, loosening it slowly. It was a long, arduous task there in the darkness. Soon he had the wire loose enough for him to slip his hands through. His wrists were cut and bruised. In the darkness he set about the task of inspecting his prison.

He took his fountain pen flashlight from his pocket, and sprayed the beam around. He was in a small closetlike room, no more than four feet square. It was absolutely bare.

"X" approached the door, knelt before it and took from his pocket the small, compact leather kit which contained a complete set of chromium tools. He held the flashlight between his knees, and went to work on the lock. It was not long before he heard a click as the tumblers yielded to his coaxing. He laid down his chromium tools, turned the knob and pulled on the door. But it did not give. The professor must have shot home a bolt or another fastening of some sort on the outside. He had not placed all his reliance on the lock. The Agent tugged at the door, but to no avail. He was effectually imprisoned in that little room.

He took from his kit a small chisel and a small, collapsible iron bar about a half inch in thickness. This bar was hollow within and contained other sections so that it could be elongated in the same fashion as a collapsible drinking cup. The Agent opened this to its full length of ten inches, and attached to the top a small hammerhead. He now had a complete hammer and chisel. He set to work upon the door. But he made little impression upon it. The solid oak resisted his efforts.

"X" did not give up. He moved around to the wall, tapped upon it at various spots until he heard the hollow sound which indicated that there was no beam here. He had seen the open door of the laboratory in the next room, and his hope was to break through the wall into the laboratory.

He set to work upon the wall with his hammer and chisel. The plaster gave easily before his onslaught. He stopped every once in a while, wondering why the noise he made had not attracted anyone. If the professor and Lola had already gone, they might have left the man, Hans, on guard. Hans must surely have heard the sound of the blows upon the wall. He might even be waiting at the other side to trap the prisoner as he was coming through. But "X" continued with his work. If Hans were waiting on the other side, that problem would have to be faced when he had broken through the wall.

CHAPTER IX

DOCTOR BLOOD SCORES AGAIN

IT REQUIRED AN hour and a half of patient, backbreaking work there in the little room with the meagre illumination furnished by the fountain pen flashlight before the Agent had succeeded in cutting a hole through the plaster large enough for him to wriggle through. Several times while he had been working, he had thrown the beam of his flashlight into the other room through the slowly widening aperture. It was the laboratory which he had noted from the corridor. But he saw, also, that the door to the laboratory was closed now. Whether it was locked or not remained yet to be seen.

The Agent's face, coat, trousers and hands were covered with plaster when he finished. He squirmed through the hole in the wall after collecting his tools. With the aid of his flashlight, he crossed quickly to the door, tried it.

The door was locked.

"X" found the electric lightswitch, snapped it on, and set to work upon the door. Once more he heard the tumblers click. He turned the knob, pulled. But the door was apparently fastened on the outside in the same fashion as the door to the closet which he had been thrust into. It did not give.

The Agent tapped the wall on either side of the door. If he could find a hollow spot here, he might be able to work through into the corridor. In the closet next door he had not been able to do this, as the whole closet was hardly more than the width of the door, with very little wall to spare on either side. Here, however, there was three or four feet of wall space. But the beams ran solidly. The wall gave forth no hollow sound. There would be no chance to cut through at any point in the wall to the corridor.

Somberly the Agent turned and surveyed the laboratory. On one wall there was a glass case with the shelves full of bottles of all sizes containing liquids of varied colors.

"X" approached this cabinet, thoughtfully studied the labels on the bottles. A smile appeared on his face.

He picked out several of the bottles, one after the other, and brought them to the work bench. Here he found a test tube, into which he proceeded to pour certain quantities from each bottle. He handled the chemicals as if he had been accustomed to using them all his life.[19] And indeed, he had. For the solution he was preparing now was in accordance with a chemical formula which he had himself designed. That formula now reposed in the secret files of the War Department of the United States. It was another contribution of the Agent's to the safety of his country.[20]

When he had finished his task, the Agent sealed the test tube, made a hole in the stopper, and inserted into it a splinter of wood which he cut from the bench. The liquid within the test tube had now assumed a sort of reddish brown hue. He laid it on the floor close to the door, and lit the splinter of wood.

Then he went to the hole which he had cut in the connecting wall, climbed back through it into the closet next door. From here he watched the improvised fuse burning down to the liquid within the test tube. When the fire reached the liquid, there came a blinding flash of light. There was the sound of tearing, splintering wood as the heavy door crashed outward. The entire building shook for a moment. A blinding cloud of smoke enveloped the room.

"X" waited a few moments longer until the smoke had drifted out into the corridor. Then he climbed through the hole and sur-

---

19 AUTHOR'S NOTE: *It will be recalled that Secret Agent "X" was a member of the Intelligence Service of his country during the Great War. His great value to that service arose partly from his profound knowledge of chemistry and the allied sciences. Once he had been enabled to score a remarkable coup of espionage by his ability to recognize the importance of a group of chemical symbols noted upon an enemy agent truck. The result of that coup had been that the Allies had been in a position to provide their combatant forces with a new type of gas mask which was proof against the new and deadly gas being used by the enemy, and whose formula the Agent had been able to discover.*

20 AUTHOR'S NOTE: *Though Secret Agent "X" loathed war more than any man living, he has often told the author that he entertains a very comfortable feeling at the thought that, if our country should be drawn into another war, the formula for this explosive would be immediately available, and it could be manufactured in sizable quantities right on the spot where it would be needed by any company of engineers in the field. The great advantage of such an explosive is that it requires no transportation from munitions factories with the accompanying danger of sabotage, and that the forces in the field need never be delayed while awaiting supplies of explosives.*

veyed his handiwork.

The solution which he had placed within that test tube, was as potent as trinitrotoluene. It had torn the heavy door from its moorings, had slitted the wall, and had given the Agent his freedom.

"X" STEPPED over the debris into the corridor. He glanced swiftly from left to right, saw no one. If anyone had been in the house, he or she would certainly have started running at the sound of the splintering door. But everything was silent now.

Swiftly "X" went from room to room in the upper corridor, found them all emptied. He descended to the ground floor. Here it was dark. "X" used his flashlight again, entered the room at the front of the hall. He found the light switch, snapped it on, and stood still in the doorway, studying the thing he had suddenly perceived upon the floor. His face was etched into a grim mask as he approached and knelt beside the body which lay there.

It was Professor Hugo Langknecht. That is, it was what was left of Professor Hugo Langknecht. His white coat shone crimson under the light. He lay stretched out on his back, at full length, dead. His glasses had apparently been knocked off in the struggle which had resulted in his death, for they lay near him, the thick lenses still unshattered by their fall to the floor.

The professor's throat was a raw, bloody, gaping wound. His jugular vein had been ripped open.

Secret Agent "X" cast a swift glance up and down the corridor, his keen ears listening for the slightest sound. There was no indication that anyone was in the house.

He dropped once more to examine Langknecht's body. There was no question but that the professor had perished in the same way as Patterson and the other ten victims. His body was drained of blood. He seemed shriveled, shrunken, and the skin of his face appeared plastered to his cheek bones.

On the floor near him there were peculiar streaks—bloody streaks that might have been left by the claws of some monster of prey. All this must have happened while "X" was confined in that closet, while he was working his way out of the laboratory.

"X's" eyes were bleak as be studied the cadaver of the psychiatrist. The Agent had suspected Langknecht of being the master of those human monsters which were committing the murders. But how to explain this he did not know.

The Agent left the body of Langknecht as it lay, and proceeded cautiously back into the hall. He encountered no one. The house was deserted now.

Outside, "X" surveyed the street, his keen eyes piercing into the shadows on all sides, making sure that the devilish cohorts of Doctor Blood had not remained behind to lay in wait for him as he emerged. The street was empty. He quickly climbed into his coupé.

CHAPTER X

BAIT FOR A TRAP

IT WAS ALMOST eight o'clock when Secret Agent "X" arrived at the waterfront street on which stood the small house where he had left Laurento. He did not drive directly up to the building, but parked two blocks away, slid from his car, and approached cautiously, invisible in the shadows of the gloomy structures that lined the street. He stopped for a long time at the corner, standing motionless, with his coat collar turned up to hide the white gleam of his shirt front.

In a doorway opposite the house where he had left Laurento, he spotted the figure of a man. Some slight motion of that watcher had attracted "X's" attention. Now the Agent's eyes roved farther down the street, noted another doorway where there was also a dark blob of blackness like the figure of a man. His place was being watched.

He had expected this. Lola must have told Doctor Blood or his lieutenant of this place. Either she worked with Doctor Blood, or else pressure had been applied to her to make her talk. For some reason, however, she had omitted telling Doctor Blood that "X" was confined in the closet in Langknecht's home.

"X" moved slowly, inches at a time, and rounded the corner. He worked his way halfway down the side street, and made sure that there were no watchers here. Then he sprinted across the street, and into a narrow alley between two tall warehouses. He made his way through this alley, hugged the rear wall of a garage until he had worked along close to the back of his own building.

Once more his figure became motionless as he studied the yard that he was in. Finally, assured that there were no watchers here, he opened the rear door of the garage with a pass key, slipped inside and felt his way along through the impenetrable darkness within. Working by his instinct alone, he found the trapdoor in the floor of the garage, which he knew would be there, lifted it up, and went down a short ladder after closing the door above him.

He swiftly traversed a narrow passage cut along the foundation wall of the garage until he came to another door, which he opened with his key. He was now in the basement of his own building. This was an emergency exit and entrance which no one knew about but himself.

He made no noise at all as he went upstairs, his keen ears attuned to the slightest sound which would show him that there were watchers within the house as well as those outside. But he heard nothing. He went through the entire house without finding anyone anywhere, he then approached the room where he had left Laurento.

He turned the knob slowly, silently, his long agile fingers moving it only a fraction of an inch at a time. He had put out the light in the hall, so that when he got the door opened just a crack, there would be nothing to indicate to anyone who might be waiting within that the door was being opened.

His eye, close to the crack, saw nothing but darkness within. He recalled distinctly having left a light on in that room.

For a long minute he kept his ear near that crack, but heard nothing. He took out his flashlight, held it ready, and kicked open the door. In his right hand, he held ready another gas gun, which he had supplied himself with from his reserve arsenal hidden in one of the other rooms. He snapped on his flashlight, swung it quickly over the room.

There was no one there.

The bed upon which he had left Laurento was empty. And at that moment he caught the sound of stealthy footsteps from the floor below.

Doctor Blood had laid a trap—but he had removed the bait. And now the trap was sprung.

THE Agent extinguished his flashlight, softly closed the door of the room and stole quietly to the head of the stairs. He sensed now that many men had entered the house. There was no sound, no shadow of movement, but his instincts told him that he was being hemmed in by adversaries.

The stillness in the house was ominous, pregnant with dreadful peril. Soon the Agent's eyes detected a slight blur of movement in the darkness of the floor below. His stalkers were coming up.

He followed the shadowy movements of the men on the floor below, counted at least four of them. They must have been outside, watching the room from which they had removed Laurento, must have been watching for the light. They knew now that he was in the house.

The Agent was sure that Doctor Blood would have made certain to prepare an unbreakable trap—for he surely suspected now that the man he was trying to corner here must be Secret Agent "X".

Even as he watched, the Agent understood what the attackers' plans were. For he saw the figure of the first man who reached the foot of the stairs raising a hand as if to hurl something. They knew he was up here, and they apparently intended to hurl another of the gas bombs similar to the one that Laurento had used in the commissioner's office.

"X" retreated swiftly from the head of the stairs, sought the ladder which led to the roof. He climbed it quickly, unlatched the skylight, and pushed upward. But it would not open. His mouth set in a grim line. He realized that Doctor Blood had not overlooked any tricks. The skylight had been nailed up from above. His escape was cut off in that direction.

Just as the Agent began to descend the ladder again, there was a tinkling crash on the floor of the landing. One of the men below had hurled up the gas bomb. Almost at once the entire corridor was suffused with a peculiar, cloying, bitter-sweet odor.

The Agent recognized it at once. It was the distinctive odor of hydrocyanic acid—quick acting, deadly. Doctor Blood was not taking any half measures with him.

"X" did not wait to descend rung by rung. He leaped from the topmost step to the floor, sped down the corridor away from the quickly spreading fumes. He tore open the door of the front room where he kept his paraphernalia and equipment, and slammed the door behind him. That would be only a feeble obstacle against the insidious gas. For the hydrocyanic would enter shortly through the crack under the door. But the Agent did not pause to worry about this.

He opened a closet, pressed a spot in the wainscoting, and a section of the wall in the closet opened outward. Behind this wall was a shallow cavity with rows of hooks upon which hung dozens of various ingenious objects. From among these the Agent selected a gas mask and respirator.

He closed the closet door, and with nimble fingers donned the gas mask. He took two or three breaths through the nozzle to be sure that the respirator was functioning properly, then he drew his gas gun and marched out into the corridor. He switched on the electric light, walked to the staircase and went down quickly. He was quite sure that he would encounter nobody now, for the men who had flung that bomb containing the hydrocyanic acid would certainly not have remained within the building.

On the ground floor he peered out through the front window, saw several dim shapes on the opposite side of the street. They were holding sub-machine guns.

Behind the mask, "X's" lips spread in a thin grin. No effort was being spared to make sure that he perished. If by any chance he should succeed in coming out through that front door, in surviving the deadly gas which by now was filling the entire house, they were prepared to mow him down with those guns.

The Agent hesitated only an instant, then started back to the rear of the house, descended to the cellar and made his way out through the subterranean tunnel which led back to the garage. Once out in the open air of the backyard, he took off his gas mask, carried it under his arm, and stole swiftly along the alley to the street.

He moved like a shadow, slipping from one blob of darkness to another, watching keenly to make sure that no one was posted on this side street. Those men were concentrated on the front. Doubtless they had scouted the neighborhood before setting their trap, had been convinced that there was no rear exit from the building.

WHEN he was satisfied that the coast was clear, the Agent slipped across the street, faded into the darkness in the direction of his parked coupé. He had escaped from the jaws of the trap. But his work was yet to be done. His unknown enemy had placed him upon the defensive, had caused him to lose valuable time in this race with death—for the Agent still bore in mind that on the following day Norman Marsh was to die. And "X's" clue had been wrested from him; all the leads which he had been attempting to work upon had been destroyed by the quick action of Doctor Blood. Langknecht was dead. Laurento had been spirited away.

There remained the woman, Lola, and Hans, if they could be found. There was also the possibility that Bates' men might turn up something on Grover Wilkerson, the demented financier. Beyond that there was nothing.

As he drove along now, he was careful to watch in his rear vision mirror. But he was not being followed. Apparently he had successfully eluded the watchers outside his house.

He listened now to the routine police broadcast which came over the short wave radio receiver on the dashboard. Somehow, he was sure he detected an edge of nervousness in the voice of the police announcer. Many of the orders had to do with the precautions that were being taken by the police to protect the doomed men. They indicated that the police still believed that Doctor Blood was employing beasts of prey to do his vicious work. One of these orders in particular was interesting.

"All cars, all cars," the announcer was repeating. "Inspect all automobiles closely. Be on the lookout for Victor Randall. He has disappeared, and it is suspected that he has been kidnaped from headquarters. Stop all cars that look suspicious, inspect the occupants. Mr. Randall must be found. It may be that his kidnapers will attempt to move him in a car. Watch all cars."

The Agent smiled as the announcer began to repeat the order. He was glad that they did not suspect his impersonation of Randall. He was also glad that they thought Randall had been kidnaped in that way. It would give him an opportunity to return to headquarters if necessary, once more in the guise of the banker. He would, of course, have to drop the personality of Arvold Fearson for the present, for it was apparent that Doctor Blood knew who Arvold Fearson was. "X" thought it quite possible also, that Doctor Blood knew he had impersonated Randall. For that master of evil would no doubt also be listening in on the police broadcast, would be quite sure that Laurento had not kidnaped Randall from headquarters.

Suddenly the voice of the police broadcaster was drowned out by a loud buzzing sound, that was repeated five times in quick succession. "X's" hand tensed on the wheel, though he did not slow down. Immediately following the buzz, Bates' voice came over the radio, saying: "Station X calling. Station X calling."

Bates must have something important to communicate, for he never used his short wave sending set unless it became imperative. It was an arrangement which the Agent had found quite convenient, for it gave Bates the opportunity of getting in touch with him, no matter where the Agent was. They used the police band, but employed a variety of codes which made it impossible for the police to understand the content of the messages.[21]

After the station call, Bates' voice continued, delivering the message. The Agent immediately recognized which code Bates was employing, and his nimble brain deciphered as it came over the air waves. He needed no paper or pencil. It was a short message, but Bates kept repeating it and repeating it. He would do so until he received a phone call from the Agent. The message was:

> "Important developments at headquarters. Our men cannot discover what is happening, as utmost secrecy is being maintained by Commissioner Foster. How shall I proceed?"

The Agent stopped at the nearest store displaying a telephone sign, entered and called Bates.

"Glad you called, sir," Bates said. "The man I have stationed at headquarters tells me that there's a lot of excitement down there. A good deal of running around. It seems that another murder has been discovered, for they phoned the medical examiner. But they wouldn't disclose what it was, wouldn't even give the reporters any information."

"I know what that is," the Agent told him. "It was up on Spuyten Duyvel Road. You needn't bother any more about getting on the trail of Langknecht. It's he who was murdered up there."

THERE was a moment's silence. Then: "Good Lord, sir," Bates exclaimed. "This Doctor Blood is bad medicine."

"Have you got any further trace of Grover Wilkerson?" the Agent asked.

"No, sir. But I've got some important information about him. One of our operatives from the middle west has just come in by plane. He tells me an item that has been kept secret from the public all this time. Did you know that Grover Wilkerson *has only one hand?*"

---

21 AUTHOR'S NOTE: Secret Agent "X" has found this broadcasting equipment very useful in the past. Adjusted to the same wavelength as the police calls the Agent is able to pick up messages from it with an ordinary receiving set which is installed in every one of his cars. Thus, if the car should be found by the police, they would have no reason to suspect that it was different from any other car. The great difficulty which the Agent encountered in perfecting this equipment was the fact that the police might be able to trace the sending set by means of direction finders. After a good deal of experimenting, "X" succeeded in devising an instrument which he terms a "disperser" which nullified the use of direction finders. Bates' organization, which is similar to that of Jim Hobart's, with the exception that it is kept entirely secret, is the only one furnished with this sending equipment.

"What?" the Agent asked.

"Only one hand, sir. It seems that about eight or nine months ago he got an infection of the left hand, and it had to be amputated. This was done in a private hospital, and the physician who did it kept it a secret from the newspapers. As Wilkerson disappeared soon after that, none of his friends or acquaintances ever had a chance to learn about it. The way our operative discovered it, was through the certificate of the Board of Health. As you know, every amputation must be reported by the operating surgeon. The certificate that our man found out there, indicates that Wilkerson's left hand was amputated at the wrist."

"That is very important information, Bates," the Agent said slowly. "You must bend all your energies now to locating Wilkerson. Keep your men out on the job day and night. Pay them double wages. And have them search down every possible clue that might lead them to Wilkerson. And warn them to be careful. Wilkerson may be dangerous."

"I'm quite sure he is, sir. The man is certainly mentally deranged, and he has a terrible hatred for society."

"I am going to be very busy for the next three or four hours, Bates. I may not have a chance to communicate with you. If anything of importance turns up, flash it over Station X. Use code 'M' the next time."

"Right, sir," Bates acknowledged.

"One thing more," the Agent added. "Do you happen to have any information in the file on a Paraguayan dancer who may be in the city at this time? Her first name would be Lola."

"Just a moment, sir. I recall clipping some items on that subject. Will you hold the wire?"

In a few moments Bates was back. "Here it is, sir. Lola Lollagi. She was a star dancer in Asuncion. It seems from these clippings that she suddenly decided to come to the United States. She arrived the same week that Professor Hugo Langknecht arrived from Germany.

"I don't know if that has any significance. She is now playing at the Gotham Theatre in the *North American Varieties*. I also have a clipping here from *La Paz*, an Asuncion newspaper which states that she left rather hurriedly, with little baggage. She had one brother, a young man who suffered from some sort of mental ailment, and had been confined in an asylum in Paraguay. That is all the information I have on her."

"That is plenty," the Agent told him. "You have given me more than I expected. Continue with the search for Wilkerson, and report to me as instructed."

The Agent was about to hang up when Bates suddenly exclaimed: "Just a moment, sir. One of the other phones is ringing. Will you hold on a minute? It may be something of importance."

"I'll wait," the Agent said.

It was several minutes before Bates returned to the phone, and the Agent had to insert another nickel in the slot to keep the connection.

Bates' voice betrayed a slight tinge of excitement. "It's one of my operatives, sir, who has been shadowing the men who were present at headquarters today. We've got dictographs planted in their homes and this operative who has been working on John Lacey, overheard him telling his wife the contents of a message which he had just received from Commissioner Foster. It appears that Foster wants all of them to meet him tonight. It seems that there is some development that is so important he can't even tell them about it in the letter."

THE Agent thanked Bates, instructed him: "Continue to have all those men shadowed. Will get in touch with you again."

After he had said good-bye to Bates, the Agent dialed Betty Dale's number at the *Herald*. Though it was quite late, she had not gone home, but had waited for his call.

"I can't meet you now, Betty," he told her. "But there is a point you may be able to help me on. Do you know anything about Lola Lollagi, the Paraguayan dancer?"

"Yes. I handle most of the interviews with women, and it happens that I was getting up a little feature article on her for next Sunday. There isn't much known about her. She has been very reticent since she came to this country, not disclosing much about her past life. Of course we know that she was a great attraction in Asuncion—"

"I know about that," the Agent told her. "What do you know about her doings since she arrived here?"

"She's very beautiful. Many men have been interested in her, particularly Oscar Stanton, the stock speculator. For the last month since she has been in this country, he has managed to meet her every night when the theatre closed, but she never permits him to take her home. They go out a little together, but that is all. The doorman at the stage entrance told me that much about her. Beyond that, little is known about how she spends her spare time. I was anticipating having a tough job dragging information from her."

"You say," the Agent repeated thoughtfully, "that Oscar Stanton has been very much interested in her?"

"That's right. But it doesn't seem as if she returns his interest."

"Thank you," the Agent said. "Suppose you go home now, and get some rest."

Betty's voice was eager, lively. "I'm not the least bit tired. If you think I can be of any further use, I'll gladly—"

"No, Betty. I think that the matter I am working on will rush through to a swift conclusion now. Your aid has been invaluable."

"Well then, if you don't think you'll need me any more, maybe I'll run over to the Gotham Theatre and try to get that interview from Lola Lollagi."

"No, no," the Agent said hastily. "Suppose you put off getting that interview for a day or so. In exchange, I'll promise you a first page scoop."

"It's a bargain," Betty laughed lightly. "I'll go home. But don't forget your promise. And—" her voice lost its banter, grew suddenly serious—"you *will* be careful? If anything should happen—" a close listener might have detected a hint of a sob—"I—"

"You must not think of those things, Betty." The Agent's voice was hard, deliberately stern. He had schooled himself long ago to repress every softer emotion within himself, to kill it, to subordinate it, to the duty he owed to society.

He walked slowly from the store, reëntered his coupé.

CHAPTER XI

RANSOM FOR BLOOD

SECRET AGENT "X" drove to another one of his apartments, changed his disguise back to that of Victor Randall. He left by a side door, and did not use the coupé again, but took a taxicab. If he had been followed without his knowledge, the watcher would continue to keep an eye on that coupé.

Once in the taxicab, the Agent gave the address of Oscar Stanton's home. Stanton was the one man who had refused to stay at headquarters for the conference with Secret Agent "X." It was Stanton who had announced his intention of paying Doctor Blood rather than rely upon police protection or upon the assistance of Secret Agent "X." The fact that Stanton was interested in Lola Lollagi further made him a focus of interest for the Agent.

When he arrived at Stanton's imposing home, "X" was admitted by the manservant who recognized him at once as Victor Randall. Randall and Stanton, of course, knew each other well.

Stanton was apparently in a state of great excitement. He greeted "X" loudly and effusively—a little too loudly, and a little too effusively, the Agent decided.

Stanton's face was flushed, his collar wilted from perspiration. His eyes did not meet "X's," but kept wandering about, never resting upon any one object. However, the hand with which he offered a whiskey and soda to the Agent was quite steady. "X" wondered if he was really as excited as he appeared.

"What's been happening to you, Randall? What's this about your being kidnaped from headquarters after Patterson was killed?"

"X" shrugged. "I don't know any more about it than you do, Stanton. He knocked me unconscious, and carried me out—must have been as a shield for him, because I came to about an hour later lying in an alley not far from headquarters." The Agent watched

The trapdoor had been nailed from the outside. Escape was cut off.

Stanton carefully as he told him this story, to see if he believed it

Apparently the stock speculator did, for he said casually: "You were pretty lucky, Randall. The others didn't get off so easy when they got in his hands. But maybe he only kills on schedule, and you're number seventeen. You have another week to live."

They sipped their drinks in silence for a few minutes. Then Stanton said in a queer voice: "What brings you here anyway, Randall? I should think you'd be traveling around with a police guard, or staying safely at home."

"X" appeared to be hesitant about speaking. Then he said: "I'll tell you, Stanton. Ever since I came to in that alley, I've been thinking about this business, wondering whether it pays to defy this

Doctor Blood. You've been talking about paying up—"

Stanton nodded. He said slowly: "I've already made arrangements to pay."

"That's why I came," "X" told him. "Suppose I also wanted to pay. Could you arrange it for me?"

Stanton held his glass arrested in mid-air. For the space of perhaps two minutes, he did not speak, but his eyes suddenly lost their shiftiness, studied "X" as if he would probe to the very depths of his innermost thoughts.

He said, rather as a statement than as a question: "So you want to pay, too. I think—it can be arranged."

"X" acted the part of Randall to perfection. He assumed an air of terrified anxiety. "Do you think he'd take my money—and leave me alone?"

Stanton nodded slowly, still studying his guest "Yes."

"When—would I have to pay it over?"

"Tonight, Randall. If you can get the money and bring it over in an hour, I will pay it over for you."

"Everything—is arranged? You're sure it'll be all right?"

"Quite sure." Stanton nodded toward a theatre ticket that lay on the end table beside him. "See that ticket? It's for the balcony box at the Gotham Theatre tonight. I go there often." Stanton's eyes again avoided "X's." "There's an actress there that I'm especially interested in—and Doctor Blood seems to know it. I'm to sit in that box, and place the package of money in my hat which I will put on the floor. After the show, I am to stay in the box for ten minutes. During that ten minutes, some one will reach in and take the money from the hat. If you bring me your cash, I'll put it in with mine, and place a note there saying it's from you."

"X" WAS tense now, his mind racing quickly. He said: "But how can you be sure that Doctor Blood will take my money, too? Or how can you be sure that he won't take my money and then kill me anyway?"

Stanton shrugged. "You'll have to take that chance. But I'm pretty sure it'll be all right. I would advise you to pay."

"Perhaps," "X" suggested, still simulating great anxiety, "I could go along with you. Then—"

"Nothing doing!" Stanton rapped out. "If you want to do this, Randall, you'll do it my way!"

"Very well," said the Agent "I'll do it your way. Anything—anything to escape the death that Patterson got!" The Agent managed to shudder in a very good imitation of extreme terror. "L-let's have another drink. Here, I'll pour it."

The Agent poured the whiskey until Stanton said: "Hold it," and then picked up the syphon of water. For a moment "X" shifted and his body screened his actions from the other. In that second, a little capsule which he had held in the palm of his hand dropped into the glass. He then poured his drink, and handed over Stanton's glass.

Stanton leaned back in his chair, looked at "X" speculatively. "You know, Randall, it's a damn good thing you've come to me. I'd hate to see you get the treatment that Lewis Forman got. It's a damned unpleasant thing to have your jugular vein ripped open, and then have some ghoul drink your blood!" He shrugged, raised his glass. "Well, let's drink to tonight's arrangement!"

Stanton took a long gulp from his glass, and put it down.

The Agent sipped his drink, watching the other. Almost immediately, Stanton's eyes began to droop, his body to sag. In less than a minute his head was resting upon his chest. He was unconscious.

Now the Agent moved swiftly but surely. First he went to the door, locked it, so that he would not be interrupted by the manservant. Then he returned to the chair where Stanton sat, extracted from an inner pocket a kit of make-up material and a triple mirror which he unfolded and set beside the kit. Quickly, maneuvering as best he could, he changed clothes with Stanton. Then his long, capable fingers set to work with furious speed, manipulating the pigments, plastic materials, and other objects in the kit.

In an amazingly short space of time he had transformed his features into those of the man who sat unconscious in the chair. He took a couple of steps up and down the room in imitation of Stanton's walk, and then talked aloud for a moment, mimicking the other's voice. Then he set to work upon Stanton. His job was easier this time as he did not have to work upon his own face but he had to rely upon memory for the features which he was placing there.

When he had finished he stood back and surveyed his handiwork. No one would have suspected that the man who sat there inertly, was anybody but Victor Randall, the man who had just come into the house. "X" had merely changed personalities with the other. The Agent now cast his eyes about the room, found a newspaper on the serving table in the corner. This he proceeded to cut into strips the size of dollar bills, and when he had a package about three inches wide, he wrapped it in newspaper and thrust it into his pocket.

Then he picked up the ticket to the Gotham Theatre, went to the door and unlocked it. Then he rang for the servant.

This moment would be a test. "X" knew that Kroon, the butler, had been with Stanton for several years. Would Kroon penetrate the disguise?

When Kroon entered his eyes instinctively went to "X," and he said: "You rang, Mr. Stanton?"

The Agent eyed him keenly, searching for some sign that the man suspected the change. But no. Kroon was entirely deceived.

"Yes," "X" told him. "Mr. Randall must have been very tired—must have been doing a good deal of drinking. He just took the one drink, and he's gone sound asleep. I must go out. Let him sit there until he wakes up. Be sure he is not disturbed. Do not come in here until I return."

Kroon bowed. "Yes, sir."

The Agent made for the door, followed by the servant.

Downstairs Kroon handed him Stanton's hat and coat, and the Agent left. He was quite certain that his orders to Kroon would be obeyed. The manservant had absolutely no suspicion that the man who had just left was not his master.

Outside, the Agent hailed a cab and said: "Gotham Theatre."

Secret Agent "X" was going to keep the appointment which Stanton had told him he had with Doctor Blood.

CHAPTER XII

ENTER—THE CLAW MAN!

THE GOTHAM THEATRE was an old house which had long been devoted to the production of legitimate plays. Musty, with the plush and gilt grandeur of another day, it now stood forlornly yearning for the old triumphs when Mansfield had trod its boards. Until recently it had been empty, with only the ghosts of its old celebrities passing wraithlike up and down the narrow aisles. Now the old house was lit up, rejuvenated—with the glittering *North American Varieties.*

The performance was more than halfway through when the Agent arrived. The orchestra was well filled, as were the balcony and the mezzanine. "X" was conducted to a balcony box. When he was seated his eyes sought the stage, but he paid little attention to what was going on there. His gaze swung back to the fashionably attired women and the well-groomed men among the audience.

Here were hundreds of people, assembled in the usual way to seek entertainment, intent on spending an evening of pleasure despite the grisly menace which they knew was overhanging the city. Tomorrow another man was slated to die, to have throat torn, his blood drained from him by mysterious human vampires; and every day thereafter for a year another man would be doomed to die in the same way. Yet these people came here to be amused.

But "X's" attention was suddenly drawn to the stage. The chorus line of flashing legs backed away from the footlights, and the music struck up a lively tune. The spotlight focused upon the wing. A gorgeous creature daringly draped in a gown of silver cloth pirouetted upon the stage.

It was Lola Lollagi.

Her beauty was dazzling as she bowed with liquid grace. A series of complicated steps carried her directly beneath "X's" box.

The setting of this scene was an old Moorish castle. The men and women of the chorus were Spanish grandees and their ladies. Lola Lollagi seemed to fit into the scene as if she had been born for it. The glittering silver cloth dress clung to her sinuous body, cut low at the neck, revealing the alabaster skin of a perfectly formed throat. Two jade earrings were the only ornaments which she wore. Her hair was combed high upon her head. She danced with incomparable grace and beauty. The simplicity of her attire made a striking contrast to the ornate settings and the glittering raiment of the other actors.

Several times she glanced up toward the box in which "X" sat. The fixed smile which she wore for the benefit of the audience remained there; but the Agent detected something else in her startling coal black eyes—something that might have been uneasiness, fear— almost terror. Was this because she resented Stanton's attentions?

Betty Dale had said that Stanton had been paying constant attendance upon the dancer; this was evidenced by Stanton's statement that he frequently visited the theatre and sat in this box. Was Lola Lollagi afraid of Stanton, or was she afraid that some third party would resent her going around with him?

That the woman must have superb control of herself was indicated by the fact that she was appearing here, able to go on with the show, after what had happened back at Professor Langknecht's house.

Lola finished her number, and retired from the stage amid crashing applause. Her last glance was leveled at the box in which "X" sat. And subsequently, while other performers held the stage, the Agent thought he could detect her peering out from the wing—inspecting him, studying him. Was it possible that she had pierced his disguise? It is harder to deceive a woman than a man. He was posing here as Stanton—a man whom she apparently knew well. Perhaps she had been able to detect some subtle difference of appearance which indicated to her that the person who sat in that box was not Oscar Stanton.

When the finale went on, the Agent took from his pocket the package of newspapers which he had cut to the size of dollar bills, and placed it in his hat on the floor.

He watched the curtain drop after the final encore, then sat quietly while the house emptied. Soon the big dome lights in the ceiling went out, leaving only the pilot light on the center of the stage. His box was shrouded in darkness.

ALL was quiet in the theatre. Five minutes passed, six, seven, eight, nine. Nothing happened. For the tenth time the second hand on "X's" wrist watch made a complete circuit.

And then the drapes at the rear of the box parted only an inch or two at the bottom.

Out of the corner of his eye "X" saw a slim, black-gloved hand reach in, pick up the package from his hat on the floor, and disappear. The drapes fell back in place.

Instantly he became galvanized into action. Moving quietly in the box, he parted the curtains and slipped through. No one was in sight. The person who had taken the money had already disappeared.

A narrow staircase led down to the orchestra. To the left, a short corridor curved around in the direction of the stage. "X" knew that the person who had taken that money had not descended by the stairs. He therefore followed the corridor, found that it ended in an iron spiral staircase. The floor above would contain the dressing rooms of the chorus. On the floor below the dressing rooms of the stars and the office of the stage manager.

Looking down into the dimly lit well of the spiral staircase, the Agent could discern a figure disappearing into the regions backstage. All he could discern was a swiftly moving flash of white skin and cloth of silver. Then the figure was lost to sight in the gloom below.

"X" descended swiftly, silently, on his rubber soled shoes. He was now on the level of the stage itself. Everything was quiet. He crossed the open space backstage, came into a wide corridor. There were several rooms along this corridor, and just as he turned into it he heard a door farther down slam shut.

He heard voices to his left, heard several "good-nights" exchanged, heard the stage door open and shut. The personnel of the play had already departed.

"X" heard the doorman tramping around somewhere at the other end of the stage. He would soon be making his rounds to make sure that everything was shipshape for the night, and that everyone had gone home. There would be a few minutes before that tour of inspection.

The Agent knew which door had opened and closed. It was the third one down in the corridor, and he was sure whose room it was. For that glimpse he had got of the silver and white had identified for him the person who had taken the money—Lola Lollagi. She must, then, be acting under the instructions of Doctor Blood.

The Agent drew back into the shadows around the bend in the corridor, waiting for Lola Lollagi to change her clothes and come out again. He felt sure that she would go at once to deliver the package. And he intended to follow her, to find just how she contacted the party who was eventually to receive that package.

As he stood there watching the door through which Lola had disappeared, his back was toward one of the darkened wings of the stage. Immediately behind him was the huge backdrop upon which was painted the representation of a golden Spanish sunset. In front of this was the tin structure which had been painted to represent the turrets of a Moorish castle. No soul moved upon the stage. He no longer heard the movements of the doorman. That worthy had probably decided that it was unnecessary to make a tour of inspection and had gone into the little cubbyhole beside the door for a snooze.

Five minutes passed. The Agent began to wonder whether there was not some other exit from Lola's room, whether she had not already departed with the package.

He set himself to wait. Perhaps she was opening the package herself. Perhaps—the thought struck him with stunning force—she was not taking it to anyone.

Although his ears were keenly attuned to sound all about, he did not hear the stealthy footsteps of the figure that crept behind him in the darkness while he watched. This figure had materialized apparently from nowhere. It crouched over, with head lowered, stalking silently; it came nearer, step by silent step. As it approached within three feet of the Agent, its head raised, revealing a queer sort of covering over the face that might have been a Halloween mask. Out of this mask, two eyes peered at the Agent

Slowly, silently, it crept upon him. The right hand held a knife. The left was a claw—a four taloned hideous-looking claw with curved, sharp-pointed talons that were poised as if ready to tear open "X's" throat.

And suddenly that sixth sense which had often come to the aid of the Agent at critical moments made him whirl about. And the masked figure leaped upon him, the taloned claw reaching for his throat!

CHAPTER XIII

FIVE MUST DIE

DEATH STARED AT Secret Agent "X" out of those two murderous eyes hidden behind the mask of horror.

The Agent dropped to one knee, twisted his shoulder about to avoid the swiftly plunging point of that glittering knife. The claw swished past, missing him by a scant hair's breadth. The talons on the monster's left hand missed "X's" throat, tore into his shoulder, ripping away the cloth of his coat, digging with agonizing pain into his flesh.

The masked monster was upon him now, and he could hear its wheezing breath. The claw flashed upward once more, the talons reached for him again.

The Agent warded off the blow with his elbow, crashed his right fist into that hideous mask. His knuckles smashed the cardboard nose, hurling the figure backwards. But in its backward fall, the claws of the taloned left hand caught in the Agent's shoulder once more, held firm and dragged him after the falling body. The two of them hit the floor together, the Agent on top. The murderous hand was powerless for the moment, being held helpless under the Agent's body. But those claws were free; they came down in another ripping blow. "X" knew now how those victims had felt when they died, what Langknecht and Patterson and the others had faced.

"X" thrust up a hand, met the other's left arm just above the taloned claw. The Agent's powerful fingers dug deep into that arm, warding the claws away from his throat. The monster struggled and twisted under the Agent's grip, exhibiting amazing, almost fanatic strength. It heaved powerfully, threw the Agent off, and scrambled to its knees.

Down came the claw once more in a vicious slash. "X" barely

rolled away in time, heard the thud of the knife as it buried itself in the soft wood of the floor. Then he lashed out with his feet, directly at the face of the monster. His heels caught the other squarely in the face, hurled him backward.

An unearthly sound that resembled a shriek of fury burst from the hidden lips behind that battered mask. The Agent scrambled to his feet, set himself to leap upon the other. From the direction of the stage entrance he heard hoarse shouts, the sound of running feet.

His eye caught the figure of Lola Lollagi suddenly rushing out of the dressing room which she had entered before. Her eyes opened wide as she saw the masked figure of the monster upon the floor, saw the person whom she believed to be Stanton about to leap upon it. Her mouth opened wide and she uttered shriek after shriek, high pitched, terror stricken. She still wore her silver gown, over which she had thrown a cloak. Under her arm she clutched the package which she had taken from "X's" hat.

The Agent caught only that single glimpse of her, and was about to disregard her, to turn and leap upon the monster, when Lola's shrieks turned into intelligible words.

"Police!" she screamed. "The police are coming!"

The masked monster struggled to its knees, and "X" turned, saw that the doorman was running across the stage toward them, followed by two uniformed policemen with drawn revolvers. He had apparently heard the struggle, had gone out to summon help.

The monster leaped to its feet, hurled itself at "X," disregarding the threat of the police. Hatred, intense and burning, gleamed from the two eyes behind the mask.

One of the officers shouted: "Stand still, or we'll shoot to kill!"

THE Agent had no wish to be cornered here, and questioned. Once more he was compelled to ward off that gleaming talon with his left arm, to protect his throat against the claws of death.

The police were almost upon them when the claw-man suddenly seemed to realize the danger. He cast a single glance at the threatening revolvers, turned a hateful gaze upon "X," and then swung about, fled down the corridor. Lola already had disappeared.

The Agent gave up all hope of capturing the claw-man. The police were close now, and their attention was all for the escaping monster rather than for him. This was quite understandable, as it would appear to them that "X" was a respectable man who had been attacked by the monster. They dashed past him, and one of the officers fired his heavy service revolver. The explosion reverberated through the theatre, but the officer must have missed, for the claw-man disappeared into the darkness.

The doorman shouted: "Get after him quick! There's a side exit there. He'll get away!"

The two officers hastened after the fugitive, and the doorman, after casting only a single glance at "X," hurried after them, eager to be in on the kill.

The Agent was left alone upon the stage. He turned, crossed quickly, made his way to the stage door, and slipped out into the alley. He heard two more shots from within the theatre, and then the frantic shrill of the patrolmen's whistles. Apparently the monster had escaped them.

The Agent hurried down the alley, out into the street which was more or less deserted by this time, walked quickly to the corner and hailed a passing taxicab.

On the West Side, "X" dismissed the cab and walked two blocks to an apartment house. Here he ascended to the third floor and entered another one of his retreats.

It took him almost a half hour to remove the disguise of Stanton, to wash the deep cut in his shoulder with antiseptic, and then to build for himself once more the personality of Victor Randall.

He must once more use that disguise, for it was imperative that he learn what plans the commissioner was making for the protection of Norman Marsh and the other doomed men.

When he was almost through with his work, the radio in the room suddenly came to life. The voice of Bates announced: "Station 'X' calling. Station 'X' calling."

Then in code, Bates proceeded to deliver a message over the air which the Agent deciphered without difficulty.

Important meeting called at home of John Lacey for 11:50 P.M. Commissioner Foster has requested Marsh, Sturgis, Larkin and Randall to be present at Lacey's home at that time. I have no means of learning purpose of meeting, and my operative reports he cannot get into Lacey's home. What shall I do?

The Agent snapped off the radio, glanced at his watch. It was 11:40—ten minutes before the time of the meeting.

He hastened downstairs, stopped in at a phone booth and called Bates. Otherwise, Bates would have continued to broadcast the message until assured that the Agent had received it. "X" then summoned a cab and gave the address of Lacey's home, which he knew to be located on Central Park West. He was ringing the doorbell of Lacey's apartment in the ornate building on Central Park West on the dot of 11:50.

"X" had had no means of telling whether the house was being watched by Doctor Blood's men or not; for opposite the building lay the gloomy expanse of Central Park, thickly wooded at this spot. A hundred eyes might have been peering out of the shrubbery along here without being perceived.

LACEY himself opened the door, and when he saw "X," he uttered an exclamation of astonishment. "We hardly expected you, Randall. Foster phoned your home as a matter of course, but we really didn't think we'd ever see you alive again. What happened to you? Were you kidnaped? How did you get away?" He fired the questions at "X" one after the other with breathless rapidity. Then, shuddering, said: "We were almost afraid you'd had your throat clawed like the others!"

The Agent made no immediate answer, but allowed himself to be led into the comfortable, high-ceilinged living room. The others were already present. Mayor Sturgis was there, as well as Norman Marsh and Frank Larkin. The original eight who had been present in the commissioner's office that morning had been reduced to five now. Patterson and Langknecht were dead, and Stanton had deserted them.

Marsh, Sturgis and the others crowded around "X" eagerly, hurling questions at him. They touched him, squeezed him, acting like hysterical schoolboys. They insisted on his telling what had happened.

He gave them a short explanation, telling them in substance the same story that he had told Stanton, taking as few words as possible.

"And now," he finished, "what is this meeting for?"

Immediately a pall of gloom descended upon them. Sturgis spoke reluctantly. "Commissioner Foster has received another letter from this devilish Doctor Blood. Read it yourself."

He extracted an envelope from his pocket, and gingerly drew forth a folded sheet of paper which he gave to "X." Like the other missive of the doctor's, it was written in blood, scrawled in a bold, large handwriting. It read:

Commissioner Foster:

You will no doubt be interested to hear that I have made a slight change in my plans. I have suddenly decided that I need one hundred and twenty-five thousand dollars. I have therefore selected the names of the next five surviving men on my list, and I request you to inform them that they must make their payments to me not later than midnight today.

If they do not pay I shall, with great regret, be compelled to order that they all perish at once. Either I receive the sum mentioned before midnight, or they will all die tomorrow. If they decide to pay, you may get in touch with Oscar Stanton, who already knows what arrangements must be made.

Yours, for a long life,

Doctor Blood.

The others listened attentively while "X" read the missive, though they apparently were already aware of its contents. When the Agent had finished it, he studied the grisly sheet of paper for a long minute, noting where the blood which had been used for ink had left stains upon the edges of the sheet.

He asked the mayor: "Has this been examined for fingerprints?"

"Of course," Sturgis assured him. "But those smudges show nothing. The man who wrote it must have worn rubber gloves."

The Agent returned the letter to the mayor who folded the sheet, and methodically replaced it in the envelope, returned the envelope to his pocket. Norman Marsh threw himself into an easy chair, and lit a cigarette.

"We've been arguing this thing pro and con for the last ten minutes before you came, Randall," he said. "Larkin and Lacey want to pay. Sturgis and I have absolutely refused. It looks like you have the deciding vote."

LACEY was pacing up and down the room nervously, chewing a cigar to shreds. He stopped suddenly before Marsh's chair, exclaimed irritably: "Stanton was right. From what this Doctor Blood says in the letter, Stanton must have paid up already. It's all right for you, Marsh. You're used to this sort of thing; and you haven't got a family to worry about either. But Larkin and I don't go in for exploring and big game hunting. All we want is to be left alone. And it's worth twenty-five thousand to each of us not to have this terrible threat hanging over our heads!"

Larkin, the newspaper proprietor, was standing with his back to the others, staring out of the window into the night. He said over his shoulder in a dull voice: "I'm with Lacey. This madman who signs himself Doctor Blood has shown that he can carry out his threats. Sturgis and Marsh can be stubborn if they want, but the way I look at it, twenty-five thousand is little enough to pay when you think of what has happened to the others." He glanced at his wrist watch. "It's five minutes of twelve. All five of us may be dead, with our throats torn open at one minute after midnight. I'm for calling Stanton right now—"

Mayor Sturgis interrupted him. "Just a minute, Larkin. There's no sense in talking this way. We're all pretty well on edge." The mayor's face was indeed gray with worry. He showed the effects of the terrible strain upon him. For, in addition to being one of those upon Doctor Blood's list, he was also burdened with the responsibility of handling the entire situation. There were fine beads of sweat under his eyes.

He ran a hand wearily across his face as he went on: "I feel much the same as you do, Larkin, but I'm holding out as best I can. We dare not give in to this man the way Stanton has. Don't you understand that it would only mean the beginning of a reign of terror throughout the country? We, here, have been unfortunate enough to be chosen by Doctor Blood; and it becomes our duty to fight him in the best way we can.

"We are *not* going to pay—and we are going to do our best to make sure that we live through the day. If we are alive by midnight tomorrow, it will mean that Doctor Blood is not as infallible as he claims to be. It will break up his entire plan, will give the rest of the men on that list of three hundred and sixty-five the courage to refuse to pay, too." His voice grew eager, urgent. "Don't you see? We've *got* to carry on!"

Lacey seemed to be somewhat impressed by the mayor's impassioned plea. He stopped his nervous pacing, said: "Well—"

Norman Marsh sprang from his chair, clapped him on the shoulder. "Come on, Lacey, snap out of it! Foster has planned to protect the five of us starting at midnight. He practically guarantees that we'll be safe."

Larkin swung away from the window, demanded eagerly: "What kind of plan?"

"Sturgis will tell you about it," said Marsh.

The mayor explained. "Gentlemen, Commissioner Foster is making sure that Doctor Blood cannot get to us tonight. We are going to place ourselves beyond his reach!"

"What will we do?" Lacey asked sarcastically. "Go up in a balloon and stay up in the stratosphere all night and all day?"

The quip provoked no answering smile from the assembled men.

Mayor Sturgis shook his head. "I am going to do better than that. We are all going to put ourselves—in jail!"

Larkin crossed the room from the window, his eyes burning feverishly. "In jail!" he repeated after the mayor. "Are you crazy?"

"X" had been silent all this time, studying each of the men in turn. He was especially interested in Lacey and Larkin. They had both been so anxious to pay up, to induce the others to pay, but suddenly, upon learning that there was a plan in the wind, they were eager to discover what it was. Neither of them was the type of man which the Agent pictured Doctor Blood to be. But both were clever, shrewd business men, and had the brains. It would be an ingenious stroke for the man who masked himself under the name of Doctor Blood to have placed himself upon the very list of victims whom he had named.

"X's" thoughts were interrupted by the mayor, who was explaining the plan. "Commissioner Foster has arranged for an escort of policemen to accompany us. We will stay in jail all night and all day tomorrow until midnight, and there will be a heavy guard placed inside and outside. Not a soul will be admitted under any pretext. If Doctor Blood can get through that guard, he will have to be good!"

Lacey seemed to be wavering. The idea appealed to him. "Of course," he said reflectively, "Doctor Blood got Patterson right in police headquarters. He might even be able to get at us in jail."

"I'm willing to take that chance," Marsh said quietly. "The only way he got Patterson was under a pretext, by sending some one to pose as Secret Agent 'X.' While we are in jail, *no one* will be admitted under any pretext."

Mayor Sturgis turned to "X." "What do you say, Randall. Will you go with us?"

"X" nodded. If these men all stuck together tonight, he wanted to be near them. Undoubtedly Doctor Blood would make an attempt upon their lives. Well, the Agent would be right there when the attempt was made. He said: "I'm in favor of it, Sturgis."

"X's" words seemed to carry weight with the others. Lacey

capitulated, and set to work to convince Larkin that he ought to throw in with them.

Finally Larkin exclaimed: "All right! I'll go with you—and I hope it works. God, I hope it works!"

"When do we go?" "X" asked.

"At once," the mayor announced. "It is two minutes of twelve—the police escort will be below now."

Lacey poured them each a drink of cognac, and then they filed out of the apartment, went down in the self-service elevator. On the way down, Lacey whispered to the Agent: "I sent the servants off for the night when this meeting was called. No one knows about it."

"X" made no comment. He could have told Lacey that the meeting was not as secret as he thought. Bates had learned of it. And it was highly possible that Doctor Blood also knew about it.

The chimes of a near-by church were just beginning to toll the hour of midnight when the five men, with Mayor Sturgis in the lead, crossed the lobby and went out into the biting cold of the February night.

CHAPTER XIV

FLIGHT FROM TERROR

THE MAYOR EXCLAIMED: "Aha—everything is on schedule!" Before the curb stood a police van. A uniformed police sergeant and four blue-coats, all with service revolvers in their hands, stood beside the van. They were tense, watchful, their eyes constantly shifting to the dark reaches of Central Park across the street.

Norman Marsh, who was walking beside "X," whispered: "Those officers are as nervous as we are. I'm beginning to have a healthy respect for this Doctor Blood of ours."

"X" smiled. "Who wouldn't have a healthy respect for him. He's in a fair way to terrorizing the entire country."

The uniformed sergeant saluted the mayor, reported: "Sergeant Mace, sir, Morrisville Precinct." He grinned sheepishly. "I've got orders from the commissioner to place you and these other gentlemen under arrest—if you don't mind, sir."

"Not at all, not at all," the mayor said. He had almost regained his usual joviality at the thought of safety. "I dare say we're the most willing prisoners you've ever had!"

Sergeant Mace saluted, motioned to one of the bluecoats who opened the rear door of the van. Marsh went in first, then Larkin, then "X," then Lacey. Sturgis followed them.

One of the bluecoats went around and sat in front beside the driver, while Mace and the other two officers climbed in to the interior of the van.

As they drove away, the single electric bulb in the wire cage in the middle of the roof of the truck cast a dim light which showed "X" the strained countenances of his companions. Larkin showed most the strain that they had been under.

"You—you think," he said to Norman Marsh, "that we'll get

there safely? It's after midnight. Maybe this Doctor Blood will—attack us on the way!"

Mayor Sturgis laughed shortly. "I doubt it. If he should be foolhardy enough to try anything like that, it would probably be the end of him." He gestured toward the bluecoats sitting near the door. Each one was grimly holding a sub-machine gun in his lap, while Sergeant Mace kept looking back through a small porthole in the rear door.

"This is really an armored car," Sturgis explained. "Doctor Blood would have to have a small howitzer to stop us. And if he attacks us with anything less than that, those machine guns will mow him down—with his beasts!"

Lacey sighed deeply. "Well, in a few minutes we'll be safe in jail. But I'm afraid I won't get much sleep tonight."

They drove in silence now for perhaps ten minutes. Then the van slowed down.

Sergeant Mace turned and announced to the mayor: "Here we are, sir." He wiped his broad face with a dirty handkerchief. "Whew! I'm glad that ride is over. I sure thought something was going to happen!"

The truck was backing up now, and in a moment the doors opened. Two of the bluecoats descended first, holding their sub-machine guns in front of them. "X" could see that they were in a sort of alley which ended in a small door at the far end. The two bluecoats walked around to the front, reconnoitered and returned, reporting that they had not been followed. It was not till then that Sergeant Mace said: "All right. I guess it's safe."

He got down together with the last bluecoat, and stood alertly while "X" and the others got out. Then he led the way down the alley toward the small door at the back.

"X" recognized the building as the old jail behind the Morrisville Station House. Its use as a jail had been discontinued about a year ago, when the new Morrisville Detention House had been erected right next to the police station. "X" had been here several times, knew that this old building backed up right against the station house.

Sturgis, who was walking beside him, whispered, "This was pretty clever of Foster. No one would suspect that we were hiding in this old jail. I begin to think we may have put it over on Doctor Blood!"

The Agent would have felt much better if he could have shared

Sturgis' confidence. He had too great a respect for the unknown individual who used the name of Doctor Blood, had seen too much of how he operated, to feel that they would be unmolested throughout the night. But he said nothing. There was no sense in undermining the courage of the others.

They entered through the small door which Mace held open for them, and the four bluecoats filed in after them.

"All right, Joe," Mace called out to the driver of the van. The gears clashed, and the van drove out of the alley as Mace closed the door behind them.

They were in a small, antiquated receiving room. A long corridor led from here into the gloomy interior.

"How about the guards?" Mayor Sturgis inquired.

"There's a half dozen inside, sir," Mace informed him. "And about fifty posted around the building. There's not a chance of anybody's breaking into this place tonight."

He led the way down the corridor. "If you will step this way, sir, I'll show you and the other gentlemen the quarters that have been prepared."

They followed him down into the jail proper, with the armed bluecoats behind them. One of the bluecoats remained at the door, on guard with a sub-machine gun in the crook of his arm.

On the way, they passed two more uniformed men, armed with riot guns.

"You've certainly taken plenty of precautions," Mayor Sturgis commended.

"Thank you, sir. We're doing our best." Mace opened another door. "If you will step in here, I will show you the accommodations. They were the best we could do on such short notice, sir."

They filed in, one after the other.

The room was square, equipped with a table and several chairs. On the table was a small lamp which cast a dim light.

"You'll be safe in here," Mace called out to them from the doorway. "The windows are all shuttered so no light can leak out."

"But where do we sleep?" the mayor demanded. "I say—"

His words were drowned out by the sound of the heavy door clanging shut. A key grated in the lock. They were alone in the room.

SECRET AGENT "X" stood tense, his eyes sweeping the room.

Mayor Sturgis ran to the door, pounded upon it. "Mace, Mace!" he shouted. "What's the matter with you! We want something to sleep on!"

The others all stood around, slightly bewildered by the sudden shutting of the door. There was no answer to the mayor's shout. Sturgis turned away from the door, looked at them queerly. His eyes, deep sunk, looked from one to the other. "Gentlemen—I am afraid I do not understand this."

Norman Harsh said puzzledly: "Neither do I. What's this—a practical joke of yours? If so, you've picked a damned poor time for a joke!"

Secret Agent "X" stood between them. "This is no joke, Marsh. I'm afraid I understand it too well."

Larkin and Lacey crowded about him, as did the mayor and Marsh.

"What do you mean?" Larkin demanded, his voice trembling.

"I mean," the Agent explained, "that we are not here under the protection of Commissioner Foster, or of the police. My guess is that Sergeant Mace is no police sergeant, and that his bluecoats are not policemen. It is a superb masquerade. Gentlemen, I am afraid that we are in the hands of Doctor Blood!"

As if to verify his words, a small wicket in the door was suddenly flung open, and a burst of demoniacal laughter pealed into the room from out in the corridor.

A distorted, ugly face peered in at them through the bars. A twisted claw of a hand, with talons flecked with blood, waved at them wildly.

The laughter that issued from that ghastly mouth was tinged with wildness, with madness. It filled the room, struck sharply at the eardrums.

Frank Larkin put a hand to his throat, staggered backward and slumped into a chair. Then he covered his eyes with his hand and began to moan.

Suddenly the grisly laughter ceased. The claw pointed at them one at a time; and a tight mad voice shrieked at them; "You've guessed it. You've guessed it. You're in the hands of Doctor Blood. Doctor Blood always gets his man!"

The Agent knew that claw. He also noted the battered condition of those hideous features. This was the man he had battled with in the Gotham Theatre—unmasked now. And he also recognized the face. It was the face of Grover Wilkerson—the demented financier, whom Bates' men were seeking everywhere, whom the police of the entire nation were on the hunt for.

The Agent's eyes were clouded as he listened to the madman's ravings. For he was convinced that Wilkerson could not be Doctor Blood. Wilkerson was a demented, dangerous, murderous paranoiac. But his very demented condition made it impossible for him to have acted in the cold, cruel, calculating way that Doctor Blood had exhibited. Wilkerson could never have planned this ingenious kidnaping trick. Wilkerson was no more than a tool.

"X's" hand was in his pocket, on his gas gun. But he did not use it. He could have rendered Wilkerson unconscious, but they would be in no better position than now. For they would still be in the power of Wilkerson's master.

The Agent's mind was racing, already planning for the immediate future, planning some means of taking advantage of the demented financier's condition.

At that moment, Norman Marsh sprang forward, a heavy blue steel automatic in his hand, leveled at the wicker window. The explorer's face was set in a grim line, as he pressed his finger upon the trigger aiming at Wilkerson's face.

The Agent acted quickly on the spur of the moment. He struck Marsh's wrist, causing the automatic to explode into the floor. Wilkerson's face disappeared from the wicker, and the steel window snapped shut.

Marsh swung on the Agent, his eyes blazing. "Damn you," he shouted. "You stopped me from killing that beast!"

The others were also staring at "X," their eyes showing strange suspicion.

The Agent tried to explain to them. "Don't you see, Marsh, we couldn't gain a thing by that. Wilkerson isn't the boss. But killing him will leave us just as badly off as we are now. It was a mistake to show our captors that we are armed. It would have been better to save that as a surprise for a time when it would do us some good."

Lacey sneered. "Sounds like a good argument, Randall, but the fact remains that that madman out there is Grover Wilkerson. He's the one who has clawed all our friends to death, drained their bodies of blood. And Marsh could have killed him if you hadn't stopped him." His voice assumed an insinuating tone. "Maybe you have some special reason for saving Wilkerson's life, Randall. After all, we don't know whom to trust in a situation like this."

Mayor Sturgis tried to soothe Lacey. "Look here, John," he urged. "You don't mean to say that Randall has got anything to do with Doctor Blood!"

"Why not," Lacey went on impetuously. "We suspected Stanton, why can't we suspect Randall. Why, look at the chance Marsh had—"

It was Marsh who stopped him. "Cut it out, Lacey," he snapped. "Randall was right, and I was a fool. Now they know we're armed. You others have guns too, haven't you?"

They all nodded, and he went on. "They forgot to search us when they brought us here. We might have had a chance to use our guns when they take us out of this room. Now they'll be more careful. Randall knew what he was doing when he knocked my gun down. I think you owe him an apology, Lacey!"

It was sometime before the air of tension in the room subsided. But the lingering seeds of suspicion which Lacey had aroused, continued to do their work. The glances which the men exchanged showed that they had ceased to trust each other. And "X" could hardly blame them. For it was entirely possible that any one of them might be connected with Doctor Blood just as they had suspected that Stanton was, just as he himself had suspected that Langknecht was.

"X" found a chair, relaxed, and closed his eyes. To the others he appeared to be sleeping. But in reality the active brain behind those closed eyes was weighing every angle of the situation. They were prisoners of Doctor Blood, and in spite of the fact that there was a police station right behind the building in which they were confined, they would all surely die if the Agent did not evolve some plan to release them.

This was a situation which called for all the resources, all the abilities, all the great daring of that man who was known as Secret Agent "X." And for once he did not feel that sense of extreme confidence which he generally experienced in his clashes with clever criminals.

For Doctor Blood was indeed the master of them all—in ingenuity, in ruthlessness, and in fiendishness.

CHAPTER XV

THE EYE IN THE WALL

THE AGENT'S THOUGHTS were disturbed by the voices of the other men in the room, which rose to a high pitch of excitement. Larkin was almost hysterically berating Marsh and Mayor Sturgis for having compelled him to go with them. "Damn you both!" he shouted. "I wanted to pay, I wanted to settle with this Doctor Blood, and you wouldn't let me. Now you've dragged me into this. We're in the hands of that madman, Wilkerson. Now we'll all have our throats torn open, and our blood drained out of us!"

"We can still put up a fight," Marsh growled. "We're all armed. They may have sub-machine guns, they may have claws, but five determined men like us ought to be able to give a good account of ourselves. To hell with this Doctor Blood. Let's sell our lives as dearly as possible!"

Mayor Sturgis was glumly silent. He let Marsh finish, and then he said: "Perhaps there's some way out of this. Maybe we can do business with this Doctor Blood. It's all my fault, gentlemen. I shouldn't have dragged you into this. But my duty as mayor—"

Secret Agent "X" did not hear the rest of what Sturgis had to say. For he had opened his eyes, and in glancing around the room noted that a tiny aperture in the opposite wall had slid open. It was no more than an inch by probably a half inch wide. But behind that opening he detected an eye peering in at them. He arose from his chair, borrowed a cigarette from Marsh and lit it. Under cover of lighting Marsh's cigarette for him, he whispered to the explorer: "Be careful what you say or do. We are being watched. Don't look around."

Marsh lowered his eyes to signify that he understood. Then he said with a great appearance of casualness: "Perhaps you're right, Sturgis. Maybe it would be better to pay up. I wonder if Doctor

Blood would take our money now."

"It's a good thing," Sturgis replied, "that Randall didn't let you shoot Wilkerson through the door, Marsh. If you had killed him, or injured him. Doctor Blood might want to take revenge on us, rather than accept our money. Now we have a chance."

Lacey was pacing up and down, again. He was about to say something, when he stopped short; for the wicker grill in the massive door was swung open once more.

They all turned to the door, remained silent as Wilkerson's ugly face appeared there again. This time Wilkerson did not press his face as close to the grill as he had before. His right hand was close to the opening, and in it he held a small metal object.

The Agent recognized this as the same sort of gas bomb which Laurento had thrown into the commissioner's room, and which the men who attacked him in his retreat had attempted to use on him. Apparently this sort of bomb could be used as a container for various kinds of gases.

Wilkerson's harsh, cackling voice addressed them. "I won't use this gas bomb unless I have to. Doctor Blood wants to talk to you, one at a time. You'll come out in turn, according to your numbers on his list. Marsh is first, Sturgis next, then Lacey, Larkin, and Randall last. Do you agree, or do I throw this bomb in and knock you all unconscious?"

The five men in the room glanced at one another questioningly. Marsh was about to say something defiant, when "X" stopped him by putting a hand on his arm. Then "X" said to Wilkerson:

"Maybe you'll tell us what Doctor Blood wants to talk to us about. And why he wants to see us one at a time?"

Wilkerson seemed to think that over for a minute, then he said quickly: "Yes, I'll tell you. Doctor Blood knows that four of you men are the ones you're supposed to be. But one of you isn't. One of you is here in disguise—he is the person who is known as Secret Agent 'X.' That man must die. The rest of you can buy your way out of here."

Mayor Sturgis started to laugh nervously. "Secret Agent 'X'! Impossible! Why, we all know each other thoroughly. I'll vouch for every one of these men!"

"And who," Wilkerson sneered, "will vouch for you?"

Sturgis flushed. "What do you mean—"

"Stop it!" Wilkerson's mad voice almost cracked with its intensity. "I hate every damn one of you. You all contributed in some way to my ruin. I'd like to claw you all. Answer quickly. Do you agree to come out one at a time, or do I throw the bomb?"

His hand, holding the small object, approached the grilled opening. Lacey shouted: "Wait! We'll go."

"All right." Wilkerson's hand disappeared with the metal object, reappeared in a moment with a pair of handcuffs which he dropped into the room. "Marsh is first. Cuff his hands behind him, and stand well back from the door. You have nothing to fear Marsh, if you are not Secret Agent 'X.' Otherwise, prepare to die."

A HEAVY key turned in the lock outside. The door started to swing open. In the hallway the twisted figure of Wilkerson was disclosed, and beside him that of the bogus Sergeant Mace holding a sub-machine gun trained on the doorway. Mace called out:

"All right, Marsh come out. If any of you others try to come with him, I'll cut you down."

Marsh turned to his companions, said quietly: "Well, see you later." He winked to them, turned and strode out of the room. The heavy door clanged shut behind him.

Sturgis and Lacey and Larkin began to talk all at once. Secret Agent "X" kept quiet. He was content to let the others buy their way out. As for himself, he must devise some means of outwitting Wilkerson and this unknown person who used the name of Doctor Blood. When his own turn came, he would not be able to avoid exposure. He could make no plans now, for he did not know where he would be taken from here. Of one thing he was sure—he would certainly make an attempt to kill Doctor Blood once he came face to face with him.

It was against the Agent's policy to kill. He avoided it whenever possible. But in this case he regarded the person who used the title of Doctor Blood as no more than a mad dog, to be shot on sight. He regretted now, that his gas gun was not a lethal weapon.

His eyes stole to the small aperture in the opposite wall. He breathed easier when he noticed that it was closed now. No eye was observing them. Suddenly he appeared to stagger, clutched at Lacey's coat.

"What's the matter?" Lacey demanded, supporting him with one hand. He led "X" to a chair, seated him in it.

"I don't know," the Agent said, making his voice sound as weak as possible. "I got dizzy all of a sudden."

Mayor Sturgis and Larkin crowded around him. Sturgis said sympathetically: "You must be under a terrible strain, Randall. You've been through more than the rest of us. After all, you were actually in the hands of one of Doctor Blood's men once before. Take it easy, Randall."

"X" kept his eyes closed for a while. He was entirely satisfied to appear to be a weakling before the others. He had accomplished his purpose. For, in staggering against Lacey as he had done, his hands had worked rapidly, efficiently, with a lightness of touch that defied detection. He had noted that Lacey was carrying his gun in an outside coat pocket. And he had made an exchange, placing his own gas gun in Lacey's pocket, transferring Lacey's gun to his own.

So swiftly, so expertly had he done it, that none of them had noticed it. Now he was armed with a weapon that would kill. And he was fully prepared to take the law into his own hands this time. If he got the opportunity, he would execute Doctor Blood in the interests of humanity.

CHAPTER XVI

STRANGE ALLIANCE

THREE TIMES MORE in the next hour the key turned in the lock and the heavy oak door swung open, revealing Wilkerson with his hideous claw, and Mace, armed with the submachine gun. Each time another man was led out. And they did not return. Sturgis was the second to go, then Lacey, then Larkin. They seemed more or less resigned to go peaceably, since Wilkerson had told them that it would be possible for them to buy their way out.

Lacey and Larkin were almost eager to make terms with Doctor Blood. Sturgis, though he felt the responsibility of his official position, seemed to be beaten. He was contrite at having dragged the others into this situation.

Larkin, who was the last to go, turned and shook hands with "X." "Well, Randall, I suppose I'll be seeing you shortly. This Doctor Blood must be mistaken about one of us being Secret Agent 'X.' I guess there'll be little difficulty in all of us proving to him that we are ourselves."

"X" made no reply, but shook hands with him, watched him leave the room. Again the oak door slammed shut.

The Agent was alone in the room. He had noted that with Lacey and Larkin, Wilkerson had not bothered to throw in a pair of handcuffs as he had done with Marsh and Sturgis. But he had seen Mace holding a pair in the corridor. Evidently they were sure enough of themselves to wait until they got each man outside now before handcuffing him.

"X" had noted the type of handcuffs which had been used on Marsh, and now, after casting a glance at the small aperture in the wall to make sure that it was closed and that he was not observed, he set to work quickly, extracted from his pocket a small case in which nestled a number of keys. From these he selected one, no more than three-quarters of an inch in length. This was a skeleton handcuff key.

"X" now replaced the case in his pocket and palmed the key. Though his hand remained open, the key rested there, held by the fleshy part of his palm. No one would have suspected that he was holding anything. The Agent took out the gun which he had slipped from Lacey's pocket, examined it to make sure that it was loaded, pulled up his right trousers leg, and stuck it in under the top of his sock. His experience had shown him that very few people when frisking a man for weapons will look there.

Hardly had he finished, when a key grated in the lock, and the big oak door swung open. "X" was slightly surprised, for less than three minutes had elapsed since Larkin had left. He wondered why they were coming for him so quickly. But it was not the distorted figure of Wilkerson which appeared in the doorway.

It was the woman, Lola Lollagi.

"X" watched her silently, with eyes narrowed as she stole into the room, casting a fearful glance behind her. She closed the door softly, so as not to make any noise, then turned, ran impulsively toward him. Her beautiful face was drawn and haggard, and her eyes betrayed inexplicable terror.

She came close to him, whispered urgently: "I know who you are. You're not Randall. You are the man that Doctor Blood has sworn to kill. You are Secret Agent 'X'!"

"X" lowered his eyelids, veiling his eyes. He said nothing.

Her slim hand reached up, gripped his coat lapel, and she shook him impatiently. "Don't deny it. You're wasting time. I'm here to help you. I know who you are, because I followed you from headquarters when you carried Laurento away. Please, *please,* don't waste time. There is so little left."

"If you are so sure about who I am," said the Agent, "why didn't you tell this precious Doctor Blood of yours. He seems to want to know very badly. You collected his money for him, you told him where Laurento was hidden. Why don't you betray me too?"

SHE dropped her hand with a gesture of despair, allowed her head to droop. "I was afraid of this. I was afraid you wouldn't trust me." Suddenly she raised her head, her large eyes met his. There was no guile in them now, only earnest pleading. "I'll tell you the truth. I'll tell you everything, because I want you to trust me. You *must* trust me." Her hands clenched and unclenched fearfully.

"X" glanced furtively at the aperture in the far wall. It was still closed. "Go on," he told her. "Talk quickly. They will soon be coming for me."

She rushed on, the words tumbling from her lips. "Everything I did, I did because I was compelled to. Doctor Blood got Laurento in his power, and did something to him that gave him this lust for blood. Then he sent him out to kill." She shuddered. "Laurento isn't the only one. He has Wilkerson, and he has others. They all do his bidding. I don't know what he does to them to make them obey him, but they go out to claw and kill at his command."

She faltered, said hesitantly: "I know you won't believe me when I tell you that I was compelled to do everything I did for Doctor Blood—compelled by the most devilish means!"

The Agent placed a hand on her shoulder, said gently: "I think I know by what means you were forced to do his bidding."

She raised her eyes, startled. "You know—"

"Yes. Let me see if I am right." He had been studying her face carefully, comparing its contours and general conformation with that of another face the picture of which he carried in his mind's eye. Now he went on: "I can see the resemblance. It is undeniable. Laurento is your brother. Doctor Blood got him in his power, did something to him that you talk about to make him lust for blood. Your brother's resistance was feeble; not mentally sound. He was confined in a sanitarium back in Paraguay for a while, was he not?"

Her eyes opened wide, her mouth fell slack. "How—how did you know?"

"If, as you believe, I am Secret Agent 'X' you must not be surprised that I should know things. But let's go on. When you learned that Laurento was in Doctor Blood's power, you appealed to this Doctor Blood to leave him alone. And Doctor Blood compelled you to serve him as the price of your brother's freedom. But he did not keep faith with you. He made your brother kill Patterson, anyway."

"That's right," she breathed. "I got my fiancé, Hugo Langknecht, to assist me when I discovered that Doctor Blood did not intend to keep faith with me. Some detective named Fearson discovered where Laurento was hidden, and somehow discovered that Hugo was interested. He went to Hugo's house, and I followed him there. We caught the detective and put him in a closet, and, as we were about to leave, Wilkerson and some of Doctor Blood's men raided the place and killed poor Hugo. I did not tell them about the detective hidden in the closet. They took me away, forced me to tell where Laurento was hidden. Doctor Blood must have guessed that you were Secret Agent 'X,' for he set a trap to catch you. But the trap failed."

The Agent put both hands on her shoulders, swung her about so that the lamp from the table cast a light upon her face. Then he demanded of her sharply: "Who is Doctor Blood? Is he Oscar Stanton?"

She shivered. "No, no! It couldn't be Oscar. Oscar has been hoping to marry me, even though I told him I was engaged to Hugo. But Oscar isn't the kind of man who could be so ruthless. He would never have had Hugo killed that way, even if they were rivals."

"Who, then, is Doctor Blood?"

She wilted, and her face paled. "I—don't—know! I have never seen his face."

"What did he do to these people—to Wilkerson, to your brother, to the others—to make them into wild beasts?"

"I don't know that—either. Most of the men that he has in his power are like Wilkerson and Laurento—mentally deranged. They are the ones who killed Prescott and Forman and the others. Somehow or other he has managed to gather around him a number of madmen, who do his bidding without question."

"All right," said the Agent "Now tell me what you have come here for."

"I want your help!" she exclaimed passionately. "Doctor Blood has Laurento here in this jail We are all his prisoners. I will help you to escape, if you will promise me to save Laurento—to take Laurento and me out of here with you. You are a man for whom nothing is impossible. You must help me in this. I do not ask you to save Laurento from the law. Let him be tried for his crime. They will not send him to the electric chair, for he is insane. But at least he will be confined in an asylum where he will be treated as a patient, instead of remaining under the dominion of this fiend who is known as Doctor Blood. Quick, is it a bargain? I will help you, if you will help me in this way."

"I promise you," said Secret Agent "X" slowly, "that if I leave this place alive, I will not leave without you and Laurento."

A smile almost of happiness suffused her face. "Thank God!" She dipped into her dress, extracted from the bodice a revolver which she handed to the Agent. "Here. It's loaded. The door is open. There are half a dozen men in the building. But I know you can win."

"I'm afraid," the Agent told her, "that it is too late. We have been seen!"

He was right. For the small aperture in the opposite wall had slid open, and a pair of dark eyes had looked through for a moment—a moment only, and then the aperture had been shut. Doctor Blood knew that Lola Lollagi was attempting to save Mr. Randall; and he must also guess that Victor Randall was none other than Secret Agent "X"!

CHAPTER XVII

MADMEN IN THE DARK

THE AGENT ACTED now without a single lost motion. He dropped the handcuff key in his pocket; there was no further use for it. The time for guile and trickery had passed. Nothing counted now but action. He stooped, retrieved his other gun from under his trouser leg, then snapped at Lola Lollagi: "Get over against the wall. I'm going to open that door and shoot my way out."

Lola sprang to one side, flattened herself against the wall. "Remember," she breathed, "you promised to save Laurento!"

"X" nodded grimly. He kicked open the door, sprang out into the corridor, a gun in each hand. Down the end of the hall he saw Wilkerson and Mace, running toward him. Wilkerson was waving his horrid claw, and shouting: "That's the man. That's Secret Agent 'X.' Get him, Mace!"

Behind them came four or five other men, still in policemen's uniform, armed with revolvers and submachine guns.

Mace stopped short upon seeing the Agent, dropped to one knee, and raised the Tommy-gun to his shoulder.

Secret Agent "X" faced them squarely in the narrow corridor, his feet planted wide apart, the two guns at his hips. His face was a calm, gray mask as he pressed the triggers on his two guns, sent lead rocketing down the corridor toward Mace and the others. He was a cool, efficient fighting machine, and each shot that he fired counted.

The attackers were taut, excited, awed by the thought that they were in conflict with the man whose name had became a legend in the underworld—Secret Agent "X." The Agent's slugs screamed from his guns before any of them could get into action with the tommies. Smoke filled the corridor, and the reverberations of the Agent's methodically exploding guns rocked the narrow hallway. Not a single shot answered him. He had fired too fast and too straight.

When the smoke cleared, it revealed the Agent, still standing, the guns still at his side, ready for more. But at the other end of the corridor men writhed upon the floor, helpless, groaning. Mace had been shot in the right shoulder. Wilkerson squirmed on the floor beside him with a bullet in his side. No single man of the attackers was left standing on his feet. The Agent, in spite of the imminent danger which had threatened, had not shot to kill; but each of his slugs had been directed at some spot that would disable his attacker.

He called out over his shoulder: "Come on, Lola." Then he advanced down the hall, watchful, wary.

The woman came out of the room, followed him at a short distance. Her startled eyes took in the wounded, writhing men. Her eyes sought the back of Secret Agent "X" and lit up with wonder. She could hardly understand how one man had been able to overcome so many opponents armed as these had been.

THE Agent stepped across the bodies, and Lola followed him. They were in the anteroom now, which led out into the street. The guard was not there. Apparently he had been one of the attackers in the corridor.

The woman exclaimed: "Those shots must have been heard. The police will be here. How will you get Laurento away?"

"No fear of those shots having been heard," the Agent told her. "The walls of this jail are entirely sound-proof. A man standing just outside wouldn't have heard a thing."

He examined his two guns. Lola's was empty, and he discarded it. The other still had a single bullet left. "Wait here," he said. "I am going to find Doctor Blood. If you hear anyone coming, run out into the alley and wait there."

He left her before she could protest, went through a small door at the right and found himself at the foot of an iron staircase which led up to the first tier of cells. From above there came to him the sound of a mad jabbering, of wild voices. Then they suddenly ceased, as another voice, cold, curt, spoke suddenly. The Agent could not understand the words, but he could tell that they came from up above in the cell tier.

Quickly, noiselessly, the Agent mounted the iron staircase. All was dark here. The cells ranged along both walls, leaving a wide cement corridor between. Faces peered at him from behind the iron doors of these cells. Strange voices shrieked at him. These were the madmen whom Lola Lollagi had mentioned. Doctor Blood kept them in cells until he was ready for them to do his evil work.

Slowly, cautiously, the Agent advanced between the two tiers of grilled doors, flashing his light into each in turn. He knew that Doctor Blood was up here, for he was sure that it was he whose voice had spoken just a moment before. Was Blood hiding in one of those cells, waiting to ambush him as he came along, or had he retreated before the advance of Secret Agent "X"?

Four cells the Agent passed, and in each he saw a mad face peering out at him. Four cells on the right, four cells on the left. Eight of these madmen, there were, and each was brandishing a claw through the bars of his door. These claws, the Agent could see now, were of metal, made like a gauntlet which could be slipped over the hand. It was with these that they ripped men's throats.

The fourth cell on the left held Laurento. "X" recognized him at once. The youth was strangely silent, his face drawn and haggard. He said nothing, did not shout or jibber like the others. "X" passed him by, peered into the next cell.

At first he could see no one in there. Then he lowered his light, and noticed the figure of a man cowering in a corner. It was Larkin. His face was white with fear, his entire body was trembling.

"God, take me out of here," he cried. "Take me away from these madmen! Let me go. I'll pay anything!"

"X" maintained silence, passed on and looked in the other cells. He saw Sturgis in the next, was about to look beyond when his eye caught the slightest hint of motion from farther down in the hall.

One of the cell doors at the end was opening silently, stealthily. The Agent dropped flat to the floor, his gun extended in front of him. His keen eyes noted the muzzle of a submachine gun poking out through the bars of the half-open cell door, detected a shadowy shape behind. Slowly that gun was swinging around in his direction.

"X" sighted carefully for a spot just above and a little to the right of the muzzle of the machine gun, and fired once. A horrible shriek answered his shot, and the sub-machine gun clattered to the stone floor. The shadow behind it resolved itself into a human body that toppled forward, crashed into the iron door, and lay still on the floor.

The Agent sprang to his feet, ran forward. He stopped when he approached the still figure on the floor, directed his flashlight downward. His lips set in a grim line as he saw the face of the man he had killed—the face of Doctor Blood.

SLOWLY he turned away, retraced his steps. As he passed Sturgis' cell the mayor gripped the iron bars of the door, shouted hoarsely into the darkness: "Who are you? Where is Doctor Blood? Let us out of here!"

"X" made no answer. He continued on until he had reached the cell where Laurento was confined. That young man stood still, white-faced, his eyes wide with consternation under the beam of light which the Agent flashed at him. There was no madness in the young man's eyes any longer—only a terrible misery. Apparently whatever it was that Doctor Blood had administered to Laurento had worn off, leaving him without that ghastly blood-lust which had made a ruthless animal of him.

"X" fitted one of his pass-keys to the cell door, swung it open. Laurento backed away, suddenly shouting: "Leave me alone! Don't feed me any more of that stuff!" His voice was thin, cracked. It aroused the other mad inmates of the neighboring cells, and the jabbering and screaming, which had ceased when the Agent fired, began once more, filled the whole tier with a wild cacophony.

"X" put out a hand to Laurento, said: "Come with me. I will not harm you."

But his voice was drowned by the shouting. Laurento feared him, probably thought he was Doctor Blood, or one of Blood's men. He had a grip on his taloned gauntlet, and he swung out at "X" with it, attempting to keep him at arm's length.

The Agent warded the blow, stepped in under it, and drove in a short blow to the other's chin. Laurento crumpled up, slid to the floor. In his weakened physical and mental condition that light blow had been enough to down him.

"X" now stooped, swung him over his shoulder, and carried him out of the cell. All the way downstairs he was followed by the mad ravings of the demented men in the other cells, by the shouts of Larkin and the others to be taken out of there.

Down in the waiting room he found Lola Lollagi sitting in a corner, her nervous fingers tearing at a handkerchief. When she saw "X" and his burden she sprang up with a glad cry and ran toward them.

"X" placed the young man in a chair. Laurento was recovering his senses. He opened his eyes, saw "X," and started up. But Lola put a hand on his shoulder, cried entreatingly:

"Laurento, brother darling! It's Lola! Your sister!"

For a moment his eyes were wild, terrified. Then they focused upon Lola, seemed to recognize her. Then he broke down. He rested his head in his hands, wept like a child.

Lola stroked his hair, glanced entreatingly at the Agent. Tremblingly her lips formed words. "What—what are you going to do with him? You promised me—"

"X" was watching the brother and sister with deep understanding.

Laurento cried out between his sobs: "Lola, Lola dear. Take me away from here. Take me away from Doctor Blood!" A spasm of revulsion seemed to be racking his body.

Secret Agent "X" said slowly: "You have nothing further to fear, Laurento. Doctor Blood is dead!"

Lola started, stared at him. "You—you know who he is? You have—seen his face?"

The Agent nodded. "I have seen his face. I know who he is." He raised a hand before she could ask the next question. "Never mind about that now. I promised you that you could take Laurento out of here. Now you must promise me two things, first."

"Yes, yes," she exclaimed eagerly. "I will promise anything you ask."

"First, you must give me your word that you will take Laurento directly from here to an asylum, the address of which I will give you. He will be well taken care of there, and if it is possible, he will be cured. After that he must agree to stand trial for his crime." The Agent scribbled an address on a slip of paper which he handed to her.

"I will do that," she whispered. "I am sure that Laurento will not be sent to jail."

"The second thing you must promise," the Agent said, "is that you will never mention what has happened here tonight. To you and to the world, I am Mr. Randall, and nobody else. Do you understand?"

There was a strange film over her eyes, as she nodded. "I understand," she said softly. "But in my heart I will always remember you by that other name. And hereafter, I shall never believe it when they say that you are a criminal!"

The Agent watched her as she led her sobbing brother out. Then he turned and walked to the rear of the jail. He could hear groans now, whimperings of pain from Wilkerson and Mace and those others who still lay wounded in the corridor. He glanced at his wrist watch. Less than ten minutes had passed since he had shot his way out of the rear room. And in that time Doctor Blood had perished. And Secret Agent "X" was the only man thus far who knew the true identity of Doctor Blood.

CHAPTER XVIII

TRAIL OF THE BLOOD LUST

IT WAS PERHAPS an hour later that the four squad cars of the raiding party from headquarters swung into the street in front of the old jail. Men, armed to the teeth, poured out of the cars. Commissioner Foster and Inspector Burks led the party down the narrow alley. With them was Betty Dale, the young newspaper woman from the *Herald*.

Commissioner Foster said testily: "I can't understand yet, how the thing happened. I never even suggested that meeting in Lacey's house. Somebody must have phoned in my name." He turned to Betty Dale. "Are you sure of your information?"

She nodded. "My source of information is absolutely trustworthy. I don't know who the man is, but I recognized his voice. He's phoned me before, and given me tips which resulted in scoops for my paper. He instructed me to get in touch with you at once, and bring you here. And don't forget, you promised to give me the exclusive on this."

"Don't worry," Foster grumbled. "If this turns out to be the truth, you'll get the exclusive all right, Miss Dale."

The small door at the end of the alley was open, and they met no opposition as they pushed through the anteroom into the corridor behind. Here they stopped short, uttering gasps of astonishment. For, lined up upon the floor were six men—Wilkerson, Mace, and the others who had posed as policemen. Their wounds had been neatly bandaged, but each was unconscious, deep in a comatose sleep.

Burks knelt beside them, exclaimed: "This is Wilkerson. We've been looking all over the country for him. They've all been put to sleep by some sort of drug!" He raised his eyes to Commissioner Foster, said slowly: "This begins to look familiar to me."

Foster returned his glance, nodded solemnly. "It looks like our work has been done for us, Burks." He was interrupted by a sudden discordant shouting and screaming from somewhere up above. Burks rose to his feet, led the way back, followed by Foster, Betty Dale and the police officers. In the upper corridor they found the electric light switch, and clicked it on. Betty Dale shrank from the sight that greeted her eyes. The madmen in the cells were shouting, jabbering, brandishing their steel talons.

"God," Foster exclaimed. "These are the *animals* that have been clawing people to death. They are men!"

"Yes," Burks added, "madmen."

They passed down the corridor, along the cell doors, until they arrived at the cell in which Mayor Sturgis was confined. The mayor's face was white and drawn, and when he saw the commissioner and the inspector, he uttered a gasp of relief.

Betty Dale watched while they unlocked the cell doors with master keys, released Sturgis, Larkin and Lacey.

"Where are Randall and Marsh?" Inspector Burks demanded.

"I don't know," Sturgis replied. "We were brought up here one at a time, searched and examined by some man with a mask, and then stuck in these cells. Marsh was brought up first, and Randall last."

Betty Dale had taken a few uncertain steps down the corridor. She uttered a cry, pointed to an inert body which lay half in and half out of an open cell doorway, with a sub-machine gun beside it.

Burks and Foster left the group of rescued men, and hastened over. They knelt beside the body, and Burks uttered a gasp of astonishment. "Norman Marsh!" he exclaimed. "Shot through the head!"

"So Doctor Blood got Marsh after all!" the commissioner said, sourly. He turned on Betty Dale. "I thought your informant told you that we would find Doctor Blood here. Where is he?"

"And what's happened to Randall?" Burks demanded.

FOR answer Betty Dale stooped, picked up a folded sheet of paper which lay beside the body of Marsh. She opened it, and handed it to Commissioner Foster without reading it. He glanced at her queerly, took the paper and scanned it. His face became suffused with a dull red as he began to understand the purport of that message. He swallowed hard, glanced at the others who had come over to crowd around him, and read aloud:

"To Commissioner Foster:

Mayor Sturgis invited me to take a hand in this case. I accepted the invitation—but in my own way. I am making this explanation because my name was taken by a murderer, and I must clear it.

Norman Marsh was Doctor Blood. If you will examine the newspaper records of five or six years ago, you will learn that Marsh headed an expedition into the Brazilian jungle. All of the members of that expedition were lost, and Marsh was compelled to live for three years with a tribe in the jungle of Brazil. This tribe is known as the Botocudos. Their religion contains a blood-drinking ritual, and Marsh became one of them. He returned to this country, recently, in order to raise a tremendous sum of money for the purpose of arming this tribe with modern weapons so that he could establish an empire in the Brazilian jungle and make himself a king.

He surrounded himself with men, mentally deranged, whom he rescued from insane asylums; such men as Wilkerson. These unfortunates were easily subjected to his influence, and by means of administering hypnotic drugs he instilled in them a lust for blood, equipped them with the sort of talons which the Botocudos Indians used in ripping open a victim's throat in order to drink his blood. These demented men are now confined in the cells on this tier. None of them, with the exception of Wilkerson, is a confirmed criminal. They should be treated as mental patients.

If you wish further proof that Marsh was Doctor Blood, you may go down to the basement where the cells for solitary confinement are located. There you will find a man named Hans, who was ostensibly the servant of Professor Hugo Langknecht, but was really in the pay of Marsh, and knew him to be Doctor Blood. By questioning Hans properly, and confronting him with the dead body of Marsh, you will have no difficulty in making him talk.

You need have no worries as to the safety of Victor Randall. You will find him in his own home, but he will remember nothing of what transpired within the past twenty-four hours.

"X".

When the commissioner had finished reading, he raised his eyes to the others. "Good God!" he exclaimed. "To think that Norman Marsh was Doctor Blood!"

Betty Dale said eagerly: "May I go and phone my paper now?"

"You certainly may, young lady," the commissioner told her. "Whoever your informant is, he has certainly done you a service.

You ought to get a raise for a scoop like this!"

Inspector Burks' face was stony, expressionless. "I hate to think," he said bitterly, "that we are indebted to Secret Agent 'X' for breaking this case. He's pretty smart, he is. But if he thinks that he can square his account with me in this way, he's mistaken. I'm never going to give up the hunt for him!"

As if to mock the inspector, from somewhere outside the jail there floated in the notes of an eerie, uncanny whistle that seemed to chill them all to the marrow of their bones.

The eyes of Inspector Burks were stormy. He recognized that whistle, raised his hand in a mock salute, and spoke into the air: "All right, Secret Agent 'X'—you have the laugh this time. But you haven't wiped out all the other charges against you. Some day I'm going to have the pleasure of watching you strapped into the electric chair!"

BOOK XV

THE CORPSE CAVALCADE

Seven corpse-faced denizens of doom swept down on the Suburban Trust. Red-tongued machine guns blasted the way for their scavenger-like leader. But that leader did an amazing thing. He brought money into the bank. And leaving it there, he disappeared with his buzzard brood...
Secret Agent "X," the Man of a Thousand Faces, the lone-wolf scourge of the underworld, had but one trail to follow. And that trail led to a gruesome gibbet—where the law and the lawless matched murder for his life.

CHAPTER I

HANDS THAT KILL

MISTY RAIN HELD the winter's pall of smoke low over the city. The narrow strip of sky, visible from the street, was like thick gray flannel. There was a vague, unfamiliar quality in the sound of things, as if the bustle of the awakening business world was muffled by some tangible shadow.

In front of the Suburban National Bank and extending for half a block beyond its brass grated doors, was a line of people. There was anxiety on every face, and the mutter of angry threats in every mouth. Men, women, children clutched tightly at passbooks, each selfishly wondering if he or she would be in time to make a withdrawal while the cash still held out.

The custodian of the Suburban National swept moodily with a broom behind the brass-barred gate. He glanced at his watch. It was five minutes to nine.

"Hey, granpa!" a man near the head of the line of depositors shouted to the bank custodian. "Open up. What's five minutes or so? We want our money!"

"Yeah," another echoed. "Good, solid money. If we get it at the bank we know it's good!"

The custodian scowled bitterly. "You'll get it! Suburban National's been open every day the law allowed. Never defaulted yet, and ain't goin' to start now! You people must be crazy. This bank's as sound as a rock!"

"You have a hard-earned twenty-dollar bill refused on the grocery bill, and you'd get scared yourself," a plump-faced woman called back. "We're getting our money while we know it's the real thing—and not counterfeit!"

Riot broke out in the rear of the line. A middle-aged man, drunk with panic, was lunging at the line, head lowered and shoulders

Suddenly it came—a roar that was a concentrated thunderclap. Hell seemed to crack open.

bucking. A blue-coated policeman stepped from the curb, seized the agitator by the collar and pulled him from the line. Another cop, swinging his stick threateningly, restored some sort of order among the depositors. But the indignant man fought free from the hands of the policeman, and lunged again at the line.

"Here, none o' that!" This time the cop was less gentle as he yanked the man back to his place. "You wait your turn like the rest or I'll give you a rap on that thick skull of yours."

The middle-aged man turned a white, frightened face up to meet the eyes of the policeman. "I've got to get in there," he pleaded. "I can't wait! It's a matter of life and death! My wife—she's got to have an operation! I've got to get money—real money. She's got to have a specialist. It's more than just grocery bills!"

The policeman's face softened slightly. But he shook his head

discouragingly. "Sorry, buddy. You got to take your chance just like the others. Back to the tail of the line."

Somewhere, a clock boomed the first stroke of nine. A shout rose from the mob of anxious depositors. There was a sudden surge forward against the gates that barred the entrance to the bank. Simultaneously with the striking of the clock, the morning parade of traffic in the street was broken by three big armored trucks that drew over to the curb in front of the bank. Some one in the line of anxious depositors saw the armored cars and shouted:

"Money! They're bringing our money!"

As if a bomb had burst in its midst the line of people suddenly broke and became a roaring crowd. The people turned in a disorganized mass and rushed towards the curb and the armored trucks. The handful of police, though battling valiantly to check the tide of humanity, were lost in the mob, their arms pinioned to their sides by the sheer weight of the frantic people.

DISREGARDING the threatening machine gun muzzles that were thrust through the slots in the armor plate sides of the trucks, the mob pressed close. Then some one in the foremost ranks of the bank depositors shouted:

"Back! Give them a chance to get out of the trucks. There'll be time enough and money enough for all!"

The crowd pressed back. A woman fainted, stifled in the jam. A policeman, poking and prodding with his stick, forced his way through the outer fringes of the crowd. He ran to the call box on the corner. Riot was impending. A squad of police would be needed in another five minutes.

The armored trucks spilled men armed with automatics and machine guns. Some carried heavy leather satchels that were linked to their wrists with chains. All of them ran, with heads lowered and collars turned up, straight towards the bank doors.

In the lobby of the bank stood a man of perhaps forty years of age. His carefully brushed, thick, white hair contrasted sharply with smooth, tanned skin and sharp black eyes. He was Abel Corin, a director in the bank and an executive in half a dozen industrial enterprises. As the armed men from the trucks entered, Corin strode forward, seized the foremost bank messenger by the arm.

"What is the meaning of this?" Corin demanded. "There must be some mistake. You men came here once this morning at the regular time. We have sufficient cash to restore the confidence of the depositors. The people have simply permitted themselves to become overexcited about the sudden flood of counterfeit money that has been discovered in circulation."

The bank messenger did not reply. Instead, he raised his head and at the same time pushed his hat back from his forehead. Like a dead, unfeeling appendage, Corin's hand dropped from the man's sleeve. His face blanched beneath his tanned skin. He retreated step by step before the slowly advancing group of armed men. Corin's lower lip became pendulous. Saliva drooled from the corners of his mouth. His eyes were terror glazed, staring into the hideous face that the leader of the men had revealed.

It was a strangely inhuman face. Thin features contributed an expression of immeasurable cruelty. Thin lips were parted in a hellish smile as utterly without humor as the grin of a skull. There was a gleam of cunning in the small eyes.

Corin suddenly overcame the paroxysm of terror that had rooted him to the spot. "The police! This is a holdup!" His hoarse voice tocsined throughout the building. He pivoted and fled through the door of the office. The hawk-faced man, shooting from the hip, drilled the window of Corin's office with a bullet from his automatic.

Then, with a gesture from their hawk-faced leader, the band of armed men broke into two groups and moved swiftly along the walls of the room where the teller's cages were located. One teller, of cooler nerve than his companions, stamped on the alarm bell. He turned his terror-white face towards his companion in the next cage. For no sound had come from the alarm bell.

"The power's been cut!" he shouted. "Try the telephone!"

Then following his own order, the teller ran toward the offices located on the balcony at the back of the bank. A tracer of machine-gun bullets chipped granite from the wall behind him. Still he ran—until leaden death caught up with him. He crumpled to the floor, where he lay twitching in a final death struggle. A sharp scream shrilled from a woman. Then a hush fell upon the bank.

THE criminal gang went about its work like a well generaled army. Every man, with the exception of the hawk-faced leader, wore a flesh-colored mask over his face. Those who carried satchels hurried into the vaults at the rear of the building. Others who were armed with Tommy guns nailed bank officials against the walls. Still others ganged across the entrance way. Two police, who had evidently been attracted by the sound of machine-gun fire, were dropped in their tracks as they entered the building.

But with all the activity, not a single masked mobster spoke a word. They seemed like fearsome, tongueless beasts who knew no language but the staccato syllables of rattling machine-gun hail.

The leader seemed to take no part in the looting of the bank. He vaulted over the marble rail that separated the cashier's booth from the central portion of the room, and approached a white-faced paying teller. The teller flattened himself against the counter and stared at the immobile face of the gang leader like one fascinated by the evil eye of a basilisk. The hawk-faced man advanced slowly, the wolfish grin on his evil face still unchanged. It seemed that he enjoyed to the fullest extent the anguish of his intended victim.

The white-faced teller found his tongue. He mouthed incoherent sentences. "Wh-what are you going to do? I played up. I—I, God! *Don't stare at me!* I couldn't help it! Did everything you told me—" And his pale hands locked over his eyes, trying to shut out the sight of that hideous, lifeless face with its leering slit of a mouth.

Then the hawk-faced monster abandoned his lethargy. He dropped his automatic upon the marble counter. The fingers of his hands crooked like steel talons. He sprang at the cringing teller, his fingernails digging so deeply into the man's flesh that they drew blood. A cry burbled in the teller's throat—became a dry rasp as the hawk-faced man increased pressure. The teller made a piteous, desperate effort to free himself from the inexorable, killing grip. But as his strength waned, the killer seemed to absorb it. His fingers dug deeper and deeper until his victim's lolling tongue was tinged with blue, and his eyes bulged from their sockets.

Then with a movement that was without apparent effort, the hawk-faced man flung the dying teller to the floor. He jerked from his pocket something that was not unlike a fountain pen in appearance. He unscrewed the cap and bared a nib of some strange, wax-like composition. Pen in hand, he knelt beside his victim and boldly traced something upon the dead man's forehead. A viscous yellow fluid that fumed as it touched the flesh flowed from the nib of the pen. As the killer arose, an ugly wound appeared on the dead teller's forehead—a figure seven burned in the flesh with acid.

Then the gang leader sprang to the center of the room in time to join his men who were streaming out of the vault, bags in hand. Outside the bank, the bandits made no further attempt to hide the masks which marked them as desperados. One lone policeman tried to keep the gang from entering the armored trucks. But the three shots from his pistol were purposely high and wide to avoid hitting innocent bystanders. He was dropped in his tracks by a snap shot from the gang leader.

While part of the gang had been inside the bank, the rear guard had remained in the trucks and stood ready for action. Up the street, just beyond the entrance of the alley, a huge van had been shunted across the street, blocking westbound traffic. This was obviously the work of the efficient criminal organization, for the cleared traffic lane offered an avenue of escape up the alley. Once there, the parade of three trucks put on full speed and roared out of sight.

The danger momentarily past, an excited tremor ran through the crowd. Where were the police? What had happened to the pride of the city, the capable John Laws? Two blocks beyond the bank an officer was busily engaged in handling a traffic jam. Evidently he was entirely unaware of the slaughter that had taken place only a few rods away. And throughout the neighborhood, the muffled roar of traffic was unbroken by the wail of police sirens.

One man in the crowd in front of the bank seemed suddenly to awake from what had been a hideous nightmare. "Our money!" he shouted. "They've taken our money from the bank! Where were the police?"

Spurred by this sudden realization, the mob moved as one man, pushing through the gates of the bank. Mr. Corin, his usually sleek hair hanging over his haggard eyes, met them with arms outthrust as if to check the crowd in its frantic dash.

"Wait!" Corin shouted, hoarsely. "Stop, everybody! You've got to listen! Your money's safe!"

For a moment, silence. Then the crowd broke into a renewed clamor.

"Go back to your homes!" Corin shouted. "The money's all here in the vaults. They—they didn't take a penny as far as we know! Incredible, but true. Some slip-up in their plans. All who wish to make withdrawals may do so, but please go away until later. Give the police a chance. There's been murder—"

"The police!" a man foremost in the crowd scoffed. "What became of the police when they were needed most? Did they answer your alarm? Have they made any effort?"

Corin shook his head sadly. "Some of them have." And he nodded at the sprawled bodies of the two policemen who had been slaughtered in the path of the criminal army. "Please! They have made a supreme effort!" His voice was choked with emotion.

"Mr. Corin's right!" A man shouted. "We'll give the police another chance. Then, if they don't get busy, we'll demand a house cleaning!"

"Mr. Corin's always right!" the crowd shouted. And with considerable more calm than they had yet shown, the people turned and moved back into the street.

CHAPTER II

THE MYSTERY MAN

IT WAS FIVE minutes past nine when a tall, gray-templed man entered the office of Police Commissioner Foster. His card—bearing the inscription: James Hunting; Division of Criminal Investigation, Department of Justice—gained him immediate entrance to the commissioner's private office.

But that card was false. And the face of James Hunting was false. For the face of James Hunting was but one of the thousand faces of Secret Agent "X."

Secret Agent "X" had just returned from Washington where he had been closely closeted with a high official whose true identity was hidden behind the alias of K9. K9 was the man who sanctioned the mysterious and sometimes greatly misunderstood activities of Agent "X." The alarming increase of counterfeiting had been the subject of their discussion. Commissioner Foster regarded "X" unsmilingly. The commissioner was justly proud of the police force of his city. That government officials should have to step in, even in case of a federal offense such as counterfeiting, was a source of annoyance to him.

"X" knew the chances he took in confronting Foster. For the police, unable to understand the unorthodox methods of Secret Agent "X," thought him to be some archcriminal. "X" had often been called upon to trick Foster in his lone battle against crime and upon one occasion, had narrowly escaped detection.[22]

However, if there was any apprehension in Secret Agent "X's"

---

22 *AUTHOR'S NOTE: It is my belief that at one time in his varied career, Secret Agent "X" was a character actor on the stage. He can, with the aid of his special make-up material, assume the features of any man. He is also capable of imitating any male voice at will. Upon the occasion mentioned above, he actually had the audacity to impersonate the police commissioner himself.*

mind, on entering the office of the police commissioner, his marvelous control of facial muscles prevented him from showing it. The grim lips, that were James Hunting's, smiled as he said:

"Good morning, commissioner. I have a matter of gravest importance to discuss with you. My name is Hunting—"

Foster's brusk nod interrupted the Secret Agent. "I've seen your card. Now, let me examine your credentials, if you please." He extended his hand across the desk.

"X" was prepared for this. In his private files he kept proper credentials for many of the disguises which he was forced to assume. He took a pass case from the inner pocket of his coat, removed a folded and official looking document, and handed it to Foster. Then, while the commissioner was looking at the document, "X" dropped into a chair across the desk from Foster.

The commissioner handed back the papers. "Everything seems to be in order, Mr. Hunting," he said, his tone a little more cordial. "I do not envy you your assignment. You may rest assured that you will have every cooperation from the police. But just what do you purpose to do that has not been done before?"

"First," replied the Secret Agent, "let me ask you a question. Is there any doubt in your mind as to who is responsible for such perfect replicas as these counterfeit bills?"

Foster gnawed his lip. "None whatever," he replied quietly. "A German engraver by the name of Joseph Fronberg—the most skillful man in his profession who ever lived—"

"And Fronberg—" the Agent persisted.

Foster looked uncomfortable. "You know as well as I do, Mr. Hunting, that Fronberg is dead. So far as we know, he committed suicide to escape capture."

"X" NODDED. "His clothes were lying on a river-front wharf. Later, an unidentified body was pulled from the water. It was consequently presumed that Fronberg was dead. Well, suppose he is. Has it occurred to you that before his death he might have produced the plates, now used in printing counterfeit money, and hidden them before his gang was captured? You remember that though the gang was wiped out, the plates were never found. But some one *has* found them and is using them today."

Foster nodded. "Proceed."

"Naturally, we must eventually find the gang responsible for this flow of spurious currency. But until such a time comes and we have learned sufficient about the activities of a criminal organization, that I am convinced is as powerful as it is efficient, I propose that all the banks in the city be closed pending the examination of every greenback in their vaults!"

Foster, overcome by surprise, sprang to his feet. "You can't believe that the banks are the source of this counterfeit money. Absurd!"

"X" checked Foster with a wave of his hand. "Not the source, but certainly some banks have served as distribution points. Do you recall that a certain well-known bank was entered not a long time ago? So skillfully was this entrance managed that no one was the wiser until it was found all the money on hand was merely worthless paper. That bank had unknowingly been distributing counterfeit money. How the counterfeit had been substituted for the real, we do not know, though I have a theory—"

And the conference between Secret Agent "X" and Commissioner Foster was suddenly interrupted by the entrance of a powerfully built, red-faced man who stormed across the room, pulping the end of a cigar between his teeth.

"Inspector Burks!" exclaimed Foster.

"Yeah, and something's gone haywire!" Burks roared. "The Suburban National's been held up, and by the time the police got there, the crooks had ambled away from the place leaving a couple of cops and a bank teller stretched out fit for a slab! Headquarters got word in plenty of time to get squad cars over there. An all-cars call went out over the police radio and not one of the cars picked it up! That was because of—" Burks checked himself. Only at that moment had he noticed Agent "X." He stared questioningly from "X" to Foster.

"You may speak freely in front of Mr. Hunting," said Foster. "He is an agent of the Federal Government assigned to investigate the counterfeit racket."

Burks did not pause to acknowledge his introduction to Hunting. "It was this way, commissioner. A few minutes before the robbery took place, nearly the whole upper police band on the radio was ripped to pieces by static—electrical interference of some sort. One of the prowl-car boys said it sounded to him as though a big electrical generator was feeding directly into the antenna. The noise was right on the police radio station's frequency and completely knocked out the voice transmission. We did not find out what was wrong until one of the police reported that he couldn't hear anything from the police radio station. And that's why the squad cars didn't get to the Suburban National until after the damage was done!"

COMMISSIONER FOSTER pushed back his chair. "That must be investigated! I want to go over the scene of the crime with you, Burks. Mr. Hunting, I'd like to have you along. One moment, please. I want to get my hat and coat." And Foster stepped into a small ante-chamber and closed the door behind him.

Burks turned and shook hands with "X," said: "It's a long way from stealing real money to making phony stuff, but there's something in this that ought to interest a federal man."

"X" raised his eyebrows questioningly. "Yes?"

"That radio noise, I mean. Maybe that comes under the jurisdiction of the Federal Radio Commission."

"You mean that the electrical interference was not an accident, not some power leak somewhere?"

Burks nodded his head vigorously. "Right. The operator at the radio station made a quick check-up. The police announcer's voice left the transmitter perfectly clear. That static was broadcast over most of the police band by some mysterious short-wave station for the one purpose of preventing the police cruisers from getting orders. Find that mysterious station and we'll find the man who planned the bank stick-up!"

Commissioner Foster entered the room, saying:

"Mr. Corin, an officer in the Suburban National Bank just phoned. It seems that the bandits came in armored trucks similar to those used by the Bankers' Express Agency. However, they were foiled in their attempt to take money from the vault. It looks as though they had had assistance from the inside."

"But there was murder!" Burks exploded. "Two of our finest men!"

Foster nodded grimly. "Let's go." And he started through the door.

Secret Agent "X" insisted on driving Commissioner Foster and Inspector Burks over to the bank in his own car. By the time they arrived, the morgue wagon had backed up to the door. Police had roped off a section of the sidewalk. Outside the cordon morbid onlookers stood in rapt attention while white-garbed attendants carried out a long basket containing the corpse of one of the victims of the ruthless slaughter.

Agent "X" followed Foster and Burks through the crowd and into the bank. The medical examiner had just concluded with the body of George Arthurs, the teller who had been murdered by the gang leader. "Over here, commissioner," said the medico. "I want you to take a look at the body before the boys move it out to the morgue."

"X," close upon Foster's heels, went over behind the counter where the body lay covered with a ripple of white cloth.

"Not a pleasant sight at all," said the medical examiner as he raised the sheet. "On first glance, it appears to be ordinary strangulation. But this killer was taking no chances!"

The face of the corpse was a frightful thing with its blue skin, swollen tongue, and protruding eyeballs. Standing out starkly on the forehead was the cruel scar of the figure seven. The throat was marked with small, bloody wounds where the killer's fingernails had bit deeply into the flesh. These wounds in the throat were points of particular interest to the medical examiner. "The reason I said this killer was taking no chances, is that I believe this man was poisoned. Strangulation wasn't enough, you understand. The rapid advance of *rigor mortis* leads me to think a certain poison was used."

AGENT "X," had he desired to make himself conspicuous, could have readily told the medical examiner that he was correct in the assumption that Arthurs had been poisoned. There was little doubt in his mind but that the fingernails of the hands that had killed Arthurs had been stained with some preparation containing the deadly drug, curare.[23]

It was a significant point, "X" thought, that every murder victim who was left with the brand of Seven upon the forehead had been killed in some manner that attacked the vocal organs immediately. A man who has been shot or stabbed may utter some dying words

---

23 AUTHOR'S NOTE: Secret Agent "X" has neglected no science in his preparation for his lone war against crime. In addition to chemistry, physics, medicine, and psychology, he has made extensive studies in toxicology. Among the interesting poisons with which Agent "X" is acquainted, is the above mentioned curare. Its physiological action is unique in that it acts to paralyze motor nerves of the body. It attacks the respiratory organs and asphyxia results. Because even a small amount of curare injected in the blood stream is fatal, it has long been used as an arrow poison among the natives of South America.

of immeasurable value to the police in tracking down the killer. The medical examiner had been exactly right when he had said that the murderer had taken no chances.

Inspector Burks shook his head wearily. "It's the Seven mob again. That gang certainly gets all the breaks!"

A soft, unpleasant laugh sounded from directly behind them. "X" turned from his contemplation of the corpse to see a tall and remarkably thin man—a man whose distinguishingly different attire, love of good living, and apparently unfailing source of income had made him a figure of importance in the social register. Lynn Falmouth was young in years and old in experience. Having fallen heir to an immense fortune, Falmouth had purchased a large interest in the Suburban National Bank as well as a number of other business enterprises.

Falmouth patted the marcelled wave of his suspiciously yellow hair. His eyes behind gold pince-nez were cold as a mackerel's. "You might add, Inspector Burks, that what breaks these criminals don't get, the police give them."

Burks' face flamed. His hands clenched. Foster put a restraining hand on Burks' shoulder.

"I am sure, Mr. Falmouth," said Foster, soothingly, "that if you knew all the circumstances, you wouldn't blame the police. I assure you that every effort will be made to track down the killer and his gang."

Falmouth smiled, and "X," studying the man intently, found much that was unpleasant in Falmouth's smile. He was evidently a man who would enjoy watching a worm squirm beneath his heel. He was fully conscious of the position his immense wealth afforded him. "I *know* every effort will be made, Mr. Commissioner. George Arthurs happened to be a cousin of mine." And with a smile that was all self-satisfaction, Falmouth turned and sauntered across to the door of an office.

Men from the morgue reappeared with a basket intended for the corpse of George Arthurs. Foster took "X" by the arm and steered him across the floor to where a group of press reporters were standing around Abel Corin, the gray-haired director of the bank. "I am anxious to get Mr. Corin's version of the holdup," Foster explained. "He's level-headed, and we can depend upon whatever he says as being fact. It might be well to sound him out on the counterfeit question, too, Hunting. Corin is a man to think things through."

On seeing Commissioner Foster, Corin nodded cordially. A

reporter, whose persistence had pinned Corin to the wall, fired another question: "An inside job, you say, Mr. Corin? Now, just a word about your suspicions in regard to the inside man. One of your bank employees, of course?"

Lynn Falmouth

Corin nodded sadly. "I regret to say that evidence points directly towards one of our tellers—a man by the name of Arthurs."

The reporter whistled. "The murdered man? That's a new angle!"

"Yes," replied Corin. "A fellow clerk who was only a few feet from Arthurs when he was strangled to death, heard a few broken sentences from Arthurs just before he died. As I have told you, our burglar alarm system had been cut off. The electric power was shorted. Arthurs was heard to plead for mercy on the score that he had done everything the leader of the gang had told him to do. In as much as Arthurs had had considerable experience as an electrician before he was employed by the bank, one may come to a logical conclusion."

The reporter nodded. "And the gang was afraid that Arthurs would squeal. Now, to what do you contribute the gang's failure to get cash?"

SECRET AGENT "X" waited for no more. It was then as he had feared. The gang had entered the bank with everything to its advantage and had left it without taking any money. It hardly sounded logical and "X" knew that he must act immediately if he expected to save the city from further spread of the noxious germs of panic.

So quietly did Agent "X" move that Foster did not notice that "X" had left his side. In the activity of police investigation, no one noticed him as he advanced to the rear of the bank where the vault was located. The door of the vault was open exactly as it had been left. Certainly there was nothing to fear from a second holdup with the bank filled with police.

Two plainclothes men stood idly by, evidently under orders to watch the vault until a routine examination of its contents could be conducted. But they, too, must have doubted the necessity of such care, for they were busily engaged in conversation irrelevant to the crime. "X" had no difficulty in entering the vault.

Unbroken sheaves of currency were racked along the walls of the vault exactly as they had been delivered by the bank messengers early that morning. "X" hurriedly broke open a pack of new twenties and dropped them on the floor. Then he took from the inner pocket of his coat a folding case. Inside, was a number of bills that he knew to be counterfeit. A careful check-up must be made. The comparison of every line of the treasurer's signature, of every detail of engraving, of each serial number must be made. He knelt on the floor and began his task, aided by the intense light of a small electric flash.

A low, scarcely audible exclamation escaped from his lips. There could be no doubt. The twenty-dollar bills in the bank vault were worth no more than the paper they were printed on. Masterpieces of the counterfeiter's criminal genius. He was about to make examination of other bills of different denominations, when he felt a cold draft of air on his back. Alert to every threat of danger, in spite of how intent he might be on any phase of investigation, "X" pivoted. The huge, circular door of the vault was swinging shut.

Instantly, he flung himself forward towards the massive, moving section of impregnable steel. A low sardonic laugh that "X" recognized sounded outside the vault and was immediately chopped off by the clang of the huge bolts as the door completed its swing. "X" found himself pushing against the door of the vault—a door that defied even his Herculean strength. He was trapped. And for what possible reason had he been taken prisoner? Surely no one had penetrated his disguise.

He passed a questioning hand over his features that were so carefully modeled in plastic material. He knew that it was impossible for anyone to discover his true identity, but it was something that he feared more than death itself. For discovery meant that he would be helplessly caught in the toils of the law—the law that hounded him though he befriended it.

What puzzled him still more was the laugh he had heard just before the door had completed its swing. For it was the low, cold laugh of Lynn Falmouth. It had been Falmouth who had trapped him.

CHAPTER III

EXPOSED

"X" KNEW THAT to shout, hoping to attract attention, was useless; for the vault was soundproof. Five minutes dragged by. Ten minutes. At last "X" saw the mechanism, that worked the bolts of the door, going into action. He dropped on the floor, nonchalantly lighted a cigarette, and permitted his eyelids to droop as though he had become sleepy with waiting.

As Commissioner Foster's head appeared in the aperture, "X" yawned. "It's about time," he said irritably. "Some one closed the door on me by accident. I might have been suffocated in here and no one would have been the wiser." He stood up. The vault door was open, but his exit was prevented by quite another barrier. Lynn Falmouth, Foster, Burks, and a man whom "X" had never seen before stood in the opening. Burks and the stranger trained automatics on "X."

The Secret Agent's jaw dropped in amazement. He tilted his hat back and scratched his head. "What the—say, it's no wonder you men have trouble in catching your criminals! Don't point those guns at me!"

Inspector Burks' eyes narrowed to mere slits. "This time we didn't have any trouble!"

"We?" asked Falmouth sarcastically. "I rather think you'll have to give me credit for this catch. I saw him sneaking over to the vault, followed, and watched him break into that money."

"X" laughed. "You should have introduced me to Mr. Falmouth, commissioner. It's my job, you know. I was merely comparing bank notes within the vault with some bills in my own possession."

Burks motioned with his automatic. "Come out of there. You'll not talk yourself out of this!"

With a careless shrug, "X" obeyed. "Washington will hear of

this, inspector!"

"True enough," said Foster. "Mr. Lyons, here—" he nodded towards the stranger—"will hear quite a bit, I imagine. Mr. Lyons is a federal man here on the counterfeiting case. You see, just before leaving my office, I took the opportunity of having you looked up. I learned not ten minutes ago that James Hunting, so far as the Washington office is concerned, doesn't exist!"

Sven Gerlak

"X" thrust his hand into his coat pocket.

"Hold that!" Burks rapped. His gun bobbed up so that his cold, narrowed eyes were centered on Secret Agent "X's" forehead. "Put your hands up in the air. I'm going to give you the once over."

"X" smiled disconcertingly. His eyes darted about the room. Police filled the bank. The front entrance was blocked. Iron-barred gates closing over the accounting rooms at the rear would prevent his escape through the back. But with the exception of a single cop, the balcony overlooking the bank proper was deserted. "X" withdrew his hand from his pocket. His fingers were clutched tightly over a small package.

"Surely you're not afraid of a package of cigarettes, Inspector Burks," he taunted. He flicked a cigarette from the pack, palmed it a split-second before he tossed the rest of the package onto the marble counter.

BURKS stepped forward until he was able to hide the muzzle of his automatic in "X's" middle. "You keep your gun on this bird, Mr. Lyons," Burks directed, "while I frisk him." Then Burks' eyes drilled the Secret Agent's inscrutable face. He said in a whisper: "I'm going to enjoy this, Mr. 'X'!"[24] And Burks proceeded to make a careful search of "X's" pockets.

The Agent's cigarette lighter, which also served as a tiny tear gas gun; a small vial of a powerful but harmless narcotic; a compact

---

24 AUTHOR'S NOTE: *Inspector Burks' fruitless efforts to unmask Secret Agent "X," whom he believes to be a master criminal, have led him to make some accusations that have at times been of considerable embarrassment to him. He had been tricked so often by Agent "X" that he cannot be censored for making such accusations in his effort to ferret out the true identity of Secret Agent "X."*

tool kit; his gas gun; and a wallet were all handed over to Commissioner Foster.

The contents of "X's" wallet created considerable disturbance. "Let me see those bills," Federal Agent Lyons demanded. And Foster had scarcely handed them over before Lyons uttered a triumphant oath. While Lyons and Foster were examining the bank notes which they had taken from "X's" pocket book, "X" passed his left hand over his mouth, took out the cigarette he had been smoking in the bank vault, and put the fresh one between his lips.

Burks was too good a policeman to allow his attention to waver toward what Foster and Lyons were doing. He watched "X" narrowly to find nothing suspicious in the way "X" lighted the fresh cigarette from the butt of the first.

"X" inhaled smoke deeply, luxuriantly. Actually, he was mentally timing the speed at which the cigarette in his mouth burned. His thumb and forefinger closed over the cigarette as if he were about to remove it from his mouth. Suddenly, his middle finger snapped out, flicking the cigarette straight at Burks.

The cigarette burst with a sharp explosion, emitting a frothy cloud of vapor that for a moment completely hid Burks' head. For the half inch of tobacco acted simply as a fuse for a small tear-gas bomb concealed within the cigarette. Such a small cartridge could not contain sufficient tear-gas to fill the entire room. It had, however, immediately rendered Burks helpless. He dropped his automatic and dug both fists into his eyes.

But Agent "X" did not wait to see other results of his surprising trick. At the moment the bomb had burst, he had pivoted and dashed toward the balcony. He took the steps four at a stride. The single policeman on the balcony came for him with gun drawn. This was exactly what "X" had anticipated. He knew that police below stairs would not dare shoot at him for fear of hitting their companion.

"X" gambled on the man on the stairs shooting hurriedly and consequently inaccurately. Hurried it might have been but certainly not inaccurate. The slug from the police special walloped squarely into "X's" chest. Ordinarily, the Secret Agent's special bullet proof vest of choice manganese steel would have rendered the shot ineffective. But the distance between "X" and the cop was short and the terrific impact of the slug striking the bullet-proof vest was centered directly above an old shrapnel wound which occasionally caused "X" pain.

Master of himself that he was, "X" could not check a wince of pain. For a moment, he staggered and seemed to waver on the brink of oblivion. Then, teeth grinding, he made a superb effort and flung himself upon the cop. The policeman was so sure of the success of his shot that he was taken by complete surprise. "X's" left arm swung up sharply, his fingers closing over the cop's gun. The point of his thumb dug deeply between the central knuckles of the policeman's gun-fist and struck a particularly sensitive nerve. The cop's fingers stiffened and his gun clattered to the steps. At the same instant, "X" drove hard and fast with his right, straight to the point of the cop's chin.

THE blow seemed to lift the cop from his feet. The point of his heels slipped on the marble floor. He began sliding down the steps. "X" side-stepped to avoid the falling cop and sprang to the balcony. He had lost precious time. Some of the other police who had received little of the effect of the tear-gas were ganging up the stairs. "X" leaped towards the rear window that looked out upon the alley.

He jerked a glance over his shoulder and saw that he would be hopelessly trapped in another moment. His eyes lighted upon a heavy desk that was used by one of the bank stenographers. Large casters were fitted into its walnut legs. "X" sprang towards it, crouched behind it, and gave it a powerful heave. The desk rolled straight to the top of the stairs, where its momentum carried it over the edge and crashing into the advancing police. The falling desk turned the group of policemen into a tangle of sliding, tumbling bodies.

"X" picked up an office chair and lunged with it towards the high-arched windows at the rear of the balcony. The pane crashed into a thousand cutting fragments. With a pang of disappointment, "X" saw that behind the frosted glass window pane were heavy iron bars. He dropped the chair and leaped into one of the private booths opening from the balcony and placed there for the convenience of the owners of safety deposit boxes. A frosted glass window at the end of the narrow booth admitted light. "X" twisted the window catch and threw up the sash. Nothing but a wood-framed copper screen was now between him and freedom.

A bullet lanced the thin wood panel of the booth. There was not a minute to lose. He kicked out the screen with his heel, threw a leg over the sill, swung full length out the window and hung for a moment from the sill. Since the balcony was between the first and second stories of the building, it could not be more than fifteen feet to the alley pavement. Kicking against the wall as he released his grip, "X" threw himself out as far as possible to avoid hitting any projections on the wall of the building. He landed on his hands and knees, and regained his balance only in time to scuttle crablike out of the way of a huge van that was bearing down upon him. Past experience had taught him to make the most of any opportunity offered, and as the truck rumbled past him he leaped to the rear platform and crawled beneath the tarpaulin that partially covered the end of the van.

In this haven of comparative safety, he immediately set about changing his make-up. Darkness and lack of makeup material made any elaborate disguise impossible. However, he removed his hat and tossed it into a corner of the van. He next took off his gray-flecked toupee that had been a part of his disguise as Federal Agent Hunting. His own natural brown hair was revealed.

His deft fingers smoothed out the lines in the make-up material which covered his face. Then standing upright in the moving truck, he removed his overcoat and quickly turned it inside out. A plaid gray lining rendered the coat reversible and, on putting it on again, it had all the appearance of a sporty topcoat. Simple as these alterations were, "X" looked like quite another person when he dropped from the rear of the moving truck a few minutes later.

Inasmuch as a few pieces of small change remained in his pocket, he boarded an elevated as the quickest means of getting to one of his hide-outs.

CHAPTER IV

DESPERATE PLANS

ON LEAVING THE elevated, "X" walked westward for two blocks. He came to a small one-car garage that jutted out from an old house that appeared to be abandoned. He unlocked the garage door and went in. The garage contained a small sedan. Using his key, "X" opened a door in the wall of the garage that led into the house. He hastened up creaking stairs and turned into a small room at the top. All the shades were drawn and it was necessary for him to turn on the light.

Seating himself before a small dressing table, "X" opened a drawer and took out a make-up kit. The disguise which he was about to assume was so well known to him that he might have made the changes in the dark. His fingers worked swiftly, building up the contours of his face with metal plates and layers of plastic volatile material.

When he had completed his task a few minutes later his face appeared to be that of a man about forty years old with commonplace features that no one would look at twice. While he was getting into another suit of clothes, he crossed the room to a small compact radio and tuned in the police band. He set the pointer of the dial for the local police radio station in hope of hearing a repetition of the mysterious "static" that had prevented police headquarters from communicating with the prowl cars.

As "X" buttoned the vest of a gray tweed suit, he heard the monotonous voice of the police announcer droning out the description of a man.

"About medium height; weight about a hundred and sixty pounds; hair, dark varying to gray about the temples; thin, slightly Roman nose; name, James Hunting. This is probably an assumed name. He is wanted by federal authorities on an alleged counterfeiting charge. All police be on the look out for James Hunting—"

"X" took a final look in the mirror above the dressing table. He wondered what Inspector Burks would think if he knew that the man known as James Hunting had become A. J. Martin, an Associated Press correspondent in the matter of a few minutes time.

Then, disguised as A. J. Martin, "X" left the house through the garage where he entered the small sedan, and drove in the direction of an office which he leased under the name of Martin. He stopped on the way, however, to telephone. On calling the Suburban National Bank, "X" left an anonymous message for Commissioner Foster. "Do not permit any of the money in the bank vault to be distributed until it has been carefully checked over," he said, disguising his voice. "I am convinced that it is all counterfeit." He did not say that it was his belief that the bank hold-up was not the failure it appeared to be. He was certain that the nefarious gang which trade-marked its exploits with the brand of the figure seven had actually looted the vault, substituting counterfeit bills in place of the real ones. Thus the criminals probably hoped to gain time for the disposal of their loot

HIS first act on entering the office of A. J. Martin was to telephone the Hobart Detective Agency and get in touch with Jim Hobart.[25] He told Hobart to meet him at the office as soon as possible. Then "X" went over to a steel index file that stood in one corner of the office. He pulled a sheet of onion-skin paper from the division marked "F."

At the top of the page was a single name "Fronberg." The rest of the report would have presented an almost indecipherable puzzle to even a cryptographer. It dealt with the particulars of the German engraver, Joseph Fronberg, who had turned his genius into the paths of crime and was thought to have headed a band of counterfeiters that persistent federal men had wiped out a few years back. Every member of the Fronberg gang was either thought to be dead or behind the bars of some federal prison with the exception of one man.

That man was a killer known as Pete Tolman. It had been impossible to tie Tolman up definitely with the Fronberg gang, though

---

25 AUTHOR'S NOTE: *The Hobart Detective Agency, to all appearances, is maintained by Jim Hobart, an ex-police detective whom "X" had befriended. Actually, under the name of A. J. Martin, whom Hobart supposed to be a representative of the Associated Press, Secret Agent "X" sponsors this detective agency.*

"X" was convinced that he had taken an active part in the counterfeiting. But Tolman, too, was about to meet his just deserts. Tolman was being held in a Louisiana penitentiary on a first degree murder charge. One of Jim Hobart's most trusted operatives had been watching Tolman for some days and had already gained information that "X" considered invaluable.

As "X" was reinserting the report sheet in the cabinet file, he heard Jim Hobart's knock on the office door.

"Come in, Jim," the Secret Agent cordially invited in the voice that was associated with his identity as Martin.

Hobart entered, smiling. "Hello, Mr. Martin. I've got some good news for you."

"X" seated himself on the top of his desk and swung one leg back and forth impatiently. "Let's have it, Jim."

"You were right about Pete Tolman communicating with some one outside the penitentiary. My man has been watching Tolman's cell after dark. Tolman gets up to the window and smokes a cigarette. If you weren't on the lookout, you'd never notice it, but Tolman isn't smoking for pleasure. He sends Morse signals! He takes a long pull on the cigarette for a dash and a short for a dot. The glow from the cigarette can be seen from outside! What's more, every message is addressed to somebody by the name of Seven!"

"Good, Jim! You be ready to leave for Baton Rouge in about an hour."

Though Hobart expected quick moves from Martin, he was a little taken back by this announcement. "What's up this time, boss?" he asked.

The Secret Agent's eyes twinkled. "No questions asked. Simply go out to that little airport where I keep my plane. There you'll meet a man in aviator togs. Obey him implicitly. His name will be Bedford. That's all now, Jim."

As soon as Hobart had left the office, "X" locked the door and set about changing his make-up. When the job was completed fifteen minutes later, "X" appeared to be a heavier man than Martin. His face was dark, brooding, and hell-scarred. A toupee that looked like a shock of unruly black hair added to his unpleasant features. He was wearing a suit of flagrant checks, a tan overcoat with exaggerated, padded shoulders, and a derby hat.

"X" LEFT the office of A. J. Martin and taxied out of the city to a small, private airport maintained in the name of Martin. He

"X" found himself pushing against the door of the vault that was swinging shut on him.

entered the hangar where his mechanic was fussing over a low-winged Lockheed monoplane.

"I'm takin' Mr. Martin's bus up," he explained to the mechanic. "Here's a note from him so's you won't think it's a steal." And "X" tossed an envelope to the mechanic. Then he went to a locker and had time to put on flying togs before Jim Hobart arrived.

"X" greeted Hobart with a deep, raucous voice that suited his rough appearance perfectly. "Guess you must be Hobart. I'm Nick Bedford, You've got your orders, so put on a flyin' suit and we'll get going."

Jim obeyed and in another ten minutes they taxied across the field into the wind. From a clean take off, "X" circled the field, pointed the nose of the plane southwest and gave it the gun.

It was nearly seven-thirty that evening when they landed at the Louisiana capital. According to information "X" had obtained through Hobart's operative, the change of guard, in the death house where Pete Tolman awaited the hangman, occurred at eight-thirty. From the same source, "X" had learned the particular habits of the two guards who were on night duty in the condemned cell. They were granted a few hours leave preceding their check-in for the night's work. Hobart's operative had been directed to shadow these two guards and make reports at thirty-minute intervals to a companion who had been installed in a private dwelling in the city. Hobart telephoned directly from the airport and learned that the two guards were at present in a small lunch-room near the penitentiary. Jim Hobart and "X" taxied to a garage where, by previous arrangement, "X" had stationed one of his own cars. Not far from the garage he had established a temporary hide-out as was his custom before entering a city on dangerous business.

"Now get this, Hobart," the Agent said, as they drove toward the restaurant where the two guards were passing the time. "I'm on orders, same as you. And what we do is wait until they come out of that hamburger house and then give 'em a blast with the guns—"

"Hold on," Hobart interrupted. "If it's just the same to you, I'll use my fists."

"Gas guns, yah sap!" "X" growled. "The boss wouldn't stand for any lead shooting." He took a pair of chromium-plated gas guns from his pocket. They were not unlike ordinary pistols in appearance. An invention of Secret Agent "X's" fertile brain, these guns could shoot a highly concentrated but harmless anesthetizing vapor. He handed one to Hobart. "Be careful with that thing and don't look in the end to see if it's loaded. What we've got to do is wait until everything's clear, then get out of the car and stick 'em up. Don't give 'em a chance. Give 'em a shot of gas right in the pan."

They were cruising past the restaurant and "X" saw two men wearing the uniforms of the prison guards hunched over the lunch counter. Another figure, standing in the shadow of a billboard, seemed intent on watching the lunchroom. "X" recognized this man as Hobart's operative. "That guy standing in front, is he your man?" "X" asked.

Jim Hobart nodded. "That's Carson."

"Right. You get out now and tell him his job's done. If we can do as well as he did—well, we'll be okeh." And "X" stopped the car long enough to permit Hobart to get out. Then he speeded the car to the next corner and turned around.

Hobart's man had no sooner disappeared than the two guards came out of the lunchroom, and started in the direction of the place where "X" waited with the car. The Secret Agent saw that Hobart was following them a short distance behind. He swung from the car and ambled leisurely towards the guards. An unlighted cigarette dangled from his lips.

"Hello, buddy," he said, addressing one of the guards. "Either one of you got a match?"

The two men stopped, and "X" saw, to his satisfaction, that Hobart was closing in from behind.

"I think I have," replied one of the guards, groping in his pocket.

"X" glanced up and down the street. Everything was clear. He jerked his gas gun from his pocket and fired directly into the unsuspecting guard's face. The man uttered a surprised exclamation. His hand got halfway to his holster. Then his legs seemed to desert him and he wilted to the sidewalk. Hobart was somewhat slower than "X." The second guard fired a wild shot before the gas from Jim's gun pitched him forward on his face.

"Quick, Hobart!" the Agent snapped. "Get your man to the car. Not a spare second!" And "X" picked up one of the guards by the middle, slung him like a sack of meal over his shoulder, and hurried towards the car. Jim followed with his man, cursing his own clumsiness.

The two unconscious men had been tumbled into the rear seat of the car and the door had been closed before "X" heard the sound of heavy footsteps. Some one was running up the street toward them. "X" looked up just in time to see a policeman turn the corner.

INSTEAD of arousing suspicion by an attempted getaway, "X" rounded the nose of the car and opened the hood.

The policeman stopped abruptly and looked up and down the street. Then he looked over to where "X" was pretending to fuss with the motor of his car. "Say, didn't you hear a shot, mister?" he asked.

"X" said: "Just my car. Carburetor is a little off, I guess. You must have the shakes tonight. What's goin' on?"

The cop's face reddened. "Well, we've got some special orders to keep our eyes open for trouble. It's on account of Pete Tolman."

"Who?" the Agent asked as though he had never heard of the name.

"Tolman, the killer. He goes on a necktie party tonight. He always was a blowhard, and he's boastin' that they'll never hang him. He's got a lot of friends in the underworld who might try to stir up a prison break or something."

"X" laughed as he climbed into the front seat of the car. "Well, Telman or whatever his name is, must be an optimist!" He gave the motor a spin and steered from the curb.

"Gosh, that was a narrow squeak, Bedford!" Jim Hobart exclaimed. "You've got nerves like ice!"

"X" bent over the wheel. His face was grim. Minutes were sliding by all too fast. At eight-thirty the two unconscious guards in the back seat were supposed to go on duty. At twelve midnight Pete Tolman was to go to the scaffold. These were two things which Agent "X" was resolved should not happen.

"X" pulled the car to a sliding stop in front of a ramshackle old house that he had previously selected because of its comparative isolation. For some reason or other neighboring houses had been vacated. The street was dark and deserted. From the floor of the front compartment of the car, "X" took out a compact traveling kit.

"I'm going into that house and open up," he said to Hobart. "Make certain that you're not being watched, then carry the two guards in after me."

With traveling bag in hand, "X" hurried up the walk that led to the door of the dark old house. He entered without a light and walked through the central hall to the back room. There, he turned on a light. The windows of the room were all boarded over, and he was certain that not a ray of light penetrated to the outside. Agent "X" opened his traveling kit and removed a hypodermic needle and a small bottle which contained a narcotic compound known only to Agent "X."[26] He had time to load the needle before he heard Jim Hobart stumbling around in the front part of the house. Calling softly through the door, he directed Hobart to bring the two guards into the back room.

When Hobart had completed his share of the task, "X" walked over to where Jim stood looking down at the two senseless guards.

---

26 AUTHOR'S NOTE: *This narcotic, only one of the battery of scientific devices which Agent "X" employs, takes effect immediately on application. It is unique in that it has no bad after effects such as are common to most of the drugs used in the practice of medicine.*

"I'm goin' to fade out now," he said gruffly. "And the next guy who'll be your boss will look enough like that sandy-haired guard to be his twin brother."

Then with a movement swift as a striking snake, "X" drove the hypodermic needle squarely into Hobart's biceps. Hobart stepped back, bewilderment clouding his face. Then before he could say a word, his legs buckled under him and he fell to the floor.

The hard-lined face of Bedford softened. His lips twisted in a smile. "Sorry, Jim," whispered the real voice of Secret Agent "X."

CHAPTER V

HOUSE OF THE DOOMED

"**X**"**ENTERED IMMEDIATELY** upon a task of seeming impossibility. First he removed the uniforms from the two guards. Putting them to one side, he opened his traveling kit and selected tubes of plastic volatile material, pigments, and plates for changing the contour of the face. Then he straightened out Hobart's crumpled form and, kneeling over him, went to work.

A few minutes later, he stood up and glanced from the face of the guard and back to the newly created face of Jim Hobart. No sculptor could have made a more remarkable similarity. He had only to select a toupee from the large stock which he carried to make the disguise complete. He noticed regretfully that Jim was about two inches taller than the guard.

"X" took out a folding triple mirror and set it up on a table in front of him. Following the lines of the sandy-haired guard's face, "X" reproduced every feature in his own make-up. He then stripped off the uniform of the sandy-haired guard and put it on. A glance at the identification card on the uniform he was wearing, told "X" that the man whom he impersonated was named Lawson.

Next, he gave both of the guards a dose of his harmless narcotic, dragged them to a closet, and closed the door.

Though Secret Agent "X" had only heard Lawson speak four words, a moment's practice enabled him to imitate the man's voice. His next task was to revive Jim Hobart. This was accomplished by injecting the antidote for his narcotic into Jim's arm. When the private detective came to a few seconds later, he stared about in bewilderment. "Snap out of it, Hobart," said "X," speaking in the voice of Lawson, the guard whom he impersonated.

"Who are you?" Hobart asked. "Where's Bedford? He drugged me!"

"X" nodded. "He was acting upon orders just as I am. You can call me Lawson. Your name, according to the tag on that uniform which you are going to put on, is Johnas. That uniform will be a little small for you, but we've got to chance it."

Used to the strange orders he had received since being employed by the man whom he knew as Mr. Martin, Hobart obeyed without hesitation. However, his shock at seeing his own reflection in the mirror was almost too much for him. "I'll never believe it's me!" he gasped. "Will—will I ever get back to normal? This may be an improvement over my face, but I still don't like it!" He rubbed his fingers lightly over his new face.

"X" said: "Don't worry. It will come off. Now, I'll take the initiative in everything. You just keep still. Don't answer anyone except in grunts. Forget that you are Jim Hobart and try to identify yourself with the guard Johnas."

"Okeh. But what's the idea?"

"We're going to prison, Hobart. Right into the death house. Come along. I'll explain while we're getting over there."

They had only five minutes to get out to the penitentiary and check in. It would be necessary to use the car.

"Get this, Jim," Agent "X" explained as the car jounced over the rocky street, "I'm going to enter the cell of Pete Tolman. Tolman is coming out. He will be wearing a guard's uniform, and it is your duty to watch him. He'll do whatever you say. Don't answer his questions, but let him know that you're a member of the criminal gang known as the Seven Silent Men. You get him back to New York in Martin's plane. Take him to Martin's office and guard him yourself until you hear from Martin. Remember, Tolman is a killer."

Hobart wagged his head. "I've got it all right. It's some risk, but it will make a knockout of a news story."[27]

They abandoned the car a short distance from the prison gates and continued on foot. They were admitted to the prison without question from the guards at the gate. "X," who had acquainted himself with the plan of the penitentiary before they had left New York, led the way straight to the cells. He approached the head

---

27 AUTHOR'S NOTE: *Jim Hobart has such faith in the man whom he knows as A. J. Martin, that he carries out any task given to him without question. He does not know the great cause in which his employer labors but believes that Martin is constantly in search of material of a sensational nature for the newspapers. No matter what queer things Martin appears to do, in the long run it is always for a good purpose. And that's enough for Hobart.*

guard and said: "Lawson and Johnas going on duty, sir."

"A rotten time you'll have of it, too," responded the head guard. "Tolman's nuts."

"Nerve broke?" the Agent inquired.

"Nope. More nerve than ever now. He just swears he'll never hang. All the other cons have been removed from your block of cells. Tolman's yelling is a little more punishment than is due them."

"The rope will soon finish that," said "X" grimly as he passed into the hall that led down between the tiers of barred cells. Hobart followed him closely without uttering a word.

A BLACK steel door closed upon the condemned block. A knock admitted them into the beehive of iron-barred cells where many a man spent his last moments in the shadow of the scaffold. The condemned men had been removed to another part of the prison.

At least there was sufficient kindliness in the law to spare them the sight of their fellow's hanging. At the end of the room was a sort of alcove, high and narrow with walls and floors immaculately clean. There stood the gallows, newly erected for the hanging of Pete Tolman.

The Secret Agent exchanged a few shallow pleasantries with the two guards whom he and Hobart relieved, watched them leave the death house, and listened to the sound of their footsteps receding down corridor. Hobart was pacing the floor nervously, glancing in the direction of the only occupied cell. From the bunk behind the bars came the sound of lusty snoring. Beyond the black door of the death house, guards paced monotonously back and forth, their footsteps sounding like a dozen death clocks, clicking off the narrow span of Tolman's life. Yet Pete Tolman seemed to be sleeping peacefully.

"X" walked over to the condemned man's cell. He cleared his throat. Tolman snored on. "X" coughed loudly. Tolman stirred and opened his vicious little eyes. He sat up and yawned. But Secret Agent "X," judging from the appearance of Tolman's eyes, knew that he had not been sleeping.

"What time is it, screw?" Tolman asked in a sharp, nasal voice.

"X" looked at his watch. "It's eight-forty-five." Then he added in a lower tone: "Are you waiting for Seven?"

At the mention of the number seven, Tolman's face became a studied blank. "X" was sure that his long shot had gone home. "Not long now until you trot up the thirteen steps," said "X" quietly. He was anxious to provoke further conversation with Tolman in hope of gaining some scrap of information.

Tolman, however, merely snorted through his high, thin nostrils, turned his back on "X" and paced to the window of his cell. Outside, the sky was tar black.

"X" quietly removed the keys from the belt of his uniform and inserted the proper one in the lock of the grating. Tolman whirled. His hands clasped and unclasped as though he was eager to kill yet another man before his death.

"X" pressed a finger to his lips, swung back the door, and entered the cell.

"What the hell!" Tolman muttered. Hope and bewilderment battled on his face.

"You want to escape, don't you?" "X" asked quietly.

Tolman looked suspicious. He didn't answer, fearing to say the wrong thing and send his hopes on the rocks. "X" walked quickly towards Tolman. His right hand was hidden behind his back. There was a flash of fear in Tolman's eyes. He backed slowly towards the wall. Had "X" approached him with gun drawn, Tolman might have put up a fight. But the invisible threat of "X's" hidden hand was too much for Tolman's ratlike courage. He dropped to the bunk, shrinking, as far from Secret Agent "X" as he could.

"Wh-what are you?" he whimpered. "D-don't stare at me! I'm goin' to get topped anyway. Y-you get out a here!"

"Who do you think I am?" "X" demanded.

Tolman's little eyes screwed up as though he was thinking very hard. "Why, you're just a guard—Lawson or something like that."

"And who else?" "X" persisted.

Tolman swallowed. His voice was a scarcely audible whisper. "You might be one of the Seven Silent Men."

THEN the Secret Agent's conjecture had been correct. The Seven gang had been in communication with Pete Tolman. It was all the information he could hope to get from Tolman. If he questioned the killer further, Tolman might become suspicious.

Without a moment's hesitation, "X" jerked his hand from behind his back. In it, he held a hypodermic needle loaded with his special drug. He plunged the needle straight into Tolman's arm. The killer squealed, tried desperately to get to his feet, then sank back as still as death.

"X" looked out of the cell towards Jim Hobart. The private detective was standing still, staring in awe at Tolman. "X" frowned, shook his head, and motioned to Hobart to continue his pacing.

Then Secret Agent "X" began his work. His nerves dictated frenzied haste. He realized that he was in the narrowest strait of his career. He knew that once he had taken the step he contemplated, nothing, *nothing* in the power of man could save him from death if the Seven Silent Men failed to do what Agent "X" expected them to do. But he must *make* sure. The hideous phantoms of panic and famine hovered over his country. The Seven Silent Men and the devils' coin they distributed must be checked.

"X" crossed to the window of the cell. Through this alone Tolman could have received communication from The Seven gang. Outside the window, "X" could hear the patient pacing of the guards in the prison yard. But standing out against the black sky, far from the prison, was a square of light. The name of a popular cigarette was emblazoned in colored lights that flashed in and out. "X" watched the sign, counting mentally the intervals between the flashes.

An exclamation escaped his lips. How simple it all was. For as he watched, he became conscious that the sign did not flash at regular intervals. It was sending out dots and dashes in Morse code. Yet the making and breaking of the circuit was so carefully handled that the casual observer would not have noticed it.

"X" translated as the message flashed out: "Seven.... Seven.... Seven," repeated over and over.

It was for this signal that Tolman had been watching. Then came a pause in the message. Not for long, however. Soon again, came halting but intelligible words:

HAVE HOPE TOLMAN LOOK IN COT FOR TWO SMALL WHITE CARTRIDGES UNWRAP AND INSERT ONE IN EACH NOSTRIL BEFORE GOING TO SCAFFOLD BREATHE ONLY THROUGH NOSE YOU WILL BE SAVED .... SEVEN .... SEVEN .... SEVEN.

"X" turned from the window. He lifted Tolman from the cot, then raised the scanty bed clothes that covered the hard pallet. Next to the thin mattress he found them—two small, white cellophane-wrapped cylinders. Putting these to one side, "X" hurriedly straightened the cot. Then he stripped the coarse prison garments from Pete Tolman's inert form. From beneath the uniform that he wore, "X" took his compact make-up kit.

For ten tedious minutes, he worked, molding and proportioning Tolman's face until it resembled the face of Lawson which "X" had assumed. The next part of his preparation called for his finest efforts. With the aid of a mirror, he transformed his own face so that it looked exactly like Pete Tolman's.

AFTER a short time, satisfied with the results of his painstaking efforts, "X" donned the trousers and coarse shirt that Tolman had worn. Then he clothed Tolman in the discarded clothes of the prison guard. He would have liked to spend more time on Tolman's disguise. He knew that he should have given Tolman some detailed instructions. However, at almost any moment, he expected to be interrupted by the entrance of some prison official. He immediately injected the antidote for the narcotic into Tolman's arm.

The killer opened his eyes. He stared about bewilderedly. His eyes met "X's" face and his jaw sagged in wonder. "It's over," Tolman muttered huskily. "They didn't save me after all. I'm dead. I'm—"

"That's enough!" "X" rapped, imitating Tolman's nasal voice. He held the mirror before Tolman's face so that the killer could see the remarkable change that had taken place.

Tolman ran a finger around the band of his collar. "Lord! I'm not me! I'm that screw, Lawson!"

"Exactly," replied the Secret Agent. "Act like him. Get up on your feet. You're going to get clear of the big house. You're going to escape, just as the Seven Silent Men promised. You're perfectly safe as long as you obey that guard out there—" indicating Jim Hobart. "If you don't do as he says, you'll pray for a return to the death cell!"

Tolman stood up and wandered to the door of the cell. "You mean I'm to walk out?"

"Yes. Lock me in the cell and keep right on pacing the floor until you're relieved from duty or until the other guard gets an opportunity to get out. If you must talk, imitate Lawson's voice as near as possible. Tell anyone who questions you that you've got a cold. You can take that make-up off when you're out of here."

"Don't worry. I'm pretty good!" Tolman assured him. Something of gangland's eternal swagger was already returning to this man who had escaped the gallows—for a time. Tolman opened the door, went out, and locked the door after him. Then with burlesqued dignity, he began pacing the floor, following the amazed Jim Hobart.

"X" looked at his watch. Two short hours until midnight. One hundred and twenty minutes until he, Secret Agent "X," innocent of crime, would face the hangman. No horrible nightmare, but stark reality, the very thought of which would send the average man mad. But "X" immediately set about disposing of all his special weapons and devices. Makeup kit, gas gun, his kit of special drugs—all must be hidden in the cot in the death cell. From here on, "X" was in other hands than his own.

His train of thought was suddenly interrupted by the opening of an iron door that led into the death house. Another guard entered, accompanied by a man in severe, black garments. The prison chaplain had come to pay a visit to the condemned man.

And all the while, Pete Tolman, wearing the garb of a prison guard, smirked behind the sky-pilot's back, already confident that he had cheated the gallows.

CHAPTER VI

JAWS OF DEATH

WITH BRAGGART GESTURES, Agent "X" scorned the ministrations of the prison chaplain. He was acting the part as Pete Tolman would have acted. He threatened to cram the chaplain's prayer book down his throat. By the time the chaplain had given up in despair, many minutes had passed slowly for "X." The impersonation of Tolman taxed his dramatic powers to the utmost.

As the time for execution approached, several workmen entered the room and proceeded to the end where the gallows stood. "X" knew that they had come to fix the four ropes, one of which would manipulate the catch on the gallows trap. These ropes would lead through the wall into a room beyond and for each rope there would be a guard to pull it. Since only one of the ropes actually opened the trap, the identity of the real executioner would be forever a mystery.

A short time later, reporters and witnesses of the execution could be heard filing into the end of the room. Even the most calloused reporter seemed awed by the proximity of the death swing and there was an almost churchly hush over the room. Then the black steel door at the opposite end of the room opened to admit the prison officials: chaplain, prison doctor, additional guards, and the warden.

Secret Agent "X" quickly inserted the two white cartridges, which had been provided by the Seven gang, in his nostrils. In another moment, he was gratified to see that Hobart and the real Tolman were ordered to leave the room. "X" felt certain that Hobart would lose no time in getting Tolman away from the prison.

As the warden approached the death cell, "X" could see that his stern gray face was beaded with sweat. He tried to smile kindly, gave it up, and resorted to a scowl that he apparently hoped would hide his emotions. For the warden's was a disagreeable task—giving the signal for the gallows trap to be released.

"Are you ready, Tolman?" asked the warden huskily.

"Well, not exactly," replied "X" in the nasal voice of Tolman. "But seein' that it's you, I wouldn't keep you waitin'." He turned to the prison doctor. "It'd be hell to be late for your own funeral, eh, doc?"

The doctor did not answer. He had spent his life learning to save lives. Now, he must stand with arms folded and watch a man die without raising a finger to save him. He did not relish his job.

"My son," said the chaplain, kindly, "I beg you to think what you are about to do."

"Ah, nertz!" the Agent snarled.

The door was opened, and "X" was marched between lines of guards towards the scaffold that stood like some gigantic beast waiting to be fed. "X" nodded at the news reporters and shouted: "Give me a good send-off, boys. Tell 'em I'm game. Slap it on in streamers: 'Pete Tolman's got guts!' That'll—that'll—"

"X" pawed nervously at his neck. The yellow pine steps that led to the platform of death confronted him. It was becoming more and more difficult to be flippant. What was more, the two cylindrical capsules that he had placed in his nose interfered somewhat with his imitation of Tolman's voice. Then, if the Seven gang failed, if something went wrong with their plans—

AGENT "X" pushed such thoughts from his head. There was only a little time remaining. Somehow, his legs carried him up the steps. The guards centered him on the trap so that in falling through he might not strike the sides and thus save his neck from breaking. Then heavy straps were tightened about his arms and legs. He found his brain groping frantically for some means of escape. He might, in his last seconds, call out that he wasn't Pete Tolman. He might demand that fingerprints be compared to prove it.

To the amazement of the guard who was strapping him, "X" uttered a sardonic laugh. Who would believe that he wasn't Pete Tolman? His disguise was perfect, his impersonation too genuine.

He saw the hangman, a citrous-faced, stocky man, picking up the black death cap that was to hide the hideous death grimaces of the condemned man. The rope dangled like a dead snake from the beam above, its noose yawning like the very jaws of death. "X" looked down upon the nervous spectators. He recognized only one face in the group—that of Milo Leads, a medical man interested chiefly in toxicology.

Not one man in this entire group could be "X's" rescuer. His jaws ached to spring apart and shout that he wasn't Tolman. He fought back the desire—as strenuous a battle as he had ever waged. He knew it was hopeless. If he was to die, if he had indeed overplayed his hand, his identity would die with him. There was no alternative.

The warden had taken out his handkerchief. He would drop it as a signal for the trap to spring. The hangman was inspecting his noose, getting ready to slip it over "X's" head.

"Peter Tolman—" the warden's voice was tremulous—"have you anything to say before you die?"

"No!" said "X" sharply. A black ring of shadow appeared on the pine boards of the platform. The noose was directly above his head. In a moment—

"Breathe only through your nose!" A warning whispered within the death chamber. Perhaps it was inaudible to any but Agent "X." But "X" knew that the warning was intended for him. He knew that somewhere among the state witnesses was a member of the Seven Silent Men. The lips of Secret Agent "X" clamped shut.

Suddenly, it came—a roar that was a concentrated thunderclap. Hell seemed to crack open. "X" had a momentary glimpse of a black line that streaked across the floor. A jagged hole broke through the concrete and a venomous looking cloud of yellow green vapor spurted from the yawning pit.

With a sound like the twang of a bowstring, the scaffold trap sprang open. "X" felt himself dropping like a leaden thing straight into the pit of swirling green mist. "Poison gas!" his mind shrieked. It burned his eyes like acid. But he did not forget to breathe only through his nose.

He had scarcely landed at the bottom of the pit before strong hands seized him. In the glow of subdued light, he saw the heads of several men—faces that were rendered simian in appearance because of the gas masks covering them. He was hurried, surrounded by men, over a rough floor in a direction unknown.

As the green mist of poison gas cleared, he knew that he was being carried through a newly constructed tunnel, evidently reaching far under the prison wall. He knew that the people in the death chamber were helpless to follow. The poison gas would see to that.

His rescuers paused only long enough to remove the straps that bound his legs. When they continued their flight up the passage, "X" panted out, "Whew! That was some narrow squeak!"

There was no reply. Only the shuffling of feet along the floor disturbed the silence.

Directly ahead, the tunnel slanted sharply upward. Warm fresh air fanned "X's" flushed face. In another moment they were in the open. A brief glimpse of his surroundings—a scattering of small houses, and "X" was lifted into a motor car. The man at his side removed his gas mask as the car rolled smoothly away.

The Secret Agent's eyes were searching the compartment trying to see the faces of the men who had saved him from the gallows. As the car sped beneath a lone street lamp near the outskirts of the city, a beam of light fell directly across the face of the man at his side. "X" could scarcely repress an exclamation of astonishment.

For the face of the man had not a single animate feature. Rather, it was like the painted, waxen face of a doll. The features were thin, the nose hawklike, the fixed expression terrifying. Only the eyes seemed part of the living man and they were deep, dark pools where nameless evil dwelt.

Suddenly, the creature at his side moved with startling rapidity. Pain knifed through "X's" arm. Fire flowed momentarily in his veins. He saw the flash of a hypodermic needle as it was drawn from his flesh. His brain suddenly became clouded. His body gained new buoyancy. He was plunged into a drugged sleep.

CHAPTER VII

ASSASSINS' COUNCIL

THE AGENT'S AWAKENING was like returning from the grave. Something seemed to explode within his body. The shock was so sudden that he found himself panting as though he had been suddenly showered with water.

He was standing upright, body rigid. For an instant, his surroundings dazed him. He was in a vast, high-ceilinged room. The walls, paneled in oak were apparently of incredible age. A huge fireplace was a maw of crackling flames. The room seemed to be without doors or windows and the only source of light was a wrought-iron chandelier that dropped from a chain from the ceiling.

"X" was in his shirt sleeves, and standing in the center of a circle of seven chairs. Six of the chairs were occupied by men wearing sombre gray suits, identical in every way. A small diamond badge, fashioned in the form of an Arabic numeral, was pinned to the lapel of each man's coat. The chairs, too, were all alike. However, the man whose badge designated him as Number One occupied a slightly larger chair than the others.

The faces of the six men were what astonished "X" more than anything else. For to a feature, all faces were alike—waxen, doll-like, hideous in their lack of human expression.

"Tolman," began the man who was designated as Number One, "you have been selected for membership in our organization for several reasons. You have an admirable criminal record."

"X" bobbed his head. "Thanks, chief," he said in the voice of Pete Tolman, better now that the capsules had been removed from his nostrils. "And thanks for savin' me from bein' topped."

"Silence! You must know that silence is our golden rule. Only because we, the leaders of a mighty order, have maintained silence have we successfully carried out every stage of our Herculean task.

"My purpose in rescuing you was a selfish one. Your service with this group will be for my own selfish purposes. However, you will find that you will be paid beyond your wildest imaginings and that you will be able to retire in a few years, independently wealthy—if you obey me in all things.

"Our battle is waged with the most powerful weapon known to man. I mean money—two kinds of money. Hard, sound currency for our friends and colleagues; spurious bills for our enemies.

"Let me enumerate your present duties. First of all, you will obtain for us the engraving plates for the production of five and ten dollar bills which were made by your old friend, Joseph Fronberg. We have all of Fronberg's plates with the exception of the ones just named. Do you know where they are hidden?"

"X" thought quickly. It was evident that Pete Tolman had been an important wheel in the old Fronberg machine. Surely he would be expected to know what had been done with the plates. He replied: "Sure, chief. Old Fronberg, hid 'em. I got a pretty good idea where they are. May take some time for me to get 'em."

"There is no great hurry, Tolman. There are other tasks of greater importance at present. There is but one man who might thwart our purposes. That man's identity is a mystery, making your job even more difficult. I speak of the man who has hidden himself behind the identity of Secret Agent 'X.' When you have found that man, you are to kill him."

"X" uttered a low whistle. "That's a tough un, chief! From what I hear he's a slick guy."

NUMBER ONE nodded. "Yet he is not as clever as I. You will have every assistance from other members of the group.

"Now, perhaps you have wondered why our group, wealthy and powerful as it is, has remained such a mystery to the police. I doubt very much if even Secret Agent 'X' has succeeded in gaining any information about us."[28]

"We are known as the Seven Silent Men because to drop the slightest information regarding our organization means death—at the hands of the law or in our own execution chamber. On occasion in meting out punishment to members who might be inclined

---

28 AUTHOR'S NOTE: *Number One was entirely correct in this statement. Though "X" is in touch with the underworld constantly through his spies and secret operatives, he had been unable to learn anything about the Seven Silent Men.*

"X" sprang toward the desk and gave it a powerful heave.

to inform, the law is our servant. Here at headquarters I have an iron-bound book. Upon its pages are signed confessions to murder.

"Every member upon initiation to our order must commit murder under the eyes of a witness and then sign his name to a full confession of the deed. If any member should be so careless as to let information drop concerning the Seven Silent Men, his confession may be promptly sent to the police. Admission to our headquarters, the one haven of certain safety, would be refused him. There is no escape for the traitor. Now you know why the Seven Men are also the Silent Men. Any question?"

"X" bobbed his head. "It's a swell idea, sure, but it looks to me as though there were only six guys in the gang."

"At present, there are only six leaders," replied Number One. "Number Six displeased us. His name was Arthurs, a teller in the Suburban National Bank. He is dead. You will take his place—*after* you have proved yourself worthy.

"You will now advance to my chair," continued Number One.

"X" obeyed. The leader of the gang reached into his pocket and drew out a pair of ivory dice and a folded slip of paper. These he handed to "X."

"The dice," he explained, "will serve as a means of designating the servants of the Seven Silent Men. You will understand when you examine them. Carry them with you always. The slip of paper is inscribed with the name of the person whom you are to murder as a part of the initiation into our order. You may look at the paper now."

Secret Agent "X" carefully unfolded the paper. His heart was throbbing with excitement. The formidable difficulties which he must overcome to outwit this archcriminal and his gang were piling up ahead of him, forming a seemingly impassable barrier. Murder! He was expected to murder—Secret Agent "X" was expected to take life when his own code seldom permitted him to use lethal weapons.

But upon looking down at the piece of paper open in his hands, he experienced a stab of pain far more cruel than a wound from an assassin's knife. For the name written upon the paper was dear to him beyond all others. It was Betty Dale, the beautiful girl reporter who had aided "X" in countless battles against crime.[29]

"X" SUDDENLY became aware that all eyes were fixed upon him. He was thankful that the plastic substance covering his face would hide the fact that he had most certainly paled at the thought of what was expected of him. However, something in his eyes must have betrayed his shock to Number One. The leader of the Seven Silent Men spoke icily.

"Does the killing of a woman seem such a disagreeable task to you? Would you prefer to return to the death house?"

---

29 AUTHOR'S NOTE: *Followers of Secret Agent "X" are by now well acquainted with Betty Dale, the courageous girl reporter, who has shared many a perilous adventure with him.*

"Cheez, no, boss!" the Agent cried. "I just ain't never knifed a woman. Give me the goose pimples at first, s' help me! But I'll do it. Just you watch me!"

"That is the better spirit!" Number One commended. "I intend that Betty Dale shall be killed, that she shall be branded with the mark of Seven, and that she shall be thrown into the river from the wharf. My idea is that such an act will force Secret Agent 'X' into open warfare. If I am any judge, Betty Dale is more to 'X' than a mere ally.

"You may wonder how this killing will be arranged. Leave that to me. Surely you realize the extent of our power. A group capable of tunneling under the walls of a penitentiary, blasting through the floor of the death house, and rescuing a prisoner from the gallows, is also capable of arranging a mere murder. And when Betty Dale is found, a corpse floating in the East River, well—" Number One uttered an evil chuckle—"Mr. 'X' will be pretty badly upset. He'll be in such a frenzy that he'll turn the city upside-down in a frantic effort to find the hiding place of the Seven Silent Men. Then—*then* he will show his hand. Then Pete Tolman's knife will know where to strike. Am I right, Tolman?"

"Sure, boss!" the Agent spoke confidently. "But you haven't told me where this headquarters is yet. Some old millionaire's dump?"

Number One's voice lost every hint of cordiality. "Do not be too inquisitive, lest your eternal silence be assured. We are rather clever at this business of ripping out a man's tongue!" Number One snapped his fingers. "Number Three and Number Four, you will attend Tolman. See that he is suitably disguised. Then take him away. He will be free to do as he pleases until his services are required to murder Betty Dale."

Two of the Silent Men rose from their chairs. "X" saw an oak panel open to reveal a scarlet-curtained doorway. Through this he was led by Number Three and Number Four into a small room hardly bigger than a closet. There he was furnished with a red wig, a sandy mustache, and grease paints—clumsy accessories of disguise that would have caused Agent "X" to laugh had there remained any humor in his heart.

When "X" had completed this clumsy disguise, Number Four approached him with a large, brutal looking hypodermic needle. He was forced to submit to several injections to nerve centers throughout the body. He felt the strange drug oozing over him.[30]

He realized suddenly, that he was going blind. His mind was strangely dulled, his sense of equilibrium upset. He was like a corpse with only the motor nerves that activated his arms and legs remaining alive. Later, he recognized the rumble of a motor. Then he knew that he was walking. But his brain was far too deadened for him to remember the direction taken or the interval of time between the administration of the drug and his sudden and violent reawakening.

---

30 AUTHOR'S NOTE: *Secret Agent "X" has never learned the exact composition of this drug, but he believes it to contain minute quantities of curare used similarly to the spinal block anesthetic so familiar to modern surgery.*

CHAPTER VIII

THE CRIPPLED SPY

SLOWLY, AGENT "X'S" sense of sight returned to him. A red mist that swam before his eyes parted and he was dazzled by the glitter of a million lights. He was in the middle of the sidewalk. Hurrying people jostled him rudely. In the street was the continual stream of heavy traffic. He realized that he was in New York—in fact, he was standing in the very shadow of the mammoth Falmouth Tower Building. It was eight-thirty P. M.

But as far as he knew, he might have been brought miles and miles from the Seven gang's headquarters. Certainly among the gleaming spires and dancing lights of the city, he would find no old house boasting such a room as the oak-paneled one occupied by the Seven Silent Men.

As he walked down the street, three newsboys came by shouting their sensational ware. The *Herald* had put out an extra. Black headlines screamed:

COUNTERFEIT BILLS IN FALMOUTH PAYROLL

"X" reached into his pocket to find it well stocked with bills and change. Evidently Number One believed in keeping his hirelings happy with money. "X" hailed one of the newshawkers and bought a paper. He glanced at the headlines as he hurried along. Much had happened since he and Jim Hobart had flown to Baton Rouge.

The caldron of trouble brewed and bubbled. Banks had closed to prevent runs. The Bankers Express Agency had been ordered to stop work because it was impossible to tell their armored trucks from those employed by the counterfeiters in the distribution of spurious money. The Falmouth Manufacturing Company had actually paid out thousands of dollars in worthless currency—money that they had supposed had come from a legitimate bank.

"X" remembered the blond, unpleasant Lynn Falmouth. Falmouth presented a baffling enigma to Agent "X." He was a character beyond fathoming, even to an astute psychologist like Secret Agent "X." Nor could he forget that Falmouth's cousin, George Arthurs, had been Number Six of the Silent Men.

Rounding the corner, "X" came abruptly on a knot of people gathered around a hollow-eyed young man who was haranguing on the failure of the government to stop the flow of counterfeit money. He flaunted a copy of the *Herald* in their faces.

"Look, brothers!" he shouted. "A supposedly reputable firm has been paying for the daily labor of hundreds of our companions. Paying not in check and not in cash. Paying them in worthless paper! Shall we stand idle as the police do? How do you know, John Smith, or you, Mary Jones, that the money in your pocket will buy the daily bread or be refused as so much waste paper?"

"X" waited for no more. He recognized the young man as Malvin Stein, an agitator who had given up his position as heir to the Stein fortune in order to air his crack-brained schemes and epic visions from soap boxes. He was a feeble orator and, had it not been that his subject was of such vital importance, he would have probably lacked an audience. Yet the incident plainly showed the spread of the germs of discontent.

"X" stepped into a rolling taxi and gave the address of an apartment building where he sometimes made his headquarters. Looking back through the window, he saw a crippled, twisted form of a man pull from the crowd and hobble into a second taxi. "X" wondered if the pitiful wreck of humanity was following him. Beggers seldom rode in taxis.

The cab containing the cripple nosed determinedly after them. When "X" ordered the driver to stop a few blocks from this apartment, he saw that the second cab dropped back to the corner, obviously to permit the begger to alight. "X" walked on towards his apartment, certain that he heard the strange, shuffling steps of the cripple behind him. Once he turned his head and saw the grotesquely shaped man dragging himself along with a diagonal gait peculiar to a certain type of paralytic.

"X" entered the apartment building—a tall, stone-fronted old house that had been remodeled for its present use. He climbed the steps to the second floor and let himself in by means of a combination lock concealed beneath the mailbox flap.

HIS first act on turning on the light was to pull down the blinds. Then, through a small hole in the curtain, he looked down upon the street. Directly opposite the apartment building, he could see the cripple. The man was squatting on the sidewalk, holding a tray of lead pencils which he offered to every passer-by.

Secret Agent "X" had previously-devised a piece of apparatus for just such an emergency. He went to a closet, unlocked it, and dragged out a strange sort of motion picture projector. It was mounted on a steel frame and in place of the usual film spools there were two flanged pulleys mounted on two arms that extended from a few inches from the floor nearly to the ceiling. Over these pulleys ran a belt of motion picture film.

He focused the projector lens directly upon the drawn blind of the front window. An electric switch on an extension cord enabled him to snap out the light of the room at exactly the same time that he turned on the projector. The illusion was perfect. The projector cast the silhouette of a man sitting in a chair directly upon the blind. From the outside it must havs appeared that "X" had suddenly seated himself in a chair and begun reading. As the belt of film turned, the silhouette made lifelike movements—turning the pages of a book and puffing on a pipe.

Then, taking care not to step in front of the beam from the projector, "X" walked into another room. There, he opened a small writing desk and produced a folded sheet of paper which he read over quickly. It was an invitation directed to Elisha Pond from Abel Corin, the wealthy bank director. It read:

Dear Mr. Pond:

As a philanthropist and public-spirited gentleman, I think you would be interested in meeting Sven Gerlak, a free-lance detective from Milwaukee. You are doubtless well acquainted with his enviable reputation for cracking down on criminal organizations. A number of wealthy gentlemen like yourself have contributed to a fund for employing Mr. Gerlak in hunting down the gang known as the Seven Silent Men.

I would be happy to have you present at a meeting in my office Thursday evening at about nine o'clock. Mr. Gerlak will be there and a subject of vital importance to our city will be discussed.

Cordially,

ABEL CORIN.

"X" returned the note to the desk and entered a small room at the back of the apartment. There he kept elaborate material for make-up as well as an extensive wardrobe. Seating himself before a three-sided mirror, he effected a miraculous change in his appearance. When he rose from the mirror he had become the wealthy, eccentric, and mild-faced man who was known throughout the city as Elisha Pond.[31]

Genevieve Leads

OPENING a window in the same room, "X" swung over the sill, hand-traveled along the ledge until he could grasp the metal downspout leading from the eaves to the alley below. He was in the act of sliding down the pipe, when a window directly opposite opened. A shrill, feminine voice screamed:

"A burglar! Help! P'lice!"

"X" hastened his descent, sliding as rapidly as he dared without burning his hands. The woman was still screaming when he found footing on the alley pavement, "X," sprinting towards the end of the alley, was forced to leap to one side to avoid running headlong into a policeman. The cop yanked at his gun.

"X" drove a smashing, paralyzing blow to the cop's gun arm. The pistol bounded to the pavement. The cop swung his nightstick over the Secret Agent's head. But "X" ducked out of the way, and led his right to the policeman's jaw. The cop was set back on his heels by the force of the blow. "X" took the advantage thus gained to duck around the corner and run up the street.

A police whistle shrilled. The answering signal came from a policeman near at hand. The sound of running feet coming towards him through the darkness halted "X." He drew himself up to the full dignity that fitted his portrayal of Elisha Pond; for Pond, although an eccentric, would certainly not be suspected of climbing down spouts and tussling with policemen.

The copper accosted "X," turned a flashlight in his face, but

---

31 AUTHOR'S NOTE: *The stock disguise of Elisha Pond, which Agent "X" frequently employs is of no less importance to him than that the A. J. Martin disguise. It is in the name of Elisha Pond that an inexhaustible fund of money, subscribed by certain wealthy and public-spirited man, is placed at his disposal.*

paused only long enough to apologize to Mr. Pond. Then he hurried up the alley to join his fellow policeman.

"X" hastened to a neighboring garage where he kept one of his cars. He backed it out, nosed into the street, and speeded downtown.

A short time later, Secret Agent "X" entered the gleaming, silvery doors of the Falmouth Tower. An elevator whisked him to the sumptuous offices where Abel Corin directed major cogs in the machine of finance. In an outer office he was met by a strikingly beautiful brunette. Her scarlet lips, and warm, dark eyes flashed him a smile of welcome. "X" stood in the doorway, fussing with a small, leather case.

Count Camocho

"Eh—young lady, if you will just take my card to Mr. Corin, I—er—"

"That won't be necessary, Mr. Pond," said the woman. "Mr. Corin is expecting you. The meeting is already in progress. Please step this way." And she led "X" through a lavishly appointed lounge and towards Mr. Corin's private office.

Though he had never seen the woman before, "X" supposed her to be Alice Neves whose name had been closely linked with that of Abel Corin. She had acted as his secretary for some time, and it was rumored that the announcement of her engagement to Corin was to be expected. Miss Neves opened the door of the inner office and then followed "X" in.

The Secret Agent glanced about the room and saw several men with whom he had come in contact in the role of Elisha Pond. Abel Corin, of course, was there, as well as Police Commissioner Foster. Suddenly the heart of Secret Agent "X" gave a bound. For seated demurely away from the circle of anxious-faced men, was Betty Dale, her reporters' notebook in hand.[32]

Never had she looked more charming. The arrangement of her golden hair seemed to lend new enchantment to her bright blue eyes. Her slim, lovely figure was attired so as to achieve that rare

---

32 AUTHOR'S NOTE: *Few men could be immune to Betty Dale's charm; certainly not the police with whom she is in daily contact in her work associated with the newspaper. The fact that she is often privileged to enter conferences denied to other reporters has occasioned considerable jealousy among periodicals which compete with the* Herald.

combination of practicality and smartness. She smiled pleasantly upon Elisha Pond, little knowing that beneath this disguise was the man whom she regarded with respect and admiration—even love, had she permitted herself to admit it.

Gray-haired Mr. Corin advanced, shook hands with Agent "X," and led him across the floor that was uniquely ornamented with colored tiles representing the playing pieces of a chess game. A short, heavy-set man whose broad face approached the flaming color of his hair was introduced to "X" as Sven Gerlak, Milwaukee's famed "Gang-buster."

COMMISSIONER FOSTER called the meeting to order. He plainly stated the condition within the city, then presented Sven Gerlak. The energetic, red-haired little man propped one foot upon a swivel chair and addressed his audience emphatically.

"A grave problem indeed!" he began abruptly, pounding the top of a desk with his big fist. "Frankly, I am at a loss to know just where to begin. The underworld, in which my secret operatives are at work, is strangely inactive, or if not inactive, it is hiding its work so well that no information can be gained. Of one thing we are sure: the leader of the Seven Silent Men terrifies his hirelings into absolute secrecy. That, I think is evident.

"But there is one man, to my knowledge, who could give us immediate assistance." Gerlak paused, removing great horn-rimmed glasses and polishing them upon his tie. "That man," he suddenly exploded, "is that mysterious person known as Secret Agent 'X'!"

This announcement created a fervor in the audience. Agent "X," in the voice that was always associated with elderly Mr. Pond, spoke up. "But, my dear sir, Secret Agent 'X' is thought to be a criminal!"

"Precisely!" exclaimed Gerlak, fixing Elisha Pond with eyes that were greatly magnified by the lenses of his glasses. "But he is a most clever criminal. There is an old adage—something about it taking a thief to catch a thief. Why, so clever is Secret Agent 'X' that he might be in this room at this very moment!"

"Has it occurred to you," said Abel Corin, as he reflectively gazed at the wisp of smoke from the tip of his cigar, "that this man who calls himself 'X' might be at the bottom of this business?"

"X" glanced at Betty Dale. The girl reporter had turned a little pale. She caught her lower lip between her teeth. He knew that Betty would have liked to speak a word in defense of the Secret Agent.

Gerlak shook his head in answer to Corin's question. "Criminal, Mr. 'X' may be, but he is not a member of the Seven. You must admit that there are no police records charging Agent 'X' with murder. The Seven gang has no scruples about blood-letting."

Commissioner Foster had to admit that the records concerning Secret Agent "X" were very few in number. "The man has been too clever," he concluded.

The meeting was suddenly interrupted by an impatient knock at the door of the office. Alice Neves answered the knocking, and the door had scarcely been unlocked before a detective sergeant burst into the room. Commissioner Foster's reprimanding glance melted with the explosion of words from the plainclothes man.

"We've picked up one of the Seven gang, sir. I knew you'd want to know—"

"Where, man?" cried Foster, springing to his feet.

"Right outside the building here. He was thrown from a passing car—dead! But you can tell by his face. It's exactly like the face of the man who held up the Suburban National. But there's something else—"

"Speak up, man!" Sven Gerlak prompted.

"Well, sir," murmured the detective, "this sounds nuts, I know. But to look at his face—well, it just isn't like a human's face at all, and yet—"

"Imagination! Sheer lunacy!" sputtered Gerlak. He sprang for the door of the office. The meeting was abruptly terminated. All crowded out of the office at Gerlak's heels. And among the others, displaying remarkable vigor for a man of his years, was Elisha Pond.

CHAPTER IX

THE SILENT HORROR

POLICE HAD HASTILY formed a cordon about a sprawling thing on the sidewalk in front of the Falmouth Tower. Following through the opening in the ring of police made by Commissioner Foster, Agent "X," Betty Dale, and Sven Gerlak came within a few feet of the corpse. Though her life as a newspaper woman had to some extent hardened Betty Dale to the sight of sudden and violent death, the sight of the face of the man on the sidewalk made her gasp.

It was, indeed, as the detective-sergeant had said, an inhuman sort of a face—the doll-like, leering visage of one of the Silent Men. The corpse was clad in a dark-brown suit, but there was no diamond insignia upon his coat lapel.

With a movement of catlike swiftness, Sven Gerlak knelt beside the body. "This is obviously the work of Secret Agent 'X,' Commissioner. The body was thrown from a passing car. 'X' has taken up the fight against the Seven Silent Men!"

"That's jumping at conclusions, Gerlak," said Foster dryly.

"This face, you see," said Gerlak, pointing at the grinning face of the corpse, "is merely a mask of something similar to wax." And before Foster could raise his voice to check the impulsive Gerlak, the private detective had given the waxen mask a quick tap with the butt of his automatic. The mask cracked from forehead to chin and fell apart in two jagged-edged pieces.

A scream from one of the onlookers; hoarse exclamations from the police; an oath from Foster. "X" turned to Betty Dale. She was braving the sudden shock of the gruesome revelation with eyes averted and lower lip locked between her teeth. Color had drained from her face.

The true face beneath the waxen mask was a hellish contortion.

Unseeing, pain-seared eyes stared from beneath beetling brows. A figure seven was burned in the flesh of the forehead. Chin and neck were covered with a beard of clotting gore. Jaws were strained open, and beyond the stained teeth was a hideous vacancy that screamed the revolting truth of the method of murder. The tongue had been torn out by the roots.

"Good Lord!" breathed Foster. "*Good Lord!* This isn't a member of the gang. This—this poor devil is Detective Fletcher of the homicide squad!"

Gerlak's dynamic energy was unchecked by the gruesome face of the corpse. His exploring fingers had yanked a slip of paper from the breast pocket of the corpse. He hastily opened the paper and read it to himself. Though he was several feet away, Agent "X" had no trouble in reading the large, clear handwriting.

My compliments, Commissioner Foster:

And accept this token of all esteem. The same fate awaits you or any others who pry into our affairs. Fletcher was unfortunate in identifying one Lewey, the Smoke, as a member of the gang which looted the Suburban National. Fletcher's success was due largely to Lewey's indiscretion. We have no room for bunglers in our organization, and Lewey has taken temporary quarters in the East River, where your police will eventually find him. Why don't you imitate our example in regard to the removal of bunglers? You've quite a number on the police force, you know.

Seven.

"X" turned suddenly and seized Betty Dale's arm. The girl's blue eyes widened in surprise. "Young lady," said "X" in the voice of Elisha Pond, "if you have any influence with your editor, do not permit him to dwell upon this incident in tomorrow's paper. The people are already beginning to lose confidence in their police force. Any hint that the police are not capable of grappling with this evil may be the brand that fires many a mob into action. Such a thing as this note which Gerlak has, has been sent for the sole purpose of goading the people to action. Do you understand?"

And without waiting for an answer, Elisha Pond, who was expected to make abrupt movements, elbowed his way through the crowd and disappeared.

SECRET AGENT "X" drove his car to a sedate old office building. There he maintained a hideout which was of great importance to him because of its location near the very center of the business world. He enacted a marvelous change, assuming one of his stock disguises—a red-haired, freckled reporter. Then he called the *Herald* office and asked for Betty Dale.

He knew that she would be at her desk turning out her story of the meeting in Corin's office and the grisly manner in which it had been terminated. When he heard Betty's pleasant but businesslike voice over the phone, he said: "Wouldn't you like to meet a gentleman of the press in about twenty minutes?"

"Who is speaking?" asked Betty, a note of cold restraint in her voice.

One of those brief, infrequent flashes of merriment appeared in Agent "X's" eyes. He puckered his lips and uttered a peculiar, vibrant whistle.

Betty gasped in surprise. "You! Why, of course, I'll meet you. Where?"

"At your apartment, please. And just as soon as you can possibly make it."

"Leaving right away," replied the girl.

"X" forked the receiver, and left the office. He drove as swiftly as traffic would permit to the modern apartment building where Betty Dale lived. Alighting from the elevator, some time later, he proceeded at once to her door. His knock was unanswered. She had evidently not yet returned from the news office.

Though special master keys would have permitted him to enter the girl's apartment, he refrained from doing so rather than run the slightest risk of jeopardizing Betty's reputation. He waited in the hall until he heard her brisk step. She took no notice of the freckled-faced man who was standing watching her. As she was unlocking the door, "X" stepped up to her and touched her arm. She was startled. Her eyes searched his face, waiting for him to speak.

"I'm Mr. Harris," The Secret Agent whispered. Then he quickly drew an "X" on the panel of the door with his finger.

"Why, Mr. Harris!" Betty smiled, falling into the little act which was obviously for the benefit of any prying eyes. For since "X" had returned from the Seven gang's headquarters, he believed that Betty Dale would be watched as carefully as the man whom the gang believed to be Pete Tolman. "Just come in, please," Betty invited. "I'm sure we can iron out that little difficulty concerning that story in yesterday's paper."

On closing the door, Betty turned around, leaned against the panel, and looked earnestly into his face, or rather the face of the reporter called Harris. Neither Betty nor anyone else had ever seen the true face of Secret Agent "X."

"Something is troubling you," she said decidedly. "A master of disguise though you may be, I can read that much in your eyes."

"X" SMILED. "It has been my great misfortune never to see you unless there is something of the gravest importance to worry about. Betty, I have now partially succeeded in establishing myself as a member of the gang known as the Seven Silent Men. Will you help me when I tell you that you will be put to the most severe trial of your life?"

Unhesitatingly she nodded her head, "I'm not very capable; not very brave, either," she replied. "But I will do my best for—for your sake." Her eyes dropped. Her face flushed a little.

"For our country's sake, primarily," the Agent corrected her gently. "I must explain to you that every member of the Seven Silent Men is compelled to commit murder. In this manner his lips are sealed against squealing on his fellow members. In my case, the leader of the gang insists that I kill some one who is very dear to me. Of course, since he does not know who I am, he does not know this. Naturally, I must pretend to murder this person, and I must coach you in the part you are to play in order to carry off this deception."

"You mean—you mean that I am the one?" Her cheeks flushed a deeper hue.

"Yes, you are the one."

For a moment, Betty was unable to speak, for the pounding of her heart warned her that if she opened her lips she would cry out: "I'm glad! I'm glad!" For though she had often guessed that this mysterious man held her in high regard, he had never openly stated that she was dear to him. Yet she knew that the important work of Secret Agent "X" must not be hindered by any emotion. When she was certain that she had complete control of herself, she asked: "What am I to do?"

"In a very few hours," he explained, "you will be confronted by a band of assassins. I will be among them. Rest assured that no hands but mine shall touch you. You will pretend to be terrified. I will pretend to stab you. You must feign death. It will be difficult, I know, but we dare not fail. According to present plans, you will be taken to the river front and thrown into the water. I would not ask you to do this if I did not know that you are an excellent swimmer. Upon striking the water, you must swim beneath the surface as far out from shore as possible. As soon as you break the surface, there will be a boat not far distant waiting to pick you up. I will make all arrangements. Are you game?"

"You know I am. It doesn't sound so very hard. But just how do you pretend to stab me?"

"We must prepare for that at once." And Secret Agent "X" took a flat leather case of make-up materials from the inner pocket of his coat. He opened it and took out a flat, rubber bladder that he had brought from his hideout. "This," he explained to Betty, "contains an aniline dye of such color and consistency as to deceive the average person into thinking that it is blood. Though the little sack contains just a small amount of the liquid dye, I hope that it will be sufficient for our deception."

Agent "X" then told Betty to sit down. With a strip of light adhesive tape, he fastened the rubber sack to her throat. Then he covered the sack with plastic volatile material, modeling like a sculptor in clay until he achieved the desired effect. Carefully tinted with pigments, the make-up material concealed the small bladder perfectly. Next he placed a thin metal plate over Betty's forehead. This was similarly covered and tinted. Thus the white skin beneath was protected from the acid with which the Seven Silent Men were accustomed to brand their victims.

"Now," said the Agent as he repacked his make-up kit, "you must not be afraid of anything, but you must act afraid. Remember that when the gang members come, I will be there, too."

Secret Agent "X" pressed Betty's hand warmly, reassuringly, and left the apartment.

CHAPTER X

A MYSTERIOUS MESSAGE

IT WAS TEN minutes later that Secret Agent "X" drove his car in front of the apartment building where the crippled pencil vender still watched. He noted, to his satisfaction, the silhouette thrown on the blind of his front window. Certainly it had served its purpose in fooling the crippled spy of the Silent Men. He promptly returned his car to its garage and hurried up the alley behind the apartment. This time, there were no curious watchers to call upon the police when Agent "X" scaled the downspout and returned through the rear window of his apartment.

His first act in entering was to change his make-up back to the Pete Tolman disguise. To this outfit he added the red wig and mustache that the Seven gang had furnished him. This done, he went into a small dining room and approached what appeared to be a sideboard. Actually, the cabinet concealed special radio receiving and transmitting equipment.

He drew a chair up before the instrument, sat down, and made several minor adjustments in the transmitting set. Then, using a telegraph key, he sent out spark transmission to a man by the name of Bates who maintained a large group of men and women employed by "X" for the purpose of obtaining information for him. Bates knew his employer only by the sound of his voice and by the special code he used in telegraphic messages.

When he heard the answering call which assured him that he had succeeded in contacting Bates, "X" tapped out complete instructions. Bates was to put every available man to patrolling the river front in small boats for the purpose of picking up Betty Dale after the murder hoax had been carried out and she had been thrown into the water.

"X" heard a vigorous knock at the door. He closed the radio cabinet, hurried into the front room, and turned off the motion picture projector. He then shoved the projector and all its accessories back into the closet and returned to answer the door.

"Telegram for you, sir," said a khaki-clad messenger as he shoved his way into the room. The messenger drove his hand into the pocket of his breeches. In the act of locating the telegram, a pair of ivory dice dropped from the messenger's pocket. The eyes of Secret Agent "X" followed the dice as they fell to the floor.

HE knew that it was not mere coincidence that the dice landed with the five and two uppermost. Agent "X" remembered the dice that the leader of the Seven had given him. He took them from his pocket and dropped them on the floor beside the other pair. They, too, rolled so that the sum of their exposed surfaces totaled seven. His shrewd eyes drilled the messenger.

The man in khaki nodded, handed a telegraph slip to "X." Upon its surface was scribbled:

"Two men will meet you with a car at the corner of this building in three minutes."

"X" winked knowingly at the messenger, pressed a fifty-cent piece into the man's hand, and opened the door for him to depart.

Secret Agent "X" required a few minutes to collect the equipment that he thought might be useful. True to his character as Pete Tolman, "X" had to carry a small dagger. Tolman preferred the knife to any other form of weapon. Then there was his own gas gun as well as small vials of drugs which he had found most useful in his battle against crime. The latter were contained in a small, velvet-lined leather case together with hypodermic needles for their injection.

Leaving the apartment building, he walked slowly towards the corner. Down the street, a car glided smoothly from the curb and cruised towards "X". A searchlight attached to the car's windshield was turned directly upon "X's" face as the car approached. At the corner, it drew up. One of the two men in the back seat lighted a cigarette. In the yellow flame, "X" made out the inhuman, waxen features of the mask which characterized a member of the gang. He walked to the car and without a word stepped inside.

Immediately, the driver shifted gears and accelerated to the center of the street.

"You are punctual, Pete Tolman," said a soft, curiously intonated voice of the man at Secret Agent "X's" side. "Might I inquire how a man so suddenly released from prison, has managed to engage an apartment so quickly? As you may have guessed, you were followed from our headquarters."

"That's easy," explained the Agent. "I leased that apartment for a girl friend of mine just a few days before the bulls picked me up. I had it paid for a long way in advance. When I goes up there tonight, whatcha think? The skirt has walked out on me! But you never catch me tearin' my hair over no dame!"

THE man seemed satisfied for he dropped the subject at once. "There has been some slight alteration in the plans of Number One. The river front swarms with police looking for the body of Lewey, the Smoke, who made his exit at the same time that Detective Fletcher did. It will be necessary to kill Miss Dale at the place where our spies say that she may be found—at her apartment."
At this announcement, "X" went cold.

"You are capable of killing without making a sound, Tolman?" asked the other man—a man whose voice "X" instantly recognized as belonging to that member of the gang whom the leader had referred to as Number Four.

"Sure," the Agent replied instantly. "They don't talk before nor after. A Chink in Frisco taught me a trick or two with the knife. No noise and not much blood, see? I use a toad sticker, give 'em just a little prick, and that's that. Some sort of poison smeared on the blade does the trick."

"Aconite?" questioned Number Four.

"Aco-what? Oh, I gets it. You mean the name of the poison. Cripes, I dunno! Some Chink stuff. It's sure death no matter what's its monicker."

As a matter of fact, there would be no poison on the knife. Agent "X's" hands were busily at work in the dark of the car. Through slits in his overcoat pocket, he had reached the little leather-covered case containing various drugs. Different shaped caps on every bottle told him which one to select. As the car sped along, "X" filled a hypodermic needle with a powerful sedative which injected into Betty would immediately depress her heart to such an extent that pulse would be detectable only by an expert. But the one danger was—she was totally unprepared for it. This, however, "X" had to risk.

Suddenly, Number Four said to his companion: "Number Three,

you are to hand Tolman one of our masks which designate the members of the Seven group. Such were the orders of Number One. He is to wear it when engaged in this job."

The soft-spoken man addressed as Number Three, handed the mask to "X". He put it on at once. Number Three and Number Four held a brief conversation in whispers. Suddenly, "X" felt a sharp, fiery sting in his left arm. A long needle had entered his flesh. Its cargo of dope was pumped into his blood stream. "X" cried out sharply: "Say, what is this?"

"Just a little something to make you relish the job," replied Number Three. "You will probably not recognize the symptoms of the drug as it spreads over your body. But if you had no appetite for killing before, you will have one now!"

Flame seemed to consume "X". He writhed with the agony of it, yet with the pain was a strange, exhilarating sensation. Muscles tightened. Fists clenched. An inexplicable voice in his mind screamed: "Kill .... Kill .... Kill!"

Then something snapped within his brain. He was plunged into a mental battle such as he had never before experienced. His knowledge of narcotics served him well. He knew the dread, fiery substance that was seeping through his body. He understood, too, the frantic desire to kill. The narcotic which had been injected in him was some preparation of hashish.[33] What was more, he knew that the effects of the drug were augmented by hypnotic suggestion that at that very moment battled to enslave his mind.

The soft-spoken man at his side immediately became as noxious as a serpent. "X" understood the honey in his voice. For the man at his side was an expert of hypnotic suggestion.

Agent "X" feverishly marshaled his superb mental control to prevent himself from falling beneath the insidious charm of the dreaded assassin's drug. A cold chill trickled along his spine. For if he permitted both the drug and the hypnotic suggestion to take effect, he would have the desire to kill, would take the keenest pleasure in plunging his knife into the lovely body of Betty Dale.

---

33 AUTHOR'S NOTE: *Perhaps the most insidious of ancient drugs that he has encountered, Agent "X" informs me, is this hashish, sometimes known as "the assassin's drug." A preparation of Indian hemp, it is used in a number of forms by such fanatical murder-sects as the Thugs and Dacoits. It brings about subjugation of the mind and lowers the morale of its users. The subject of hashish and its evil use has hardly been touched by Occidental scientists.*

CHAPTER XI

THE MURDER HOAX

IT WAS CLOSE to midnight when the car stopped at the rear entrance of the apartment where Betty Dale lived.

"Number One thinks of everything," the soft-voiced man explained. "That the custodian should be dead drunk tonight is not a coincidence."

They got out of the car and one of the men unlocked the door with a key that had probably been obtained from the drunken janitor. The hall was deserted, and they had no difficulty in entering the automatic elevator, and mounting to the third floor.

In front of Betty's door, the trio stopped. The man who was known as Number Three listened a moment at the door. "There's a typewriter going inside. The noise of it will mask the sound of our entrance." He fitted another key into the lock, twisted it slowly, and flung open the door. An automatic sprouted from the fist of Number Three.

Agent "X," bathed in cold sweat, weakened by the terrific mental battle he was still waging, went unsteadily into the room.

Betty Dale sprang up from her desk. Her face blanched. She smothered a scream with the back of her hand, and retreated slowly step by step as the three sinister figures approached. "X's" iron will alone forced him to spring ahead of his companions. He was like a wolf eager for the kill. With the two gang members at his back, he brandished his drawn knife in such a manner as to draw a letter "X" in the air.

The glimmer of recognition in Betty's eyes would have been noticeable to only Secret Agent "X." His long left arm flung out, strong fingers seizing her shoulder, dragging her to him, smothering her scream against his chest. Betty kicked mercilessly at his ankles, pounded his back with small fists.

The knife in the Secret Agent's hand darted upwards. The terror at that instant in Betty Dale's eyes was involuntary. Yet it cut Agent "X" to the quick, unnerved him so that he dropped the knife as soon as the deed was done. The blood-colored dye, gushing apparently from the soft flesh of her throat, was almost too realistic. Still he held her tightly, teeth grimly clenched over his lips lest he open his mouth and cry out a word of encouragement.

Her struggle had abated somewhat. She was playing her part like a veteran actress. "X" snapped a look over his shoulder. The two waxen-faced witnesses were standing back near the door. They could not possibly have detected "X's" movement as he drew out the small hypodermic needle which he had prepared. He thrust the fine, sharp point deeply into her shoulder. He pressed the plunger to the limit. This was something that he had not prepared Betty for. Doubt and pain of the needle-thrust battled in her eyes as they raised appealingly to meet his face—a face that was as hideous and inhuman as those of his companions.

That appeal was more than Agent "X" could resist. Beneath the mask, his lips parted. "Courage," he whispered, his voice sounding alarmingly loud behind the hollow of his mask. But it was doubtful if Betty could have heard it even so. The powerful sedative had already taken effect. Her eyes, still open, were glazed. Terror had frozen there as unconsciousness had crept upon her. Her body became limp in his grasp.

He let her fall as gently as possible and still retain a semblance of callousness in the action. She lay on the carpet, a pitiful, huddled form, throat darkly stained in contrast to her pale face. So realistic was the picture, that "X" went cold with horror. He feverishly wondered if he had won the battle with the insidious hashish.

"X" stooped, picked up his knife, and wiped its edge on his handkerchief. With the swaggering air that was characteristic of Pete Tolman, he turned to the silent figures at the door. "That job's done. Neat, too, if I do say so myself."

THE men in the doorway bobbed their heads. Then Number Three advanced to where Betty lay. He gave her body a push with his foot. Wrath that was almost beyond control boiled within Secret Agent "X". Yet he swallowed it and watched with bated breath as the man knelt beside the girl and seized her wrist in his long fingers.

"A good job, Tolman," he commended. "No pulse. Sometime I

would like to make an analysis of the poison you use. It would be an interesting study."

Number Three then took from his pocket something that appeared to be a fountain pen. When he had unscrewed the cap and "X" had a chance to observe the special non-metallic nib, the Secret Agent quickly guessed that this was the instrument used for branding the gang's victims with acid.

"Hey, wait a second," the Agent interrupted. "This is my job, and I'll put all the finishin' on it. Let me do that."

Number Three turned. At the back of the eye cavities of his mask there was a suspicious gleam. "Do what?" he asked softly.

"Why, mark the dame with the good old Seven trade-mark. Ain't that what you're goin' to do?"

Number Three stood up. "You have been in prison for quite a time now. Just how did you know about that?"

"X" knew that in his eagerness to prevent Betty Dale's lovely face from being forever marred by an acid burn in case Number Three's pen should slip beyond the boundaries of the plastic material which "X" hoped would protect her, he had made a false step. "Why," he explained glibly, "didn't I read the papers tonight while waitin' for you fellows to give me the high-sign? There's nothin' much in them except about the Seven Silent Men."

Number Three shrugged. "If you want to do it, I can see no objection. It is of the greatest importance in this case. Secret Agent 'X' must not have the slightest doubt but what this is our work. Only then can we be certain that he has turned his attention to the Seven. Number One hopes that his rage at the assassination of this girl will lead him to fight in the open. Go ahead." He handed the acid pen over to "X" and withdrew towards the door.

"X" knelt beside the still, silent form of Betty Dale. The powerful sedative had simulated death so effectively that the sight unnerved him. "Just what kind of a figure seven do you want?" he asked to hide his hesitancy.

No answer. "X" glanced over his shoulder. Then he stood up slowly, turning towards the door. His two companions had disappeared. He stepped quickly to the door, pulled it open, and looked out into the hall. They were nowhere in sight. This was an unlooked for opportunity. He would have a chance to revive Betty, perhaps. Still, he was extremely puzzled at the actions of the two gang members. Had they discovered that he was an impostor? Surely in such a case they would not have deserted him. It would have been to their advantage to kill him on the spot, silencing him forever.

Still baffled by their untimely retreat, he was about to return to Betty, when his sensitive nostrils caught a vague, pleasant odor—the faintest hint of feminine perfume. He stepped farther along the hall only to learn that the strength of the perfume increased. Perhaps some one who occupied a neighboring apartment had passed along the hall. But surely that would not have occasioned the hasty retreat of the two masked men.

"X" returned to where Betty lay. He drew from his pocket the small case in which he carried his narcotics. He selected the vial containing an antidote for the drug which he had injected. He was in the act of loading the needle when he heard footsteps on the stairs. He paused, held his breath. If the two gang members returned at this critical moment—

HE ran silently across the room, shoved back the blind that covered the front window, and looked out upon the street. Two black cars were drawn up in front of the building. In the light that emanated from the door of the building, he could see that they were cars belonging to the police. Shadowy figures could be seen moving along the sidewalk. The place was rapidly being surrounded.

"X" sprang to the door and twisted the key in the lock. Then back to the unconscious Betty. With haste that did not sacrifice care, he made the injection of the antidote in Betty's arm. Then, to hasten her revival, he followed it with a small dose of adrenalin, which he was in the habit of carrying at all times.

Almost at once, the bloom of life returned to Betty's face. Her eyes met his face and stared bewilderedly. "X" uttered his characteristic whistle very softly. Her lips curved in a tired smile.

"X" lifted Betty to her feet. "We've got to hide," he said. "Something's wrong. This place will be alive with police in a few seconds. Is there anyone in the building whom you can trust implicitly?"

"Trust?" she murmured. Evidently the effects of the drug had not completely worn off. "X" seized her shoulders and gave her a gentle shake. "You've got to help me," he said earnestly. "Surely you've some neighbor who will permit you to remain in hiding until this thing's over. Don't you see? Some one has informed upon the Seven gang—told the police that they had come here to do murder. If it gets out that you are alive, the gang will know that I am an impostor."

Betty nodded understandingly. "On the next floor, there's a

young woman who works as a buyer for one of the stores. She's away nearly all the time. I have the key to her apartment so that I can keep an eye on things. She wouldn't mind—"

"Quickly, then. Get the key!"

Betty turned into her bedroom, and "X" stepped to the door. He pressed his ear to the panel and detected a movement in the hall outside. He drew his gas gun from a hidden inner pocket. With extreme care, he turned the key and eased the door open a crack. By the light of the hall lamp, he saw a slender, smartly dressed blonde woman pacing nervously up and down and muttering something about: "Why don't they hurry! Oh, why don't they hurry!"

"X" pushed the door wide and stepped into the hall. He took a step nearer the blond woman and thrust his gun forward. Then he coughed slightly. The woman turned quickly, the long skirt of her evening gown swirling. At the sight of the immobile, grinning mask that "X" wore, her mouth opened to scream. Instantly the gas gun in Secret Agent "X's" hand hissed like a snake. The woman's scream was suddenly choked by the powerful gas. Her body stiffened and she fell full length on the floor.

But the sound of her fall was enough to hasten the police. Feet were pounding on the stair. The cold, piercing scream of a police whistle sounded. "X" turned. Betty Dale had just come through the door. The key to her friend's apartment was in her hand. The sight of the blond woman stretched out on the floor stopped her.

She would have asked some question had not "X" pressed a warning finger to her lips. Seizing her by the arm, he hurried her across the hall to the elevator. Fortunately, the car was still at the third floor. "X" pushed Betty inside, followed her, and pressed the button.

The elevator mounted, stopping smoothly at the next floor. Together, Agent "X" and Betty hurried across the hall. "X" took the key from Betty's nerveless fingers and unlocked the door. Inside, he turned on the light, closed the door, and made a hasty inspection of the apartment. Satisfied that it was empty, he returned to the girl.

"Keep in hiding until you hear from me," he cautioned her.

"But you—you haven't a chance of getting out of here! The place must be surrounded—"

"Don't worry," he interrupted her cheerfully. He stepped back into the hall and closed the door behind him. On the floor below he could hear the police. They had probably entered Betty's apartment.

Below stairs came a sharp command. "Search the next floor. We've got them cold. They'd have to have wings to get out of here."

"X" sprang into the elevator, slammed the door, and pressed the button for ascending. The car did not move. He pressed again and again. He tried the other buttons on the control panel. The police, he knew, foreseeing that the elevator might be used as a means of escape, had cut the power probably not more than a few seconds after he and Betty had entered the apartment of the department store buyer.

Through the frosted glass window of the elevator door, "X" could see the shadowy forms of men walking around in the hall. He was caught as nicely as a rat in a trap.

CHAPTER XII

ESCAPE

TO STAND THERE helpless in the elevator waiting for the police to find him was an absurdity. "X" knew those efficient, painstaking men from headquarters. He knew they would leave no stone unturned in their search. Furthermore, "X" feared that their search would lead them to the apartment where Betty Dale was hiding. Because the Seven gang must think that Betty had been killed, he knew that it would never do for the police to find her unharmed. There was but one way to prevent the police from looking farther. He must show himself, using the waxen mask he wore as a means of decoying the police from Betty's hiding place. "X" slid the door of the elevator open a crack. Five plainclothes men were standing in the hall questioning a pajama-clad man.

"There's a woman downstairs who's been knocked out cold," a detective sergeant by the name of Mallon was saying. "X" knew that Mallon referred to the blonde woman who had taken a lungfull of the charge from his gas gun. "Did you hear anything?" the sergeant went on, addressing the man in pajamas.

The man shook his head. "I was asleep."

"Riley," Mallon rapped, "you and Jennings block off the fire-escape. Jones, Henniger, and I will finish up on this floor."

From the crack in the elevator door, "X" saw two of the detectives turn down the hall towards the fire-escape. Mallon and his two men crossed the hall to the door of the apartment where Betty was hiding. Agent "X" sent the elevator door slamming open. He sprang into the hall, gun in hand. At the sound of the opening of the elevator door, the police turned. But "X" fired first. His gas gun was effective at even a distance of twenty feet and there could be no doubt but what at least one of the detectives would succumb to the anesthetizing vapor.

Mallon received the very center of the gas discharge. The automatic in his hand blasted a hurried, ineffectual shot as he spilled forward on his face. One of the other detectives, staggering forward, hampered his companion. "X" gained the stairway. As he sprang up the steps, a detective got in two quick shots. One struck the iron banister of the stairway and buzzed off harmlessly. The other burned across the calf of the Secret Agent's leg.

Gaining the top of the steps, "X" ran straight towards the fire-escape at the back of the hall. He felt certain that any police following him, would think that he had continued to the next floor.

Stepping out on the iron stairway, "X" looked down in the alley below. He could see the two detectives that had been sent to watch the fire-escape. They both looked up as "X" stepped out onto the escape. Imitating the voice of Sergeant Mallon, "X" shouted: "Hold your fire, Jennings. It's Mallon. I'm coming down."

"X" knew that the gloom of the alley would hide him for the time being and he depended upon his skill as a mimic to maintain the illusion that he was Detective Mallon. He ran down the steps, but as he came to the last flight, one of the police turned a flashlight full upon "X's" face, or rather the waxen mask that covered it.

"That's not Mallon!" shouted one of the men. "It's one of the Seven gang!"

But as soon as the light struck his eyes, "X" vaulted over the iron railing of the escape. It was a twelve foot drop. "X" landed squarely on the back of the surprised detective. Together, they rolled over, the dick clawing at his gun with one hand and trying to ward off the blows that "X" was driving into his mid-section.

The other detective, afraid of hitting his companion, dared not fire a shot. He blasted his whistle and jumped into the fight. One man was on top of "X". The Secret Agent got an arm free for a short, savage punch to the detective's jaw. It was a terrific jolt, actually lifting the detective. "X" rolled to one side, picked himself up and at the same time drew his gas gun. He swung around to meet the second detective who was ready with his gun drawn. The crash of the cop's pistol drowned out the spurt of "X's" gas gun. But while the slug whined inches from the Secret Agent's head, the charge of the gas found its mark.

"X" BROKE into a run, zig-zagging in and out of the shadows. Gun hail followed him. Lead flattened against the walls of buildings, ricocheted, snagged wooden telephone posts. Nothing stopped him. Nothing *could* stop him unless at the end of the alley he found the police waiting for him.

As he reached the corner, a moving car pulled up sharply. A powerful searchlight cleaved the darkness of the alley like a scimitar. It blinded "X"; it made him a perfect target for his pursuers. With the car blocking his exit from the alley and the police closing in on him from behind, escape was impossible. Suddenly, the searchlight was turned off. A harsh voice called:

"Get in here, Tolman! Do you want to get chopped down!"

Unmistakable, that voice. It belonged to the leader of the Seven gang. It was Number One himself.

Secret Agent "X" leaped for the open rear door of the car and had hardly landed before the motor picked up speed and the car leaped into the street. Bullets whanged against the steel sides of the car. But the car was as perfectly armored as the trucks which the gang used in delivering its counterfeit money.

Looking through the rear window of the car, "X" saw that an opaque cloud of smoke fumed from the exhaust pipe. The car was spreading a chemical smoke screen that would make pursuit impossible. Then "X" noted that another of the Silent Men shared the back seat with him. There were two more in the front—one of them was certainly the big boss himself.

Number One was driving, for he called over his shoulder, "Did you think we had deserted you, Tolman?"

"Right!" the Agent rapped in the nasal snarl of Pete Tolman. "And a lousy trick it was. Seems as if you'd take more care of a man who's of so much value as I am!"

"Softly, now, Pete," Number One soothed. "I was so anxious for your welfare that I myself chauffeured the car that brought you and the two other brothers to the apartment. Numbers Three and Four tell me you did a good job. It is unfortunate that a woman came so near to ruining your good work. Numbers Three and Four saw a very lovely blonde woman in the hall and nothing would do but what they must follow her!"

Number One was all scorn. "You see, that woman was the wife of Number Four, here. What is more, Number Four has the bad habit of drinking too much and babbling in his sleep. His wife overheard him talking about the plans for tonight's little job. Because she is a mercenary woman, instead of going to the police with her information, she tried to blackmail her husband.

"Imagine! So she tipped off the police in an effort to frighten

Number Four into giving her the money. What is more, she will hold on to her information, that her husband is a member of the Seven group, until she does squeeze the money out of him. Now, what would you do in a case like that, Tolman?"

"Me?" "X" laughed. "Why, I'd finish that! I'd give Number Four the works!"

Number One said softly, "No-no. He is far too valuable a man for that. It is the woman who is to get 'the works' as you put it. And his punishment for not catching her tonight and bringing her to me, is that he must kill her with his own hands. What do you say, Number Four?"

A groan escaped the man at "X's" side. "I—I won't do it," he muttered fiercely.

"Oh, but you will!" Number One insisted. "See what you will gain. The object of your affection is quite another person than your wife. You will be glad to get rid of her, really."

Number Four moodily murmured his assent. "True enough. But after all, to kill my own wife—"

"The alternative," said Number One, "would be exquisite torture at the hands of the bishop. By tomorrow night, you will be perfectly willing to do as I bid you!"

Secret Agent "X" felt the man at his side shudder. He knew that already Number Four had resolved to kill his own wife rather than be a subject to the mysterious tortures of which Number One spoke.

"And," Number One continued, "tonight by special messenger, your wife will receive the amount of money she demands for silence. Tomorrow, she will receive silence itself—eternal silence."

The gang leader had stopped the smoke which had plumed from the car. The motor was idling now, the car barely moving. "X" saw that they were in a run-down section of the city.

"By the way, Tolman," Number One asked, as the car pulled over to the curb, "did you manage to brand the forehead of the girl whom you just killed before the police intervened?"

"Sure, boss," the Agent lied. "It was a good job. But say, are we gettin' out of here?"

Number One laughed. "Wouldn't you like to know!"

"X" suddenly felt a sharp stab of pain in his arm. He turned towards Number Four. The man was about to apply his hypodermic needle to yet another portion of the Secret Agent's body. He knew that they were preparing him to go to the gang headquarters. Or had they discovered his deception? How did he know whether the needle had contained drug or deadly poison?

His senses were already dulling. He had presence of mind to look at his watch this time. It was nearly two A. M. Somewhere, seemingly far distant, Number One was speaking:

"And tomorrow, when Secret Agent 'X' reads in the papers that Betty Dale has been found murdered by the Seven—"

The sound faded. "X's" sight dimmed. But his mind was drumming out the alarming thought, "You are trapped…. You are trapped." For "X" knew that when the morning papers did not speak of the murder of Betty Dale, Number One would know that he had been tricked by Secret Agent "X".

CHAPTER XIII

THE BLACK BOOK

WHEN "X" REGAINED full possession of his senses, he found himself in a small room, bare as a prison cell, and without doors or windows. It was lighted by a frosted electric fixture in the center of the ceiling. He stood up, patted himself all over to make sure that none of his special devices had been taken from him. Evidently, he was trusted by the leader of the gang and had not been searched.

He was about to inspect the room, hoping to ascertain the method of entrance, when a sliding panel opened to admit one of the Seven Silent Men. This man, dressed in the usual dark suit, and wearing the doll-like mask, was marked by a diamond badge fashioned in the form of a figure two.

"Howdy, Number Two," said "X" genially. "I was just wonderin' when somebody was goin' to show up. This box would get on your nerves after a few hours."

"Yeah. Well, there's plenty in this house to drive you nuts," replied Number Two, slurring his syllables in a manner that "X" associated with underworld characters.

"Say, you speak my language," said Agent "X". "You're a top guy."

"Well, in this outfit, Number One's the top guy, and get that in your noggin. He sent me here to get you. You've got to put it down in writing."

"You mean sign a confession in the chief's record book?"

"You get ideas quick," replied Number Two. "And from then on, Tolman, you're in it up to your neck."

"Wait a minute," said "X" peevishly, "How come everybody in this joint knows me and I don't know anybody except by their number? How come they haven't even opened up as to where this shack is?"

He had raised the knife for a killing thrust just as "X" sprang into the room.

"Don't be so curious," growled Number Two as he led "X" through the door. "You'll get a number soon enough. As far as knowin' where this dump is, you know as much about that as I do. Nobody but One, Three, Four, and Seven knows just where it is. Oh, The Bishop, he knows, but he's screwy. Five guys out of a gang that's got more members than you can count, ain't many. I get drugged the same as you when I'm brought into headquarters. But we better get hikin'. Number One don't care about being kept waiting."

They were walking down a narrow corridor, arched and beamed

after the ancient Gothic pattern. With the exception of the cell in which "X" had been held, the entire house seemed to be of incredible age. And it was as silent as a tomb. Not a murmur penetrated from the outside world.

"Who's this Bishop?" asked the Agent. "This dump gets more like a church every time I get a squint at it. Now you tell me you've even got a Bishop!"

"Church!" an ugly laugh roared from Number Two. "Church of hell, maybe!" Then he added, as though he feared that he might have been overheard by some one who was easily offended: "Oh, they treat you right enough. Pay your money down in good hard cash. It's pretty sweet. Better pay and no more risk than if you was on your own, runnin'—" Number Two checked himself. "The Bishop, now, you'll know him when you meet him. He'd get kicked out of any church just on account of his looks!"

THEY had come to the end of the passage and a door swung open at a touch from Number Two. The room they entered was similar in appointments to the rest of the house. At an antique desk, sat Number One. Standing directly behind his chair was another of the Silent Men—Number Seven. Number Two also remained in the room.

The inscrutable eyes of Number One looked "X" up and down for a moment without speaking. Then he said: "Well, Tolman, how do you like it?"

"Not so hot," the Agent replied promptly. "A lot of dope jabbed in you. You go croak some dame, and where does it get you?"

A low chuckle from Number One. His hand glided across the desk and opened a large drawer. The eyes of Secret Agent "X" followed that hand and saw that the drawer was packed with bills—new, crisp greenbacks of large and small denominations. "This is where it gets you, Tolman," replied Number One. "Come here and help yourself."

"X" hesitated. Either Number One and the Silent Seven were wealthy beyond even the dreams of Midas, or there was some sort of catch connected with it.

"What are you waiting for?" demanded Number One.

A scratchy laugh from the Agent. "Ah, you're puttin' somethin' over on me! Ain't those bills phony?"

"You should know, Tolman," replied Number One. He dug both hands in the drawer and dipped out as much money as he could hold. He tossed bills carelessly across the desk. "X" advanced cautiously and picked up several bills. He looked at them carefully. Without doubt they were genuine. "Gosh, boss, t'anks!" And Agent "X" began cramming money into his pockets.

"Money, you see," Number One exclaimed, "means nothing to me." His powerful fingers closed crushingly on a wad of century notes. "Money in itself is worthless. It is what it will *buy* that is important—men, souls, *power!*" He stood up quickly. "Tolman," he said, "you've proved yourself a man worthy of my organization. You have only to sign the confession that has been drawn up for you, and you are one of us. Follow me."

Number One crossed the room and threw back scarlet portieres, revealing a small closet. In the closet was a writing desk of ancient design and upon it a large record book with an iron cover. The gang leader opened the book. As "X" approached, he noted that all of the page was blank with the exception of a small space at the bottom where the confession to the murder of Betty Dale had been drawn up. Agent "X" guessed that the other confessions had been written in invisible ink to prevent "X" from learning the identity of the other members of the gang. He supposed that his own confession would vanish in the same manner that the others had done.

With seemingly great deliberation, "X" read the confession to the murder of Betty Dale. Actually, his eyes were taking in the closet and its contents. He noted that set in the two walls at either end were two rows of bullseye lenses. Certainly Number One would have provided a means of guarding his book in case some member attempted to destroy it. The lenses along the walls led "X" to believe that some arrangement of the electric eye, the photo-electric cell, watched over the book day and night.

He delayed no longer, but picked up the pen on the desk, and signed the name "Pete Tolman" with a flourish.[34]

NUMBER ONE nodded his approval. Then he reached into his pocket and brought out what appeared to be an ordinary penny. He handed it to "X" who examined it carefully.

---

34 *AUTHOR'S NOTE: Before ever attempting the impersonation of any man, Agent "X" is always careful to acquaint himself with every detail of that person's character. He has learned that one of the most important tricks of disguise is to master the handwriting of the man to be impersonated. "X," in my opinion, has a natural penchant for forgery and could have made a fortune at that profession had he turned to crime rather than criminology.*

"It is a convenient way that we leaders of the organization have of recognizing each other when outside the headquarters," explained Number One. "You will observe that a number is punch-stamped on the face of the coin—the number six, in your case. This badge may be carried in the pocket without arousing suspicion. Naturally, we cannot wear these diamond-studded badges, such as I have on my lapel, out in the street."

"I getcha," said "X."

"As I have no further use for you at present, you will be conducted from the headquarters. Your time is your own until tonight at eleven o'clock when you will appear in dinner clothes at the home of Mr. Lynn Falmouth."

"Cheez, boss, do I have to put on a monkey suit?" asked "X" in apparent dismay.

"That is imperative. You would not be admitted otherwise. You will be there for the protection of another member of our group who has a job to perform. In case you're needed, you will be called upon. There will be many people present—quite a number of our own organization as well as several of our hirelings. And I warn you to be on the lookout for Secret Agent "X." If he has any suspicions as to the identity of any member of our group, this party may attract him."

"Will you be at this blow-out, boss?" asked "X."

Number One drew himself up proudly. "If I were to go to that party, not even Agent "X" himself would recognize me. You must not attempt to learn my true identity. Only two persons in the world know who I am!"

Number One returned to his desk and pressed a button. Evidently, the room was perfectly sound-proof, for "X" heard neither bell nor buzzer.

"Later," Number One went on, "you may be called upon to obtain the plates for the printing of five and ten dollar bills which were hidden by Joseph Fronberg. At present, we have all the counterfeit money necessary for immediate needs. Rest assured that a few hours from now, this city will be mine—police and all officials will be under my thumb. Those who serve me well will be rewarded. For those who fail me, there is justice and execution as the law demands—or the *Bishop!*"

"X" noted that at the mention of the Bishop, Number Seven, who had been all the time standing behind the leader's chair, shuddered slightly. Who was the Bishop that men trembled at the name?

But "X" was given no time to reflect on the identity of this mysterious being. The man who was designated as Number Four entered the office, and "X" knew that he would be doped with the strange drug that deadened his body while his brain remained alive. He had only time enough to look at his watch before the dreaded needle was thrust into his arm. It was seven o'clock, and he supposed it was morning.

CHAPTER XIV

"CALLING SECRET AGENT 'X'"

WHEN AGENT "X" again regained the use of his eyes, he found himself wandering aimlessly outside his own apartment. He looked dazedly up and down the street. There was no sign of the lame begger who had followed him on the previous occasion.

He entered the building and took an elevator to his own apartment. He wanted to think. His problem, instead of slowly unraveling, was becoming more tangled every hour. So far, he had been completely successful in only one thing—Number One had been entirely fooled by "X's" impersonation of Pete Tolman. But that triumph, he knew, would not be long lasting.

He spent the rest of the day in ascertaining the extent of the deadly virus of discontent that the Seven gang had spread throughout the city. There had been numberless riot calls. Business had been tied up. Panic was impending in Wall Street. Nothing could be done to dam the flow of spurious currency, save close the doors of every bank and business house which distributed large quantities of money. The city was teeming with federal men, all busy in sorting real money from counterfeit. The populace was enraged. Nearly half the money in the working man's pocket was found to be spurious.

Turning on his radio for a few minutes, "X" was surprised to hear a familiar voice coming from a local radio station. It was the voice of gray-haired Abel Corin:

"Calling Secret Agent 'X,' the People of New York calling Secret Agent 'X.'"

With a puzzled frown on his face, Secret Agent "X" listened to every word that Corin uttered.

"Secret Agent 'X' if you are within the sound of my voice, know that my fiancée, Alice Neves, has been kidnaped by the Seven Silent Men. If you have a spark of human feeling about you, move heaven and earth to return her to me. This is much more than a personal appeal. I am speaking for thousands who are suffering at the hands of these ruthless criminals. Sven Gerlak, the noted detective, has advised me to call on you. He adds his appeal to mine. You can help us if you will!"

And there Corin's message ended.

IT was eleven-forty when Secret Agent "X," still in the guise of Pete Tolman, drove his car beneath the porte-cochère and crossed the veranda of the stately old Falmouth mansion. He had been careful to add the red wig and mustache that had been given him at the Seven headquarters.

For all he knew, the Seven headquarters might be located in the dark and lofty turrets of Falmouth House itself. In the lower stories of the house there was certainly nothing sinister. All was gayety, scintillating lights, rhythmic music. The dignity of the old walls was occasionally mocked by shrieks of drunken laughter. Even before Agent "X" entered the door he knew that glasses had clinked far too often.

A butler whose stiff attitude would have put a clothes-prop to shame, took the Secret Agent's hat and coat.

"Good evening, Mr. Six," the butler whispered.

"Cheez, you, too!" the Agent exclaimed. The butler put a warning finger to his lips. Lynn Falmouth was approaching, crossing the reception hall on somewhat unsteady legs. His too yellow hair was faultlessly brushed, his tie a knot of perfection. Nevertheless, "X" believed that unless his host slowed down on his liquor schedule, he would be unable to wish his guests good night.

An ugly scowl spread across Falmouth's brow as he approached. He turned toward the butler.

"Nothing wrong, sir, I hope?" the butler asked with the deepest concern in his voice.

"This person—" Falmouth gestured indefinitely towards "X"— "I've never seen him before!"

"No, sir? But you invited him, Mr. Falmouth. This is Mr. Church, the author."

Falmouth's pale hand partially suppressed a drunken guffaw. He staggered over to "X" and pawed the latter's shirt front. "Sho shorry, old man. Should have guessed by the fit of your clothes. Author's privilege—wearing mussy clothes. Shtill can't remember of meeting a Mr. Church, but whatever Lewish says tonight goes. Come on, old fellow." And taking "X" by the arm, he led him into the next room where dance music swayed thirty couples across a polished floor.

Falmouth beckoned to a servant who was bearing a tray of tall, chill drinks. Falmouth offered Agent "X" a glass. "Have one with me," he invited cordially.

Agent "X" accepted a glass. He had avoided speaking to his host because he had not been able to decide whether he should attempt to sustain the character of Church, the author, which had so suddenly been thrust upon him, or whether to retain the role of Pete Tolman. If Falmouth or anyone at the party happened to be a member of the Seven gang, then "X" dared not speak in any other manner than that of Pete Tolman.

He decided that Falmouth, at least, was too drunk to notice much difference. As he clinked glasses with Falmouth, he said, "Sure, t'anks," in the nasal twang that was an exact imitation of Tolman's voice. He thought for a moment that he detected a flash of suspicion in Falmouth's cool blue eyes. Was Falmouth's drunkenness merely clever acting? At any rate, he was very much relieved when Falmouth said, "I've got to leave now, old man. Musht see that everybody has a nishe time. But I'm putting you in good hands." Falmouth's liquor-cracked voice raised in a boisterous halloo: "Oh, Genevieve!"

A tall, strikingly beautiful blonde woman broke away from a circle of admirers and came smiling towards Falmouth.

"Genevieve—" Falmouth stumbled over the name—"want you to take care of Mr. What's-his-name, here. Mister—mister, this is Genevieve—Genevieve—"

"Genevieve Leads," prompted the blonde woman.

Secret Agent "X" muttered some sort of an acknowledgment. Actually, he had trouble speaking at all. For the tall blonde woman was the same whom he had seen in the hall outside Betty Dale's apartment. It was she who had tipped off the police. It was she who had tried to blackmail her husband on information that he had inadvertently dropped concerning the Seven Silent Men.

"X" UNDERSTOOD now how the Seven gang obtained its powerful drugs. Milo Leads, this woman's husband, was one of the greatest toxicologists in the country. It was Milo Leads who drugged the gang members before they were taken from the Seven headquarters. It was Leads who had engineered the escape of "X" from the deathhouse. Milo Leads was Number Four in the gang.

For a longer time than he realized, Agent "X" had stared at this amazingly beautiful Genevieve Leads. With a provocative smile on her lips, she suggested that they dance.

"Sure, er, Miss, er Genevieve," the Agent stammered. He took the lovely creature in his arms, and dancing with the clumsy, familiar embrace that he thought best fitted his identity as Pete Tolman, he steered her towards the center of the floor.

Genevieve Leads was enduring him, nothing more, so well did Secret Agent "X" play his part. The farce continued for another chorus before "X" danced his partner towards French doors opening on a softly lighted conservatory.

"How'd ja like to sit the rest of this out with me, baby—I mean, lady?" he asked.

Determinedly, she disengaged herself from his arms. "I think not. I think Mr. Falmouth is looking for me—" Her voice tapered off evenly as her eyes compassed the dance floor in search of Lynn Falmouth.

Secret Agent "X" permitted his hand to slip down the length of her bare, white arm. His fingers locked tightly over her wrist. Mrs. Leads fixed him with a frigid look. "Please, Mr.—"

"Church is the name, but most everybody calls me Bill."

"I don't think I care," replied Genevieve Leads. But her austere glance seemed to have no effect upon "X." He drew her closer to him, holding her with his strange, magnetic eyes. "Chee, kid, you can't give me the air like that!" He thrust his head forward in a pugnacious attitude so that his lips were only a few inches from her ear. His lips scarcely moved, but his whisper was clearly audible to the woman.

"Mrs. Leads, I must talk to you. You are in deadly danger!"

The abrupt change of his voice, the power of persuasion in his tone, seemed so utterly out of place with the underworld character whom he impersonated, that Genevieve was astonished. For a moment, she could not speak. Then:

"Did you say something, Mr. Church?"

A dancing couple swung near to where they were standing. "X" was surprised to see that the man was short, red-haired Sven Gerlak, the Milwaukee detective. Gerlak's small eyes darted from "X" to Mrs. Leads. "X" raised his voice to imitate Tolman's.

"Sure I said somethin'. You and me is goin' out in this greenhouse." And "X" jerked his head towards the conservatory. He fairly dragged Mrs. Leads through the door.

With his arm tightly locked through hers, Agent "X" swaggered through the room. Here flowers and ferns of varieties found in tropic countries blossomed and grew for the delight of Lynn Falmouth and his guests. "X" lighted a thick, black cigar and puffed out a huge mouthful of smoke. "Some dump, I'd say," he commented.

"You like it?" Obviously, she understood that he was but making conversation for the benefit of a couple who occupied a small divan that had been placed in a shadowy corner.

"X" led Mrs. Leads to a similar divan at one end of the room. They sat down. His powerful fingers closed gently, impersonally upon the woman's hand. His right arm went about her shoulders. It was his purpose to deceive anyone at the opposite end of the conservatory into thinking that he had engaged Genevieve Leads in amorous conversation.

"Mrs. Leads," the Agent whispered in a deadly seriousness that his presuming smile did not betray, "you must leave this house at once. Take my advice and go at once to the nearest police station. Get in touch with Inspector Burks and tell him everything you know about your husband and the Seven Silent Men."

A frown of perplexity crossed the woman's forehead. "Who are you? A detective?"

"That is beside the point. If you remain here you will most certainly be killed—and by your husband's own hands. He has his orders to kill you. He dare not disobey."

MRS. LEADS uttered a laugh that was harsh and altogether out of tune with one so attractive. "My husband? Do you think he would dare lay hands on me in this house?"

"How do you know that you are not in the headquarters of the Seven gang right now? Do you know who the leader of the gang is?"

She was very serious, and "X" knew that she was speaking the truth when she said: "I do not. Certainly, the leader isn't Milo Leads! He couldn't be the head of anything except some rotten laboratory!" There was venom in her words, and Agent "X" guessed that her marriage to Milo Leads had been anything but a happy one. Leads was noted for his ability to get into scandalous difficulties with other women.

"You will heed my warning if I tell you that there is more than one member of the Seven gang here tonight?" Agent "X" urged. "Why even the butler is in their employ." His voice suddenly mounted. His alert eyes had caught sight of a man moving behind the wall of ferns at the side of them. "Chee, baby, you're a swell looker!" he said in the voice of Pete Tolman.

The man suddenly stepped out from behind the ferns. He was tall and undeniably handsome. Yet there was craft in his eyes that glittered darkly against his olive skin.

The dark man flashed a smile, bowed low, and addressed Mrs. Leads. "Ah, the charming *Senora* Leads!"

Mrs. Leads stood up quickly. As "X" glimpsed her smile, he knew that she was already captivated by the continental manner of the man.

"Count Camocho!" she exclaimed. "Where have you been all evening? You have not been hiding from me?"

"*Si, senora.* I have been hiding lest your beauty turn this poor brain of mine. Ah, but I could resist no longer." The man who had been addressed as Count Camocho turned politely to the Agent. "I have not yet had the pleasure of meeting you."

Mechanically, "X" took the hand of the Spaniard. The feel of those soft fingers sent a sensation of revulsion over "X." For Camocho was a crook of international reputation.

"I am sorry to intrude, *senor*," said the count, "but I believe Senora Leads has already promised this next dance to me."

Dance? Would it be a dance of death? Was Camocho merely making an excuse to get Mrs. Leads away to some dark corner where Milo Leads, Silent Man Number Four, waited to kill her?

"X" placed himself directly between the woman and the count. He thrust out his jaw and seized Camocho roughly by the coat sleeve. "She don't want to dance with you!" Agent "X's" hand started towards the pocket where he kept his gas gun. If he could get Camocho out of the way, he would take Mrs. Leads from the house if he had to carry her.

"Don't go for that gun, Pete Tolman, or I'll drill you!"

THE command in a voice that was as soft and cold as snow came from directly behind "X." He turned slowly to face Lynn Falmouth—Falmouth, whose every symptom of drunkenness had disappeared, whose chilly eyes narrowed over the bead of a revolver.

"X" took a step towards Falmouth. The latter's gun jabbed threateningly forward. "I'm rather a good shot, Tolman," said Falmouth. "And even if I miss you, Inspector Burks who has just entered the room will not."

"Right, Mr. Falmouth!" came unmistakably in Burks' voice.

"X's" eyes compassed the room. As soundlessly as if they had been conjured from the shadows, plainclothes men entered the room. Each carried a gun. "X" was rimmed by deadly, steel eyes that were focused directly upon him. The inspector and his men could not know that they were actually assisting the Seven gang in their plot to kill Mrs. Leads. He could not tell them. For to the police, he was Pete Tolman, a killer many times over, who had escaped from the death-cell of the Louisiana penitentiary.

Inspector Burks stepped forward. He was carrying a pair of handcuffs. "Put out your hands, Tolman," he ordered. "We'll have to hold you in New York until the Louisiana authorities are notified. That red wig of yours and that mustache might have fooled a lot of people, but not Mr. Falmouth. He recognized you from your picture in the paper the minute he set eyes on you."

Secret Agent "X" had no choice in the matter. He thrust out his hands to receive the cuffs. As they nipped Agent "X" and Inspector Burks together, Lynn Falmouth seemed to relax. He smiled his unpleasant, one-sided smile.

"You really couldn't think I'd have let a person of your stamp enter this house unless I had recognized you and planned to trap you." He turned to Genevieve Leads. "Sorry I had to impose this fellow's company on you, Genevieve, but I thought if anyone could distract his attention while the police were getting here, you could. Count Camocho, Mrs. Leads looks a little tired. No doubt this has been something of a shock to her. If you will take her into the next room—"

"*Si, Senor* Falmouth. I shall be delighted." And offering Mrs. Leads his arm in a courtly manner, Count Camocho led her from the room. "X" knew that she was walking to certain death, yet he was powerless to stop her. Had he told the police what he expected to happen, they would have laughed. For he was Pete Tolman, a clever killer who would try any trick to gain his freedom.

CHAPTER XV

THE THIRD PENNY

SECRET AGENT "X" had been carefully searched by Burks' men. He was firmly linked to the wrist of the inspector by means of the handcuffs. Yet as he was led from the Falmouth home, he felt that he was not entirely helpless in spite of the police guns that were leveled at him. In his free left hand, he had palmed a small, round object that was hard as a marble. He had slipped the little ball out of his pocket at the very moment that Inspector Burks was putting the bracelet on his right wrist.

That hard little marble was made of compressed paper pulp, hollow inside, and heavily loaded with compressed magnesium powder. Protruding from its surface was a stubby little fuse. As he approached the police car, Agent "X" was still puffing on the cigar he had lighted in the conservatory. In spite of the fact that he had been frisked, Agent "X" was prepared to surprise the police. The only thing that prevented his trying for an escape at that moment was Inspector Burks.

As far as Burks knew, this man whom he supposed to be Pete Tolman was firmly welded to his wrist. Nevertheless, the cautious inspector kept his eyes constantly upon his prisoner. But "X" knew that his time would come. It would be extremely awkward for Burks when it came time to enter the police car. It would be impossible for him to watch his prisoner then.

They stopped at the side of the police car. The driver was already at the wheel. A second car behind the first was already being loaded with men. One of the detectives entered the rear seat of the car in which "X" was to be taken down to headquarters. There remained room enough for Burks and "X" in the back seat. Behind Agent "X" was another detective, but the Secret Agent knew that the gun in this man's hand would be as useless as if it had never been loaded. This detective who brought up the rear would not dare to fire into the car for fear of hitting one of his companions.

As Burks stepped into the car, dragging "X" after him, the Secret Agent moved like lightning. His left hand came up towards his cigar. At the same time, the joints of his right hand compressed to such an extent that he jerked free from the bracelet.[35]

Before the inspector could realize that his man was free, there came a deafening, stunning explosion. The car was swallowed in blinding, silver light. And when Burks recovered from the shock, both doors of the car were open and his prisoner had disappeared.

The Secret Agent's movements were simpler than they seemed. He had touched the short fuse of the magnesium bomb to the glowing tip of his cigar. He had dropped the little bomb on the floor of the car at the same time that he pulled free from the handcuff. Before the explosion came, he had marked the exact location of the latch of the opposite door, and in that moment when the police were stunned and blinded, he had opened the door and dived out the other side of the car. The magnesium bomb was comparatively harmless, though as was afterwards apparent, the explosion had singed the inspector's eyebrows.

As Agent "X" zigzagged across the lawn, darting in and out of the shadows cast by the numerous clumps of shrubbery, a tracer of slugs followed him from the second police car. But he was far out of range and running like a rabbit.

He doubled back towards the house with a twofold purpose in view. The house where Falmouth had betrayed him to the police was probably the last place where the police would expect to find him. Then, he hoped that he was still in time to save Mrs. Leads.

Crawling along behind the foundation planting of the old house, "X" came upon a wooden trellis upon which a stout, well-rooted ivy vine climbed up the wall of the house. Far across the lawn, he could hear the police beating through shrubbery. He must act quickly before they closed in on the house. Without further hesitation, he dug his fingers into strong, bare tendrils of the ivy vine and crawled up.

---

35 AUTHOR'S NOTE: I once persuaded Secret Agent "X" to demonstrate this escape trick which he explained he had learned from a Hindu fakir whom he had met during his travels. It consists simply of muscular expansion of the wrist at the time the hand-cuff is put into place and muscular contraction when it is desired to remove the cuffs. This is followed by an extremely difficult compression of the joints of the hand in order to permit the cuffs to drop off. It is necessary for Agent "X" to practice this feat daily in order for him to be certain of accomplishing it in case of emergency.

He knew that his ascent was dangerous. The vines in winter were dry and treacherously brittle. However, he gained the second story window without mishap. The casement was unlocked, and though the room beyond was lighted, it was also empty. He swung back the window and climbed over the sill. Passing the lighted window, he knew that he was in comparative safety.

HE crossed to the door, opened it cautiously, and peered out into the hall. Below stairs, dance music had been uninterrupted. Noisy laughter echoed throughout the house. Evidently, the gayety of the party was picking up. "X" stepped into the hall and started down its winding length. He had not proceeded more than half a dozen steps before he heard the sound of a door opening directly ahead of him.

Two men came stealthily down the hall. "X" sprang back into a darkened doorway. Looking around the corner of his hiding place, "X" immediately recognized one of the men as Milo Leads. The famed toxicologist was wearing evening clothes. His face was extremely pale and gaunt. And walking beside Leads was a broad-faced Japanese, also in evening clothes. The Japanese, however, did not continue towards Agent "X" as did Leads. Without a word to the toxicologist, he turned off into a small dressing room.

"X" watched Leads. Did he look like a man going to commit murder or like a man who had recently committed murder? If he had not yet killed his wife, then "X" knew that he probably would never have the opportunity.

Quickly knotting a handkerchief over the lower portion of his face, "X" sprang into the hall directly in the path of Milo Leads. And as he leaped, his right fist drove out. The blow landed with full force just behind the toxicologist's ear. Leads hadn't a chance even to groan. His long legs sagged under him and he collapsed on the floor.

Agent "X" sprang up the hall in the direction from which Leads had come. He glimpsed the Japanese in the small dressing room putting on his coat. Evidently, the wide-faced yellow man was going to leave the party. Ahead of him, "X" saw a pin-point of light coming through a keyhole in the door at the end of the hall. "X" ran for the door, knelt, and looked through the keyhole. He could see some one moving about the room—a man whose rotund body was strangely familiar to "X."

As though some sixth sense had warned him, the man in the

room glanced apprehensively over his shoulder straight at the door where Secret Agent "X" watched. Then the man walked across the room to a door in the opposite wall, opened it quickly, and disappeared beyond.

Agent "X" stood upright. A puzzled frown knotted his brow. For the round little man that he had seen within the room was none other than Sven Gerlak, Milwaukee's ace private detective.

"X" seized the doorknob, gave it a twist, opened the door and stepped into the room! Involuntarily, a gasp of horror escaped his lips. For lying in the center of the room, her evening gown torn as though she had engaged in a desperate struggle, was the body of Genevieve Leads. Her face was swollen and blue-black. Her mouth gaped hideously. The marks of fingers that had killed were on her white throat, and the brand of Seven was on her forehead.

On the other side of the body, "X" saw something that he pounced upon and examined closely. It appeared to be nothing more than a penny. But punch-stamped upon its surface was the number three. It was the badge of one of the Seven. "X" pocketed the penny. His own penny insignia had gone with the wallet the police had taken from him when he had been searched. Probably this penny had been dropped by one of the gang when the murder had been committed.

"X" was about to leave when he heard the sound of voices in the room adjoining. He crossed to the door and pressed his ear to the panel. He recognized the voice of Count Camocho talking in whispers to some one. He could not distinguish the words. But when the second man spoke, "X" immediately recognized the voice as that of the underworld character he had met in the Seven headquarters—the man who had worn the diamond insignia of Number Two.

"It's a hell of a note, count," Number Two was saying. "I've seen the dame alive. Number One thought it was funny that there was no report of her death in the papers. Then I seen her at the window just above the apartment where she's supposed to live. The chief is plenty sore! He's detailed me and the doc, and you, too, to light out after Tolman. He think's Tolman's crossed him. He's goin' to take up the dame himself. Then the doc went and lost his penny so he's got no chance of gettin' back into headquarters. I tell you, if some of us don't get a taste of the Bishop before ten hours go by, it'll be a surprise to me!"

The two members of the gang were directly outside the door now, and "X" heard the count's reply: "The doctor might have dropped his badge in this room when they were struggling with *Senora* Leads. Let us search, my frien'."

"X" waited for no more. The count's hand was already on the doorknob. "X" sprang across the room, hurdled the body of the murdered woman, and got through the door into the hall. The Agent's heart was pounding like a triphammer, for he knew that the "dame" to whom Number Two had referred could be none other than Betty Dale. Then his deception had been discovered. He was being hunted by the Seven Silent Men.

CHAPTER XVI

A CLUE

"X" WENT INTO the room at the opposite end of the hall through which he had entered the house. He closed the door behind him and stepped over to a mirror. He took the handkerchief from his face and examined his make-up critically. Removing the red wig and mustache, he looked exactly like Pete Tolman. Lack of time permitted only slight alterations—the reshaping of his nose and smoothing out lines in his cheeks.

Then he turned once again to the window and climbed out on the ivy trellis. The breaking of a dried ivy tendril hastened his descent. He picked himself up from the bushes, waited a moment to see if the noise of his fall had warned anyone inside the house. But the noise within would have drowned out any disturbance that "X" had created.

He ran across the lawn to the circular drive where his car had been parked. He leaped in, started it, and turned directly across the lawn in order to avoid the slow procedure of backing and wheel twisting in order to get out of the line of parked cars.

As he sped through the gate into the street, several policemen tried to stop him. Shots from their pistols struck his tires, but had no effect upon his speed. For beneath the fabric of his special tires was a ply of woven chain armor. "X" knew well that the police would give chase, but he had a long lead on them even before they were started, and the terrific power of his car widened the breach between them every time he opened the throttle on a straightaway.

Soon he was lost in the traffic of theatre-goers returning to their homes. He made further provision against being halted by touching a concealed lever beneath the dashboard. This lever operated strands of piano wire which flipped his license plates over. On the reverse side of these plates, a new set of numbers was deceptively painted.

A short time later he pulled up in front of the apartment building where Betty Dale lived—where he hoped she *still* lived. He leaped from the car and bounded into the entrance. He sprang to the elevator and pressed the fourth-floor button. Out into the hall, he hurried to the door of the apartment that Betty Dale had appropriated. He did not wait to knock; but using one of his chromium master keys, which he had taken from his car, he opened the door.

The searching eye of his flashlight swept the room. It was completely empty. He opened the bedroom. The bedclothes had been disturbed. Dainty lingerie was scattered about the room. He turned to the kitchenette. It, too, was empty. Betty Dale was gone.

But with all the keen disappointment that knifed the Secret Agent, there was one ray of hope: had the Seven gang killed Betty in the apartment, they would have left her body there. Perhaps she was still alive. Perhaps they were holding her, hoping to draw Agent "X" into a trap.

"X" turned into the hall and whisked down to the street floor in the elevator. Across the entry way and out into the street he went. He was walking towards his car when someone hailed him with:

"Oh, Mr. Robbins!"

"X" PIVOTED and saw a familiar figure coming towards him— old Thaddeus Penny, a blind man who peddled packages of chewing gum in the streets.[36] Though it was nearly two A. M. old Thaddeus still carried his tray with a few packages still remaining. He was walking as fast as he could towards the Secret Agent.

"Sorry, I haven't time to talk with you, Thaddeus," said "X" kindly, as he put his hand on the handle of the car door.

But the blind man's hand fastened tenaciously on "X's" coat sleeve. "I know you're a detective now, Mr. Robbins," the man piped in a thin, quavering voice. "What were you doing comin' out the Falmouth Building after two o'clock yesterday morning? Nobody but detectives, criminals, and these good for nothin' playboys are out at such indecent hours."

"I wasn't coming out of the Falmouth Building at that time, Thaddeus," replied "X." "What makes you think I was?" He was

---

36 AUTHOR'S NOTE: *The reader may remember Thaddeus Penny who appeared in "The Case of the Waiting Death." On that occasion Thaddeus gave "X" some information of inestimable value. Thaddeus knows "X" only by the name of Mr. Robbins, an identity which he assumed when he once befriended the old blind man.*

extremely interested in the old blind man's deductions.

"Oh, don't try to fool me, Mr. Robbins. I'd know your step anywhere. I was out tryin' to get a few pennies from the theatre folk and I heard you come out of the Falmouth Building just as I was passing. I'd have hailed you except that there was two other men with you and I thought—"

Agent "X" gripped the old man's hand. "You're sure of that, Thaddeus? Positive?"

"Sure and positive. Say, your voice sounds tight, like maybe you was in some sort of trouble."

"Right, Thaddeus!" the Agent rapped. He pressed a crumpled five-dollar bill into the old man's hand. "You've helped more than you'll ever know!" And Secret Agent "X" leaped into his car. The blind man's super-sensitive ears never failed to identify "X" by his walk. If, then, as Thaddeus Penny had said, he had come out of the Falmouth Building, he had done so when he was under the influence of the Seven gang's powerful drug. It was possible that the headquarters of the gang was somewhere in the mighty Falmouth Tower, in the very heart of the city.

Secret Agent "X" headed for his apartment hideout. Motor open, he drove skillfully and at the same time planned a schedule of preparation that he hoped would cover every possible emergency. At his apartment, he changed his make-up and assumed one of his stock disguises, that of Roger Cole, a middle-aged business man. He thought that this disguise would be less apt to attract suspicion than any other when he was prowling around the Falmouth Building.

Many important business enterprises were controlled from the Falmouth Tower. Business men came and went at all hours of the night. The coat of the suit he put on had many secret pockets, and these he loaded down with special devices that he thought would prove helpful. Among them were a small galvanometer for detecting the presence of electrical current, a cubical black box with a dimension of about two inches, a small make-up kit, gas gun, and a case of special drugs. Beneath his coat he carried the waxen mask which had been given him at the headquarters of the Seven Silent Men.

Thus prepared, he left at once for the Falmouth Tower.

Five minutes later he was standing within the shadow of the mighty structure, that was like a steel gimlet boring through the sky. Lights burned in many of its thousand windows. Flood lamps, advantageously placed, gilded its gleaming metal trim, and touched what seemed to be from the sidewalk a tiny cupola at its top. Actually, this cupola was a magnificent penthouse.

Sales corporations, life-insurance companies, brokerage offices, offices of almost endless variety could be found in the building. Where, though, in this modern structure of steel, stone, and chromium would he find an ancient, oak-paneled room such as he had seen at Seven headquarters?

Far above the last gleaming light, was a belt of darkened windows that encircled the building. "X" smiled grimly.

Entering the building, "X" stepped to one of the elevators. The elevator boy stared at him sleepily and enquired, "What floor, please?"

"Straight to the top," replied Agent "X." And the car speeded on its seemingly endless climb.

WHEN the car came to a stop and the door was opened, "X" looked out upon a row of frosted glass windows of offices—some without any lettering on them, indicating that they had never been rented.

"Is this as far up as you go? Isn't there anything higher?" "X" enquired.

The boy scowled. "Sure, Mister, but you don't want an elevator. You want an airplane or one of those stratosphere things. Are you gettin' out or do you plan to move in here permanent?"

"X" fixed the boy with his peculiarly magnetic eyes. "Think," he said softly; "is this the top of the building?"

The youth flushed. "There's another floor and a penthouse yet, but it's never been finished. It won't be either. Take it from me, this building will never pay," he said importantly. "Not a lot of these offices are rented and there's not enough to pay them to finish the top of the thing. But I can't stay here all night, mister."

"Any way of getting up to the unfinished part?" "X" persisted in spite of the youth's impatience to be gone.

"Nope. You can't leave the unfinished part of a building open. It would be dangerous. Curious guys—" with a marked look at the Secret Agent—"would try to get up there and fall through most likely. If I was you, I'd go to the Alps!"

"X" stepped out into the hall. Few of the offices showed signs of occupancy. He couldn't search them all without arousing suspicion. He was inclined to believe that the floor above was a longer way towards being finished than the elevator boy had said. However, he did find a narrow hall at the end that because of its labyrinthian turns warranted special investigation. Guided by his flashlight, he came upon a door lettered with the one word "Private."

The Secret Agent took one of his master keys from his pocket, inserted it in the lock, and opened the door. Immediately his heart leaped with renewed hope. For directly behind the innocent-looking office door was a second panel of solid steel. It presented an unbroken surface apparently without keyhole or lock. However, a moment's search revealed a small, circular indentation at the lower part of the steel panel at one end. "X" knelt and examined it closely. It looked as though a penny had been pressed into the steel while the panel was yet in the molten stage.

Every outline of the one cent piece was clearly visible with the exception of the fact that a peculiar design was embossed in the exact center of the surface. Providing himself with his pocket magnifying glass, "X" saw that the design was composed of the Arabic numerals one, three, four, and seven—each laid directly on top of the other.

Instantly "X" remembered what he had overheard in Falmouth's house. He had heard the underworld character known as Number Two say to Count Camocho: "The doc has lost his penny and can't get back into Seven headquarters."

The purpose of the indentation was then clear to "X." It was some sort of an electrical lock that opened when a penny was pressed into it. However, only a penny with the numbers one, three, four, or seven could have been placed in the opening because of the design in the center.

Agent "X" quickly removed the waxen mask from beneath his coat and fastened it over his face. Then he took the penny-badge bearing the number three from his pocket and fitted it into the little circular indentation. His heart was thumping with excitement as he pushed it home. Without a doubt he had passed through that door before, but then in a drugged state and in the company of one or more of Number One's trusties.

As soon as he had pushed the penny into the lock, a spring snapped. The coin jumped back into his hand, but the steel panel was slowly sliding back into the wall. Beyond, a pale blue light illuminated a room about eight by ten feet in size. Without hesitation, "X" stepped in.

CHAPTER XVII

THE ENEMY'S CAMP

SO SMOOTHLY, SO silently that no one but a man of "X's" unusually accute senses could have noticed it, the little room began to rise. It was then, as "X" had guessed, an electric elevator. On stopping, the door slid open with the same silence. "X" stepped into a barren room and a steel panel, similar to the one which he had just succeeded in opening, closed upon the elevator.

Sliding doors directly in front of Agent "X" opened, revealing a short hall. Around the bend of the hall, moving with a shuffling, diagonal step that Agent "X" immediately recognized, came a hideous figure. It was the crippled begger who had spied on "X's" apartment. Bleary eyes glared from beneath the overhanging tangle of his dirty gray hair. If the cause of his limping had come from paralysis, then the same disease had left its mark on his face.

His mouth was twisted to one side in a permanent, bestial snarl. His red tongue gaped between exposed teeth. His cheeks and chin were pitted with loathsome, open sores. The peculiar posture that his crippled limbs imposed upon him caused his powerful arms to dangle in front of him, lending something simian to his appearance. "X" saw that his gait, which could only be described as diagonal, was produced by extending the right leg at an angle and pulling its mate up to meet it.

The hideous monster of a man sidled up to "X." He seized the Agent's arm with a grip which actually brought a wince of pain to "X." "The sign," he mumbled from his crooked mouth.

"X" hesitated. He felt that the cripple's strange eyes were stripping off his mask, discovering him as the spy that he was. He had never been told any sign in particular used by the Seven gang. Anyway, he had to take a chance. He took from his pocket the numbered penny and handed it to the cripple. As he did so, he noticed the monster's hands.

The fingers were knotted, big knuckled. Flesh had been eaten away from the fingertips until they were raw-looking and sponge-pitted. No vicious, flesh-corrupting disease had done that to the man's fingers. The fingertips had been eaten by acid—perhaps to prevent any chance of his fingerprints being recognized.

He fumbled the coin back into Secret Agent "X's" hands. "Come, Number Three," he grumbled. He dragged himself around the corner and down the hall. "X" followed closely and noted that the cripple unlocked a second door at the end of the passage by means of a penny exactly the same way as "X" had opened the door of the elevator. However, "X" saw that the face of the cripple's penny was centered with the strange design that combined the numbers one, three, four, and seven.

The room beyond seemed like the lounge of some exclusive club. Perhaps twenty men sprawled in chairs or leaned over card tables. And they were all criminals—men with police records, denizens of the underworld easily recognized by Secret Agent "X" who knew nearly every face in the rogues' gallery. They paid not the slightest attention to "X," but he noted that their glances followed the cripple with surreptitious, timid glances.

Through another door of immense thickness, the noise of the criminals in the lounge was muffled completely. Up a short hall, they turned into the Oak Room with its antique paneling and crackling, open fire.

IN a small office just beyond, "X" saw Number One sitting behind his desk. He neither moved nor spoke. Dim light did not pierce the sunken eye-holes in his mask, and "X" could not discern the slightest sign of life in the man.

"Number Three," announced the cripple in a surly voice.

"I suppose, Number Three," came coldly from Number One, "that you have not brought Tolman with you?"

"No, sir," replied "X" imitating as closely as possible the soft, velvety voice that he remembered as belonging to Number Three.

"If I were a just man," Number One went on quietly, "I should hand you over to the Bishop, here, for a taste of the knout."

"X" looked at the hideous cripple. This creature, then, was the Bishop. The cripple's bleared eyes burned as if he anticipated, with pleasure, beating Number Three with the knout.

"However, present circumstances make it necessary for me to have every available man ready for instant service in case the populace does not respond to our present methods of persuasion. The revolt I have so carefully nurtured—" Number One stopped, uttered a sharp command: "Bishop, are you still here? Go! I must talk to Dr. Kousha in private!"

Dr. Kousha! Then Number One took Agent "X" for Dr. Kousha. Well did "X" remember the name. Kousha, a Japanese professor of psychology whose plottings in his own country against the military party had caused him to flee from the island empire. So Kousha had found his way to America. Probably, he was the broadfaced Japanese whom "X" had seen with Milo Leads not more than an hour ago.

How eagerly Number One must have snapped up Kousha for membership in his criminal council. For Kousha was a man entirely without scruples, a brilliant scholar, and a skilled hypnotist. It was easy for "X" to see how weak characters might have been enmeshed in the sinister web of the Seven gang by means of Milo Leads' drugs and Kousha's diabolical hypnotism.

When the door had closed behind the Bishop, Number One asked: "Just what would you propose be done in order to ferret out this Secret Agent 'X' and prevent him from hindering our progress?"

"X" answered promptly: "I would broadcast by radio, communicate with Agent 'X' and tell him that you have Betty Dale here at headquarters. That would most certainly draw him from his hiding place."

After a moment's silence, Number One replied: "I heard Corin's appeal to 'X' over the radio. I wonder if he succeeded in putting 'X' on the job? But even Secret Agent 'X' could not find our headquarters. We dare not tell him that Betty Dale is here and further inform him where our headquarters is."

"Then, I should arrange to have Secret Agent 'X' meet several of our men," the Agent suggested. "He should give himself up as a prisoner in exchange for the freedom of Betty Dale."

"I shall think it over," replied Number One. "Having the girl in our power is the first step towards the removal of 'X.' We might use our own transmitter—" His voice tapered off in a mumbled soliloquy.

Certain now that Betty Dale had been taken by the Seven gang and was yet alive, Agent "X" inched towards Number One's chair. He was well armed and he felt certain that he could overcome

Number One. Under the threat of death, he might be able to make the gang chief tell where Betty Dale was held prisoner.

BUT the very simplicity of what he was about to attempt put "X" on his guard. Surely Number One had some insidious, hidden weapon, some powerful defense to hold his lieutenants in check. For Number One must live in daily fear of his life. His payment for servitude was lavish, but he was a cruel master. He must have made enemies among his own men.

Four feet only separated "X" from the criminal chief. Still, Number One had not moved. Somewhere, a gong rang out. "X" wondered if Number One had sensed danger and was signaling for help. A crackling noise sounded somewhere as though an electrical circuit was being switched on or off. "X's" right hand sought the pocket where he carried his gas gun. He knew that he was taking desperate chances, but it was now or never. He leaped towards the silent, motionless figure. His left hand shot out, seizing Number One by the throat. His right brought the gun up to the gang leader's head.

"X" was about to speak, to demand the instant release of Betty Dale. Suddenly, he realized that the throat of Number One was as cold as death and that it was hard and unyielding. Nor had the gang chief made a single move to defend himself against "X." The man-thing in the chair with whom "X" had been talking was nothing more than a dummy, weighing all told not more than fifty pounds.

"X" sprang back. No wonder he had been permitted to speak to Number One alone. Somewhere in the building or perhaps miles away, Number One had spoken to "X" by means of a telephone and loudspeaker system. Probably the equipment was concealed in the dummy itself.

"Number One," said "X" softly, "do you hear me, Number One?"

There was no reply. Evidently the circuit had been switched off. Perhaps the gong that "X" had heard had been a signal to call Number One's attentions to some matter that required immediate attention. "X" was alone in Number One's office, and in the little closet at one side of the room was the iron-bound book of records that could spell doom for the Seven Silent Men.

"X" approached the little closet cautiously and pushed back the curtains. The book lay exactly as it had been when "X" had signed the name of Pete Tolman to the confession of the murder of Betty Dale. It seemed but a simple task to reach out and touch the book. But "X" knew that certain death lurked in that closet. It was a man-trap constructed so as to protect the record book of the gang. "X" guessed that invisible infra-red light rays passed between the bullseye lenses at either end of the closet.

He knew that the slightest interruption of those rays, by even passing his finger across their path, would break an electrical circuit. He could only guess at the result. Probably some deadly weapon was hidden behind the walls of the closet.

But Secret Agent "X" was prepared for the occasion. He took from his pocket the small galvanometer for detecting electrical circuits. He moved it slowly around the inner frame of the doorway, watching the needle of the instrument. Suddenly, the needle dipped, telling him that beneath the wooden door frame ran a wire carrying current.

Moving the galvanometer slowly in the vicinity of the spot where the needle had first dipped, "X" determined that a wire led from the closet under the polished wood flooring and straight toward the gang leader's desk. In this way, he discovered that the wire led up the inside of the leg on Number One's desk, struck a small, brass ash tray and doubled back the way it had come.

Upon examining the ash tray, he learned that the glass lining rested on a delicate spring. The slightest weight, such as the butt of a cigarette, laid on the ash tray would operate the switch that broke the electrical circuit. "X" set his galvanometer down on the ash tray, thus breaking the circuit that operated the electric eyes which guarded the iron book.

Then he hurried back to the closet and opened the record book. He leafed through pages cluttered with figures that represented the huge financial strength of the gang. Then he came upon the page of confessions. Except for the heading "Confessions" written in black ink, and the lines that allotted seven divisions of the page where the gang members had signed, the page was blank. "X" knew that invisible ink had been used as a further protection. The confessions could easily be brought out by treating the page with heat or chemicals.

"X" was not interested in reading those confessions. They were for the police and the law courts. For "X" had learned the identity of most of the gang leaders and had even gone so far as to deduce the name of Number One himself. He simply ripped the sheet from the book, rolled it into a neat cylinder, and enclosed it tightly in a small, black cubical box which he had brought for that special purpose.

Putting the box in his pocket, "X" returned to the desk and closed the circuit that guarded the closet. He had no more than returned the small galvanometer to his pocket, when a man entered the room. He wore the waxen mask of the Seven gang leaders and until he spoke was indistinguishable from any of the others. Then "X" recognized the voice of Count Camocho.

"Good news, my frien'!" cried the count. "We have been successful in the capture of Secret Agent 'X'!"

CHAPTER XVIII

THE TORTURE TEST

"**X**" **IMMEDIATELY ADOPTED** the soft voice of Dr. Kousha. "No! How was it possible?"

"He was found by Number Two and myself," declared Camocho proudly. "We were about to give up in despair and return here, when we saw the man who looks like Pete Tolman standing in the window of a downtown office—the office, curiously enough, of the Hobart Agency. We went up to the office to find that this Agent 'X' who tricked us into believing he was Tolman, was with another man. Number Two strong-armed the other man. I drugged Tolman and brought him to where Number Four was waiting for us, since Number Four knows where this headquarters is."

"I see," said "X" thoughtfully. He knew that the man who had been in the office with Tolman was Jim Hobart. "And I suppose," he said to the count, "that Number Four drugged you and Number Two in order to bring you here."

"Of course—of course," said the count impatiently.

"But what makes you think Tolman is Secret Agent 'X'?"

The count shrugged. "Number One says that he is. If he were not, why would he have taken the trouble to merely pretend to kill Betty Dale? My one mistake in getting this Tolman was that I didn't get a chance to kill the man who was with him in the office. You see, the noise of our struggle had attracted so much attention already that we had all we could do to bring Tolman here without being caught.

"But you need not say anything about this to—" Camocho stopped. He was looking beyond "X" at the dummy that was seated behind the desk. "Sometimes," the count said shakily, "that dummy deceives me. It would not do to let Number One know that we could not kill the man who was with Tolman!" Camocho waved towards the door. "Come, we must not keep Number One waiting. He is making one of his few personal appearances in the Oak Room. There, we will pass judgment on this Tolman or *Senor* 'X' or whatever his name may be."

"X" followed Count Camocho into the Oak Room. There, all of the seven chairs were occupied with the exception of the two that awaited Camocho and himself. Tolman had been strapped into the sixth chair where he sat trembling and darting furtive glances about the room. Tolman's thin ratlike face was as pallid as paper.

Number One nodded at the Agent. "I am sorry our conference was so abruptly terminated, Number Three. I had to hurry here in order to be present when the prisoner was brought in. This man, who to all appearances is Pete Tolman, is none other than Secret Agent 'X.'"

"That's baloney!" screamed Tolman. "It's a frame, that's what!"

"Very clever acting, Agent 'X,'" said Number One to Tolman. "But you are already too well acquainted with our methods to suppose that it will save you. You have learned too much."

"I don't know a damn thing!" shouted Tolman. "All I know is that you fellows got me out of stir and shut me up in a stuffy office that wasn't much better."

NUMBER ONE looked at Agent "X." The latter had taken the chair that awaited him. "What do you say, Number Three?" Number One enquired.

"X" replied, "The man may be telling the truth." For killer though Tolman was, "X" had no desire that he should suffer the tortures which Number One might inflict upon him.

"We shall very soon find out," declared Number One. He turned to Number Seven who occupied the chair at his left. "You may retire," he said. "Tell the Bishop to bring Betty Dale into this room."

Number Seven left the room. For nearly two minutes, the council chamber was as silent as the grave. Then a door opened. All eyes turned towards the door, but none stared as eagerly as Secret Agent "X."

The Bishop entered, his scarred and misshapen hands locked over a rope. Tied by the wrists to the rope, was Betty Dale. A sensation of rage that he could scarcely restrain passed over "X." Her face was the picture of beauty and terror.

Number One spoke, again addressing Tolman: "Do you know this woman?"

Tolman's beady eyes darted towards Betty. "Naw, never seen her before!"

Number One turned to Betty. "Miss Dale, not only did you escape the death which I decided should be yours, but you also escaped the brand of Seven which should have been implanted on your forehead. As a means of persuading Secret Agent 'X' to speak, we are about to remedy the omission of the brand. Acid would have been used formerly, because we find it inconvenient to carry a branding iron with us wherever we go. But seeing that you are alive, I believe that the pain of your flesh burning with a hot iron will have more effect on Secret Agent 'X' than the acid would." He nodded towards the Bishop. "Bring the branding iron!"

Agent "X" sprang to his feet. "Number One," he called sharply, "if this woman must suffer, I beg to be permitted to inflict the torture myself."

Number One regarded "X" suspiciously for a time. "Just what personal enmity do you have against this woman?"

"None whatever," replied the Agent. "But I hope to redeem myself for the gross negligence on my part which permitted Agent 'X' to fool me into believing that Betty Dale was dead. Permit me to be the instrument of her torture."

Number One considered for a moment. "This is somewhat out of keeping with your character, doctor," he said. "But I shall not pry into your affairs. Perhaps you have a personal grievance against Secret Agent 'X.' That is of no concern of mine, in as much as it does not have anything to do with this organization. You have my permission. But remember, the branding iron shall not touch the girl if Agent 'X' should decide to talk."

"Go ahead and fry her, if you want to!" screamed Tolman. "I don't know anything about Agent 'X' or the Seven gang. But—" he added craftily—"I do know somethin' that I'll trade you to get out of this mess. You're not so damned clever as you think."

Ignoring Tolman, Number One turned to the Bishop who had just entered with a red hot iron held in a pair of tongs. "Give the brand to Number Three," he directed.

AGENT "X" stepped over to the Bishop. The monster, who had apparently looked forward to the torture with sadistic delight, yielded the iron to him only after another sharp command from Number One. "X" turned and walked slowly towards Betty, the hot iron outthrust before him. Betty opened her lips as if to scream, but suddenly choked back the cry. For the Secret Agent had drawn in the air an almost imperceptible letter "X."

Agent "X" bent over the girl, holding the iron as close as he dared.

"Wait, Number Three," commanded Number One. He got up from his chair and walked across to Pete Tolman. That moment, when all eyes were fastened upon Number One and Tolman, gave "X" his opportunity. He had noted as soon as the girl had been brought into the room that the plastic material, with which he had insulated Betty's forehead, was still intact. He knew that the material had sufficiently poor conductive qualities to prevent the heat of the iron from reaching her skin.

"Don't be frightened, Betty," he whispered softly as he bent over her. "Keep your eyes closed. Scream at the proper time; then pretend to faint."

Betty nodded her head slightly. "X" saw her fists clenched. She was bravely preparing herself for the ordeal to come.

"Secret Agent 'X,'" said Number One to Tolman, "consider carefully the torture you are about to inflict upon Miss Dale. A word from you will prevent that. I must know how much you have learned about our group, and how much of that information you have turned over to the police. Then, I am extremely curious to know just who you really are."

Tolman laughed madly. "You think I'm nuts enough to go to the police with anything? Every cop's on the lookout for me. You're nuts!"

Number One signaled the Agent. "Proceed with the torture."

Very slowly, "X" brought the glowing iron towards Betty's forehead. She screamed, closed her eyes, and at the instant the hot iron sizzled against the plastic material that covered her forehead, she became limp. "X" could not tell whether her unconsciousness was pretense or not. As he jerked the iron away, the scar of the brand in the plastic material was so realistic that he could not suppress a shudder.

Pete Tolman was unmoved. "Give her the limit, chief," he muttered, "and just see if I give a damn!"

Number One shrugged his shoulders impatiently. "Number Five, take the girl to Number Seven. When she has revived, we will see if the Bishop can get any information out of her. As for this man—" indicating Tolman—"either he has the nerves of iron and the heart of stone, or he is not Agent 'X.' Bishop, you will remove him to the execution chamber. Number Two, Number Three, and Number Four will accompany me. Perhaps on the scaffold, this man will talk!"

The Bishop backed up to the chair in which Tolman was tied. He hoisted chair and man upon his powerful back. Number One led the way through a sliding panel, down a short hall, and into a square, barren room. In the very center of the room, a scaffold had been constructed. The Bishop and Number Four, whom "X" knew to be Milo Leads, untied Tolman's legs and dragged him up the scaffold steps.

Tolman shouted vile epithets and struggled desperately. But he was like a child in the mighty arms of the Bishop. Tolman's legs were rigidly tied. Then he was centered on the trap door. The Bishop busied himself with the rope, while Number One went over to the lever that operated the trap door.

Suddenly, the Bishop seized an instrument not unlike a pair of pointed tongs. He leaped upon the helpless Tolman and thrust the point of the tongs between Tolman's teeth. Held helplessly in the arms of Number Four and Number Two, Tolman could not jerk his head away. "X" understood the purpose of the tongs now. They were pivoted so that the Bishop could slowly force his victim's jaws apart. Tolman's screams echoed and re-echoed about the chamber. The Bishop seemed to relish the torture and would have prolonged it had Number One permitted him to do so.

THEN the Bishop picked up the rope and "X" saw that in place of the noose was a sort of clamp. For a moment, "X" was so astonished by the brutality of the scene that he was unable to speak. He saw the crippled madman thrust the clamp into Tolman's mouth. Tolman's screams were gagged. Slowly, the Bishop tightened the clamp on Tolman's tongue.

"X" knew the fiendish murder method employed by the Seven gang. He knew that in another moment, Number One would open the trap. The force of Tolman's fall would actually tear his tongue from his throat. The result could well be imagined. Even if Tolman withstood the shock, he would slowly bleed to death, would be strangled by his own blood lodging in his throat. Then Tolman's body would be dropped in the street as an appalling example of the fiendish cruelty of the Seven Men; as a graphic symbol of the silence they imposed.

The Secret Agent's sense of humanity overrode his better judgment. Tolman was a killer. The law would have hanged him. But

Secret Agent, "X" could not stand idly by, watching a man hang by his tongue!

"X's" hand crept towards the pocket where his gas gun was kept. He would use it if he had to. But first, one desperate effort to talk Tolman out of such a fate. As the Bishop backed away from Tolman in order to stand clear of the trap, Agent "X" shouted:

"Stop!"

All eyes turned towards him. "X" resumed the soft-spoken manner of Dr. Kousha. "Number One, have you considered how valuable this man may be to us? Do you remember what he said a moment ago about knowing something he would be willing to trade for his life?"

"Sheer bluff," rapped Number One. "He knows nothing. By what authority do you retard the punishment to which I have sentenced this man?"

"X" looked up at the platform of the scaffold. Tolman's agonized eyes stared beseechingly. His tongue was slowly turning black, so tightly had the torturous clamp been screwed.

"I have no authority," said "X" quietly. "But if this man is Pete Tolman then he may know where those five and ten dollar engraving plates, which Fronberg hid, are kept."

"True," said Number One thoughtfully. "But I doubt if it will be necessary to issue more counterfeit money. I have very nearly accomplished my ends. Still—"

The door of the execution chamber was flung open by one of the gang. "X" knew by the diamond studded number on his lapel that he was Count Camocho.

"*Senor!*" cried Camocho, "*Senor* Number One! You have succeed! You have accomplish!" he shouted, in his excitement forgetting to take his usual care in his grammar.

Number One strode across the room and seized Camocho by the shoulders. "What do you mean?"

"I mean that New York is yours! I receive a radiogram stating that a great body of people of all classes are gathering in a parade! They will march the streets. They will shout! They will fight! It is revolution!"

Number One turned, looked enquiringly about the room. Then he fixed the excited Camocho with his eyes. "*Who sent that message?*" he asked with cold emphasis.

"Why—why, Number Three," Camocho stuttered. "Number Three—who is Dr. Kousha!"

CHAPTER XIX

"HE IS 'X'!"

SECRET AGENT "X'S" heart leaped into his throat. Dr. Kousha had been unable to get into the Seven headquarters because he had lost his penny-badge which would have admitted him. But he could still communicate with Number One by radio.

Number One asked: "But where is Number Three at this time?"

"At the counterfeiting headquarters in Jersey. He radioed from there since he was unable to come in person."

Number One turned slowly towards "X." "Take off your mask," he demanded icily.

"Impossible!" shouted the Agent. "Surely the secret of my identity must be kept from some of these men here. Number Five must be mistaken. Perhaps it is some trick." But while he talked, "X" was gauging the distance to the door. His fingers closed upon the gas gun in his pocket. He knew that his life was not worth a penny. But the black box in his pocket was dearer to him than his life. If he could only find a way to get that to the police. It contained evidence that would put an end to the Seven Silent Men for all times to come. Then, there was Betty Dale. What would happen to her?

"Take off that mask!" Number One insisted.

"X" saw that Number Two had come down from the scaffold and was edging towards the door. If that door was closed, he would be hopelessly trapped. From complete immobility, every muscle and sinew in the Agent's well knit body sprang into life.

He hurled himself towards Camocho who barred his way. So fast did he move that the Spaniard had not time to duck the powerful upward swing of "X's" right arm. The blow met Camocho's chin and flattened him to the floor. "X" gained the door just as Number Two snatched an automatic from his pocket. The Agent's gas gun spurted. The powerful anesthetizing gas struck Number Two squarely in the face. He staggered back on his heels. Even before Number Two had struck the floor, "X" was racing down the passage beyond.

But on the instant he gained the Oak Room, a panel slid back. Pouring through the opening, as eager as hounds unleashed, came a score of gangmen—the hard-faced hoods "X" had seen in the lounge on entering the headquarters. Number One had evidently signaled to them and opened the door of the oak room by remote control.

Down the passage came Number One's crisp order: "Take him alive. He is Secret Agent 'X'!"

The criminal mob was upon him. "X" met the first man, seized his out-thrust arm in a jujutsu hold and threw him over his shoulder. Then he plunged into the midst of the mobsters, his arms working like twin windmills. His fists slammed into the noxious faces, cracked jaws, pounded fleshy bodies. Men went down before his pitiless onslaught; yet where one man fell, there were two to take his place.

"X" fought nearer and nearer the fireplace, dragging half the weight of the mob with him. He snaked one arm free from a hood's grip, brought it up to his pocket, and seized the black, cubical box. He had only a split second of freedom, but he used it well. His aim was perfect. He threw the box containing the Seven gang's confessional record straight into the blazing fireplace.

And not a moment too soon. The full weight of the gang was upon him. Blows were telling, exhausting even his superb strength.

He was thinking of Betty Dale now. He *must* save her. The vision of the Bishop's foul hands pawing over her loveliness while he planned some sadistic torture for her, drove "X" to desperation. He fought like one gone mad. His fearful blows wrecked one man after another. Again, he got his hand into his pocket, this time to clutch the penny which would open the doors of the headquarters. Now, if he could slip one of those tear gas bombs from his pocket, he might gain a moment in which to rush from the room, a single minute in which to find Betty.

Something came hurtling through the air. Before he had time to duck, the missile struck Agent "X" on the forehead. The waxen mask he wore was shattered to fragments. His brain swirled, his eyes swam in red mist. But on the instant that he fell, he had presence of mind enough to put that all-important penny in his mouth. His tongue clamped down on it hard, holding it flat against his teeth. Oblivion caught up with him.

A PLEASANT sensation brought Agent "X" to his senses. Soft, cool fingers were gently stroking his hands. At first, he was under the impression that he had been thrown into the same room with Betty Dale. He opened his eyes. His head felt swollen, his mind feverish. He looked around a room barren of furnishings and without doors or windows. And he was alone. The hands that had caressed his brow were then but figments of his imagination.

He lay on the floor and for the moment relaxed. Then he drew a deep breath and slowly hauled to his feet. There was a strange, metallic taste in his mouth. He remembered the penny which he had put in his mouth just before he had been knocked out. He returned it to his pocket.

Then Agent "X" made a slow and careful inspection of his little prison. But though his rapping knuckles could detect the position of the sliding door panel, there was no electric lock into which he could fit the penny.

He had been carefully searched. All his weapons had been taken from him. None of the secret compartments in his clothing had remained unexplored—with one exception. "X" dropped to the floor. Unless Number One was more clever than he appeared to be he would not have thought of examining "X's" shoes.

The Secret Agent gripped the heel of his right shoe and quickly unscrewed it. Inside the heel was a compartment where he concealed small objects that had at times been extremely useful to him. His heart gave a bound. The contents of his heel had not been tampered with. The small opening contained a miniature tube of his make-up material, a little vial of his special narcotic and two small, hollow needles.

He took out the vial together with one of the needles. With extreme care, he loaded the needle with enough of the drug to knock a man out and keep him unconscious for some time. Removing a small, leather plug from the toe of his shoe, he inserted the needle in the socket revealed.

If he were to kick some one, plunging the needle into that person's flesh, enough of the drug would be driven into the blood stream to knock a man out in a few seconds. It was a ridiculously small weapon, impotent beside the mighty organization he was up against. Still, it was the only weapon remaining to him. He resolved that it should give a good account of itself.

He had hardly time to replace the heel of his shoe before the door of the cell opened and Number Four, who was Milo Leads, entered. Behind him were four armed gangsters.

"Okey, you!" said one of the men gruffly. "Up on your feet. Do you walk or do we drag you?"

Secret Agent "X" did not utter a word. He stood up, and two of the men seized him by either arm. He might easily have pricked one of them with his doped needle, but now was not the time for his counter attack. Agent "X" knew that if his plan was to succeed he must wait until his efforts would create the greatest surprise.

GUARDED by the four men and followed by Leads, "X" was taken from the cell, down a short hall and into the execution chamber. In the room were Number One and his hideous aide, the Bishop. The crippled man mounted the scaffold steps, his ugly mouth twisting in a grin.

"X" saw that the floor below the scaffold was stained with blood. He knew why his execution had been delayed. Had Pete Tolman been the last victim, or had it been—

"X" dared not think lest his mind suggest that Betty Dale had been the last to mount those scaffold steps.

"Secret Agent 'X'," said Number One, "I had hoped that you would be a more worthy opponent. I regret that our little encounter has to terminate so abruptly and, for you, ignominiously. Your removal is imperative. Therefore, I sentence you to hang—by the tongue!"

Two guards dragged "X" up the scaffold steps. The Bishop centered him on the trapdoor. "X" saw that Number One had walked to the end of the platform supports to where the lever that operated the trap was located. Two gunmen, with automatics drawn, stood at the bottom of the steps. One guard covered "X" with his gun while his companion picked up a piece of rope, preparatory to tying "X's" arms and legs.

At the moment that the man with the rope stooped to tie the Secret Agent's ankles, "X" kicked out with his right foot. The doped needle caught the guard in the calf of the leg. The gunman tumbled back against the legs of the man with the gun.

"X" leaped clear of the trapdoor, evading the clumsy fingers of the Bishop. The two guards at the foot of the stairs fired instantaneously and started up the steps. But Agent "X" swung around, leaped over the railing of the platform for a ten-foot drop that landed him directly upon the shoulders of Number One. Both "X" and the gang chief went sprawling. "X" recovered his feet in a moment, ducked behind a supporting member of the scaffold, seized the lever that operated the trap, and gave it a yank.

The trap sprung. Two men dropped through the opening, arms and legs sprawling as they struck the floor. An automatic, dropped by one of the criminals, slid within six feet of "X." He sprang for it, swept it up not a split second before a shot gouged wood from the piece of scaffolding only inches from his head.

"X" swung out from under the scaffold. A gunman, who had dropped from the steps, raised his automatic. Though he disliked lethal weapons, Agent "X" did not hesitate a moment. He fired two quick shots. The first shot took the gangster in the thigh. The second crashed the lighting fixture in the ceiling. The room was plunged into darkness.

"X" knew well the location of the door. Yet he supposed that all shots would be aimed in that direction. He ran silently on his rubber soled shoes across the room until he encountered the wall. Darkness was splintered with gun flame. Shots crashed, and reverberated throughout the room. "X" waited his chance. The gunmen were shooting at random now, hoping that a chance shot would find its mark.

"X" sprang for the door and swung it open. The sound of the opening door drew fire instantly. As "X" leaped through the opening, slugs screamed about his head. He slammed the door into place, ran the length of the hall, and into the Oak Room.

There he stopped. It would take many valuable seconds to locate the door that led into the lounge. Even so, the lounge would not be where Betty Dale was held prisoner—providing that she was still alive. Two doors beside the one through which he had just passed were open. One, he knew, led to the gang chief's office—a cul de sac, he knew. The other opened on a narrow flight of steps.

Though he did not know what was at the top, "X" chose the stairs. Behind him, he could hear Number One roaring out commands to his men.

AT the top of the steps, "X" ran squarely into one of the Seven who was just coming out of a small room. Unhesitatingly, "X" swung. His gun connected with the man's head directly behind the ear. The man dropped quietly at Agent "X's" feet.

"X" seized the man by the collar and dragged him into the room from whence he had just come. The room was empty, and "X" saw at a moment the purpose for which it was intended. A large bench held the layout of a powerful radio transmitter.

"X" kicked the door shut behind him, knelt beside the man he had just knocked out, and removed the wax mask. Beneath was a face unfamiliar to him. Because of the man's pugnacious aspect and scarred cheek, "X" knew that here was a man who had risen from the underworld to the criminal empire of the Seven Silent Men. Probably he was the raucous-voiced individual who was known as Number Two. Evidently the medical skill of Milo Leads had succeeded in reviving Number Two after "X" had blown the charge from his gas pistol into his face.

"X" dragged the unconscious gang-man to a closet and locked him in it. Then he put on the waxen mask which he had removed from Number Two and sat down at the radio transmitter.

The door of the radio room opened and a waxen face was thrust through the aperture. "Did the *Senor* 'X' or what is he called come up here, Number Two?" asked the man—evidently Count Camocho.

"Nix," growled "X." "Has he given you the slip again?"

Camocho cursed and slammed the door without answering. "X" turned to the controls of the radio. His practiced eyes swept the layout. The transmitter was a flexible outfit capable of covering the police bands as well as the true short waves. Used with a continuous spark gap arrangement, it might well have been the cause of the electrical disturbance which had tied up police radio communication. "X" plugged in a microphone, adjusted dials, and turned switches. He watched the various meters on the panel climb. The transmitter was now adjusted for the particular frequency used by the police radio prowl cars.

Placing the microphone directly in front of him, "X" spoke distinctly and softly: "Calling all cars. Secret Agent 'X' calling all cars. *Listen!* The headquarters of the Seven Silent Men is on the top floor of the Falmouth Tower Building. A secret entrance is provided, leading from the last floor occupied by business offices. This entrance is a door marked 'Private' at the end of a short hall. Move at once!"

Because he was not sure that this particular radio channel was clear, "X" carefully repeated the message three times. Since the radio room, like the rest of the Seven headquarters, was perfectly sound-proof, he had no way of knowing whether or not police squad cars were racing towards the Falmouth Tower. Why should they obey him at all? Agent "X" was thought to be a criminal. He was simply hoping that in their desperation the police would heed.

CHAPTER XX

THE BISHOP

"**X**"**OPENED THE** door cautiously and tiptoed down the stairs. At the bottom of the steps, he paused. The headquarters, which had been the scene of such furious activity only a few moments before, was now filled with a sinister, foreboding hush. "X" was about to step from the stairway into the Oak Room, when the sound of the voice of Number One checked him:

"Leads, we've played a desperate game, you and I. We've played it well. The streets are filled with people, begging for me to take over the city and steer it—straight to hell!" Number One chuckled. "Even the mayor has agreed to resign if I will become city manager and rid the country of the Seven Silent Men. I'm ready to leave this place forever!"

"Are you sure you haven't forgotten something?" asked Leads anxiously.

"Not a thing. Most of the professional gunmen whom we hired have been locked in the execution chamber. It is upon their heads that the blame for all these crimes will rest."

"But when the police swarm over this building, they will—"

"Find death," interrupted Number One. "The building is mined. An electric time fuse is waiting to be started at any moment. Nothing will remain that can possibly give a clue as to who the Silent Men were. Silence has been our golden rule. Now that our work is done, it will guard us so that we may enjoy the fruits of our labors."

"And the girl, Betty Dale?" asked Leads. "What have you done with her?"

Number One laughed. "I have left her here, *as I shall leave you.*"

"What do you—"

A single shot crashed out. Agent "X" leaped from the stairway into the Oak Room. A door had opened and shut behind Number One. A wisp of gun smoke crawled through the dead air over the body of Milo Leads. Leads's face twitched in agonized death writhings.

Had he desired to do so, "X" might have pursued Number One. But his chief concern was for Betty Dale. For all he knew, she might be in the maniacal hands of the Bishop. He sprinted across the Oak Room to the door that led into the passage approaching the execution chamber. A piteous scream lent wings to his feet. He skidded around an abrupt corner and came suddenly upon an open door. Beyond was a small cell and inside was Betty Dale.

The girl was struggling in the arms of the Bishop. The mobster's right hand was clenched over the hilt of a long knife. His left hand held the girl in its merciless grip. He had raised the knife for a killing thrust just as "X" sprang into the room.

The Bishop turned with a snarl, lowered his head, and like a maddened bull rushed upon "X." The Secret Agent side-stepped, avoiding the criminal's knife thrust. He led with his left fist to the Bishop's jaw. The maniac recoiled, shook his head, and rushed again. "X" brought the barrel of his automatic down with terrific force to the Bishop's head. The man's crooked legs melted beneath him. He sank to the floor.

"X" sprang to the support of Betty Dale. She stared for one searching moment up at the wax mask. A little joyful sob burst from her throat. "It's you! I know it's you!"

"X" gathered her in his arms. "Pull yourself together, Betty," said "X" gently. "We've got to get out of here. *You've* got to save the police!"

She raised her head. "I don't understand," she said, blinking back tears of relief. "But whatever you say—"

A strange murmur filled the cell. "X" turned and saw that the crippled man was stirring slightly and muttering. The Bishop's voice grew stronger. "Vait," he whispered. "Don't beat me, Carl. I am your brudder, Joseph; yet you beat me!"

"X" CROSSED quickly to the cripple's side. He saw that the man's eyes were staring vacantly, insanely at the ceiling. "I cannot help it if my mind is no goot," the Bishop whispered. "I do not know vhere I hid der odder plates. I could make more if you had not pour acid on my fingers. My fingers—" the Bishop held his scarred hands above his head and stared at them—"My fingers are no goot now because of acid. You vant to destroy them so the police cannot catch me. Who vould know me now that I am sick and crippled? Better you should have saved for me my hands!"

Betty looked inquiringly at "X." "What does he mean?"

"X" shook his head silently. The Bishop was speaking again. "Carl, my brudder, vhy do you hurt me because I can't remember. All der plates I give you but the vons I forget—"

"X" took Betty's arm. "We haven't any time to waste. Number One is waiting to get this place filled with police. Then he is going to try and blow this building up—if he gets the chance!"

"Then you know who Number One is?" Betty asked as they hurried out into the oak room.

"X" nodded. "He is Carl, the Bishop's brother. And of course the Bishop is the German engraver, Joseph Fronberg—the counterfeiter whom the police think is dead. But we haven't time, Betty!"

"X" hurried her to the sliding door and unlocked it by means of the penny with the number three stamped on it. Soon they were in the secret elevator, speeding downward. When the car came to a stop, "X" pulled off the waxen mask he had been wearing and concealed it under his coat. He opened the door and led Betty out into the hall. Outside the building, a police siren was wailing.

"X" seized the girl by the arm. "Betty, there will be police here in any moment Tell them that the building is about to be blown up. Get them to get the people out of here. Have them send out warnings—"

Agent "X" stopped suddenly. An elevator had just bobbed to the floor level. It was loaded with police. He had no time to talk with them. He sprang towards the stairway and bounded down the steps. Flight after flight he passed until he came to the tenth floor—leased entirely by Abel Corin's firm. He entered the general office where a telephone switchboard girl was just taking her place for the morning's work.

Aside from this girl, the office seemed deserted. She stared, amazed, at the man who ran across the general office towards the sumptuous reception hall that fronted Mr. Corin's office. She called on him to stop, but Secret Agent "X" seemed to have suddenly gone deaf. He charged the door of Corin's private office, smashed it open with a heave with his shoulders, and closed it behind him.

CHAPTER XXI

SECONDS OF DOOM

ABEL CORIN JERKED around from the cabinet before which he had been standing to see the man who had just broken into his office and was now striding across the chessboard patterned floor.

"What is the meaning of this, sir?" the business executive demanded. His eyes dropped to the automatic in the Agent's hand.

"Good morning, Carl," said Secret Agent "X" mockingly.

"What do you mean, sir?" demanded Corin. "You've made a mistake. My name is Abel Corin."

"It is Carl Fronberg," "X" insisted "Carl Fronberg, the man who would turn the city into an underworld empire for his own evil purposes."

Corin laughed. "What fantastic tale is this?"

"The truth. The Bishop told me—the Bishop who is Joseph Fronberg, master of counterfeiting. Diseases warped your brother's mind and body. You destroyed the only means the police had of identifying him—his fingerprints. As far as the police were concerned, Joseph Fronberg was dead. But *you* took the plates which he had made before his sickness. With your head for organization, you built up the greatest counterfeit gang that I have ever run across. I think it more than likely that you were the brains behind the original Fronberg gang instead of your brother, Joseph. No one seems to know where you got your start in business, you know. It might well have been from counterfeiting."

Corin's eyes narrowed. "Who are you?" he asked, softly.

"I think you know," replied the Agent. "You have been trying to get me to face you openly for some time now. Here I am. Curiously enough, with all your juggling of wax masks and numbers in an attempt to conceal your identity, it was the floor of this office which gave you away!"

Corin stared speechlessly at the floor.

"As soon as I heard the name by which you called your crippled brother, I knew who you were," said the Agent. "For the peculiar, diagonal gait of that cripple resembled nothing so much as the movement of a certain playing piece on a chess board. The bishop piece in chess can move diagonally only! Chess suggested that name for your crippled brother. And the very floor of this office screams that you are a chess enthusiast! Carl Fronberg, alias Abel Corin, is also Number One of the Seven Silent Men!"

Corin's eyes were scornful. "And now where are you, Mr. 'X'? Are you any nearer your objective than you were at first? Who would believe your story? Turn me over to the police? Man, in one hour from now *I* shall be the police!" He strode across the room and flung open the front windows. "Do you hear them? Thousands of people keyed to revolt! They are pleading for me to save them!"

Agent "X" could hear well enough. Wind screamed down the canyon between the lofty buildings and sucked up the roar of a thousand throats. The name of Abel Corin was on every lip.

"Do you hear?" shouted Corin, and in his anger his voice slipped to a higher register so that it sounded exactly like the voice of Number One. "They are shouting: 'Let Corin run the city and wipe out counterfeiting!'"

Corin sprang to his desk, seizing it as though he were about to tear it to pieces. His words came quick and sharp like a string of exploding firecrackers. "New York is mine! How New York once laughed at me, Carl Fronberg, an immigrant! It called me 'Dumb-Dutch!'" Corin twisted the name into a venomous snarl. His face was purpling with rage. "I've made New York pay for that name it gave me—Dumb-Dutch! But I changed my name. I trampled on the mob without them knowing it. I've *twisted* and *squeezed* and *pinched* millions from them. And they will pay more and more! In these two fists of mine I'll hold the power to crush the people or watch them grovel. I, Carl Fronberg, once a ridiculed immigrant, shall have the power of an emperor!"

Corin's voice hushed to burlesque seriousness. "Go to the window, Mr. 'X' and shout that Abel Corin is a thief, a murderer. Do you think those morons out there will believe you—you who are hunted like a rat by the police?"

Only then did Secret Agent "X" speak. He nodded his head soberly. "You're absolutely right—about them not believing me. *But,* there is one man they will believe."

"Who?" shouted Corin.

"Abel Corin," replied "X" calmly.

CORIN sneered. "You poor fool! Do you suppose that because they are going to trust me with the managership of this city that my conscience dictates that I should confess my crimes to them?"

Secret Agent "X's" eyes narrowed. "You *have* told them, Abel Corin." The deadly seriousness of his voice made Corin tremble.

"What do you mean?" he gasped.

"X" smiled slowly. "You are afraid, aren't you, Corin? You always were a coward at heart. Your thirst for vengeance, your greed for power, gave you a sort of synthetic courage. Yet always, you were the coward, hiding behind a woman's skirts. You made Alice Neves your dupe. You played upon the sincere affection with which she regarded you, criminal though she may be. Every message that you sent over the radio or wrote on paper was signed with her name—the inverted Seven. The very name of your gang was developed from her name—for Neves becomes Seven when inverted. You made her take risks you would not take. You—"

A sob cut through the Agent's sentence. From the little closet off Corin's office, came a pitiful figure. It was Alice Neves. She wore a man's dark suit of clothes. The diamond insignia, the number seven, was on the lapel of her coat. Her blue black hair was streaming. She walked straight towards Corin, pointing an accusing finger at him. "Is that true, Abel? Is what this man says true?" she asked huskily.

Corin shook his head. "It's absurd!"

"But it's true! You're lying to me. Abel. After I stole, lied and cheated, even *killed* for you." Then Alice Neves moved so quickly that even "X" was not alert enough to stop her. He saw the flash of something that glittered like silver in her hand. He uttered a harsh cry, sprang towards her. But the girl's hand had darted up. The long, thin knife was driven straight into her left breast. She tottered and fell full length behind Corin's desk.

"X" forgot Corin for the moment in his anxiety over the woman. He dropped to his knees, hoping that her self-inflicted wound was only slight But he did not need a moment to determine that her wound would be fatal.

"It is better so!" came Corin's harsh voice.

"X" looked up. A smile of self-satisfaction had spread across his face. "With Alice gone, and Leads gone, and my brother too mad to tell—"

"But you have told!" cried Agent "X." "You and every other one of the Silent Seven committed murder and signed a confession in the record book. The witness who watched you sign your confession must have been Milo Leads, since he was the only man beside the Bishop who knew your true identity. Milo Leads was your right-hand man. If it had not been for Leads' dope and duplicity, you would not have gone far towards your objective.

"From your conversation with Leads, I gathered that you held some threat over his head—something else beside the exposure of the murders he was responsible for. Leads was always in trouble with some woman. He was fundamentally a weak character. When Leads saw the possibility of huge monetary returns, he gladly fell in with your scheme rather than have you expose his true character.

"And remember that inside of an hour, the confessions of every one of your gang will be in the hands of the police."

Corin laughed. "But I destroyed that record book. None could touch it but me because of a battery of machine guns hidden behind the panel of the closet in which it rested. Had anyone else touched the record book, he would have been instantly riddled by bullets!"

"X" NODDED. "I thought of that. I took the trouble to trace out the electrical circuit that operated your machine-gun trap and turn it off before I removed the confessions from the book—"

Corin's face went suddenly from purple to ashy gray. He chewed his lower lip. Then, suddenly, a crafty gleam stole into his eyes. His hand dropped to the desk. One finger poised over a brass ash-tray. He pushed the tray to one side, revealing a black-handled electrical switch. "X" saw that tiny wires ran from it across the desk and to the large cabinet at the other side of the room. The Secret Agent's heart pounded in his throat.

"Now, will you surrender, Mr. 'X'?" asked Corin. "I started a time fuse going just a few minutes before you entered. In this office is enough T.N.T. to blow the entire top off this building. But I have only to touch this switch under my hand, and the time fuse will be cut out of the circuit and the building will be blown to pieces at once! Now, do you surrender?"

"X" knew that Corin was in deadly earnest. The man dared not risk standing trial as the leader of the Seven gang. He preferred sudden death. But "X" knew that if Corin touched that switch and the building was blown to bits, thousands of innocent people might be killed. Not the flicker of an eyelash betrayed the thought that was going through Agent "X's" mind at that moment.

His eyes were steadily fixed on Corin's face. But the automatic in his pocket was nosing straight towards Corin's right arm. He knew that the pain of a bullet in the arm would cause Corin to jerk his hand back—a reflexive action that it would be impossible to resist. He squeezed the trigger of the automatic with extreme care. He could not miss at such a distance.

A sharp, metallic click—nothing more. The automatic was empty. But Corin had heard that click. It startled him. "X" saw the man's finger drop towards the switch.

In those seconds when destruction seemed evident, Agent "X" moved faster than he had ever moved before. He leaped towards the desk. His left hand clawed at Corin's hand. His right fist drove upwards towards Corin's jaw. Corin fell backwards to the floor, dragging switch and wire with him. He was unconscious—but he was lying directly on top of the fatal switch.

For a moment, Agent "X" was too dazed to comprehend what had happened. He stared at Corin, wondering vaguely why the building had not blown up. Had Corin been bluffing? He sprang to the cabinet before which Corin had been standing on "X's" entrance. He opened the door. His eyes lighted upon a perfectly wired bomb large enough to blow up half of the city.

He pivoted, staring at the still form of Alice Neves. Blood crawled from the knife wound in her breast, but there were also little strings of blood trickling down her lips. "X" crossed over to where she lay. Across her mouth, but not touching, were two ends of a wire. "X" followed the wire with his eyes. It led to the switch beneath Corin and over to the cabinet of explosives. He knelt beside the woman, took her hand in his. Her pulse could hardly be detected, but her eyelids flickered back. Her lips moved in a husky, death whisper: "Did—I redeem myself—Mr.—'X'?"

There was a faint smile on her lips even after she was dead. Then Agent "X" knew why the bomb had not exploded. Alice Neves had found the wire leading to the bomb not far from where she had fallen. She had bitten the insulation from the wire, then broken it with her hands.

"X" sighed softly, got to his feet, and went to work. Removing the vial of narcotic from the heel of his shoe, he gave Corin enough to keep him unconscious for several hours. Then he took the waxen mask he had carried beneath his coat, and put it over Corin's face. The police could not fail to recognize Corin as Number One now!

And very quietly Secret Agent "X" left the office.

IT was two hours later. Thermite, that hottest of all substances, had enabled the police to melt through the steel door that guarded the Seven headquarters. Burks and his men had swept the place clean of criminal life, for, as Number One had said, many of the underworld hirelings had been locked in the execution chamber. The body of Milo Leads, together with the tongueless remains of Pete Tolman, were taken to the morgue.

Still marveling at the completeness of the gang's hideout, its electrical devices, and its sound-proof construction, Inspector Burks was suddenly interrupted by the entrance of a young man wearing the uniform of a telegraph messenger.

"Special message for Inspector Burks!" shouted the young man as he crossed the floor of the Oak Room.

"Here!" snapped Burks. He snatched the envelope from the messenger and ripped it open. Enclosed was a neatly typed note. It read:

Dear Burks:

You will find signed confessions to various murders committed by the Seven, in a small, asbestos box in the fireplace of the Oak Room. This should aid you materially in rounding up the gang. The confessions are written in invisible ink. Three of these seven leaders have already paid with their lives. Abel Corin, the actual brains of the mob, will be found in his office. I believe you will find secret telephone lines from Corin's office to the Seven headquarters above.

Most of the stolen currency as well as a large amount of the counterfeit bills will be found in the gang's headquarters. Go to Jersey to find the plates and presses from which the phonies were printed.

Concerning the construction of the Seven headquarters: I have taken some pains to learn that Lynn Falmouth, the owner of the building, rented the unfinished top section to a Mr. Jephard who purposed to turn it into a studio for a local broadcasting company. You will understand the truth of this when you examine the sound-proof construction, the private elevator, the Oak Room which might well be used as a main studio. But Jephard could not find sufficient funds to put the studio into operation. As is actually the case, the place was never really intended for anything else than a headquarters for the gang. Mr. Jephard was simply an agent for Abel Corin.

The pretended kidnaping of Alice Neves, the sponsoring of Sven Gerlak, the holdup of the Suburban National Bank, in which Corin was interested—were all tricks to divert suspicion.

My regards to Lynn Falmouth, who has a flare for amateur criminology as well as an ability to throw whoopee parties—[37]

Thus, whimsically, the message ended. And though there was no signature, Burks knew that the note was from Secret Agent "X." Grim and tight-lipped, Inspector Burks hurried from the Seven headquarters. He was bent on following the messenger who had brought the note. How had the young man known where to reach Burks? Why had he so discreetly withdrawn without waiting for the usual tip?

In the street outside the Falmouth Building, Inspector Burks found his answer. For as he elbowed through the crowd, eyes sharpened for the sight of the messenger's uniform, a strange, eerie whistle, weird yet mingled with a note of mockery, pierced the excited murmur of the crowd.

With an imprecation on his lips, Burks returned to the building. For he knew that that whistle had come from the puckered lips of Secret Agent "X," standing perhaps only a few feet from the inspector and looking for all the world like one of the thousands of people in the street.

---

[37] *AUTHOR'S NOTE: The reader will perceive that there was no mention of Joseph Fronberg in this mysterious message. Such is the quality of Agent "X's" mercy. Recently, on visiting a friend who was ill in a local sanitarium, I met one of the patients—a man who answered Agent "X's" description of the Bishop, Joseph Fronberg. The crippled man was undergoing medical treatment of both mind and body. On inquiry, I learned that the man who paid for this cripple's treatment was the eccentric individual known as Elisha Pond.*

BOOK XVI

THE GOLDEN GHOUL

Secret Agent "X's" far-flung, crime-crushing organization brought him whisperings of a fiend who meted out a death worse than death—a monster who called himself the Ghoul, for this Ghoul made men living prisoners in an amber colored shroud of their own dead flesh. And even Secret Agent "X," the man of a thousand disguises, a thousand surprises, was checkmated when he pried into the Ghoul's palace of pain.

CHAPTER I

FANGS OF DEATH

NIGHT HAD INVADED the city. In the living room of suite 10B in the Hotel Empire a dozen powerful electric globes shed searing-white light. The doors were locked; the shades were drawn. Gilbert Warnow had ordered it so. Night must not enter here.

There was a certain tenseness in the stale, stagnant air that was almost electric. Though Gilbert Warnow napped in a luxurious lounge chair, it was a sleep that brought no rest, that was often broken by nervous leg twitchings. The anxiety of the past three days and nights showed plainly on the deep lines that crossed his gray face. Three police detectives sat wakeful in chairs about the room, and smoked or idled through the pages of magazines.

The muffled sound of a buzzer was like a stab to the frazzled nerves of Gilbert Warnow. He sprang out of his chair, stood stiffly, unblinking eyes darting about the room.

On his feet at the sound of the buzzer, Detective Malvern spread his hands in a gesture that was intended to pacify Mr. Warnow. "Everything's okeh," he said. "Just somebody at the door."

But Warnow was not to be comforted. He whispered inaudible words, his eyes followed the somewhat jumpy movements of Detective Malvern as the latter unlocked the door of the living room and crossed a small foyer. Gilbert Warnow's Chinese valet, Ah-Fang, was about to unlock the hall door when Malvern's ham of a hand swept the Oriental to one side.

"I'm tending to this, chink," Malvern said bruskly. He yanked open the door to confront nothing more formidable that a small, square hat box on the door sill. The box was tagged for Mr. Warnow. The corridor was empty.

Malvern slammed the door and, carrying the box at arm's length, returned to the living room. Ah-Fang, his inscrutable slits of eyes

never leaving the box, followed Malvern soundlessly on slippered feet. An excited clamor arose in the living room as soon as Malvern had entered.

"Get that box out!" Warnow's tight voice snapped. "A bomb—"

Malvern shook his head. "Too light." He regarded the box suspiciously. "You get way back in the corner, Mr. Warnow. We take the risks. That's what we're paid for. Keegan!" he rapped to one of his men. "Cut this cord for me."

But before Keegan could obey, Ah-Fang stepped forward. A gleaming tongue of steel darted from the sleeve of his black silken jacket, and lashed across the cord. Malvern scowled into the broad, yellow face. "What you doin' with that knife, chink?"

Ah-Fang regarded the detective unblinkingly. "Always carry knife for the protection of honorable sir, and own worthless flesh."

Malvern grunted, peeled paper from the box, nipped up the lid and sprang back. Nothing happened. The box seemed to be stuffed

Agent "X" raced on, hard on the heels of the death's head.

with tissue paper. This paper, Malvern gingerly lifted. A curse snarled from his throat. The three detectives and the Chinese, who seemed possessed by insatiable curiosity, pressed around the table and stared into the box.

Resting on a cushion of yellow silk was what appeared to be a life-size mask. It had a hellish, pain-racked appearance—eyelids were sunken yellow veils; cheeks, chin, and nose were the color of amber. A downy mustache fringed the upper lip of a mouth that was distorted by a silent scream.

"What the hell!" gasped Keegan. "Looks like a Halloween false-face."

The lean hand of Ah-Fang darted into the box, explored the surface of the mask to find it hard as stone. His finger grasped the mustache and gave it a vigorous twitch. He raised his eyes to meet Keegan's face. "Humble opinion that this is face, but not false."

"What the devil are you gettin' at, chink?" Malvern grumbled. Then he called: "Come over here, Mr. Warnow. What is this thing?"

Gilbert Warnow approached hesitatingly and peeped over Ah-Fang's shoulder. "Good—God!" he breathed. He struck his eyes with his shaking hand, shutting out the sight. "That—that isn't a mask. That's the *face* of Steven Bainbridge! The Amber Death! That's a warning from the Ghoul. *He* wants me to know how I'll look after—after—" And Gilbert Warnow dropped into a chair.

"Perhaps," Ah-Fang suggested in his odd, crackling voice, "it is an act of wisdom to take backward glance and learn who sent unpleasant box."

MALVERN sprang to the phone, called the hotel desk, and got in touch with a plainclothes man who had been posted in the hotel lobby. He issued brisk orders for the tracing of the package. He clamped the phone in place, turned, with an oath, and snatched the hideous death mask from the hands of the inquisitive Ah-Fang. Malvern turned the gruesome object over. He could see clearly the marks made by the knife that had been used to peel the hard, amber-like flesh from the bone of the skull. With an exclamation of disgust, he dropped the filthy, dead thing back in the box.

"The Amber Death!" he whispered. "That's what got Ivan Trasker and this—this poor devil, Bainbridge. The job of that damned extortionist, the Golden Ghoul!" He twisted around facing Warnow. The wealthy manufacturer was staring at his own twitching fingers. "How much was the Ghoul trying to stick you for, Mr. Warnow?"

"Seventy-five thousand," Warnow muttered mechanically. "And I can't raise it. God help me! The Ghoul doesn't give enough time. This is my second warning. And it's pay up, or be like—like—" He gestured helplessly toward the box.

"Don't take on like that, sir," said Malvern, almost kindly. "Nothing can get in here, not even a mouse—"

"Gilbert Warnow."

Malvern snapped a glance from one to the other of his fellow detectives. "Who said that?" he demanded.

Out of the air that had suddenly become pregnant with disaster, came a voice.

"Gilbert Warnow!" The voice, disembodied, and mere whisper though it was, was compelling. All eyes turned toward a single point of focus—the radio in the corner. But the pilot-lamp behind the radio dial was not turned on.

"Gilbert Warnow." A third time came the voice. "Does life mean so little to you?"

Warnow was standing upright. His fingers clutched at his own throat. His eyes burned with a feverish light. "Good Lord! *The Ghoul!*"

"You have disobeyed the Golden Ghoul, Gilbert Warnow," the voice sighed. "You had instructions *not* to call in the police. Yet I know that there are detectives in your room at this very moment. What madness leads you to believe that you can escape the Ghoul? I am all-powerful. My decree is inexorable. There is no escape. You were offered your life for a price. And you have failed to pay. Bolted doors, latched windows, police! Do you think that *I*, who am invulnerable and invisible, care for the police? Die, then, as Bainbridge died, *and within the hour!*"

A hoarse, fear-maddened voice grated from the throat of Gilbert Warnow. "Ghoul! For the love of heaven, wherever you are, listen to me! I can't pay! Give me more time!" And Warnow's voice rose to a shriek that filled the room with its terrific cadence. "Time, Ghoul, only a little more time!" He dropped into a chair. He pressed moist palms to his throbbing temples.

"I must be going mad! The Ghoul spoke to me—in this room."

Ah-Fang padded across the room to the radio, thrust his arm behind the console, and pulled it out again. "This foreign devil machine voice of Ghoul."

Malvern ignored the Oriental. "You're perfectly safe, Mr. Warnow." His voice lacked conviction. "Ten stories above the street—"

WARNOW blurted out: "I wish to hell you were all rich! Maybe you'd know what it is to be hounded to death .... Get out, all of you! If I'm going to die, I don't want a squad of half-witted police standing about!"

Malvern shook his head. "Sorry. We're here on special orders from Commissioner Foster. We're stayin'. I'm going to call a doctor. Your nerves are shot."

Ah-Fang shuffled toward the door. "Ah-Fang call doctor."

"Ah-Fang'll stay right here!" roared Malvern. "Keegan, get a doctor."

"Please." Warnow stayed the detective. "If you must have a doctor in, get Dr. Luigi on the floor above. He's my friend."

"Okeh," Malvern complied. "Make it Luigi."

Malvern walked over to the radio. "Here, Connelly," he called to the other detective, "take a look at this radio. You know something about them." He pulled out the cabinet from the wall and Connelly ran his hands over the tops of the tubes.

"Must have been the radio. Tubes are warm."

"Was own humble opinion," Ah-Fang volunteered.

Malvern silenced him with a look. "Too darn clever, these Chinese!"

Keegan suddenly opened the door to admit a small, well-knit person with dark skin and polished black hair. He carried a small satchel in his hand. He was followed by a broad-shouldered man with graying hair above an impressively high forehead.

"Luigi!" exclaimed Warnow. "Thank heaven you've come!" He rose weakly to his feet and shook hands with the dark-haired doctor. To the broad-shouldered man, he said: "Hello, Gage. Why're you here?"

The man called Gage smiled pleasantly. "Just dropped in for a chat with the doctor when your call came in. What's the matter with you, man? You look all in."

Warnow wearily shook his head. "No sleep for days. Heard a voice calling me out of empty air—"

Dr. Luigi smiled slightly. "Your nerves are frayed, Warnow. You can't expect to live without sleep." He snapped open his satchel and took out a hypodermic needle. "I am going to give you a little morphine. Then I want you to go to bed and rest."

"Rest! Would you rest when your life hangs by a thread?"

"Yes. I am resting. Relaxing, at any rate."

Warnow's jaw dropped. "Lord! You don't mean—"

The doctor nodded. "I mean I either raise seventy-five thousand dollars, or the Ghoul tries his Amber Death on me." Luigi prepared the hypo with professional dexterity, rolled back Warnow's sleeve, and made the injection.

The broad-shouldered Lionel Gage patted Warnow on the back. "Buck up, old man. I know how you feel. You see," he whispered, "between Wall Street and the Ghoul, I'm pretty well stripped myself."

Warnow would have said something had not Luigi checked him. "Not another word, Warnow. You go to bed. Sleep as long as you can. And remember, the police have tackled racketeers before now. The Ghoul's just a racketeer with a flare for sensation." He got up, and started toward the door. "Come along, Gage. Warnow's got to rest. He'll not get it as long as you are talking Wall Street with him."

Detective Malvern laid a hand on Dr. Luigi's arm. "You mean to tell me the Ghoul has threatened you?"

Luigi nodded with magnificent unconcern. "I'm not worried. You'll get the Ghoul before he gets me."

Having said good night to Warnow, Lionel Gage followed the doctor from the room. Warnow, accompanied by his Chinese valet, started for the bedroom.

"Just a minute, Mr. Warnow." Malvern held up an arresting hand. "I wouldn't go in there alone with that chink if I were you."

"With Ah-Fang? Nonsense!" Warnow regarded his servant affectionately. "Why, I'd trust him above anyone in the city—even you."

MALVERN shook his head doubtfully. "Well, maybe *you* can trust him—" He pushed ahead of Warnow into the bedroom, crossed rapidly to the bathroom and made a careful search. Not content with that, he looked into Warnow's closet. Ah-Fang had led his master to the bed and was in the act of unlacing Warnow's shoes.

Almost hostilely Warnow glared at Malvern. "Please go," he ordered. "I assure you that I'll be perfectly safe with Ah-Fang. I insist!"

Reluctantly, Malvern crossed the room. At the door, he said: "Remember, we'll be right outside." And with a black look at the Chinese, "Get that, chink?"

Ah-Fang bobbed his head and, as the door closed, continued to assist Warnow to undress.

After a moment, Warnow asked: "Have you ever heard of a man called 'X'?"

The Chinese shook his head. "Remarkable small name."

"A remarkable person. Most remarkable. Probably, he's the only man in the world who could save me from the Golden Ghoul."

Ah-Fang looked at his employer. "Where I find this man?"

"I—I don't know." Warnow yawned."Feel sleepy. . . .One never knows where Secret Agent 'X' is. Might be anywhere. Can be anybody." Warnow's eyelids dropped. "I could tell him something that might help. There's a blonde—" Warnow thrust pajama-clad legs beneath satin covers, yawned again. "She doesn't belong here. Seen her somewhere—" Warnow's head sagged. He could scarcely support himself. The drug was rapidly taking hold of him.

"Wait!" the Chinese whispered. "Not sleep—yet. Ah-Fang get water." He left the bedside, hurried into the bathroom, and drew a glass of water. He was on his way back when a series of sounds, coming one on top of the other, nearly caused him to drop the glass. There was a metallic snap, a ripping of silk, and a shrill scream of pain and terror mingled in hideous cacophony.

The yellow man sprang into the room and over to the bed. There, Gilbert Warnow writhed in mortal agony. His hands were tearing at his throat. The pillow, upon which Warnow's head rested, had been ripped wide apart. Down from the pillow flurried into the air. Veins on Warnow's neck were swollen. His eyes protruded. Two needles, mounted like fangs in the steel jaws that had snapped from the pillow, were deeply imbedded in his throat.

A hideous change was slowly, inevitably creeping across Warnow's face. His flesh was becoming as yellow as that of his Chinese servant

The door of the room burst open. Malvern's face was the color of raw dough. "What the hell!" he ripped out. He stamped to the bed and sent the Chinese spinning across the room. He took hold of the jaws of the trap that had been hidden in the pillow and strained them apart. Over his shoulder he shouted frantic orders:

"Get Dr. Luigi! Watch that damned chink. Connelly, call Inspector Burks. Fourth time the Ghoul's struck this week!"

Malvern lifted the trap and stared at it as though he could not believe his own eyes. It looked something like a pair of ice tongs—the long, pointed members so edged that they had cut through the pillow when a central impelling spring had been put to work by a trigger device in the center. Two hypodermic needles were fitted to the points of the tongs, so that when Warnow's head had struck the pillow just above the trigger, the spring had driven the needles up through the pillow and into Warnow's throat.

"The most hellish device I've ever seen!" gasped Malvern. "Whole damned trap sewed right up inside the pillow. Keegan! Don't stand there like an ape. Get the doctor!"

At the phone in the outer room Connelly could be heard calling Inspector Burks. But Keegan seemed unable to obey the order that had been given him. His eyes were riveted on Warnow. "Good Lord!" he whispered. *"Look at his face!"*

CHAPTER II

CORPSE OF THE LIVING

TERROR WAS IN full command of Gilbert Warnow's bedroom. Like a man fascinated by the eyes of a serpent, Detective Malvern bent over the body on the bed. Keegan, too, though his left hand was clamped over the wrist of Ah-Fang, had eyes but for one thing—the face of the man on the bed.

Warnow's face was undergoing a horrible and inexplicable metamorphosis. His face was screwed into a knot of agonized supplication. Facial muscles were fixed as though death already possessed him. His fingers, which had been working convulsively, no longer moved; rather they seemed to be frozen into gnarled, yellow claws.

Blood no longer colored his flesh. His skin at every tick of the clock became a deeper, more transparent yellow. His eyes were immobile beneath hardening eyelids; yet in his eyes life still burned and pupils stared accusingly at Detective Malvern.

Malvern's fingers passed down the dying man's arm, touched a yellow hand, and recoiled involuntarily. "Good God!" came his husky whisper. "His hands are hard as rock! Yet he lives! Here I sent Connelly for Inspector Burks. Told him this was murder—but is it murder? No life outside, but beneath that shell—"

Keegan bent forward eagerly. His right hand brushed Warnow's cheek. Had he been watching his charge, he would have noted a crafty expression stealing over the face of Ah-Fang. The Chinese moved with something approaching the speed of light. His right leg came up in a quick kick to the back of Keegan's knees. Keegan went down in a heap.

The yellow hand of Ah-Fang slipped through his grasp, flattened, and sliced the air in a blow that landed at the base of Detective Malvern's brain. It was a blow that could have killed had it not been checked by the superb muscular control of the yellow man.

Malvern staggered forward. His knees encountered the edge of the bed. He pitched forward across the form of Gilbert Warnow. On his knees, Detective Keegan snatched at his automatic. Two shots lanced through the panel of the bedroom door, which had already closed behind the Chinese.

Through the living room into the hall, like a soundless, moving shadow, raced Ah-Fang. Before he reached the door at the end of the hall, a key was in his hand. In another moment, he was inside the room, and a lock clicked behind him.

To watch the movements of Ah-Fang was to witness a transformation almost as startling as that which had occurred in the bedroom of Gilbert Warnow. No sooner had he entered the room than the shuffling gait of an Oriental changed to lengthy strides that devoured the distance between the door and a small dressing table. Already his thin yellow fingers were doing wonders to his face—raking down his cheeks, tearing off pieces of what appeared to be yellow flesh.

Bits of transparent adhesive that held the eyelids of the man aslant, so as to attain the appearance of a Chinese, were torn away. A glossy black toupee disappeared into a small bag open on the dressing table. A pigment-neutralizing substance was rubbed into his hands, returning them to their natural whiteness.

For a brief interlude, the mirror reflected the man's true face—a smooth, youthful forehead surmounted by brown, wavy hair; eyes that were hypnotic, steely points; lips and chin that were a startling combination of youth and maturity. There was in his entire aspect a certain fearlessness, a deadliness of purpose that marked him as a man far above the average in courage and resourcefulness. It was the real face of the incomparable Secret Agent "X".

EARLY that evening, the real Ah-Fang had been waylaid by a stalwart, rough-looking character who had thrust a peculiarly shaped gun into the Chinese's face. A jet of powerful anesthetizing vapor had shot from that gun.[38] Ah-Fang had slipped into unconsciousness and had been whisked away in a powerful motor car.

For the stalwart man was none other than Secret Agent "X" con-

---

38   *AUTHOR'S NOTE: Followers of the "X" chronicles will recall this gas gun as one of the weapons frequently used by the Agent. His dislike for all lethal weapons led him to perfect this harmless anesthetizing gas. The gas pistol itself has an effective range of about twenty feet. The same gas is enclosed in small bombs which the Agent usually carries in his pocket for emergency use.*

cealed behind another of his masterly disguises. No identity was too difficult for him to assume. His special plastic volatile compound could be molded to resemble the contours of any face. His own formulated pigments, clever toupees, face-plates, and other elements of make-up, had enabled him to create for himself the exact replica of the face of Ah-Fang. And when he had mastered the peculiar speech of the Oriental, he had gone to the suite of Gilbert Warnow—Gilbert Warnow, who awaited death at the hand of the fiendishly clever extortionist known as the Golden Ghoul.[39]

The skilled fingers of Secret Agent "X" produced lightning changes in his face. He dared not lose a second of time in carrying out the daring scheme he had contrived. On turning from the mirror a few minutes later, he had achieved another of his brilliant disguises.

He seemed a heavier man withal, powerfully built and red of face. He had had the audacity to assume the character of Inspector Burks of the Homicide Department, knowing full well that within a short time the real Inspector Burks would enter the Hotel Empire to investigate the living death that had claimed Gilbert Warnow.[40]

Having removed every trace of his make-up materials from the table, "X" opened the door of the room and stepped into the hall. He nearly bumped into Detective Keegan who was striding down the hall, hand on the butt of the gun in his pocket.

"Inspector Burks!" Keegan exploded. "You got here fast enough."

A puzzled expression, neatly counterfeited, crossed the face of the man who appeared to be Inspector Burks. "You called me? What about? I just dropped in to see how Warnow was getting along. What's the matter, man? You look like you'd seen a ghost!"

"I have!" Keegan insisted. "I've seen the Ghoul! Warnow's Chi-

---

39 AUTHOR'S NOTE: *The Secret Agent's ability to assume any type of character, and imitate the voice of any man has enabled him to enter many secret places that would otherwise be denied him. His wealth, knowledge of foreign languages and unequaled ability to defend himself has made him at home in any surrounding. He has many friends among many peoples, and he is the only white man ever to be admitted into that powerful Chinese society know as the Ming Tong. Through Lo Mong Yung, venerable head of the Ming Tong, "X" gains much information not afforded the men who compose the Police Force.*

40 AUTHOR'S NOTE: *It will be remembered that on a previous occasion recorded in the novel entitled THE SPECTRAL STRANGLER, "X" impersonated Inspector Burks. The Agent possesses such a remarkable memory for detail, that once he has mastered an impersonation he can, at a later date, recall each characteristic, facial expression, and voice inflection of that person in case circumstances required him to impersonate that person for a second or third time.*

nese house-boy must be the Ghoul. He was the only one in the room when Warnow was killed. He must—"

"X" seized the detective's arm. "Warnow killed? You stand there and tell me that the Ghoul got into that locked room with my best men laying for him?" He didn't wait for Keegan's answer but sprang down the hall towards the suite occupied by Gilbert Warnow. "X" had chosen the perilous

Dr. Luigi

disguise of Inspector Burks because he wanted to have complete freedom to do as he pleased in Warnow's rooms. There were valuable clues to be collected before members of the police force got a chance at them.

AT the hall door of Warnow's suite, Detective Malvern sat in a chair and held his head. Evidently he had not yet recovered from the effects of the blow "X" had given him. However, he stood up and saluted a little dazedly as "X" brushed past him into the living room. "Stay where you are, Malvern," he ordered. Then crossing to the bedroom door, he twisted the key in the lock.

He turned at once to the radio console through which the voice of the Ghoul had spoken to Warnow. With a tiny pen-flashlight in his hand, he made a hasty inspection of the console. His eyes narrowed as they encountered a small, flat, black package at one end of the cadmium-plated radio chassis. He noted that aerial and ground leads were fastened to the black packet and that feed wires led back to the radio set proper. A small timing device was attached to the power line and evidently could be set to turn the set off and on automatically.

The black packet, "X" guessed, was some new sort of short-wave converter that had been attached to the radio set by some one in the Ghoul's organization who had access to Warnow's room. This would have enabled the Ghoul to speak to Warnow through the medium of one of the hundreds of short-wave transmitters located throughout the city.

"X" was in the act of removing the black converter when he noted, at one end of the chassis, a twisted wire hairpin. A close examination led him to believe that it had been used as an improvised screw driver in making the necessary connections to the converter.

"X" pocketed the converter in a secret pocket located in the lining of his coat.[41] Then he went to the bedroom, unlocked the door and stepped inside.

Beside the bed where lay the stiff, yellow form of Warnow, was Dr. Luigi and Detective Connelly. Without a word, as one awestruck by the appearance of Gilbert Warnow, the Secret Agent approached the bed. Warnow's face retained the same rigid, terrified aspect. His eyes were open, but the eyeballs had also turned the yellow of amber and looked dry and brittle.

"Another yellow corpse!" the Secret Agent exclaimed in perfect imitation of Burks' voice. He stretched out his hand and flicked the yellow cheek with his forefinger. It was like snapping a piece of cold china.

Dr. Luigi regarded "X" with dark, serious eyes. "Not a corpse, Inspector. The damnable part of it is that inside that hard, amber shell of a body beats a living heart! Behind that yellow mask is a living brain! You and I have no conception of the torture through which that living brain is passing. Warnow is entombed alive in his own body! That is what my fellow countryman, Dante, called inferno!"

"Poor devil," the Secret Agent murmured sympathetically.

"And life may go on for hours, even days. There seems to be a sort of stricture in the throat that would prevent him from taking nourishment. Unless he has a better brain than most men, this living death must drive him to madness."

"X" stared at the living corpse a moment longer. Then he said: "Connelly, take Dr. Luigi out of the room. I want to be alone here a moment."

Connelly looked wonderingly at his superior. It was an odd command; but who was he to question the authority of Inspector Burks.

"X's" first action on being left alone with the corpse was to pick up the trap that had been concealed in Warnow's pillow. The movements of "X" were difficult to follow, so rapidly did he work. Time had already ticked along too fast. At any moment, the real Inspector Burks might enter. Inasmuch as there was no possible exit from

---

41 AUTHOR'S NOTE: *In the countless garments that comprise the wardrobe of Secret Agent "X" there are many secret pockets so placed as to enable him to carry many pieces of special equipment. Agent "X," about to set forth on one of his perilous undertakings, might be likened to a stage magician who often appears before his audience with as much as thirty pounds of paraphernalia concealed about his person.*

the bedroom save through the living room, "X" could not hope to escape without encountering the inspector if he came before "X" was through with his investigation.

IT took him but a moment to remove the two hypodermic needles that had been fixed in the jaws of the trap. These he wrapped in a piece of gauze and dropped into a hidden pocket inside his coat. Then he left the room, and locked the door behind him. In the living room were Malvern and Connelly. Dr. Luigi had vanished.

Ah-Fang

"Malvern," rapped the Secret Agent, "anyone come in to see Warnow?"

"Lionel Gage came in for a while with Dr. Luigi," replied Malvern.

"And the servants?"

"Just the hotel chambermaid and that chink who was with Warnow most of the time. The chink gave us the slip. When we get him, we'll learn something. Why, he had every opportunity to plant that trap!"

Malvern was interrupted by a violent crash that emanated from the bedroom where lay the living corpse. "X" and the detective leaped at the same time to collide at the locked door of the bedroom. With Burks' characteristic roar, "X" shouted Malvern out of the way, twisted the key in the lock, and leaped into the room.

The window pane was smashed to bits. "X" saw the legs of a man who was poised on the window sill. He sprang toward the window, fingernails raking the cloth of trouser legs just as the man leaped into space. "X" leaned far over the window ledge in an effort to see the falling body. But there was nothing—nothing ten stories below, except the deserted street.

"Inspector Burks, sir!" shouted Malvern. "Look! It's gone!"

"X" turned. Alert as was his brain, it was impossible for him to comprehend all that had happened in these few minutes. A large canvas sack was on the floor. A seam in the sack was ripped and leaden shot strewed the floor. And on the bed was the impression—*only* the impression—of a human body. The living corpse had vanished.

Suddenly, "X" sensed something that spelled immediate peril for himself. In the living room, two men were talking—Keegan, and a man whose voice was familiar to "X". How familiar! It was the voice of the real Inspector Burks.

As quickly and as silently as a cat, "X" sprang to the door of the bedroom. With a movement so rapid as to be almost imperceptible, he snatched what appeared to be an ordinary automatic from his pocket. He leaped into the room, faced the man whom he was impersonating so artfully. Inspector Burks cursed and stabbed for his gun. But halfway toward the pocket of his coat, his hand stopped. He knew that Agent "X" had the drop on him.

In flawless imitation of Burks' voice, Agent "X" said: "Put up your hands, Secret Agent 'X'!"[42]

---

42 AUTHOR'S NOTE: Though under the secret sanction of a high government official in Washington, the nature of "X's" crime fighting methods, differing radically from those employed by the police, has led Inspector Burks and other police officials to regard "X" as a dangerous criminal. Burks, acquainted with the Agent's ability to impersonate, must have known immediately on confronting this counterpart of himself, that once again he had met Secret Agent "X." It was decidedly to the Agent's advantage, in this instance, to pretend to believe that Burks was Secret Agent "X" in disguise. The element of surprise has been responsible for the success of many offensive and defensive moves of Secret Agent "X."

CHAPTER III

THE TRAP IS BAITED

THE FACE OF Inspector John Burks purpled. For a moment, he could only splutter an intermingling of oaths and incomplete sentences. "You've got the nerve to point that gun at me and tell me I'm not Burks? Malvern, grab that man, if you don't want to be back on the beat in the morning! Keegan! Connelly! Don't stand there like—like—"

"Malvern," commanded "X", and it was baffling to hear an exact echo of Burks' voice coming from the mouth of another, "take that man's gun. He's Secret Agent 'X'. No one else would have the nerve to stand there and tell me that *he* is Inspector Burks."

Of the three detectives, not one made a move toward either of the twin inspectors. They were seeing double, and looked it.

"You're going to stand there and let this rank farce go on while the most dangerous man in New York sticks me up with a gun?" roared Burks. "By heaven, I'll prove I'm Burks! Connelly, you ask that damned impersonator what your first name is. He won't know, and I will!"

"X" realized that he was trapped. He hadn't the faintest idea of what Connelly's first name was. He resorted to sheer bluff. He stepped within inches of the inspector and tilted his gun up at Burks' face. "You drop that gun, Mr. 'X'," he growled, "or I'll feed you lead!"

A smile started spreading across the broad face of John Burks. "Yeah, well you ought to point that gun of yours lower. That gun of *yours*, Mr. 'X', doesn't feed anybody lead!"[43]

---

43 AUTHOR'S NOTE: *Inspector Burks has encountered "X" often enough to know, to his cost, the effects of the Agent's gas gun. However inasmuch as Burks has often charged "X" with murder and believe him accordingly dangerous, he must be credited with considerable courage for this attempt to call the Agent's bluff.*

Burks' gun-hand, that had been dangling at his side still clenched over his weapon, came up fast. "X" knew in an instant that his gas gun would avail him nothing against Burks; for the inspector was holding his breath.

When the shot from Burks' gun came, "X" swayed but inches to one side, turned, as the bullet tore through his coat sleeve, and falling to the floor on his side, fired a full charge of the anesthetizing vapor straight at the trio of wide-mouthed detectives who stood behind him. Instantly Malvern pitched forward. Burks must have thought for a moment that his shot had gone wild and struck Detective Malvern. But he had little time to think or plant a bullet in Secret Agent "X's" body. "X's" legs swung up in a scissors hold that took Burks at the knees.

Burks collapsed, shouting, grasping frantically at the air. "X" squirmed over, sprang to his feet, and streaked through the door. He came very near to knocking over a uniformed hotel chambermaid who had evidently been listening at the door. Though he had only a fleeting glimpse of the girl's face as he flashed down the hall, that face was indelibly stamped on his memory. He had seen her somewhere before, and she had been wearing something quite different from the uniform of a Hotel Empire chambermaid.

But there was not a moment to lose. That charge from his gas gun could not have rendered both Connelly and Keegan unconscious as well as Malvern. Then there would be Burks to reckon with—Burks who was doubly dangerous because previous encounters had left him wise to many of the tricks which "X" resorted to.

DOWN the hall, "X" saw the door of an elevator-car sliding open. Behind the glass door of the cage, he could see a squad of men from police headquarters—print men, photographers, and other specialists who had followed on the heels of Inspector Burks. It was then that "X" conceived an audacious little plan. With the real Inspector Burks almost at his heels, "X" leaped into the elevator in the midst of police officials whose promotion would have been immediate could they have knowingly laid their hands on Secret Agent "X."

"Wrong floor," he panted in the voice of John Burks. "Next floor up. Make this thing move, operator!"

The elevator boy slammed the door, pushed the starting lever. The police plied "X" with excited questions, ignoring entirely the fact that Burks or some other member of their own force was frantically thumbing the elevator signal-bell on the floor below.

As the car shot upwards, "X's" hand drove into the pocket of his coat. His fist came out tightly clenched over something. As the operator opened the door, "X" rapped out an order. "Everyone stay in the car a minute."

The Secret Agent stepped into the hall; but as he did so his right fist shot out, knocking the elevator starting lever to the up position, and at the same time releasing a fragile glass capsule that he held in his hand. As the elevator shot upward, there was scarcely so much as a surprised exclamation from the men within the car. The glass capsule that "X" had smashed on the floor contained enough harmless anesthetizing vapor to render the men unconscious almost instantly. By now, they were probably at the top of the building where the safety device would stop the elevator. And Agent "X" was comparatively free to pursue his course of investigation.

His first task was to get to Dr. Luigi's suite. It was the last place the police would expect to find the man they were hunting. In addition, the suave Italian doctor was an object of intense interest to "X" because of his close association with Gilbert Warnow, and because he was a frequent visitor at the Warnow suite.

Another moment found "X" knocking at the door of the suite of Dr. Luigi. It was located directly above that leased by Gilbert Warnow. It was not Luigi, however, who opened the door. It was the broad-shouldered, gray-headed Lionel Gage.

"Well, Inspector Burks!" Gage puffed the words out with mouthfuls of pipe smoke. He regarded "X" for a moment. "And how is Mr. Warnow making out?"

"Dr. Luigi in?" the Agent inquired, ignoring Gage's question.

Gage shook his mountainous head. "Just stepped out to pick up a friend who was going to discuss a plan—"

"I must see Dr. Luigi," the Secret Agent interrupted. "I'll wait for him here."

Lionel Gage courteously ushered the man whom he supposed to be Burks into the room. When the door had closed, "X" said: "Then Luigi didn't tell you that Warnow had been murdered?"

"Been murd—" Gage's face was blank with astonishment. "Good Lord, no! With your men in the room? It's incredible!"

"X" nodded. "That's the way with the Ghoul. And he's always got by—so far. Strange, though, that Dr. Luigi didn't mention it. Like a medical man. They are habitually reticent."

Scowling, Gage puffed furiously at his pipe. "No doubt but what Warnow's death caused the consternation Luigi exhibited when he returned here. He immediately put on his coat and rushed from the room. I had previously outlined a plan which we hoped would outwit the Ghoul—a rather costly plan, I'm afraid." Gage examined the polished toes of his oxfords.

"Just what was your plan, Mr. Gage?" The Agent inquired.

"I'd rather not divulge it at present," was the reply. "If I did, it might seem that I am attempting to appear heroic. The far-reaching power of this Ghoul infuriates me so that I am tempted to go to any length in an attempt to check him." He took hold of "X's" arm, gripped it, and stared earnestly into "X's" face. "Any length—" his voice dropped to a whisper—"if it costs me my life."

"That is, of course, commendable of you, Gage. And if you are not yet ready to confide in the police, there's no way I can force you to speak. I must urge, however—"

GAGE interrupted with a shake of his mountainous head. "Not yet. I've no doubt that this plan of mine will have publicity soon enough!" A slight shudder passed over his broad shoulders.

Agent "X" glanced about the room. "I suppose that Dr. Luigi, being a medical man, has a private phone?"

Gage nodded. "Right here." He opened the door of a tiny office half filled with a huge desk upon which were two telephones.

"X" nodded his thanks. "I have a call to make." He entered the room and closed the door behind him. He was considerably disappointed at not finding Luigi at home. The doctor's actions had aroused his suspicion. In close contact with Warnow, Luigi might well have had a hand in the crime. With the disappearance of Warnow's body there was no possible way in which to prove that the doctor's hypodermic injection had not been something quite different from morphine. But while the Ghoul's sinister progress remained unchecked, "X" knew that the loss of a single second might be vital.

His chief point of query was not Dr. Luigi, but the girl in the chambermaid's uniform whom he had found listening at the door of Warnow's room. "X" had penetrated her disguise; knew that far from being what she seemed, the girl was a strikingly beautiful blonde known by a number of aliases, one of which was Drew Devon. Famous behind footlights, and in divorce courts, "X" guessed that Drew Devon concealed behind glamour the fact that she was a dangerous woman; that she figured in more serious enterprises than profitable *affaires du coeur*.

It was probably that she was the blonde woman referred to by Gilbert Warnow just before Luigi's drug had caused him to doze off. "X's" best source of information in regard to Drew Devon would be Betty Dale, the lovely girl reporter of the *Herald* who had assisted "X" in so many of his perilous battles against crime.[44]

Though he knew his position to be perilous; though he realized that the Ghoul's forces were working in the hotel itself, and might have managed to tap the telephone wires, he felt that information concerning Drew Devon was too important to neglect even for a short time. Accordingly, he called Betty Dale's apartment.

"Miss Dale?" he enquired in a whisper that could not have been heard outside the little room.

"This is Miss Dale speaking," came a clear, beautiful feminine voice. Yet pleasant as was that voice, a scowl crept across the forehead of Agent "X". Some sixth sense flashed a warning to his brain. Here was a situation that called for all his amazing powers of rapid lucid thinking. There was something—some almost imperceptible inflection in the girl's voice that sent the blood pounding through his arteries. Betty Dale was in danger. For the woman who was speaking to him at that moment was not Betty Dale.

"Who is speaking, please?" came the feminine voice that so artfully impersonated Betty.

"Impossible to talk now," replied the Agent "Will call you in ten minutes." He forked the receiver and flung from the room. Gage, seated in a chair and puffing at his pipe, turned as "X" entered the room. "Can't wait any longer for Luigi," explained "X" hastily, and hurried into the hall.

On the floor below, he could hear Burks' thunderous voice as he evidently attempted to locate the runaway elevator and its unconscious cargo. If Burks stayed on the floor below, there was yet a thin chance of "X" getting clear of the hotel. He thumbed the elevator signal button and, as the car came to a stop, sprang inside. "Basement garage, and no stops!" he rasped out.

STANDING as far back in the cage as possible, "X" saw the irate Inspector Burks standing directly in front of the door of the eleva-

---

44 AUTHOR'S NOTE: *Followers of the amazing exploits of Secret Agent "X" doubtless recognize in Betty Dale the name of an old friend. Her character, her beauty, as well as the sincere affection that Betty Dale has for "X" have been sources of inspiration to Secret Agent "X" throughout his career as a public defender.*

tor shaft. But evidently the elevator boy was too impressed by the importance of his passenger to take any note of what was going on outside the rapidly descending car.

From the elevator, "X" stepped into the garage. He entered the lavatory and, with a master key which he took from his pocket, locked the door behind him. Never had he moved faster than he did in the next few minutes. Spurred on by the danger which threatened Betty Dale, his fingers fairly flew as he opened a compact make-up kit which he always carried. How the Ghoul had learned of his association with Betty he did not know. But master criminal that the Ghoul was he would naturally try to find his chief opponent's most vulnerable spot and such investigation must have led to Betty.

When he had concluded his makeup job, Agent "X" appeared the very picture of a timid, inoffensive young man. His name, the one under which he had engaged his hideout in the Hotel Empire, was Roscoe Jennings. In another moment he had obtained his car from the hotel garage and was on his way.

As "X" turned into the street, he noted a gleaming touring car in front of the hotel. Two men were alighting—one of them the sleek-haired Dr. Luigi, and the other a swarthy, beetle-browed man known in the empire of finance as Daniel Calvert. Oddly enough, "X" thought, he had last seen Calvert's ugly face on the front page of a sensational tabloid, figuring in a story involving a good deal of scandal and the blonde charmer, Drew Devon.

Ten minutes of fast driving, and "X" was at the door of Betty Dale's apartment. But a moment was required for him to select the correct master key from the collection he always carried. Stealthily, he fitted the key in the lock, opened the door, entered, and closed the door behind him.

A woman started up from in front of a small telephone desk, and regarded "X" with wide, violet eyes. She was tall, statuesque, and garbed in a becoming dark suit. A wealth of platinum blonde hair was arranged in soft waves on her head. Her features were regular, undeniably beautiful.

"What do you mean by this, sir?" she demanded, her voice brittle.

"X" saw that her slender white hand was fingering behind her toward a small, pearl-handled revolver on the phone table. The Agent's gas gun seemed to leap from his pocket. He saw that the only way to deal with this woman was to confront her with immediate, personal danger. His tongue dripped ice as he said:

"Make no mistake. I would not hesitate a second to put a bullet through your brain. Where is Miss Dale?"

Drew Devon leaned carelessly back against the phone desk. She folded lovely hands in front of her, and regarded "X" through veiled eyes. Her lips curved in an alluring smile. "What do you intend to do with me?" she asked. "I should have known better than to pit my tiny strength against you, Secret Agent 'X'!"

"X" STEPPED within inches of the woman. He picked up the pearl-handled revolver from the telephone table and dropped it into his pocket. His gas gun tilted toward Drew Devon's face. "Only once more—where is Miss Dale?"

For a moment, Drew Devon's self control deserted her. Her cheeks drained of their natural color. Then her upper lips lifted slightly in an almost imperceptible sneer. Her violet eyes were looking past Agent "X".

Instantly, the Secret Agent sensed danger behind him. He pivoted. With the silence of shadows, three men had entered the room. There was something in the bizarre color selection of their Oriental clothing that suggested that they were men of the Far East. They wore black domino masks through which slant eyes gleamed evilly.

There was a tense moment, void of sound and motion. Then a knife blade in the yellow hand of one of the men flashed into prominence. "X" went into action. A charge from his gas pistol was centered on the face of the foremost Chinese. The man staggered, fell backwards. "X" came to grips with the others. A swinging, upward thrust of a knife and the hilt met the wrist of the Agent's right band, sending his gun to the floor.

Behind the fury of the hand-to-hand encounter, "X" saw Drew Devon run from the room. "X" caught the wrist of one would-be assassin and gave it a quick twist. The knife clattered to the floor. The Chinese writhed from "X's" grasp, and streaked for the door. "X" tried to follow, saw a shadowy something hurtling through the air toward him. He ducked a split second too late. A small walnut table, thrown from the hands of the remaining Chinese, struck him on the head. For a moment, it seemed that he must lose consciousness. But he mastered the pain, forced aside the mist that swam before his eyes—to find the room empty.

"X" ran into the hall. The Chinese had left as silently as they had come, and had taken their unconscious companion with them. "X" went back into the apartment. On entering the bedroom, he knew that his quick action had frustrated the criminals' plans by a narrow margin. Betty Dale was lying on the bed, bound and gagged, but apparently unharmed.

Her blue eyes searched his face wonderingly as he unknotted the cords that bound her. He smiled gently, quickly drew the letter "X" in the air with his finger.

"You!" she gasped, as soon as the gag was out of her mouth.

"Tell me, Betty, what happened? How did that Devon woman get in here?

Deft fingers unconsciously rearranging her golden hair, Betty hurried her explanation: "She came here about half an hour ago, knocked at the door, and said she had important news for me. Drew Devon is always good for the front page, so I thought myself lucky to get a chance to talk to her. But when she stepped in, a man leaped through the door behind her. He had a gun. Together, they forced me back into this room and tied me up. I knew it was you they were trying to get at. I was afraid for your sake. Then the man said he was going to send three of his 'boys' to pick me up, and he went away, leaving Drew Devon."

Agent "X" smiled a little sadly. "I am afraid that my association with you results in nothing but an untold amount of trouble for you."

Betty sat up on the edge of the bed, placed her small hand impulsively on his arm. "Please, please don't think I mind—not at all, if you're safe. But what does it all mean?"

"Tell me about the man who came with Drew Devon. What was he like?"

"He wore a black mask," the girl told him. "But I would know him anywhere. He was so—so evil-looking. His right eye was turned out so that it didn't match its mate. And I saw that there were only three fingers on his right hand. His skin was yellow, yet I do not think he was a Chinese or Japanese."

"Come into the living room, Betty," the Agent suggested. "Undoubtedly Drew Devon was sent here by the Ghoul."

"The Ghoul!" Betty repeated with a shudder. "The Amber Death?"

"X" nodded. "The Ghoul is no ordinary criminal. The fact is, he is the most—" The Agent paused. Across the living room, he noticed that the light gleamed on some sort of a pin that was partially imbedded in the nap of the rug. He crossed to it and picked it up. It proved to be a hairpin of the same pattern as the one he had found in Warnow's room. Without a doubt, Drew Devon, in the guise of a chambermaid, had had a hand in preparing Warnow's room for murder.

"X" looked at his watch. It was nearly two A.M. "Betty," he said earnestly, "I must not conceal from you the fact that you are in the deadliest danger. The Ghoul will not make a similar attempt tonight. He is far too clever to repeat his tricks. But if he guessed of the friendship I have for you, he is *certain* of it after this night's work. You must be extremely careful. Stay as near the newspaper office as you possibly can. That will be the safest place for you."

"And you? What are you going to do?" she asked with concern.

"I am going now."

And Betty, who respected the wisdom of this man whose real face she had never seen, made no effort to pry into his affairs.[45]

---

45 AUTHOR'S NOTE: *Never having seen the Agent's true face, "X" has been compelled to devise signals by which Betty Dale may identify him.*

CHAPTER IV

VOICE OF THE GHOUL

THE FOLLOWING AFTERNOON, three distinguished gentlemen left the impressive portals of the Bankers' Club. They were Lionel Gage; Robert Cass, whose timid appearance and manner of speaking effectively concealed the fact that he was a lion of finance; and eccentric old Elisha Pond, whose generous attitude toward many charities had endeared him to thousands of people. On the lower step of the club building, they paused. The timid appearing Robert Cass seemed reluctant to leave his companions of the luncheon hour, and loath to discontinue the discussion of the subject of their conversation.

"Then you have not been approached by the Ghoul, Mr. Pond?" Robert Cass enquired as he lighted a fresh cigar.

"Indeed no," replied Elisha Pond with a vigorous shake of his head. "And I assure you that the fiend will be sadly disappointed if he makes a demand on me."

Lionel Gage shook his head dismally. "It's a terrifying business. I doubt if you realize the seriousness of the matter, Mr. Pond. The police are absolutely up against a stone wall. The power of this Ghoul is amazing—almost supernatural! Only this morning, so the papers say, the police, acting on a tip of some sort, conducted a raid that netted the capture of four men believed to be in the Ghoul's gang. But before they could reach headquarters they had not four criminals on their hands, but four corpses! The gang committed suicide by some sort of trick."

"And last night," said Cass, "the police were frustrated in an attempt to save Ramesey Hurst, the radio manufacturer. But the Amber Death was concealed in Hurst's cigarette case. Then there was the Gilbert Warnow affair. I declare—" Cass stopped. His thin fingers clutched at the sleeve of Mr. Pond's coat. "Wasn't that some one calling you?"

Pond bobbed his head in agreement. "Most decidedly—"

"Elisha Pond," a voice interrupted the aged eccentric.

Cass pointed silently at a flashy touring car that was parked in front of the club. Though the car was empty, the radio under the dash seemed to be turned on. From the concealed loudspeaker, the sepulchral voice of the Golden Ghoul boomed:

"Elisha Pond. This is the Golden Ghoul calling Elisha Pond."

MEN and women on the sidewalk swarmed around the car, muttering excitedly. They had read of the Ghoul in the papers, and attributed much of what they read to sensational writing. But now they were actually hearing him speak.

"If Elisha Pond is within the range of my voice," the Ghoul continued, "let him be warned. The toll that he must pay for his life is seventy-five thousand dollars. I shall not bother to speak to him again about the matter. However, he may expect instructions through the mail as to how and where this price of his immunity from the Amber Death may be paid." The voice sighed into silence.

A confused Babel of voices arose from the knot of people about the car.

"Whose car is that?.... That's the Ghoul's car.... Where are the police? Never here when they're needed.... Ought to be able to trace the car by the license...."

But the general criticism of the police was entirely uncalled for. Hardly had the voice concluded speaking before a broad-shouldered cop shoved his way through the crowd. But of all the people standing about the flashy car, Elisha Pond seemed to be the least concerned.

"So much mumbo jumbo," he was heard to remark to his companions.

"But Mr. Pond!" exclaimed Cass. "You can't afford to neglect a warning of this kind! It would cost you your life. If you have not thought of yourself, think of the thousands who would miss you."

Elisha Pond snorted.

"Mr. Pond," said Gage seriously, "I consider you a man of great good sense, and courage. There will be a meeting of men, whom I hope are as courageous as you are, at my house tonight. We are going to discuss a plan that will undoubtedly defeat the purposes of the Ghoul. I would be most happy to have you join us. Say, about ten o'clock?"

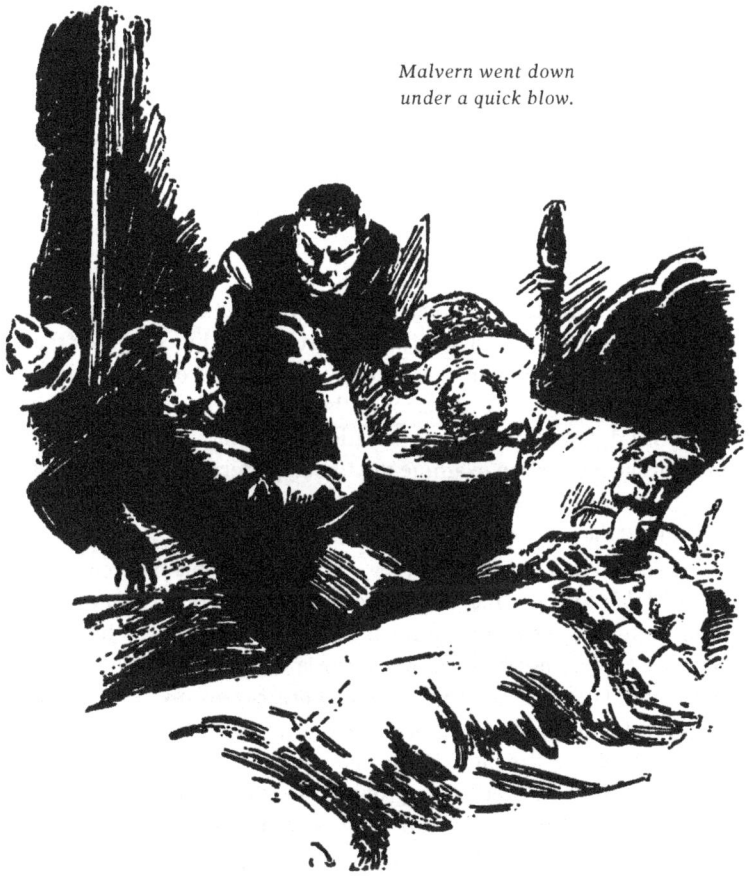

Malvern went down under a quick blow.

Elisha Pond bobbed his head and hurried off. Beneath his apparently aged exterior, a young heart beat high with new hope. Behind his wrinkled face the brain of the most amazing criminologist of our time was hard at work. There was a glint of humor in his brilliant eyes. Little did the Ghoul know, for all his cunning, that in threatening Elisha Pond, he had threatened his arch enemy, Secret Agent "X".[46]

That morning, Secret Agent "X" had spent in putting his vast

---

[46] AUTHOR'S NOTE: *None of the Agent's stock disguises are more important to him than that of Elisha Pond. It is in this name that an inexhaustible fund, subscribed by certain public-spirited wealthy men, is placed at his disposal. From this fund, he obtains money with which to pay the vast army of men and women in his employ. He is free to use the money according to his own judgement.*

crime-fighting machine into operation. Jim Hobart, who directed the operations of a group of private detectives employed by "X," had been ordered to release Ah-Fang, former servant of Gilbert Warnow. Ah-Fang had been held prisoner during the Agent's impersonation of the Chinese valet. "X" believed that Ah-Fang might have had a hand in the murder of Gilbert Warnow, and his instructions to Hobart were to have one of his men shadow the Chinese and record his every movement.

TO Bates, another important cog in the Agent's machine, had fallen the task of investigating the shortwave radio converter that "X" had taken from Warnow's suite.[47] Bates had been directed to put experts to work to determine the wave of the Ghoul's radio station and if possible learn its location. A scientist in the Bates organization was also to examine the two hypodermic needles which "X" had removed from the pillow-trap to learn, if possible, what substance they contained.

As he hurried along the street toward one of his hideouts, "X" noticed that the building directly across from the Hotel Empire was made conspicuous by the fact that a large balloon was anchored to its roof. He had noticed several of these balloons in various parts of the city lately. They were moored there, ostensibly, to advertise some little known product, and their surfaces were covered with lettering. But to the alert brain of Agent "X," these balloons together with the mysterious bag of shot he had found in Warnow's bedroom, formed an important clue as to the means in which the Ghoul performed his amazing kidnapings.

However, he had plans that had to be carried out immediately, foremost of which was to contrive an interview with the dangerous Drew Devon, beautiful, poisonous tool in the hands of the Golden Ghoul.

The apartment house in which Drew Devon lived cast a long shadow by the time Agent "X" arrived. He had taken considerable pains to produce an entirely new make-up. He was the very picture of opulence. Chubby cheeks were traced with a network of tiny red lines that might have indicated high blood pressure brought on by too much good living.

---

47 AUTHORS NOTE: *Similar to the Hobart Detective Agency, which "X" secretly commands under the alias of A. J, Martin, is the Bates organization. However, while the Hobart group appears to be an ordinary detective agency, the general public does not known of the Bates group,*

As he alighted from his car, "X" noticed a familiar figure approaching a taxi that was parked in front of his own car. It was the swarthy-faced Daniel Calvert whom he had seen with Dr. Luigi on the previous night. And Calvert had come from the apartment house where Drew Devon lived.

"X" busied himself around his own car, seeming to pay no attention to Calvert. As the wealthy financier got into the cab, "X" distinctly heard him say: "Back to the Great Eastern Bank, driver."

As soon as Calvert's cab had pulled from the curb, "X" entered the building. A few moments later, he was adjusting his tie in front of the door of Drew Devon's fifth-floor apartment. When the beautiful blonde opened the door, a toothy smile spread across "X's" face. He allowed a dazzling diamond ring to show on the third finger of his left hand. Drew Devon's slight frown disappeared. Here, to all appearances, was the sort of person she thrived upon.

"Miss Devon?" enquired "X" politely.

Drew Devon smiled, nodded, and accepted a visiting card that introduced "X" as Jason Longworth, a name that meant millions in Chicago.

"It is my intention, Miss Devon, to back an entirely new musical revue that a promising young author-composer has brought to my attention. That young man was particularly anxious that no one be selected for the leading part until I offered you the post. Frankly, if I may say so, I realize now the wisdom of my young friend's choice."

"Please step in, Mr. Longworth," Drew Devon invited. "As you probably know, I have rather abruptly, but wilfully, terminated my stage career. However," she added with an alluring smile, as she closed the door behind "X," "I am always ready to listen to a new proposition."

Back to the door, "X" made a move that was nothing else than legerdemain. He twisted the key in the lock without Drew Devon knowing it. His voice, which up to now had dripped honey, became flinty. His right hand came out of his pocket holding a bent and twisted hairpin.

"You realize, Miss Devon, that I have only to turn this over to the police together with information as to where I found it, and a very beautiful woman takes her place in the electric chair!"

Most of the pink faded from Drew Devon's pink-and-white complexion. Her eyes widened. "Wh—who are you?" she whispered huskily.

"You have seen my card. I am Jason Longworth, a life-long friend of Gilbert Warnow. I happened quite by accident upon this hairpin. Discreet inquiry led me to believe that it was you who were the instrument of Warnow's death. Be assured that I will move heaven and earth to see that my friend is avenged. You are a servant of the Ghoul. But I am charitable enough to believe that you are a victim of circumstances. Is my assumption correct?"

DREW DEVON nodded slightly. It was as though she feared some unseen eye might observe her admission.

"Very well," continued the Agent. "I am willing that my knowledge concerning your part in this matter shall forever remain a secret. In addition, I am willing to pay you enough money to leave this country and insure yourself an excellent living elsewhere. Can we do business?"

Drew Devon's poise did not desert her as she crossed the room to a small table. But "X" noticed that her hand trembled slightly as she drew out a chair. "Please sit down, Mr. Longworth. Perhaps we can come to some agreement."

"X" seated himself on the opposite side of the table. He studied the woman's face carefully. Outwardly, she appeared the picture of harassed woman-kind. But beneath the mask—what?

Drew Devon examined her polished nails critically. "I am," she began, "as you say, a victim of circumstances. I would do anything within my power to free myself of the slavery of him. But I am afraid—afraid of him I dare not name."

"X" reached inside his pocket and drew out a neat packet of currency. "Would fifty, one thousand dollar bills overcome that fear, Miss Devon?" he asked shrewdly.

Drew Devon started. Perfect as was her control she could not conceal the avaricious gleam in her eyes as they met that stack of bills. She made an attempt to conceal her eagerness in a sudden movement. She picked up a silver cigarette chest, opened it, and passed it to Agent "X." He declined without hesitation. He had sensed beneath Drew Devon's lovely face the guile of a Borgia. Aware of his distrust, she shrugged slightly, selected one of the cigarettes and put it between her lips.

"So you want me to risk my life—even my sanity—to tell you the name of—of him of whom you speak," she said reflectively.

"X" watched the woman narrowly and saw her do a peculiar thing. Whether, in a moment of suppressed excitement, she made a mistake or whether the act was intentional, he couldn't tell. But

Drew Devon flicked a lighter and applied the flame to the cork tip of the cigarette. She inhaled deeply and allowed feathers of smoke to dribble from her scarlet lips.

"Mr. Longworth, you will probably find the name of the man you are seeking in tonight's paper. If you will read the story which will undoubtedly concern a gentleman by the name of Elisha Pond, you will find his true name." She leaned far over the table. Her cigarette returned to her lips. She drew deeply, regarding her companion with a curious gleam in her violet eyes.

Suddenly, it happened. There was a snap like the breaking of a violin string. The cigarette in the woman's lips had disintegrated. A tiny dart, propelled by a coiled spring, had been released from the inside of the cigarette. In a split second it had sprung the short distance between Drew Devon and Agent "X." The dart, at that moment, was deeply imbedded in what appeared to be the cheek of Secret Agent "X." He sprang out of his chair, staggered to one side, and pitched over backwards to the floor. Legs and arms twitched convulsively. Then he lay very still

An evil smile twitched the lips of Drew Devon. "Now, Mr. Longworth, read this evening's paper—if you can!" She picked up the sheaf of bills from the table and tucked them into the bosom of her dress.

THERE came a knock at the door. From beneath lowered eyelids, Secret Agent "X" watched Drew Devon as she walked across the room. Actually, the dart, which was evidently poisoned, had not touched his flesh. The point of the deadly little missile had entered the plastic material that covered his cheeks, but had come in contact with one of the metal faceplates which he had used to achieve the plump contours of the face of Jason Longworth.

He knew now why Drew Devon had lighted the cork tip of her cigarette. The dart and the spring that propelled it had been concealed within that cigarette. Had "X" smoked the cigarette, he would have lighted the right end. In that case, the poisoned dart would have shot down into his throat.

It was a deadly contrivance worthy of the criminal genius of the Ghoul himself. He watched the beautiful figure of the woman gracefully crossing the room. Hers was the callousness of a master murderer. Was it possible that she was the Ghoul whose infallible schemes and terror tactics were slitting the fattest purses in the city?

Drew Devon opened the door of the room a crack, silently nodded her blonde head, then opened the door to admit a man. She closed the door behind him and locked it. The man who had entered was extremely tall and thin. He was dressed in the height of fashion. The lean hands, visible below the cuffs of his dark coat, were yellow, and "X" noticed that one finger on his right hand was missing.

"You are ready to go with me, Drew?" the man asked in a voice that could be described only as metallic.

"All ready, Bobby. Having transacted a rather neat bit of business. Do you suppose you could manage to have some of the boys dispose of this carrion for me?" She took the arm of the man with the yellow hands and turned him so that he faced the recumbent form of Agent "X."

Without so much as a flutter of an eyelid, "X" regarded the man through the curtain of his eyelashes. The man's face, too, was the yellow of old ivory, but his features were regular and Caucasian. He would have been handsome in an effeminate sort of way, if it hadn't been for his right eye. This eye, turned far out, gave an ugly, inhuman cast to his face. He was obviously an Eurasian.

"Who is he?" demanded the man with the ivory face.

"Jason Longworth," Drew Devon replied. In front of a mirror, she was putting on a rakish looking hat. "A friend of Warnow's who thought I could be persuaded to tell things—things I don't know."

"How did you manage this?" asked Bobby as he approached "X."

"Oh, I've ways of protecting myself," she said lightly. "Is he dead yet?"

The man knelt. With one yellow finger, he peeled back "X's" right eyelid. Had not the Agent been the master of his own nerves that he was, he could not have managed to roll his eyes back under this severe test.

"No," replied he of the yellow hands. "But he is scarcely breathing. Don't you think it would be wise for me to thrust my knife into his throat?" He allowed "X's" eyelid to snap shut.

Drew Devon laughed. "No! Decidedly crude. He won't last much longer. Are we going to Ah-Fang's, or not?"

"With you in a moment." The man called Bobby availed himself of the diamond ring on the finger of Secret Agent "X," and then joined Drew Devon at the door.

No sooner had the couple left the apartment than Secret Agent

"X" was on his feet. His photographic memory had recalled the face of the man with Drew Devon. He was known simply as China Bobby and operated a supposedly respectable Chinese-American restaurant—one of the show spots in Chinatown. But "X," who was as familiar with the records of Scotland Yard as he was with the New York police records, knew that China Bobby had obtained the money with which to back his elaborate restaurant by operating a profitable dive in East End London. He was an exceedingly dangerous person, if his past history could be believed, and a man crafty enough to be the Ghoul himself.

"X" TOOK but a moment to twitch out the dart that would have spelled his death had it entered his flesh; then he opened the door, and cautiously followed Drew Devon and her half-caste companion.

Dusk had deepened. From the door of the apartment building, he watched them step into a small black sedan. As the car started from the curb, he flung from the apartment and sprinted for his own car. He had the engine turning in a moment, and flashed off down the street following the speck of red light that marked the car of China Bobby. "X" weaved in and out of traffic until he was directly behind the Eurasian. When the black sedan turned into a less traveled side street, "X" was forced to slow down and permit the car ahead to gain on him.

In a poor section of the city, the car pulled to a stop in front of a once pretentious house. But the place was dark now and seemingly deserted. "X" speeded to the end of the block, rounded the corner and came to a stop. He got from the car and walked with apparent unconcern back toward the dark old house which Drew Devon and her companion had entered.

The house exhibited no more outward signs of life than when he had first passed it. But in the shadow of a sagging board fence that separated the house from the adjacent lot, he saw a man. Though there was not sufficient light to recognize the man, "X" believed him to be one of Jim Hobart's sleuths. Drew Devon had stated that they were going to Ah-Fang's place so it was logical to assume that this shadow was the man put on the Oriental's trail by Jim Hobart.

"X" crossed the small, unkempt yard and walked silently around the side of the house. Still no sign of life. Judicious use of his flashlight, however, enabled "X" to find a cellar window that would require little effort to open. With a small jimmy of special chrome steel, "X" had the window open in a minute.

With the utmost care, he wriggled backwards through the opening, and dropped soundlessly to the floor. The finger of his flashlight explored the basement—evidently a clearing ground for years of trash accumulation. He picked his way through the litter, climbed the stairs, and found himself in the kitchen.

A panel in the door leading from the kitchen to another part of the house had warped out of place and a narrow line of light shone beneath it. On tip-toe, "X" approached the door and peered through the crack. Squatting on a box behind an old round dining-room table was the man whom "X" had so artfully impersonated the night before. It was Ah-Fang, Warnow's valet. Drew Devon and China Bobby were standing. The woman regarded Ah-Fang through scornful eyes. It was China Bobby who was speaking in his odd, metallic voice:

"You think that I was born yesterday, Ah-Fang?" he demanded angrily. "Why, I wouldn't pay that price for number one *Li Yuen*, let alone that rooster brand of mud you put out!"

"Do not imagine, son of two races, that you can bargain with Ah-Fang," said the Chinese. "You not pay my price, no *Pen Yen*. What is more for persuasion, unless you buy from me, I inform to police."

A laugh hissed in China Bobby's throat. "That's likely! You go to the police! Why, I've half a mind to put a bullet in your thick skull and walk off with every *Fun* of the stuff in the house."

ON the other side of the door, Secret Agent "X" believed that he had run into what promised to be an ordinary underworld squabble. It was evident from the conversation that Ah-Fang operated a depot for smuggled opium. China Bobby, it seemed, had evidently reverted to his old occupation of running an opium den. "X" was about to turn away from his peephole when words from Ah-Fang checked him.

"I do not make reference to your occupation as master of House of Black Smoke. I was thinking of telling police that you serve another—he who calls himself the Ghoul."

With an oath, China Bobby's hand drove into his pocket and brought out a blunt-nosed automatic. "Know too much, don't you, Ah-Fang? Well, there's a cure for that!"

Drew Devon put a restraining hand on China Bobby's arm. But the half-caste shook her off angrily. "X" saw a knife slip from Ah-Fang's sleeve. China Bobby's gun roared. The knife dropped from the fingers of Ah-Fang; an expression of surprise flashed across his face. He slumped to the floor, a little stream of blood trickling down his forehead.

Again China Bobby laughed. "Come on, Drew. We'll have to move. The cops—"

Hardly had the half-caste spoken the word before a police whistle blasted just outside the house. With an oath, China Bobby sprang for the door, dragging Drew Devon with him. From his listening-post at the kitchen door, "X" turned. Outside the house came the sound of running feet. The back door was suddenly thrown open and a heavy figure blotted across the doorway. A ray of light glinted against gleaming metal—the silver shield of a policeman.

The cop's flashlight bit through the gloom, caught the fleeting form of Agent "X" as the latter leaped to the opposite wall of the kitchen.

"Comin' out of there now, or do they bring you feet first?" growled the cop. The spot from his light danced a little nearer to Secret Agent "X". Creeping along the wall, eyes locked on the manhunter in the doorway, "X" encountered the sink. His groping finger touched the rusty surface of a tin can. He snatched it up and hurled it against the opposite wall The policeman's light followed the clatter. His gun spat lead, shooting at the sound. But almost as soon as the can had left his fingers, "X" leaped toward the door.

A quick kick to the policeman's wrist and the gun was knocked from the copper's hand. "X" led a powerful, paralyzing blow to the cop's solar plexus. The man went down in a heap. "X" hurdled both the cop, and the steps, landed in the back yard, and sprinted towards the fence. He vaulted over, and ran down the alley.

Behind him another police whistle sounded. There came the roar of a starting motor, followed by two quick shots. Ahead of him, a car speeded by the mouth of the alley. Though he had only a glimpse of that car, he recognized it as the black sedan belonging to China Bobby. There were two persons in the front seat. Drew Devon and the Eurasian had escaped.

CHAPTER V

SUICIDE PACT

ON HIS WAY to a near-by hideout, Secret Agent "X" bought an evening paper from a boy. Tucking it under his arm, he hurried on up a dismal street, entered a red-brick dwelling, and hurried up worn stairs to the second floor to enter a room which he rented under one of his numerous aliases.[48] He had nearly an hour before it was time for him to go, in the guise of Elisha Pond, to the special meeting called by Lionel Gage.

From beneath an iron bed, "X" took a small leather-covered case containing a compact short wave transmitter and receiver. He put the case on a table, manipulated various knobs and switches. Using a telegraph key that was incorporated in the transmitter, he called the headquarters of his secret organization directed by Bates. An answering call came almost at once; and "X," using a code known only to him and Bates, sent this message:

"What have you on record concerning Dr. Claudio Luigi?"

While waiting for Bates to look up the information, "X" spread the evening paper out on his knees. He remembered that Drew Devon had told him that he might find the name of the person who was the Ghoul in the evening paper. He could hardly expect a word of truth in the woman's statement. Probably she had no more idea than he who her employer, the Ghoul, really was.

She had been compelled to kill time while waiting for her cigarette to burn down to the point where it would discharge the poison dart. However, the Agent was always thorough.

---

[48] AUTHOR'S NOTE: Agent "X" has established hideouts in every section of the city to which he may retire to change his disguise or obtain new materials and devices. Because of the constant peril in which he works, it is necessary for him to be on constant lookout for new strategic locations for these mysterious quarters of such vital importance to his method of procedure.

"X" saw in the paper that once again the Amber Death had struck—this time a wealthy newspaper publisher. As they had rushed his slowly ossifying body to the hospital, the ambulance had been held up by a gang of masked men and the Amber Death victim had been kidnaped. Again the law had been outwitted. Farther down the column was:

GHOUL WARNS ELISHA POND

Knowing most of the details even better than the newspaper men, "X" skimmed over the story. One paragraph, however, attracted his attention. It gave out the startling information that the Ghoul's warning had come from a radio in a parked car owned by Daniel Calvert. Police investigation had shown that a compact short-wave converter had been attached to the car radio. Calvert, who had arrived to take possession of his car some time later, denied any knowledge of the short-wave device.

"X" remembered that at the time, Daniel Calvert must have been in the apartment of Drew Devon. Possibly, Calvert had parked his car in front of the club, and taken a taxi to Drew Devon's apartment just to prevent his being trailed by some newspaper reporter anxious to dig up more about the scandal in which the financier and Drew Devon had been featured. More than likely, one of the Ghoul's men had added that short-wave converter to Calvert's car radio. Still, Calvert was a man who would bear watching. His dealings in Wall Street had been none too clean.

At that moment, the information from Bates came through. Dr. Luigi had been born and educated in Bologna, Italy. He was a specialist in dermatology and had a large practice among wealthy people of the city. Bates further informed "X" that all efforts to locate the Ghoul's headquarters had been fruitless. The extortionist's sinister whisper had passed out into the ether through an ultra-short waved transmitter which permitted great range with a minimum power. All attempts to find out what substance the hypodermic needles, taken from Warnow's room, had contained were also failures.

"X" RETURNED the radio equipment to its hiding place and proceeded at once to assume the disguise of Elisha Pond.

Half an hour later, he alighted at the porte-cochere of the palatial home of Lionel Gage. It was Gage himself who admitted "X"; for, as Gage explained, he had deemed it wise to dismiss the entire staff of servants for the night. In the magnificent glassed-in conservatory "X" greeted the six men present—among them the swarthy Daniel Calvert, the suave Dr. Luigi, and the timid Robert Cass. The others were all men whom "X," as Pond, had frequently come in contact with.

When cigars were well lighted, a tall, blond man, hardly out of his forties, stood up. He was Anthony Bernard, whose family had for generations found a fortune in the iron and steel industry. He paced the floor nervously for a few moments, chewing his cigar ragged. "Well," he snapped at last, "what's this wonderful proposition of yours, Gage?"

Lionel Gage's dark eyes turned from Daniel Calvert to Dr. Luigi.

With a vigorous jerk of his shaggy head, Dan Calvert rapped out: "Tell 'em, damnit!" He leaned far forward on the edge of his chair, and glared about the circle of anxious faces.

Gage, nervous and ill at ease, ran a finger around the inside of his collar. "You gentlemen understand that we are all marked men," he said huskily. "We've either been threatened by the Ghoul, or have bank accounts that would prompt one to expect to hear the Ghoul's voice at any time."

Bernard's jaw sagged. The chewed cigar dropped from his mouth unnoticed. He glanced apprehensively into the shadowy corners of the room as though he half expected to hear the Ghoul call him by name.

"We've all been threatened," Daniel Calvert's unpleasant voice croaked. "Or haven't we?" he demanded crossly. "I have. Paid, too, like a damned ass! But—" his voice dropped to a crackling whisper—"a man likes to live!"

"I haven't," Bernard muttered.

"Haven't what?" Calvert glared at the younger man. "Sit down, Bernard! Enough to give a man the shakes just watching you pace up and down, and mutter like one in a trance."

Bernard flushed. "I said I haven't been warned by the Ghoul."

Robert Cass jerked a nervous glance at his watch. "This won't get us anywhere, gentlemen—sitting here bawling at each other. Let's have the plan. Anything that will trick the Ghoul."

Calvert snorted. "This plan is *anything*—the last resort. The police are stumped. They can't swear out a warrant against a voice."

Gage explained his plan:

"The Ghoul will continue his damnable practices just as long as they net him anything. If we don't pay, we become living corpses—live brains within dead bodies." He repressed a shudder. "The Ghoul is an infallible power. There is only one escape. Only one way to check the Ghoul's nefarious scheme before he confiscates most of the wealth of the city, perhaps the wealth of the country. That is not to pay the Ghoul a single farthing from here on!"

Anthony Bernard wheeled on Gage. Color had completely drained from his face. "Not pay!" he muttered hoarsely. "Man, are yon in your right mind? Cass, Pond, Luigi, all of you—is there a man among you who has not dreamed of the Amber Death? Good Lord, gentlemen, in my sleep I've seen this face—" and his trembling bands raked across his cheeks—"this face reduced to a contorted yellow thing, the face of a living mummy!"

Dr. Luigi got up, laid a restraining hand on Bernard's shoulder. "Get a grip on yourself, Bernard," he said sternly. "No time to play the coward."

Bernard's right hand came up flatly against Luigi's cheek. The sound of the slap cracked throughout the room. The mark of Bernard's fingers flamed Luigi's smooth, dark skin. Daniel Calvert catapulted from his chair. His thick, outthrust arms shoved Bernard back to a chair.

"Sit down, you fool!" he roared.

Panting, pale with anger and shame, Bernard sat down. "Sorry," he mumbled.

"Please, gentlemen," said Dr. Luigi, straining to control his voice, "let us hear the rest of the plan."

"Yes, the plan! Go on."

GAGE continued: "It is a plan that requires courage, but for the common good, we must be the ones to defeat the Golden Ghoul. As Bernard has said, the police are helpless to fight this thing they cannot see. This person called Secret Agent "X," who I am inclined to regard as a myth, has evidently had no better luck than the police.

"Here is my proposition. Tonight, each of us will sign an agreement not to pay one cent of tribute to the Ghoul. This agreement will be published in every paper in the country. Furthermore, to show that we are in earnest, and to deprive the Ghoul of the pleasure of torturing us with his Amber Death, each of us must agree to commit suicide when the Ghoul next makes a demand upon us!"

"You're crazy!" Bernard leaped to his feet. It was only with considerable effort that he restrained another nervous burst of temper.

"And you believe," Elisha Pond asked mildly, "that meeting defeat from a handful of men will cause the Ghoul to give up extortion entirely?"

"That is my belief, Mr. Pond," Gage spread out a sheet of paper on his carved walnut desk. "I have the agreement which I have just outlined. May I have the honor of being the first to sign this declaration of our independence?"

"You may—and be damned!" cried Anthony Bernard. "I'll pay if it lands me in the bread line whenever the Ghoul speaks to me."

"If it would avail us anything to sign," Robert Cass said as if he were giving the question considerable thought. "But death, whether by the Amber Death or by putting a bullet through my own head—" He was seized with a fit of shaking that prevented him from continuing.

"I didn't say anything about a bullet," said Gage as he signed the suicide pact with a flourish. "I have a poison that Dr. Luigi tells me is perfectly painless—even pleasant. One gradually dozes—"

"Anthony Bernard." A cold dispassionate voice echoed throughout the room.

Cass's thin hand seized the sleeve of the Agent's coat. "Look!" He pointed at a heavy radio console at the end of the room. This time, whoever had attached the short-wave converter to Gage's set had made no attempt to conceal the fact that the Ghoul's voice came from the radio. The pilot lamps made a ghostly eye of the airplane dial on the radio.

"Anthony Bernard," repeated the voice, "this is my first warning. It shall be my last. I will give you two days in which to raise seventy-five thousand dollars. If you succeed, I will permit you to live. Fail, and your life is mine."

"Good Lord!" gasped Bernard. "The Ghoul! Two days to live—"

Again came the voice. "Two others are marked for the Amber Death. Elisha Pond, what have you done toward raising the money I demanded? You defied me. You shall be punished. And to him who opposed my strength with his puny will, I give certain death. Lionel Gage, I have spoken to you." The voice sighed into silence.

A half-mad smile, ghastly in its untimely glee, twisted the lips of Anthony Bernard. "Now, Gage, where's your courage?"

Gage passed a quivering hand over his high, pale forehead. But his jaw was set with deadly determination. His right hand plunged into the pocket of his coat and pulled out a large hypodermic needle.

"Stop him!" shouted "X." With a celerity that belied the aged appearance of Mr. Pond, "X" sprang across the room. He caught Gage by the wrist—too late. Gage had emptied the entire contents of the syringe in the flesh of his neck. His fixed eyes stared at Pond. "All over now," he panted out "Doesn't take much nerve. Painless—"

A scream of pain retched from Gage's throat. He fell to the floor writhing in agony. His hands clenched and unclenched. Facial muscles contracted in a hideous grimace. *And very, very slowly, a tinge of yellow crept upwards across his face.*

"Look! His face. It's the Amber death!" shouted Cass.

"So that's the *painless* poison!"

"Didn't Luigi give it to him?"

Like an enraged panther, Bernard sprang toward Luigi. "Traitor! You're the Ghoul!"

THE Italian suddenly paled, sidestepped to escape the lunging Bernard.

"Kill Luigi! Kill the Ghoul!"

And suddenly the room was drowned in darkness. Every light in the house seemed to have gone out at once. Men uttered high-pitched, feminine-like screams of terror. The glass roof of the conservatory was smashed to bits. Pieces of broken glass fell in tinkling rain upon the tiled floor. And through the opening in the roof, dark, agile shadows dropped.

Hoarse blasphemies cascaded from the mouth of Daniel Calvert, and mingled with a hideous, pain-ridden shriek.

"Dio Mio!" Luigi's voice. "The Amber Death!"

And above the noise of bedlam, the Ghoul's voice whispered orders.

Across the room, "X" saw a gleam of phosphorescent light—a death's head drawn in luminous paint. The death's head danced around the room. That luminous face—perhaps it marked the Ghoul himself. "X" sprang across the room toward the face of fire, encountered a writhing tangle of arms and legs.

The blade of a knife raked his arm. Thin, clawlike hands dug at his throat. "X" let go with his right at a shadowy foeman. He twisted free. Not ten feet from him gleamed the death's head. He leaped toward it, saw the dark form of a man who bore the ghostly emblem. "X" tripped over a sprawling body, caught his balance and raced on, hard on the heels of the illusive wisp of phosphorescent light.

In front of him, his quarry crashed through French doors, stopped, encountering the wall of the next room. "X's" fingers crooked like the talons of a striking hawk as he seized the creature by the throat. But his man was possessed with the strength of desperation. He twisted and turned in the Agent's grasp. He drove hard, short blows to the Agent's chest. Yet "X" clung to the man with the tenacity of a bulldog.

A faint, gurgling cry from the man he was slowly inevitably choking into insensibility. "Ghoul! I'll—pay—"

That agonized cry knifed through the Agent's heart. He had made some mistake. He released his grip, snapped a flashlight from his pocket and played the brilliant ray upon the face of the man he had tried to throttle. It was the terrified face of Anthony Bernard. Even in the light of the flash, he could make out the tracing of the death's head on Bernard's shirt front.

"You. Pond!" gasped Bernard. "You the Ghoul?"

"No—no, Bernard! Where did that mark on your shirt come from?"

"You're crazy! Nothing on my shirt!"

"Look," the Agent commanded. He snapped off the light for a moment.

Bernard gasped. "Why—why how did it get there?"

"Some one marked you so that the Ghoul could find you in the dark," the Agent explained. "Could your valet have marked that shirt?"

"Incredible!" Bernard exploded. "Why, I've had Ho-Yang for years."

"A Chinese! Undoubtedly, Bernard, your valet is in the Ghoul's gang. Had I not chased you out here, you would have been in the Ghoul's power."

"But I was to be given two days to raise the money," Bernard objected.

"X" nodded. "Merely to put you off your guard, I think. The Ghoul has a different method. He does not work as most extortionists do. The Amber Death first. Later, you pay—under the torment of the living death. That is his method."

Though "X" had not noticed it before, the entire house was

A knife blade in the hand of one of them flashed into prominence, and "X" went into action.

shrouded in an awful silence. "X" took Bernard by the arm, and dragged him through the French doors and into the conservatory. "X" played his light about the room. The place looked as though it had been struck by a small hurricane. Broken glass covered upended furniture and was strewn over the floor. But, as "X" had expected, there were a number of canvas, shot-filled bags lying around the floor. But there was not a single human being in sight. The Ghoul's work had progressed in its usual efficient manner. The master criminal seemed to be everywhere. His nefarious schemes seemed infallible.

Suddenly "X" snapped out his light. A little gasp from Bernard. "What's the matter."

"Hush," the Agent cautioned. "The door on the right. It's opening. Quiet, now.'"

The door creaked. Cautious footsteps padded across the floor. Bernard, his hand on the Agent's arm, was shaking like a leaf. "X" waited until the footsteps came closer. Then the beam of his light sliced through the gloom to center on the frightened face of Robert Cass.

"Cass!" Bernard exploded.

Relief passed over the little man's face. "You there, Bernard! Thought the Ghoul took you along with the others." He hurried over to where "X" and Bernard were standing. "I managed to hide in that closet. Couldn't see much of what went on. Some of the mob climbed back up the ropes to the roof. Others just seemed to disappear."

"X" nodded his head. The bags of shot accounted for those sudden and mysterious disappearances. And he knew from the cries he had heard that Calvert and Luigi had both fallen victims of the Amber Death. Probably, they had been removed to the Ghoul's headquarters. What had been the fate of the others, he did not know.

"Hadn't we better inform the police?" asked Bernard.

"Definitely, no!" the Secret Agent replied. "We must all go to our respective homes at once. I do not trust the police. They have been so successfully defeated in every attempt made against the Ghoul, that I suspect some man, some one high in the police force, is the Ghoul himself!"

This statement was obviously false. While "X" had a theory concerning the identity of the Ghoul, this theory included no one on the police force. But he knew of no other way of convincing Bernard that he should not go to the police. Already a desperate plan was forming in "X's" mind. It was a plan that would endanger Bernard, perhaps, but it was one that might enable "X" to come face to face with the Ghoul.

In his car a few moments later, "X" watched Cass and Bernard drive off in their own cars.

CHAPTER VI

KILLERS FROM THE CLOUDS

THE AGENT'S CAR followed that of Bernard unerringly through the streets. Steering with his left hand, his right worked miracles with the plastic material that covered his face. Wrinkles disappeared under his skilled fingers. Features took on an entirely different shape. A black toupee replaced the one which had been a part of his disguise as Elisha Pond.

A few minutes later, "X" stopped his car a short distance behind the parked machine of Anthony Bernard. A glimpse of his face in the rear-vision mirror told "X" that his disguise was perfect. Bernard would never know that the man who was following him to his apartment was the same Elisha Pond who had experienced the Ghoul's raid that night.

Hurrying up the walk that approached the apartment building, "X" just managed to enter the same elevator with Bernard. The latter was obviously worried. His glance hurried around the walls of the ascending cage as though hunting for some avenue of escape in case the Ghoul put in another miraculous appearance.

At the sixth floor, Bernard got out and "X" followed him closely. The Agent, aware that the Ghoul struck at the most surprising times, dared not let the millionaire out of his sight for a moment, even though his movements should arouse Bernard's suspicion.

It was not until Bernard was in the act of fitting his key into the lock of the door, that he seemed to notice "X." He turned quickly, frightened eyes searching the Agent's face. But "X" was not watching Bernard. His eyes were riveted on the brass doorknob of the apartment. Dull antique finish as was the knob there was a tiny spot of reflected light that gleamed like the eye of a snake at its very center. As Bernard started to reach for the knob, "X" sprang forward and knocked Bernard's arm down to his side.

"Be careful, Mr. Bernard!" the Agent cried. "Danger!"

Startled almost beyond speech, Bernard shrank back against the wall. "Who—who are you?" he muttered feebly.

"That is not important," replied the Agent. "Simply rest assured that I have your interests at heart." Standing to one side, "X" took hold of the doorknob between thumb and forefinger. He turned it slowly, his eye on the tiny hole that centered the knob. As the lock clicked, a needle stabbed halfway out of the knob, and discharged a stream of clear, yellow liquid on the floor.

Drew Devon

"Good Lord!" Bernard husked. "Poison! It would have been injected into the palm of my hand!"

"X" knelt, touched a drop of the liquid with his finger, and conveyed it to his nose. He sniffed cautiously.

"Not poison," he corrected slowly. "The Amber Death. Some one in the Ghoul's crowd substituted this trick doorknob for the one that was originally on here. Now, Mr. Bernard, I think you are comparatively safe." The Agent stood up, flung open the door, and followed Bernard into the room. He locked the door from the inside.

"Are you a detective?" asked Bernard.

"X" smiled. "You can regard me as something of the sort."

Bernard dropped into a chair, for his legs seemed too shaky to support him. "The second attempt on my life tonight. Gage, Luigi and Calvert—all fell into the hands of the Ghoul."

"X" REGARDED Bernard critically for a moment. Then he went into the bathroom to return with a glass containing some colorless liquid. "Drink this, Mr. Bernard," he ordered.

Bernard seized the glass and drank half its contents. Almost at once, a marked change came over his face. His eyes, once wide with terror, began to look drowsy. He tried to stand up. "You—you tried to poison me! I—I—" And he collapsed, unconscious.

The Agent was certain that the Ghoul's next move would be to send somebody for Bernard, who by this time would have been under the influence of the Amber Death had not "X" acted quickly. Such had been the Ghoul's method of procedure in the case of Gilbert Warnow, and others.

"X" picked up Bernard bodily, carried the unconscious millionaire into the bedroom, and stretched him out on the bed. Then, having made sure that the blinds were drawn, he began working on Bernard's face. From his pocket make-up kit, he took yellow pigment and plastic volatile material.

Lionel Gage

He made no actual changes in Bernard's features, but with his plastic material he built up muscles and added lines so as to achieve the appearance that Bernard was in great pain. Then with the yellow pigment he carefully colored Bernard's face and hands.

The result was that Bernard looked for all the world like a victim of the Ghoul's Amber Death.

"X" turned out all but a single lamp and walked quietly from the apartment.

Having located the stairway, "X" climbed to the top floor of the building and from there into the attic. There he found a ladder reaching up to a trapdoor in the roof. It was on the roof that he took up his vigil.

It was nearly midnight. Far below, the late traffic was hushed beneath a blanket of fog. And above, night and the mist had created a dismal gray void. Neighboring buildings were tall, uncertain shadows. The breeze, "X" noted, blew seaward. It was from the west, then, that he could expect the danger. For Secret Agent "X" was probably the only man in the city who understood how the Ghoul and his gang managed their mysterious entrances and exits.

"X" hid himself behind a fan-tailed ventilator and for perhaps fifteen minutes remained perfectly motionless. Then without a sound, a man dropped, apparently from the clouds, to land lightly on the flat roof of the building. Though "X" could not see very clearly through the gloom, he knew that a rope extended from the man up to a balloon.

This balloon, "X" had deduced, was what had become known in the world of sports as a jumping-balloon. They had been introduced in Europe some time ago, were considerably smaller than an observation balloon, and were so inflated as to exert slightly less pounds lift than the weight of the persons who intended to travel with them. The balloon-jumper, hanging beneath the bag, had only to jump into the air and the buoyancy afforded by the balloon converted the jump into a gigantic stride that sometimes carried the balloonist a hundred feet in the air.

It was by means of these small balloons that the Ghoul's men had entered Warnow's bedroom, and the conservatory of Gage's house. The true purpose of these balloons, which had been moored throughout the city, was concealed by the fact that each balloon carried some sort of advertising matter.

"X" had guessed from the first that the bags of shot dropped by the Ghoul's balloon jumpers acted as ballast and were dropped whenever it became necessary for the balloon to gain additional lift. He could see similar ballast bags tied to the belt of the man who had just alighted on the roof. Probably, the man had leaped from the roof of a neighboring building.

"X" watched the balloon-jumper fasten the mooring rope of the balloon to the edge of the eaves, saw him drop a coil of rope over the edge of the roof, and commence his descent. As soon as the man's head had disappeared, "X" hurried over to where the balloon was moored. He saw that a special mooring clasp had been provided—one which resisted the upward pull of the balloon but one which could be released by the slightest horizontal pull on the line which had been dropped over the eaves. The operator had only to stand on the window sill, give his line a quick, outward jerk, and the balloon would be released. A powerful jump, and the man could soar high into the air and possibly cover the distance of a block or so to alight on some neighboring roof.

"X" took a knife from his pocket and quickly sawed through the mooring rope. The line snapped and leaped into the air to disappear in the gray dome above. Then, having made sure that the line over the eaves was made fast, "X" began a hand over hand descent towards the window of Anthony Bernard's apartment four stories below.

HE had climbed down perhaps fifteen feet when he felt a sudden jerk at the line. Looking up, he saw the round silhouette of a man's head leaning gargoyle-like over the eaves. A powerful beam of light drilled down through the darkness, and centered upon the upturned face of Agent "X." A harsh laugh from the man on the roof.

"X" saw the broad blade of a knife flash in the man's hand. He knew that to climb back that fifteen feet before the knife slashed through that line would be impossible. Already, as he swung there, eight or nine stories above the pavement, he could feel the rope vibrating like the strings of a violin beneath the sawing knife of the man on the roof.

There was but one thing to do—and small chance of it succeeding. "X" loosened his grip on the line, dropped like a plummet, felt the rope burn through his fingers. Then came that instant of sickening sensation when the rope became a limp, snaky thing falling with him. The knife had won.

Even in that moment when the primitive fear of falling would have paralyzed another man, "X" kept his head. At the moment that the rope broke, "X's" right arm shot out. His fingers crooked to grasp the steel awning-support that extended out a little way from the wall directly over Bernard's window. For a fraction of a second, he hung there, saw the masked man beside Bernard's bed turn, draw a knife and spring toward the window. "X" swung up his legs, kicked forward with all his strength, and threw himself through the open window.

He landed on his heels, fell over backwards, with the masked assassin on top of him. The killer's knife flashed silver fire in its descent, and was stopped by the Agent's hand when its point was but a fraction of an inch from his throat. With a quick twist, "X" brought his left arm around over the man's head and gave a jerk that threw the killer over on his back.

"X" rolled, following his opponent, and landing with both knees on the man's chest. His thumb pushed sharply between the center knuckles of the man's knife hand. The killer's fingers sprang apart and the knife clattered to the floor.

A single blow from the Agent's fist would have put the man out for a long time; but before he could deal that blow, the second balloon-jumper had dropped a rope, slid down it, and swung through the window. "X" sprang to his feet then dropped almost to his knees as the second man's knife sang its death song over his head to bury its point three inches in the woodwork of the opposite wall.

"X" snatched out his gas gun and, as the man leaped toward him, jerked the trigger. The gas pistol hissed. A cloud of the powerful anesthetizing vapor blotted across the assassin's black mask. The man received the full concentrated force of the gas and lurched forward to fall a few feet from "X".

But in that brief moment when the gas gun had knocked the second man unconscious, his companion had bolted from the room. "X" could hear the sound of his feet padding down the hall outside the apartment. "X" did not pursue the escaping criminal. He had captured one of the Ghoul's hirelings, and expected to be able to make that man talk.

His first act was to remove the man's mask. Beneath was a narrow, ratlike face with white skin blued about the chin by a stubble of black beard. He recognized the man as Jeff Lucko, who had cut his name in several crime records. He carefully searched the man's pockets. He found a few coins, a deck of cocaine, and a small bit of cast brass. The last-named article interested him. It appeared to be a tiny hand not more than an inch in length, and he further noted that the little finger had been removed. This little brass hand "X" put into his pocket.

FROM his pocket medical kit, "X" removed a powerful stimulant and a hypodermic syringe. He made an injection of the fluid into Lucko's arm, and while waiting for the man to revive, he contemplated the possible value of the little brass hand. It was obviously a badge or a pass. "X" remembered that China Bobby had had only three fingers on his right hand. It was very probable that "X" would be able to make use of that bit of brass later on.

Jeff Lucko stirred slightly, opened his eyes, and stared up into "X's" face. Then his beady eyes wandered toward the bed. He licked dry lips. "Well?" he challenged.

Agent "X" fixed the man with his strange, magnetic eyes. "Lucko," he said softly, "you're in a spot. I'm the only person who can help you out."

Lucko sat up. "Who the hell are you, mister?"

"The man you tried to kill. My name is of no importance to you. The point is, do I turn you over to the police or will you answer my question?"

Lucko didn't answer. He looked past "X" and twisted a button on his coat.

"You know, Lucko, there's quite a price on the head of anyone associated with the Ghoul—dead or alive. You were caught with the goods. Your jumping-balloon must be moored up on the roof right now. I've only to give you a shot of an effective narcotic, and then call the police."

"You got me wrong, mister." Lucko shook his head. "You're off your nut if you think I killed this guy here."

"A lot of people are going to think you killed Bernard," the Agent lied. "But if you tell me who the Ghoul is and where I can find him, you get an even break to skip the country, and pocket money besides."

"The Ghoul!" Lucko muttered fearfully. "Don't try to get none of that stuff out of me. I don't know nothin'!"

"X" shrugged. "Maybe you don't know who he is, but you can tell me where to find him."

A ghastly grin spread over Lucko's face. "Nix. Get wise, guy. You couldn't worm that dope out of anybody with a hot iron!"

"X" slipped a small black leather case from his pocket and removed a small vial from it.

Lucko, who had been watching every movement the Agent made, said: "Save that stuff. Mister. I'm fit for the slab right now!"

A puzzled frown flashed across "X's" forehead. His eyes skated down Lucko's coat, and rested upon a telltale vacancy. The button with which Lucko had been toying, was missing. "X" seized Lucko by the shoulders and shook him. "That button! What did you do with that button?"

A sickly grin spread across Lucko's face. "That button? You won't see that again. It was one of the Ghoul's pet tricks. Loaded with enough cyanide to knock over a horse. Don't fool with me. I'm—I'm—" Muscles of the hood's face tightened, drawing his features into a mask of pain. "I failed.... The Ghoul knows everything... He'd have—got me.... The Amber Death—livin' hell—"

A convulsive tremor shook his entire body. A sigh rattled in his throat. The man was dead.

More than ever before "X" realized the power of the criminal with whom he battled. It was the power of fear. Lucko had preferred certain doom to living torment of the Amber Death.

So the Ghoul had won another hand. The single trick that "X" had taken had been the saving of Bernard's life—a valuable trick, to be sure, but it took "X" no nearer his goal.

"X" turned to the telephone, picked it up and called police headquarters. In a flawless imitation of Bernard's voice, he said: "Quick! Send somebody to my apartment. There's a man here. He's killed himself.... This is Anthony Bernard speaking. I've got to have—" A gurgling sound that to the desk sergeant must have sounded as though Anthony Bernard's conversation had been interrupted by the clutching fingers of a strangler. "X" dropped the phone on the table, confident that his message would bring quick results.

With sure, deft movements, he removed the make-up material from the face of the unconscious Bernard. Then he dragged the millionaire from the bed to the table where the phone had stood, and dropped him on the floor. When the police arrived, it would appear that Bernard had been attacked by some one when he was in the act of phoning the police.

CHAPTER VII

HOUSE OF BLACK SMOKE

SOME TIME LATER, in Chinatown, a white man was seen to leave the door of a three-story brick house which contained the offices of the powerful Chinese society, the Ming Tong. This young white man was dressed in the height of fashion. His pale face bore the unmistakable marks of mild dissipation. But those weak, pale features served only to hide the true face of Secret Agent "X".

"X" because of a great service he had once rendered the Mingmen, was the only white man ever to be admitted into their society. That night he had sought Lo Mong Yung, venerable father of the Tong. He had asked questions and learned something concerning the Eurasian, China Bobby, which would have caused considerable alarm had the same information reached the ears of the city's vice and narcotic squads.

Beneath China Bobby's respectable restaurant, "X" had learned, the Eurasian carried on a flourishing opium traffic, making use of strange underground rooms that many years ago had been closed and sealed by the police.

Was China Bobby a member of the Ghoul's gang, or simply a human spider spinning a web to snare the rich and unwary? It was very probable that he was both. Ah-Fang had accused him of serving the Ghoul. Betty Dale had told "X" of the man who had aided Drew Devon in her attempt to kidnap Betty; undoubtedly he was China Bobby. The Eurasian's opium den might well serve as a catch-pool for the Ghoul's prospective victims.

Agent "X" proceeded down the street from Ming headquarters to an ornately fronted building, brilliantly lighted even at this late hour. From its plate-glass doors, framed in gilt and gleaming lacquer, came the thin and tinkling strains of flute and moon-lute. An emblazoned sign proclaimed that this was the Chinese-American restaurant operated by China Bobby, late of Limehouse, London. There wealthy, sensation-seeking patrons, and sightseeing tourists gather at all hours of the night to sip tea and scented wines and partake of foods more American than Chinese.

Through these gaudy doors passed Agent "X" to deposit his hat and stick with a smiling Chinese girl who had forsaken the dress and mannerisms of her ancestors for those of her Occidental sisters. A swarthy-faced person with features that were unmistakably Latin, led "X" to a small gilded table at one side of the room.

There, "X" ordered wine more to be rid of the waiter than for any other reason. He relaxed in his chair and languidly puffed on a cigarette. Outwardly, he appeared the very picture of boredom; but beneath drooping lids, his eyes missed nothing of what went on about him. He scrutinized every one of the restaurant's habitues.

While he was making a pretense at sipping his wine, he saw a young, nervous-acting man push back from his table, whisper a word in the ear of the waiter, then walk toward a door at the rear of the room.

A few minutes later, "X" followed the young man's example, pushed open the door at the rear, and entered a room into which no light penetrated. For a moment, he stood perfectly still, listening to the sound of approaching footsteps. Suddenly, an ornate, pierced brass lamp above his head was turned on. He found himself confronting the Latin-American who had met him at the door of the restaurant.

"X" uttered a cracked, drunken laugh and put his hand familiarly upon the shoulder of the Latin. "'S funny, everytime I open a door in thish place I find you. Your name'sh goin' to be Albert. Now what I want, Albert, ish one lil old pipe and pill to put in it."

The man frowned. "I am sorry, sir. You are laboring under a misapprehension."

"X" WAGGED his head. "No such thing. Just laborin' under a yen to twisht up a few."

"I don't understand you, sir. Perhaps you had better go back—"

"X" clapped the man on the shoulder. "Sure, you gotta be careful. But not with me, no shir! I'm a genuine, bonifie' *Yen Shee Kwoi*," he said using the term for opium smoker which, though Chinese, was familiar to nearly every addict. "Here, maybe, maybe thish lil old thing will put me right with you." He fumbled in the pocket of his vest and brought out the tiny brass three-fingered hand which he had removed from the pocket of Jeff Lucko.

Recognition glimmered in the Latin's eyes. He bowed his head. "Of course, any friend of China Bobby's is welcome. Just follow me."

The man led the way to a door at the end of the hall. He unlocked the door, and pointed to a flight of winding steps that extended down beneath the surface of the earth.

"Here," the Agent thrust a five-dollar bill into the man's hand, "just a lil token of my eshteem, Albert. Happy dreams!" And on seemingly unsteady legs, he began the descent of the stairs. Behind him, the door closed with an ominous clangor.

The circular staircase ended in a stone arched doorway. There "X" was met by an ivory-faced Chinese wearing American evening clothes. He looked "X" over from head to foot as if trying to determine his worth—in dollars. "X" would have passed the Chinese had not the latter stopped him.

"Just a minute, sir," said the Chinese in perfect English. "You are of course not familiar with our methods. I have never seen you before. You will pay me before entering the dressing room. The price is sixty dollars."

"Oh, sure," replied "X" cheerfully. He pulled out a roll of bills large enough to make even the Chinaman blink. He peeled off the required amount, tossed the bills to the yellow man and stumbled through the door. There he found another Chinese attendant who offered to assist "X" in putting on a suit of embroidered silk pajamas.

"X" cursed the attendant from the room; then, as he staggered across the room, he purposely tripped over the cord of the only lamp in the small dressing-room. He knew that he would be expected to disrobe and put on the pajamas; for the true opium smoker usually spends at least twenty-four hours in his bunk after smoking his two pipes. "X" had feared that he would be watched through some secret opening while he was supposed to be in the act of undressing, and he had certain equipment in the pockets of his clothes that he dared not discard.

Under cover of darkness, he pulled the pajamas on over his clothes and buttoned them tightly around his neck. Since he had apparently entered the place somewhat the worse for drink, this action would not have aroused suspicion had it been discovered. With his knife, he slit the sides of his pajamas so that he could get his gun and other material at a moment's notice.

He had scarcely completed this preparation, before the door

of the dressing room opened and another attendant entered. This man was a Chinese and wore a plain silk, sack-like garment that reached nearly to his heels. He bowed low before "X", and ushered him through a door into a large circular room.

Never before had Agent "X" seen such a place of beauty put to such a damnable purpose. The ceiling was a low dome formed by branches of a single carved tree, the trunk of which rose like a pillar from the center of the floor. Whether this tree was wrought of wood, metal, or of plaster composition, he could not tell. Bronzing metal in greens and golds tinted the profusion of artificial foliage that covered the ceiling.

And from the black, overhanging branches, tiny yellow lanterns shed light as pale moonbeams. Twined about the black trunk of the tree was a green dragon similarly wrought. From its nostrils and open mouth, wisps of incense smoke drifted lazily to mingle with the heady perfume of opium.

ABOUT the walls of the room were twenty or more bunks built into the walls. Some were closed off by filmy curtains of lustrous Oriental silk. Others were wide open, revealing the sprawled forms of their occupants. Some were wealthy men known to "X". In a few of the bunks were women, once beautiful but now reduced to frowzy abandonment, twitching in dreams induced by the black smoke.

"X" was led to an open bunk upon which he dropped. The attendant departed. Somewhere in the apartment sounded the dreamy silvery tinkle of a bell. A panel, between two bunks directly opposite "X" slid open and closed again behind the svelte figure of a young Chinese girl. From across the room she appeared a creature of fragile, jewel-like beauty.

She busied herself for a moment over a tiny, teakwood table. This table she picked up and brought over to where "X" reclined. He watched her through somnolent eyelids. Hers was a flawless ivory complexion; yet, aside from her slanting eyelids, her features were more Caucasian than Chinese. A dark red poppy nestled in her dusky hair. As she raised her eyes to meet the Agent's face, he noticed that her eyes, instead of the usual sloe-black eyes of her race, were deep blue.

She lighted the smoking-lamp, rolled a bit of opium gum from a box to the needle point of a *yen hok*. This she twirled in the flame of the lamp, watching the blue flame sputter. When the roasting was done, she deftly put the pill of opium into the brass bowl of an ivory-stemmed pipe.

"I have not come to smoke and dream, little flower of Chung Kwoh," the Agent whispered to her in Cantonese.

The girl continued her occupation, paying no more attention to his whispered words than she did to the groans and nightmare mumblings that droned from the sleepers. But this fact only confirmed what "X" had suspected almost as soon as he had laid eyes on the girl. She was no more Chinese than he was.

He accepted the brass-bowled pipe from her slender fingers, set the bit in his mouth and puffed once or twice, taking care not to allow the poisonous smoke to enter his lungs. He watched the girl narrowly as she prepared the second pill of opium. His hand thrust in under his pajamas and took out the tiny brass hand from his pocket. In a slightly amused voice, he addressed the girl in English. "As I said some moments ago in what should have been your native tongue, I am not here to smoke opium."

The girl jerked, nearly dropping the opium she had been roasting. Her violet eyes regarded "X" questioningly. He allowed opium smoke to dribble through his lips. "I have come with a message for China Bobby."

A shadow of suspicion crossed the woman's ivory face. "He is not in, sir," she replied coldly. "If you do not desire to smoke, I advise you to go and make room for another."

"I must see China Bobby. It is about the man who prevented the removal of Anthony Bernard from his apartment some hours ago."

Cautiously, she said: "If you were one of us, what sign would you give?"

"X" OPENED his hand, disclosing the tiny replica of China Bobby's maimed hand. "This," he said, knowing full well the chances he took. For if this bit of brass was not the pass to China Bobby's headquarters, he would undoubtedly be disclosed as a spy.

"Why did you not show me this in the first place?" she demanded. "Come then. China Bobby is waiting for you."

"X" followed the graceful figure of the pseudo-Chinese girl across the floor of the opium palace to the ornate sliding panel through which she had entered. Pressing on the eye of a gilded dragon that centered the panel, the girl gained admittance. She led "X" into a narrow corridor the walls of which were hung with heavy silken draperies.

At the end of the corridor, she pushed open a door and bade him enter. "X" walked into a room that was the exact opposite of the Oriental atmosphere which dominated the rest of the building. Here was the latest in modern office furnishings. Evidently, China Bobby took greater pride in his white blood than in his yellow.

The half-caste was seated behind the desk, busily scratching off a note with a modern fountain pen. He did not raise his sleek head at "X's" entrance, but simply waved him to a chromium waiting-chair against the wall of the room. "X" saw that the girl in Chinese costume had not entered the half-caste's office.

An electric signal, somewhere in China Bobby's desk, burred. He extended his pointed forefinger to a small electric switchboard, and pressed a button. A panel in one side of the room opened and closed quickly as a thin, emaciated Chinese with long stringy mustaches entered. China Bobby turned his head.

"Greeting, Yu'an," he said in Cantonese. "What is your business?"

"Master, I have had the privilege of saving thy worthy life this night."

"So?" China Bobby scratched with his pen.

"I have killed Ah-Fang when he came seeking your blood."

China Bobby whirled in his chair. "What the devil do you mean?" he broke out in English.

The man addressed as Yu'an replied in halting English. "He came with bared knife. He would have killed you."

China Bobby glanced quickly at "X," and reverted to speaking Cantonese, supposing that "X" would not understand. "I thought him with his ancestors some hours ago. Perhaps my bullet was not blessed with good fortune. Perhaps I only wounded him. What have you done with the carrion?"

Yu'an pointed significantly at the floor with a long forefinger.

China Bobby nodded his head. "You have done well, Yu'an," he replied. He reached into the drawer of his desk, took out a soiled ten dollar bill, and handed it to the Chinese. The man bowed, and retired through the panel by which he had entered. The Eurasian put aside his pen and faced "X". His sensitive nostrils dilated. Because of the fact that his right eye turned far to one side, "X" was scarcely aware that the man was looking at him.

"Who sent you here?" he demanded in his metallic voice.

"The man whose name I dare not speak," replied "X" cryptically.

He thrust his hand deep into the slit he had made in his pajamas and grasped the butt of his gas gun. They were alone in the room. Not more than ten feet separated him from the half-caste. It would be a simple matter to overcome the man, force a confession from him, learn the identity of the Ghoul, and quickly conclude the matter.

"And what message did *he* send?" asked China Bobby.

Without the slightest display of muscular effort, "X" tensed himself for a spring that would carry him to China Bobby's desk.

"I was to tell you that Anthony Bernard was saved by the activity of Secret Agent 'X'. 'X' must be sought out, and killed."

"And the Ghoul said that?" a smile flickered across China Bobby's effeminate lips. "How do you know that I am not the Ghoul?"

Now was the moment for action. China Bobby had detected falsehood. Perhaps the half-caste *was* the Ghoul, contrary as that might be to the conclusions "X" had already drawn. But at the very moment when "X" would have hurled himself upon the Eurasian, China Bobby's hand shot out and touched one of the buttons on his switchboard. Instantly, the steely nerves of Agent "X" received a terrific shock.

The metal chair in which he was seated became literally alive with crackling electrical charges. And try as he might, "X" could not break the invisible bonds of current that held him to the chair. He was helpless, racked with pain that was like the thrusts of a thousand needle points. At any moment, the diabolical Eurasian might move the switch, increasing the amperage to a point where "X" would die—die like a common criminal in the death-cell of Sing Sing prison.

CHAPTER VIII

THE GRAVELESS DEAD

FOR A TIME, the Eurasian grinned with sadistic mirth. Then his voice rose above the hum of the electric current that had caught even the wily Secret Agent in its invisible web.

"These are Chinese police methods, Mr. Detective," China Bobby said. "You must admit they are some improvement over your methods of truth learning. An extremely high voltage at relatively low amperage prevents the current from doing you any serious damage. But always, the current is variable. Will you taste a little more?" He touched the button on his switchboard and the current increased, shooting tingling splinters of fire through "X's" entire body.

The Agent's face was contorted as though the pain was almost unbearable. Actually, he was watching a narrow slot in the wall which had opened when China Bobby had turned on the current. Through the slot, dark eyes watched the captive in the electric chair.

"Now," said China Bobby, "perhaps you will explain how you managed to enter here? Who sent you?"

"X" shook his head. "You're wasting time."

China Bobby laughed and stepped up the torture current another notch. "Now, your name!"

"X" writhed, unable to take his hands from the metal arms of the chair. "Martin Smith," he groaned. "Good Lord, man! Stop it! You're killing me!"

"And who is Martin Smith?" demanded China Bobby.

"Federal agent—narcotics."

China Bobby nodded. "And what becomes of spies, Martin Smith?"

"Get shot," the Agent gasped. "You couldn't do that. Too merciful."

"True," said China Bobby slowly, as though he was considering what more terrible death his sadistic cunning might devise. "We have our stinging ants, always anxious to be put to work. Or perhaps you could be lashed with nettles. That's rather unpleasant. Then, of course there's the Amber Death in which men die to live a brief eternity of mental torment. Or again, I might burn you in that chair." With an evil smile, China Bobby stepped up the current another notch.

"Turn off that current."

A voice had whispered from the walls of the room in which they were seated. The half-caste turned pale, and jerked his head toward the slot in the wall which "X" had been watching. He murmured something and cut the switch. "X" felt muscles and nerves relax. He stared at the slot in the wall and the glittering eyes behind it. They were the eyes of the Ghoul.

AGAIN came the voice of the Ghoul, this time speaking in Cantonese, obviously with the intent that "X" should not understand.

"That man is lying to you. If he is not the one known as 'The Man of a Thousand Faces'—then he is one of his servants. He would not speak the truth were he to be lashed with scorpions. But if he is the man I think he is, then there is *one* who can make him talk. We shall learn later on. If he were to see *her* in the ant pit, he would talk. But there are other matters that require my attention. Let him be held a prisoner in the cells below. I would have speech with you alone."

"Yes, master," said China Bobby. There was no mistaking the whipped-cur attitude with which he regarded the Ghoul. It seemed to "X" that each of the Ghoul's words had been a leaden weight descending upon the Agent's shoulders. The Ghoul's insinuations had been unmistakable. By some ruse, he had managed to lure Betty Dale into this devil's den.

Pressing the buttons on his switchboard, China Bobby summoned two men. One of them was the emaciated Yu'an; the other a broad-shouldered, black-haired Irishman addressed as Morgan.

"Take this man to the cells," China Bobby ordered. "Search him first."

Morgan prodded "X" to his feet with the muzzle of his automatic. "No funny business, now," he cautioned.

Yu'an ripped off the pajamas "X" wore, then relieved him of his gas gun. Supposing, no doubt, that it was a regular automatic, the Chinese put the gas pistol in his own pocket. "X's" compact make-up kit, pocket tool-kit, master keys, medical kit and other special equipment were laid on top of China Bobby's desk. Then, seizing "X" between them, they dragged him through a doorway and into a short hall that ended in a flight of stone steps descending to a sub-cellar. As they were going down the steps, "X" debated whether or not to try and jump Morgan's gun. He had overpowered armed men many times before. But to hope to be able to quietly knock both Yu'an and Morgan unconscious before they could sound an alarm, was too much. He must not take unnecessary risks. There was more at stake now than before. For Betty Dale had fallen into the power of this master criminal.

The stone steps ended in a veritable catacomb of damp, brick-lined rooms. Iron gratings covered darkened cells—cells which at that moment might have been housing Calvert or some of the others who had been taken from Gage's house that night.

Morgan threw open a door, flung "X" to the damp floor, and slammed the grating. There was the click of a lock and the sound of receding footsteps, as Yu'an and Morgan returned the way they had come.

Though Yu'an's search had seemed thorough, "X" was not entirely stripped of his resources. The Chinese had left him such innocent little devices as a fountain pen and a cigar lighter. Then in the heels of his shoes were little compartments where he carried a tiny tube of make-up material, a vial of powerful narcotic, and a number of finely tempered tools. The lining of his coat had several accessories, that Yu'an had overlooked, sewed into it.

HIS first act was to take the fountain pen from his pocket. It resolved itself into a small but powerful flashlight. With this, he took stock of his surroundings. Cold brick walls and a floor through which moisture was seeping, a wooden bench, nothing more. He approached the door and turned his flashlight on the lock. For a moment, escape seemed impossible.

The lock on the door was a pattern he had seen but a few times in his life. It was an ancient Chinese pin-lock, entirely different from western locks and in some ways superior. It consisted of two separate parts—a socket, and a wedge-shaped piece of flexible steel that fitted into the socket. The shackle, which in this case passed through the iron grill and a ring welded to the door frame, was simply a straight pin. The keyhole was so shaped that only one key could fit it. The key would be so channeled as to pull the wedge-shaped members of the steel together and at the same time force the lock open. There were neither tumblers nor movable cylinders. It was a veritable Waterloo for even a professional lockpick. "X" knew that the tools he carried in the heel at his shoe would be absolutely worthless.

It was then that he remembered a part of his equipment which he was seldom called upon to use. In a moment he had stripped off his coat, torn a strip from the lining, put in his hand, and pulled out a flat little bag of cloth. From the other side of his coat, he pulled out a similar bag. Each bag contained a small quantity of powder of his own compounding, so combined as to render ordinarily dangerous chemicals safe to carry.

"X" tore through the corners of each of the bags. Then he emptied the contents of both bags into the keyhole of the Chinese padlock. He retired to the end of the cell, turned out his flashlight, and waited. Brought into contact with one another, the two chemicals would combine in a complex chemical reaction producing terrific heat. The substance was very similar to that known by welders as thermite.

After perhaps a minute, the entire cell was engulfed in a blaze of dazzling white light that emanated with a hissing sound from the lock of the door. After the flare had subsided, the lock was a white-hot mass of twisted metal. "X" well knew that no tempered steel could withstand such temperature. He picked up the wooden bench and knocked open the grating. Then he stepped out into the dark passage.

He had no time even to examine the neighboring cells under the gleam of his flashlight before he saw a dot of light hurrying down the corridor towards him. "X" stepped aside, flattened himself against the wall. He heard the footsteps of a single man coming toward him. Evidently some one had heard him escaping from the cell. A few feet from "X", the man came to a stop, staring in awe at the open grating.

"X" sprang toward the man, his cigarette lighter in his hand. The man turned at the sound and stabbed for his gun. But before he could get it out, "X" had pressed a button on the side of the lighter and a fine spray of anesthetizing vapor shot from the lighter. At the same time, he wrenched the man's automatic from his hand. The Ghoul's servant staggered, choked on an oath, and fell forward at "X's" feet. His flashlight crashed to the floor and went out.

"X" turned the beam of his own light on the man's face. It was the dark-haired, broad-shouldered Morgan. The Secret Agent dragged him back into the cell. There, he made a careful search of the man's pockets. The search revealed nothing that would be of use to "X" save a bunch of keys. Probably, Morgan was the Ghoul's jailor.

In another moment, "X" was out of the passage and running toward the stairway. He took the steps two at a time, and came to a stop at the door that lead into China Bobby's office. A moment he hesitated. There was no sound within the office, yet the half-caste might still be at work at his desk. "X" drew the automatic that he had taken from Morgan. He tried the door and found it unlocked. Cautiously, he inched it open.

The room was empty, and on the desk lay the Agent's special equipment that the searching fingers of Yu'an had taken from him. Quickly, he removed the contents of his makeup kit, medical kit, and tool-kit. He thrust the rest of his equipment into his pockets and was putting his amplifying device away when he heard the murmur of voices on the other side of the left-hand wall. He tiptoed across the room, his sound amplifying device in his hand.[49]

He placed the microphone against the wall and held the box to his ear. Manipulating a rheostat on one side of the box, he clarified the sound, and made the words audible. The Ghoul was speaking and evidently to China Bobby:

"That Morgan has failed. Furthermore, our spies believe that last night he tried to get in touch with the police. He is trying to sell out. Inasmuch as we must get rid of him, I intend to use him as a subject of experimentation. Vardson, the chief chemist, has developed a new phase of the Amber Death that does not penetrate so rapidly and hence does not reach the vital organs so quickly. It means better control for us and longer torment for our victims—and more money. You understand, China Bobby?"

"Yes, Master," replied the half-caste meekly.

"Then in a few minutes you will send the man Morgan to the laboratory on some trumped-up errand. Later, we shall see to this girl reporter. From her we may be able to learn something definite regarding the man who stands between us and the wealth of the nation."

---

49 AUTHOR'S NOTE: This amplifier resembles a small camera. In the box of this efficient piece of apparatus is a stage of amplification, as well as an extremely compact reproducer. The microphone is attached to the box by means of a covered wire lead. A rheostat serves to control the intensity of the sound.

CHINA BOBBY started to say something. However, "X" did not listen for more. He sprang back to the steps leading down into the catacombs. Without the aid of his light, he hurried down the steps. As he ran along the narrow tunnel, he flashed his light from one cell to another, trying to locate the one occupied by the unconscious Morgan.

In two of the cells, he saw nondescript underworld characters chained to the wall, evidently being disciplined for some slight mistake they had made while serving the Ghoul. In another cell, "X" saw the body of Ah-Fang, one-time valet of Gilbert Warnow. He had evidently only suffered a scalp wound from the bullet China Bobby had fired at him that night. Probably, he had come seeking to be revenged on the half-caste only to be murdered by Yu'an.

Entering the cell in which he had been imprisoned for so short a time, "X" knelt beside the unconscious Morgan. For a brief interlude, he studied every angle of the man's face. Then setting up the small mirror that he had taken from his pocket make-up kit, he proceeded, in the uncertain light of his flashlight, to disguise himself as Morgan. In spite of the adverse conditions under which he worked, the effect was marvelous. After he had changed clothes with the gunman he felt that he could pass for Morgan even under the eyes of the Ghoul.

In a corner of the cell, "X" hid as much of his paraphernalia as he possibly could. He retained the automatic which he had taken from Morgan; it was a weapon that would arouse no suspicion in case he was searched. He also loaded a small hypodermic needle with an anesthetizing drug, and concealed the needle in an inner pocket of his coat. Having slipped a new charging cylinder into the anesthetizing gas chamber of his lighter, he considered himself prepared to meet the Ghoul.

"X" had already deduced something of the process by which the Ghoul turned men into hideous, living mummies. He knew that certain aldehydes, particularly formaldehyde, produce peculiar changes in the proteins of the human body. That formic acid played some part in the preparation of the mysterious chemical compound the Ghoul employed, had been indicated by China Bobby's reference to stinging ants and nettles. Both were natural sources of that acid. "X" believed that the Ghoul's Amber Death simply enabled him to change the colloidal protein on the human body into synthetic amber. The Ghoul embalmed his victims alive.[50]

It was as he hurried up the steps leading from the Ghoul's prison cells that his disguise was compelled to undergo its severest test. A beam of light in the hands of a man at the top of the steps flashed directly into his eyes. "X" stopped, and steeled his nerves for the ordeal that was to come. For he had seen Morgan only twice, and heard him speak once.

"Morgan!" China Bobby's cold metallic voice sounded hollow as he shouted down the stairs. "What have you been doing down there?"

"Oh, it was that dick we took in, sir," the Agent explained, relying on his memory to recall the voice and manner of speaking of the man he represented.

"What's the matter with him?"

"He was making all kinds of a fuss. So I conked him on the head, and he'll be out for a bit of a nap."

China Bobby stood aside to permit "X" to enter the office. He followed the Secret Agent, closing the door behind him. "The Ghoul," China Bobby said, "places a good deal of trust in you, Morgan."

"Glad to hear that," replied "X".

"As you probably have heard, we are going to kidnap the mayor shortly, and force him to appeal to the people of the city for a huge sum of money to be paid to the Ghoul for his release. You understand what *kind* of release!" China Bobby chuckled. "The Ghoul wants to see you."

"X's" jaw dropped. He simulated surprise. "Y-you mean I am to meet *him* face to face?" But while he had spoken to the half-caste, his mind considered this new enterprise of the Ghoul. Kidnap the mayor. Then Mayor Grauman would be subjected to the Amber Death.

China Bobby smiled. "I cannot say as to that," he replied. "But come with me. I will show you to the laboratory." China Bobby touched a button on his desk. One of the many sliding doors in

---

50 AUTHOR'S NOTE: Though a clever chemist, "X" has never been able to learn the complete formula for the Amber Death. He compares it, however, to the secret embalming method used by the Russians in embalming the body of Lenin, their national hero. As the reader may know, the body of Lenin is preserved because of some colloid-chemical reaction has converted it into solid amber. "X" explained to me that the Amber Death is, strictly speaking, not a poison, but an agent for promoting a definite chemical change within the body.

the room opened. He led "X" through this and down a labyrinthian corridor to stop in front of a steel door. There was a Chinese dragon lacquered on the center of the door. The half-caste said: "You have only to press the eye of the dragon and you will be in the laboratory." He turned and retraced his steps.

Without hesitation, "X" pressed the dragon's eye. Immediately, the lights in the passage went out. The entire floor seemed to tremble beneath him and move down so gradually that he was scarcely conscious of it. A panel flipped open in front of him, and he faced a brilliantly lighted room. Boldly he stepped into the room and the panel closed behind him. In amazement that his masterly control could not disguise, "X" stared about the room. And in a row along the wall, the graveless dead stared back at him.

A veritable museum of accursed art! A silent hell. The laboratory of Satan himself. Daniel Calvert, Lionel Gage, Dr. Luigi, Gilbert Warnow and others who had mysteriously disappeared in the last few days—all were there, standing erect, their stiffened bodies yellow shells of amber. And inside those hardened bodies, they lived and knew the torture of the damned. But aside from himself, "X" saw no other truly living thing within the room. On shelves and in cabinets about the room were rows of chemicals and apparatus.

As "X" looked about the room, a cabinet against the wall swung back, revealing a doorway. A man dressed in a surgeon's white gown entered the room to be followed by six vicious-faced men of both yellow and white races.

"X" recognized the man in white. He was Dr. Vardson, a scientist and medical man who had recently been deprived of his license to practice. Probably Vardson was responsible for the development of the Amber Death.

Although he knew the scientist, "X" asked timidly of the man in white: "Are you the Ghoul?"

A MAD cackle of a laugh broke from the scientist's lips. "No, I am not the Ghoul!"

"Are you concerned about my presence, Morgan?" the cold, inhuman whisper of the Ghoul breathed from empty air. "Know then that I am always with you. Nothing that you do, or have done, has escaped my notice."

"X's" eyes roamed around the chamber. Between a pair of powerful electric lamps in the ceiling, he saw the conical diaphragm of an ordinary radio speaker. Through this the Ghoul spoke. "X" realized the seriousness of the position in which he had placed himself. Hoping to meet the Ghoul face to face, he had been willing to risk meeting even the Amber Death. But the Ghoul, always shrewd, always cunning, took no personal risks. He remained the disembodied voice, the invisible presence. "X" was not in the hands of the master criminal, but in the hands of his paid assassins.

"Morgan," said the Ghoul, "we have developed a new phase of the Amber Death—a milder form that will give us better control. So many of our victims have died from the Amber Death before we had a chance to give them a thorough milking. It is my intention that we shall kidnap the mayor, keep him under the influence of the Amber Death, and make the city pay for his release—his release from life, that is. It will be my master stroke. We will gut the treasury of the city. You understand?"

"X" shook his head. He knew that the Ghoul was simply trying to distract his attention from the fact that the pack of criminals was slowly forming a circle about him. "Don't get much of this," he said, stalling for time. "How can you get money from these rich slobs after you've given them the Amber Death?"

The Ghoul laughed. A note of pride crept into his whispering voice as he said: "Few understand that. The common extortionist threatens his victims with death, if they do not pay. But I have learned that men will pay money to be allowed to die—when one makes the burden of life more terrible than any conception of death! The secret is combining life with death. The statues you see around the room are living brains within dead shells. Even you must understand the torture of living within a sarcophagus of your flesh!"

Like wolves circling the dying fire, hungry eyes on the hunter they will tear to shreds, the Ghoul's murderers moved restlessly about Secret Agent "X"

"You will notice," the Ghoul went on, "that the right hands of all these living statues are as yet unaffected by the Amber Death. This enables them to write orders of my own dictation and sign them with their names. Such orders direct the payment of money and negotiable securities to my own agents. Each time they pay, they are promised release from life. But eventually, the creeping Amber Death claims them all."

Out of the corner of his eye, "X" watched the men who were closing in on him. He could see that they did not relish the prospect of meeting the broad-shouldered Morgan in open fighting. Yet they feared the Ghoul above everything else, and they would obey him.

"Why don't your victims hear what you've just said to me and refuse to pay, knowing that you have no intention of living up to your promise?" asked "X". His right hand was in his pocket, fingering with his cigarette lighter.

Again the Ghoul laughed. "Their torture is increased by the fact that I have carefully sealed their ears. They hear only when I desire to speak with them. And they are blind. Dead bodies, living brains, eternal darkness. It is little wonder that they pray for death!"

"X" knew that in another moment, the criminal horde would be upon him. He took out his lighter, fingered it absently. Suddenly, he leaped upon the nearest man. A mere puff of vapor from the lighter, and the man bowled over.

A command shrieked from the loudspeaker in the ceiling. "Take him alive!"

A horde of yellow and white humanity suddenly descended upon "X". He snapped out the automatic he had taken from Morgan. Much as he disliked lethal weapons, he shot quickly and accurately. His first bullet crashed through the thigh of an ugly Chinese. He twisted in the grasp of thin, steely hands, dealt powerful blows with his left fist, tried to wrench his right arm free from the hold of another man in order to get in more telling shots.

And mingling in the general turmoil, behind the line of danger, "X" glimpsed another figure—a man whom he had not seen in the room before—a man whose entire head was swathed in a yellow veil that concealed his features. He saw, too, even as he fell to the floor, a tiny, round black button fastened to the lapel of the veiled man. And the veiled man's hands—one was white, and the other the sickly yellow of the Amber Death! The mystery of the Ghoul was solved—too late?

For at that moment, a sharp pain knifed through "X's" left leg. The Ghoul's voice came again—not from the speaker in the ceiling but from the man with the yellow veil.

"Vardson, you fool!" The Ghoul shouted. "You've used the wrong needle! That one contained the old form of the Amber Death—not the new! You've made a mistake. Morgan may die before we can complete our experiment!"

A strange numbness was creeping over "X's" body. His blows were becoming less effective. There was cold pain in his left leg as though muscles were gradually knotting. Many times in his career he had knocked at the door of death. But now the door had opened. The Amber Death, the death that was worse than death, was upon him. Minutes marched, approaching that time when he would no longer be a man, no longer Secret Agent "X," but a helpless, living, yellow mummy.

CHAPTER IX

DANGER BELOW

HIDDEN BEHIND HIS minions, the Ghoul shouted his orders. "Clear the room. To the cells with Vardson. He shall taste torture! Put Morgan in the second laboratory! Go—all of you!"

"X" felt himself dragged across the room. A door sprang open, and he was thrown to the floor. The door closed. He could hear men running before the furious commands of the Ghoul; could hear the screams of the half-mad Vardson as he was dragged to the place of his punishment. Then, all was silent.

"X" stared about him. This second laboratory was smaller than the other. At one end he saw the black panel of a radio transmitter. Evidently, it was from here that the Ghoul's warning messages originated. He saw, too, apparatus for transcribing phonograph records. Experimental chemical and electrical apparatus littered the room. Shelves were laden with drugs and chemicals. It was toward these shelves that "X" looked for some tiny ray of hope.

With a mighty effort, he dragged himself to his feet. The pain of the contracting muscles in his left leg would have been unbearable to the average man. He limped to the shelves that lined the wall. His feverish eyes devoured the labels one by one and paused on a small vial of adrenalin. Rummaging in a drawer with hands that were already unfeeling, he found a hypodermic needle. Hastily, he filled the syringe, rolled back his sleeve, and made the injection. Almost instantly, the natural stimulant began to take effect. But it could not halt the creeping death.

He only hoped that it would give him fifteen minutes' strength before the final rigor set in. In that time, he must find the Ghoul.

But he was without a weapon. He had lost Morgan's automatic in the battle in the laboratory. He was looking about the room for some sort of an instrument that would spell death for the Ghoul,

A command shrieked from the loudspeaker. "Take him alive!"

when a sound at the other end of the laboratory caused him to turn around.

A door flung open and he saw the slight, lovely figure of a woman running toward him. It was the blue-eyed, pseudo-Chinese girl who served in China Bobby's dope den. She stopped five feet from him and stared, wide-eyed with horror. "Bill, darling!" With a sob, she flung herself into his arms and clung passionately to him. "I heard that the Ghoul no longer trusted you," she sobbed out. "I was afraid—afraid he might use the Amber Death.... Your hands—already yellow!"

She turned from the Secret Agent. "Don't worry. There's a way out! You have to oxydize the chemical producing the Amber Death. If you get it in time, everything will be all right. That's how they prevent the Amber Death from reaching the extortion victim's right hand." She fairly flew around the room, dumping chemicals into a glass beaker. "Watch the door, Bill. I'm through with the Ghoul! If he comes in here, kill him!"

The strange, unexpected entrance of the girl could be explained only by the fact that Bill Morgan was evidently some one who was very dear to her. As soon as she had entered the room, "X" recognized her voice. In fact, he had suspected from the very first that she was Drew Devon so disguised as to lend Oriental atmosphere to the opium palace and at the same time enable the Ghoul to have a person he trusted watching over the opium den at all times.

"X" watched Drew Devon work. She was mixing a strange concoction. He knew that if she failed in her efforts to halt the creeping death, he would have not only lost his life but also the chance of ridding the earth of the Ghoul. He looked down at his hand. The flesh was faintly tinged with yellow. He knocked the back of his hand against the edge of the work table. It rapped out like a wooden thing and there was no feeling in it.

Pale beneath the yellow paint she wore on her face, Drew Devon turned toward him. She filled a huge hypodermic syringe with the pinkish fluid from the beaker. She peeled back both sleeves of his coat, jabbed the needle into his flesh, and pumped the pinkish liquid into his blood stream.

"The other arm, quickly," she whispered. And again the needle went home.

A TINGLING sensation raced through "X's" body. But he had yet to regain his old strength. Drew Devon hurried back to the shelves, filled a clean beaker with liquid from a bottle, and handed it to him. "Drink this," she commanded.

He took the beaker and drank gratefully. It had contained some stimulant not altogether unfamiliar to "X".

"Feeling better?" she asked with a smile.

"A lot," "X" replied. Already the stiffness had passed from his legs and arms. "Where'd you learn—"

"Vardson taught me," she said quickly. "I've helped him in the laboratory. But we mustn't stay here."

"Right! I'm goin' back after that damned Ghoul!"

Drew Devon seized both of his arms. "Bill! You can't! Come, we'll go to my room, until I can plan a way for us to escape. You can't match wits with the Ghoul! Oh, I've risked everything to save you. I can't lose you now. Next time, he might throw you into the ant pit as he has Vardson. Come quickly!"

Holding him by the hand, Drew Devon led him through a door, and into a hall. At the end of the hall and down a short flight of steps, she stopped in front of the door of her room. Taking a key from the pocket of her Oriental garb, she unlocked the door.

It was a small room, but comfortably furnished. She forced "X" to sit down into a chair. Going to a table, she selected a cigarette, lighted it, and regarded him through half-closed eyes for a few minutes. Suddenly, she got up, crossed the room and kissed him impulsively. She sat down on the arm of the chair and dropped her arm over his shoulder. Her face close to his she whispered dreamily:

"Don't know why I love you, Bill. Don't know why I staked everything on saving you."

"X" looked into the lovely face and frowned. "Love me as much as you did that rich slob of a Calvert?" he demanded.

Drew Devon recoiled from him, stood up. "Bill! Jealous, after all I've done for you? You know I hated Calvert. I had some old letters he'd written me. I was trying to collect five grand on them, and he wouldn't come across. The piker! Satisfied?"

"X" shook his head. "Not yet, Drew."

The girl's yellow-tinted forehead crimped into a tight frown. For a moment, fury possessed her to such an extent that she could not speak. When she had found her tongue, she spoke in an icy whisper: "So, I am Drew, am I? An error on your part! So I save the man I think to be Bill Morgan, and he calls me Drew—a name he has never known me by! Now, I know you—Secret Agent 'X'!"

WITH the speed of a striking snake, her hand darted inside her garment, and reappeared with a small, black automatic. The pistol cracked almost as soon as she had drawn it. But at the first movement of the girl toward the hiding place of the weapon, "X" had leaped to his feet.

He swerved slightly to the right and the shot spent itself on the wall behind him. She had no time to pull the trigger again before "X" had seized the gun and twisted it from her hand. He turned the muzzle toward her.

"Tell me where Betty Dale is!" he demanded.

For a moment, Drew Devon's eyes were riveted in terror on the gun in the Agent's hands. Then a smile curved her lips. "I do not think Secret Agent 'X' would kill a woman. I am taking advantage of your gallantry."

"X's" left hand sought the pocket of his coat, and flashed out again. The hypodermic needle, which he had filled previous to his impersonation of Morgan, stabbed into the woman's arm. A shrill cry of terror died in her throat as she fell forward into "X's" arms.

He carried her to a little closet at one side of the room, and placed her on the floor. He removed the black wig the woman wore and slipped it into his pocket. Then he took a pair of Oriental pajamas, similar to the ones Drew Devon wore, from a clothes hanger in the closet. These he concealed under his coat.

He turned next to the woman's dressing table. Removing the small tube of plastic volatile material from the heel of his left shoe, he lost no time in making slight but effective alterations in his make-up. He added deep lines in his cheeks, a crook in his nose, and removed the black wig which had been part of his Morgan disguise. Then armed with the little automatic he had taken from Drew Devon, he opened the door and stepped into the hall.

"X" knew that he would have to go down into the prison cells on the floor below. It was there that he must first look for Betty Dale. At the end of the hall, instead of opening the door that led into the second laboratory, he turned to the door at his left. This door yielded when he used one of the keys that he had removed from Morgan's pockets. Down another short hall he came to what appeared to be a blank wall.

A careful search under the beam of his flashlight revealed a tiny black button near the base of the panel. He knew that this was a door leading into China Bobby's office—the connecting link between the half-caste's dope den and the underground realm of the Ghoul. Without further hesitation he pressed the button. An electric signal burred; the panel slid back.

The office of China Bobby was empty. "X" went to the half-caste's desk and examined the switchboard that he had seen China Bobby use. It was covered with perhaps a dozen different buttons, each one marked with a letter. He had to take a chance on the button marked "C" opening the door into the cells in which the Ghoul kept his prisoners. At a touch of the button, another panel slid back and "X" recognized the dark stone stairway that led to the catacombs below.

As he hurried through the door, a sharp clicking sound behind him, stopped him. He shot a glance over his shoulder, but saw no one in the office.

"X" ran down the steps. That clicking sound had worried him. It might be some sort of a signal that would send a troup of the Ghoul's men hard on his heels.

As he entered the row of cells, the stale air was knifed by a giggling shriek of stark madness. From directly ahead of him the cry had come. He hurried forward, flashlight darting from one cell to another. Suddenly, he stopped. Yawning in the floor, in front of him, was a pit covered with an iron grating set in the floor. "X" sent his light beam down into the opening, revealing a scene of revolting horror.

In the pit, the mad scientist, Vardson, ripped his garments from his back; tore at his own flesh with his fingernails. The man was a raving maniac—a product of the Ghoul's torture. The floor of the pit was like a single moving, red shadow. Stinging ants! Vardson's body teemed with noxious, stinging little lives. A myriad of tiny legs scurried across his face, into his eyes.

THAT such might be the fate of Betty Dale spurred "X" into action. Vardson was beyond help. But Betty—

He stopped only long enough in the cell where he had left the unconscious Morgan, to regain his special equipment. Then he was out into the narrow passage again, the searching beam of his light darting from one cell to another.

As the passage branched abruptly to the right, "X" came upon a little cell apart from the others. Through the iron grating, he saw the form of a woman extended at full length on the wooden bench. It was Betty. Her eyes were closed, and she was breathing heavily. She must have been drugged, for without the assistance of narcotics no one could have slept within the range of the tortured Vardson's screaming voice.

With feverish haste, he unlocked the cell door with one of Morgan's keys. Under the light of his flash, he searched his pockets and laid out strips of transparent adhesive, makeup material, yellow pigment, and the wig and pajamas he had taken from Drew Devon. He knelt beside the sleeping girl. His fingers worked quickly and skilfully.

With the transparent adhesive tape, he stretched the flesh around the girl's eyelids so that her eyes attained the slanting appearance of a Chinese. Then he spread on plastic volatile material and yellow pigment over Betty's face. And when he had completed his task, Betty looked the exact counterpart of Drew Devon when the latter was disguised for service in the opium den. He completed the disguise by putting the black wig over Betty's blonde curls.

Then he gave her a stimulating hypodermic that brought her out of unconsciousness in a few seconds. The girl sat up, stared about her with terror-filled eyes. She met the strange face of the man who had worked miracles with her appearance. Her lips formed the unuttered question: "Who?"

"X" smiled reassuringly. "Don't you know me, Betty?" He drew the letter "X" on the bench.

She gasped. "How did you get here?"

"Tell you later," he said. Picking up his pocket mirror, he held it before her face. "While you're getting used to being a pretty Chinese lass, you can tell me by what trick the Ghoul brought *you* here."

She stared for a moment in astonishment at her new features. Then: "I received a call from a man whom I thought was the city editor. He told me to go over to China Bobby's restaurant, that another reporter would meet me there. It was a woman I had never seen before who met me. It must have been one of the Ghoul's gang, because she led me back through a door and into a room where there was a man with a golden veil over his face. He asked me all sorts of questions about you. I didn't say anything. He said something about putting me with the ants or something like that. Some one carried me down here. I was drugged. I don't remember anything else."

The Agent's eyes burned with fury as he thought of what might have happened to Betty. "Just the kind of a trick the Ghoul would try," he said. "Do you remember Drew Devon? Think you can impersonate her? You've *got* to. You *must* get out of this rotten hole."

"But you? What will happen to you?"

KNOWING the generous nature of the girl, "X" knew that she valued his safety above her own. If he was to persuade her to leave him in this moment of great danger, he knew that he would have to give her some responsibility outside the Ghoul's headquarters. "My work is not yet completed here," he told her. "Your task is to warn the mayor."

"The mayor!" she exclaimed. "You mean the Ghoul might use

his Amber Death on the mayor?"

"X" nodded. "And if the Ghoul succeeds in his plan, who knows but what he will next turn his eyes toward Washington! But you must hurry. You'll have to put on these Oriental pajamas to make your disguise complete. Quickly, now. Everything depends upon the speed with which we act. If you stay here, the least the Ghoul will do is torture you in an attempt to gain some information."

Betty needed no urging. She had already slipped out of her dress, and was putting on the pajamas. She had scarcely fastened the jacket of the garment when a whispering sound broke through the darkness. It was the voice of the Ghoul. It seemed to be coming from the hall right outside the cell.

"Spy, do you presume that at this very moment I am not watching you?"

Betty uttered a frightened little gasp. She clutched the Agent's arm. "What was that?" she whispered.

"The Ghoul," he replied softly, "has loudspeakers located everywhere in this place. He isn't watching. He can see no better through this gloom than we can. It's the colossal egoism of the man. He must have seen me enter this prison from that peephole he has in the wall of the office."

"But if he knows you're down here, why doesn't he send some one after you?"

"X" did not answer that question. He knew that that was exactly what the Ghoul would do, or had already done. His mind was busy, trying to see a way out of their difficulty. He took Betty by the arm and led her through the door of the cell. He turned out his flashlight and handed it to her. "Don't use it until you leave me," he said. "We'll work as far toward the steps as we can. Don't trip over that grating in the floor."

A low moaning sound came up from beneath their very feet. Then the stagnant air was rent by an hysterical laugh. Vardson, in the ant pit.

Betty clung closely to the Agent as he piloted her through the darkness. "Leave you? Do you think I could leave you—now?" came her tremulous whisper. But the element of concern for the Agent in her voice dominated any indication of personal fear.

"X's" heart was pounding like a triphammer. For all he knew, the darkness shrouded some diabolical trick of the Ghoul. His arm encircled Betty's shoulders. For a moment held her with fierce tenderness. Then reason mastered sentiment. He pressed Drew Devon's automatic into her hand. "Shoot to kill, if you have to," he told her as they moved slowly up the passage. "In this same direction, you'll find a flight of steps leading out of here. If the door at the top isn't open, you'll find a little black button right at the bottom of the door. Press it. Once in China Bobby's office, you'll have to experiment with the switchboard to find the button that opens the front door leading into the opium den. Don't worry. I'll probably be right behind you."

Again the Ghoul's voice whispered along the corridor. "Spy, Secret Agent 'X,' or whoever you are, my eyes are upon you. My hand is lifted to strike!"

Betty tried to suppress a shudder.

"Be brave, Betty," the Agent whispered. "He may try some sort of a trick. But remember, *you* are Drew Devon. If we are cornered, you must pretend to struggle with me. You must cry out that I am Secret Agent 'X'."

A little sob broke from Betty's lips. "No—no! I will never do that! Not for all the mayors and presidents!"

"X" STOPPED, seized the girl's shoulders, and held her tightly. "Betty!" he whispered sternly. "And I always thought that I could rely upon you! You must do exactly as I tell you if the Ghoul's men come. It will give you an opportunity to get through the lines. Your disguise is perfect. In the part of Drew Devon, you cannot do otherwise than denounce me. And remember, when you reach China Bobby's office, I will be right behind you!"

"But you can't hope to escape!"

"I *can* escape, only if you play your part. Hush!.... There's some one coming up the passage behind.... Remember your part—struggle, cry out that I am Secret Agent 'X'.... Wait—"

Breathless, they listened in the darkness. Soft, padded footsteps sounded behind them. And in front of them, the rasp of a door opening. Husky whisperings. They were between two squads of the Ghoul's men.

Suddenly, a barrage of light-beams shot through the darkness in front of them. And from behind, men came running. "X" turned and seized Betty with his left arm. His right hand closed gently but realistically over her throat. She struggled, kicking and screaming. "Help! This man is Secret Agent 'X'. Help!" she cried.

And as the twin squads bore upon them, "X" pushed Betty from him and toward the door. He turned to meet his foremost foeman, knowing that the man would not dare use his gun for fear of hitting the girl he supposed to be Drew Devon. "X's" fist smashed into the man's jaw, sent him reeling backwards.

The agent ducked under a descending knife, seized the man by the waist, picked him up bodily, and threw him back over his shoulder. As he fought with silent fury, he saw a bright flash of color move through the criminal band, and streak toward the steps. Betty had played her part well. She was on the way to safety.

But the girl gone, "X" knew the criminals would not hesitate to use firearms. Though he wore a bullet proof vest, he knew that at such close range he could not hope that vulnerable parts of his body would escape the flying shot. But he had prepared for that crucial moment. Beating back his nearest opponents with Herculean blows of his left fist, his right hand plunged into his pocket and closed upon a little glass capsule that had been enclosed in his medical kit.

He took a deep breath, sprung aside to avoid a knife-thrust, and dropped the fragile glass bubble on the floor of the passage. There was a sharp pop and instantly a cloud of gray vapor rose from the floor. A man directly in front of "X" spilled forward on his face. "X" hurdled him; brushed aside another staggering, choking man; drove his fist into the surprised face of another, and he was free. He ran up the passage, pounded up the stone stairway, and sprang into China Bobby's office.

The half-caste was there, his back toward "X." He was holding Betty by the arms, evidently thoroughly convinced that she was Drew Devon.

"But, Drew," China Bobby insisted, "you can't go out in the streets in broad daylight in the outfit of a Chinese girl. It might lead the police to investigate these cellars."

Betty, over the Eurasian's shoulders, saw "X" as he stealthily approached. Perhaps China Bobby saw the anxiety in the girl's eyes, for he immediately released her, turned, and snatched at the gun in his coat pocket. But as China Bobby turned, "X" leaped. All the strength of his lean, hard body was behind that long upper-cut that landed on the point of the Eurasian's chin. China Bobby hardly had time to utter a groan as he fell to the floor.

"X" seized him under the arms and dragged him to a little curtained closet. It would not do for the Ghoul to look through the peek-hole and see his chief lieutenant laid out on the floor. Then "X" joined Betty at the desk. With his finger, the Agent pressed the switch button marked "F." This, he believed, was the switch operating the front door of the office. As the panel slid back, he saw that his conjecture had been correct; beyond was a beautiful yet terrible temple of the black smoke. Some of the silk-curtained bunks were still occupied by dreaming addicts. "X" led Betty across the room, into the entryway, and up the spiral staircase to the rear door of the restaurant.

Looking out through the door of the restaurant, "X" saw that China Bobby's legitimate employees were busily engaged in preparing the restaurant for the evening.

"Go at once to the mayor and warn him," the agent whispered in Betty's ear. "But do not go to the police. A police raid at such a time would ruin all my plans. The Ghoul would escape."

"You're not coming with me?" she said, a look of dismay passing over her ivory-tinted face.

"X" shook his head. "My task has only begun." And, as he watched Betty hurrying toward the door, he looked through the plate glass front of the building. It was evening. He had, then, spent over twelve hours in the catacombs beneath China Bobby's restaurant.

CHAPTER X

THRONE OF THE GHOUL

"X" HURRIEDLY RETRACED his steps to China Bobby's office. Slipping into the closet where he had concealed the Eurasian, he stood his pocket mirror against the wall and began working on the most difficult disguise he had ever attempted. For a man of "X's" ability, the features and flesh tints of China Bobby were not difficult to duplicate; but there were two physical defects in China Bobby's appearance that it was almost impossible for anyone to imitate—the missing finger on his right hand, and the fact that some muscular trouble had turned one of his eyes far to the right.

Yet, even as he worked, molding plastic material on his face to resemble the contours of the Eurasian's face, a plan suggested itself to "X" by which he could overcome one of those difficulties. It would be painful, and perilous, but without attempting it, he could not hope to succeed in impersonating China Bobby.

Having changed clothes with the Eurasian, "X" slicked down the hair of his black toupee so that it resembled the polished hair of the half-caste. Then he made an injection of a harmless narcotic in China Bobby's arm—enough of the drug to keep the man unconscious for eight hours or more. He pocketed the Eurasian's gun and immediately left the office.

He had little fear of being apprehended in the dark passages that honeycombed the basement floor below. Instinctively, he groped his way through the gloom, returning to the second laboratory by the same route he and Drew Devon had used in leaving it. He found the laboratory empty. In fact, the entire building had sunk into a silence that somehow foreboded disaster.

In the laboratory, he procured a length of thin, copper wire, a small dry cell, an induction coil, and a tiny push-button switch. He worked one wire lead under the plastic volatile material that covered his face. The end of the wire he fastened above an important nerve center near his right eye. Having completed the circuit, he concealed all wires under his coat and pocketed battery, induction coil, and switch. His right hand, thrust into his pocket, operated the little switch for making and breaking the circuit.

He then approached a cabinet, the glass front of which would mirror his face. Pressing the switch, something happened that would have appeared nothing short of miraculous when observed by a person unaquainted with artificial stimulus of nerve centers of the body. "X's" right eye jerked sharply to the right and remained fixed in that position as long as his finger depressed the switch. His left eye was free to move in any direction. It was extremely unpleasant and interfered with his vision, but he knew he had only to lift his finger from the switch and his eye would return to its normal position.

He had scarcely completed his preparation before the whispering voice of the Ghoul sounded within the room. "All will come to my room at once. Important instructions."

"X" swung into the hall. He had not the slightest idea where the Ghoul's room was, and he feared that failing to find it, he would be apprehended at once. As he hurried along the corridor, he almost bumped into the sinister Chinese known as Yu'an. Instantly, "X" depressed the switch in his pocket that sent the artificial stimulus to his right eye. Imitating the metallic voice of China Bobby, he said in Cantonese: "The master summons us, Yu'an."

"And he is possessed by anger at the failure of his plan to take the spy," replied Yu'an. "Many men have been tracked in the prison cells below." He bowed slightly and stepped aside for the man whom he supposed to be China Bobby to go ahead. For a moment, "X" feared that he made a serious error. China Bobby was the Ghoul's lieutenant. Perhaps China Bobby alone knew the exact location of the Ghoul's chamber.

"X" SHOOK his head and motioned Yu'an to go ahead. "This night it is I who am your humble servant, Yu'an. For have you not saved my unworthy flesh from the assassin's knife in killing the vengeful Ah-Fang?"

Yu'an bowed and to "X's" immense relief, accepted the honor of leading the way to the Ghoul's chamber.

They entered the central office of China Bobby. One of the panels was wide open. They entered to find a company of perhaps a score of men already assembled. They were men of the East and West, dangerous men who had police records. Walls and ceiling of the room were covered with bright gilt. Gold-painted armchairs were arranged facing a golden dais. Kneeling motionless at the foot of the dais were two gorgeously robed Chinese girls, each holding a bowl of green Chinese porcelain from which wisps of fragrant incense mounted toward the ceiling. A veritable curtain of gray mist, probably produced by some chemical reaction taking place beneath the dais, partially concealed a golden throne-like chair on the dais.

Somewhere, a gong sounded a low, vibrant note. The mist thickened, became almost impenetrable; but behind it, "X" noticed some slight movement waved the mist curtain. Perhaps a door had opened to admit the Ghoul.

A white man next to "X" whispered an oath. "Look!"

The mist cleared away, and seated on the golden chair was a man. A robe of yellow silk draped his shoulders and fell to his feet. A skull cap of the same material, topped with the coral bead of a mandarin, covered his head. The yellow veil that "X" had seen before dropped from the cap and covered his face.

For a moment of awful silence, the hidden eyes behind the veil seemed to be upon the men at the foot of the dais. Then, from behind the veil came the whispering voice of the Ghoul: "China Bobby, stand up."

"X" calmly obeyed. He was confident of himself. He had purposely chosen to impersonate China Bobby because the Eurasian's defective eye made such an impersonation seem nothing short of impossible.

"Did anyone pass through your office after I sent the men down into the catacombs to look for a spy?"

"No, master," replied "X".

"Very well. Since there are only two ways to leave these headquarters and one of them is known only to me, the spy must still be here. It is of no matter. He shall not escape."

One of the white men, bolder than the others, spoke up. "If that spy you talk about was the guy known as Secret Agent 'X', there'll be matter enough."

"Silence, Cramer!" commanded the Ghoul. "I have called you men here for final instructions. As you know, the hour of my master stroke draws near. Tonight, you will proceed to the country home of the mayor. You will bring him alive to this place. Yu'an shall be in charge of the expedition. All arrangements have been made. Balloons have been moored at convenient spots. There will be fog, and positively no excuse for failure! You understand?"

"Nope." It was the man called Cramer who spoke. "I'll be damned if I see how you're goin' to get at the mayor. He's been scared to death somebody will bump him with the Amber Death. He's got bodyguards and all sorts of 'lectrical stuff strung around his place. Too damned much risk."

"Cramer," the Ghoul whispered, "I do not like your attitude."

"Nor me yours. This whole gang of yellow-bellies is scared of you and your fake tricks. It's a neat little old racket for you, but where do we come in? Your pay's too thin. You keep all the big sugar for yourself. We take all the risks. You sit there and push buttons. Never show your face."

The Ghoul waited until Cramer had finished. He leaned far forward in his chair. "Would you like to see my face, knowing that to look into my eyes means certain death?"

"Hooey!" Cramer turned around and looked at his companions. "Any of youse got the guts to oust this guy? He's got most of the swag hid around here somewhere. Must be more'n a million bucks."

Not a man stirred.

"Cramer!" commanded the Ghoul. "Look at me!"

THE man turned his head and confronted the Ghoul boldly. From beneath the yellow robe, a thin, yellow hand moved. With tantalizing slowness, that hand crawled up toward the yellow veil. The members of the gang were breathless. Some of them turned their eyes away as if they believed that the Ghoul could really kill with a glance.

Slowly, the thin fingers peeled back the veil. A gasp of stark terror breathed from the lips of every man in the room. For the face of the Ghoul was a yellow, dead thing with living eyes behind slanting lids. A round bullet hole had tunneled the creature's forehead. It was unmistakably the face of Ah-Fang, Gilbert Warnow's Chinese valet.

A hoarse cry ripped from the throat of Cramer. He sprang half out of his chair, uttered a strangled oath, and pitched forward on the floor.

The veil dropped over the hideous face of Ah-Fang. Yet "X" was not deceived. He had detected a movement of the Ghoul's left hand beneath the silken robe. Almost at the same time, he had seen a hidden needle snap out of the arm of Cramer's chair, and enter the gangman's arm. Doubtless this needle had been poisoned. Probably a similar needle was in the arm of every chair in the room and each controlled by some sort of push button on the Ghoul's chair.

"Now," said the Ghoul, and his whisper did not hide the note of triumph in his voice, "there will be no more disobedience. Go all of you. From now on, Yu'an, who thought he killed me, is in command."

The gong boomed hollowly again. Smoke fumed up from the dais and enveloped the form of the Ghoul. One by one the men filed from the room, and close behind Yu'an walked Secret Agent "X".

So Yu'an had thought he had killed Ah-Fang. Surely, thought "X", the Chinese had more intelligence than to believe that Ah-Fang had come to life again. Was it possible that the Ghoul had made a death-mask from the flesh of All-Fang's face and had actually worn it to further the horror-hold he had upon his men? If so, then the Ghoul had earned his name. "X" had seen the fleshy death-mask that had been sent to Warnow. It had been mummified, turned to solid synthetic amber by the Ghoul's deadly chemical weapon. It was probable that he made the mask he wore in a similar manner from the flesh of Ah-Fang.

But he had no time to cogitate on the subject at that moment. The Chinese, Yu'an, was in China Bobby's office passing out weapons to the men who were to assist in kidnaping the mayor. As "X" entered the office, Yu'an approached him, handed him a knife, and whispered: "It is with great joy that I learn that you, my friend, are to accompany me on this expedition of great danger."

"X" bowed in silence, accepted the knife, and tucked it into his sleeve. He had already resolved that Yu'an's joy should be short-lived indeed.

CHAPTER XI

THE MASTER STROKE

FOG HUNG HEAVY over the suburban estate of Mayor Grauman. Its vaporous tentacles twined around the chimneys that stood up from the slate roof like so many little minarets. Behind the fifteen-foot wall that surrounded the house, the mayor had sought sanctuary after a week of tiresome official duties. That wall was topped with a complicated network of wires that were connected with burglar alarms. Yet he must have known that no wall, no alarm had yet been devised that was proof against the Ghoul.

That night, there was no sense of security in the mayor's heart. The Ghoul had promised to strike. Only once had he failed.

On the last stroke of twelve, the iron gates that surrounded the mayor's grounds swung open. A big car whisked through to the highway and the gates clanged shut behind it. The car had not proceeded along the road more than a quarter of a mile before its lone occupant saw a blur of headlights through the fog directly ahead. He touched his light switch once, twice—a little signal that had been worked out beforehand.

Then he braked his car alongside of three others that were parked on the shoulder of the road. He got out. Headlights shone on the vizor of the man's cap. He was the mayor's own chauffeur.

Behind the wheel of the foremost car, a thin, yellow face with long, drooping mustaches gleamed with faint ivory luminosity in the light from the car's dashboard. It was the face of Yu'an, the Ghoul's henchman.

The chauffeur saluted. "The mayor has been warned. A guard of state police is on its way. Within fifteen minutes they will be on hand to take him back to the city where he will be kept in the prison for safety's sake."

Yu'an's eyes became mere slits. "Who warned him?" he asked.

"A Chinese woman," replied the chauffeur. "She came here wearing a pair of embroidered pajamas. She delivered the warning to the mayor's two bodyguards."

An almost imperceptible smile flitted across the yellow face of the man beside Yu'an—the man who looked like China Bobby. Betty Dale had succeeded in warning the mayor. "X" could only hope that this warning would prevent the Ghoul's plan from being put into effect. But in another moment, he was disappointed. Yu'an told the chauffeur that they would strike at once.

The men got from the car, and Yu'an divided them into four parties—three groups of three men and the fourth group composed of the remaining members of the gang. This fourth group was detailed to waylay the police. The other three groups were to go at once to three strategic points where jumping-balloons had been brought and moored under cover of darkness.

Agent "X", in the disguise of China Bobby, was one of the three in the group led by Yu'an. Beside the thin-faced Chinese, "X" trotted toward the knoll at the east side of the wall surrounding the mayor's grounds. There, faintly visible in the gray sky, a dark, round shape tugged at its moorings and swayed in the night breeze. It was a jumping-balloon.

"As soon as I have landed on the other side of the wall," Yu'an said to "X" and the third man, "you will both be ready to meet me at the other side of the estate. Because of the strong wind, I will be able to jump only in one direction." Yu'an was fastening the line from the jumping-balloon to the leather harness about his waist. To this harness were fastened canvas bags of shot which would be dropped when Yu'an laid hands on the mayor. These bags compensated for the weight of the second man when the jump was being made.

"When I return with the mayor," Yu'an explained to the Secret Agent, "you, my friend, will fire this flare pistol." He thrust into "X's" hands a pistol with a hard rubber butt and a thin metal barrel. "It will be a signal for the car to drive to the spot of my landing."

"X" was standing close to the Chinese. His right hand gripped the knife that was thrust up inside his sleeve. His nerves and muscles were tense, ready for the instant when everything depended upon his quick and accurate movements. Yu'an flexed his knees, testing the buoyancy of the balloon. A strange, eerie note, like the cry of an owl, tocsined across the sky.

"The signal," whispered the Chinese. "The other balloons are ready." He answered the signal with a similar cry. His knees flexed until he was almost squatting on the ground.

SUDDENLY, he sprang into the air. And at exactly the same moment, Agent "X's" knife flicked across the cord that held the ballast bags. As Yu'an shot into the air, "X" dropped his knife and seized the Chinaman's harness. Adding the force of his own leap to that of Yu'an, the balloon shot up through the damp, swirling gray fog.

"X" saw Yu'an's thin fingers whip out a knife. He saw the keen blade flash downward. "X" let go with his right hand and caught Yu'an's knife wrist firmly in his own grasp. The Chinese wriggled like an eel, trying to break that hold, trying to shake the Agent off. Sixty feet below, as the balloon gained the peak of the parabola which it traveled, the roof of the mayor's house bulked darkly against the mist-enshrouded earth. And at the end of the rope of the now descending balloon, "X" and the Chinese fought their silent battle. "X's" legs scissored about the knees of Yu'an. His ankles crossed, locked into place.

For a split second, he released his grip on the man's harness to swing his left arm up around Yu'an's neck. He strained upward until his full weight was upon the Chinaman's shoulders. He wrenched the knife from Yu'an's hand, only to have the Chinese yank an automatic from his pocket. The gun came up quickly. "X" drove a short hard blow at the side of the Chinaman's head—a blow that did not land. The gun in Yu'an's hand—was it an automatic, or the Agent's own gas gun? If it was the former, he could not hope to escape the shot; for the barrel was pointed straight at his head.

Suddenly, the slanting roof house became something more than a mere dark blot. "X" was evidently of much lighter build than the mayor, and the lack of ballast had permitted the balloon to travel farther than had been planned.

"X" sent another blow to Yu'an's head. The pistol blew just as they bumped lightly against the roof and started sliding down toward the eaves. The anesthetizing vapor hissed into the Agent's face, but he had been prepared, had held his breath. But the Chinese, knowing nothing about the weapon in his hand, had not been prepared. The cloud of gas dissipated; but, even so, it was of sufficient power to knock out the unwary Chinese. The gas gun dropped from his fingers, slid down the slates, and fell over the eaves.

"X's" foot encountered the edge of a small skylight that evidently opened into the attic of the mayor's home. Still clinging to the harness about the Chinaman, he maneuvered his foot so that they might slide farther down the roof to a point where they were stopped by one of many chimneys that sprouted from the roof.

Loosening the line at Yu'an's belt, "X" moored the balloon to the chimney. With his pocketknife, he cut the Chinese away from the harness and propped him against the chimney to prevent him from rolling off the roof. What became of Yu'an when he at length awoke was no affair of Secret Agent "X". The Chinese would not have the jumping-balloon to aid him, for "X" had already planned how he would use the balloon in his scheme to save the mayor. For the mayor would be kidnaped that night, but not by the Ghoul if "X" had anything to say about it.

Aided by the traction afforded him by his rubber-soled shoes, "X" crept slowly back up the slates toward the skylight. Catching the frame of the skylight, he extended himself full length on the roof. With a special chrome steel jimmy, which he took from his pocket, he worked the inner latch of the skylight loose and swung the cover back on its hinges. He crawled up so that he could seat himself on the edge of the opening. Since he had given his flashlight to Betty, he had no way of knowing what lay below.

He snaked his body through the opening, caught the edge of the skylight frame with his fingers, dangled there a moment, and dropped. His feet struck something that instantly gave way in a crackling, splintering smash that must have been audible through the house. The attic of the mayor's house had not been floored, and "X's" weight had been too much for the plaster. He picked himself up from a mess of broken plaster and splintered lath. He had no idea where he was.

The room was blackness itself. He stumbled forward and encountered a wall. Groping along the wall, he came to a door frame. His fingers closed over the doorknob. He gave it a twist, flung the door wide, and stepped into a hall.

As "X" moved down the hall toward the stairway, a pistol shot rang out through the night. From the foot of the stairs came a cry of terror. As "X" bounded down the stairs, he saw a man stagge across the hall tearing at the hilt of a knife that protruded from his chest. The front door was standing wide; and on the veranda two of the Ghoul's cutthroats, who had evidently cleared the wall with their jumping-balloons, were struggling with one of the mayor's bodyguards.

"X" was about to go to the assistance of the guard when a heavily built, gray-haired man ran through the door and into the hall. It was the mayor. There was a revolver in his hand, and before the Agent could make a move to stop him, the mayor turned his gun on "X" and fired. The bullet whined above the Agent's head. "X" leaped upon the mayor before he could shoot again and twisted the revolver from his hand.

"Quiet!" "X" hissed. "Your safety depends upon speed and quiet."

"It's a trap!" shouted the mayor at the top of his lungs. "You're not a policeman. You're the Ghoul. A Chine—"

The mayor's sentence choked off. "X's" hand had darted from his pocket. His cigarette lighter spat its last charge of gas straight into the mayor's face. The man tottered forward, fell across the Agent's shoulders. "X" lifted him bodily, and started up the stairs. If the mayor's bodyguard could hold off the Ghoul's other jumping-balloonists, "X" hoped to be able to clear the mayor's grounds and take the mayor to a place of safety.

IN the hall, "X" pressed on the light and found the attic steps without difficulty. How he was going to get the mayor up on the roof where the jumping-balloon was moored, he did not know. He hoped to find some sort of a ladder that would reach the skylight. But in this he was disappointed.

The attic was empty save for a couple of old trunks resting across the joists. There was, however, a gable jutting out from the steeply slanting roof. "X" walked across the joists and entered the gable. He unlatched and opened the casement window that centered it. Looking down, he saw that there was perhaps five feet of roof between the casement and the eaves—a narrow enough margin when a man starts slipping down the slates of a steeply inclining roof.

But "X" had no intention of slipping. In a moment he had removed his belt from the loops of his trousers and fastened it beneath the mayor's arms. This gave him a good handle by which to hold the man.

"X" stepped over the sill, holding to the window frame with one hand and dragging the mayor with the other. In this precarious position, he shifted his grip to the edge of the gable roof. With infinite care, he worked the mayor out onto the roof. Then he began his perilous ascent, keeping close to the gable.

Gaining the ridgepole of the house, "X" saw that the chimney to which he had moored the balloon was directly below him and opposite the gable. He had nothing to do but release his grip on the ridgepole and slide down until the base of the chimney stopped him.

Yu'an was still there, huddled against the chimney. "X" strapped the harness he had removed from the Chinese to the mayor. Then he attached the mooring line of the balloon to the harness. Still holding to the belt beneath the mayor's arms, he released the balloon from the chimney. The upward pull of the bag enabled him to hoist the mayor to his shoulders without difficulty. He then stepped far enough to one side so that he could clear the chimney and poised himself for the leap.

From his vantage point, "X" could see that the Ghoul's men had encountered the state police. He could hear the sound of machine-gun fire. A sudden gust of wind tugging at the bag, caused "X" to lurch forward. He kicked out. The balloon climbed into the air. But that moment of off-balance had spoiled his jump. The ground was coming up to meet him faster than he had anticipated. He jerked up his legs to avoid the wall; but as the balloon settled, "X" felt his back brush the wires at the top of the wall.

Distantly, the burglar alarm system raised a mad clangor of gongs. Floodlights, connected with the circuit, blazed through the misty dark. A beam struck "X" full in the face as he settled to the ground. Somewhere, close at hand, a shadowy form moved. "X" kicked out with all his strength in an effort to send the balloon once more climbing into the sky. But at that moment, strong arms locked about his legs. He made an effort to release the mayor. But before he could do this, a horde of men poured from the bushes and threw themselves upon him. And gleaming in the beam of a floodlight, "X" saw the golden veil of the Ghoul himself.

CHAPTER XII

BETRAYED

HOPELESSLY OUTNUMBERED, SECRET Agent "X" resorted to strategy as the only way out. There was much to explain that seemed inexplicable if he was to clear himself in the eyes of the Ghoul. He stopped struggling and shouted: "Master, what is the meaning of this? Is this my reward for carrying out your orders?"

"Let him up," the Ghoul ordered, "but keep him covered with your guns."

The weight of many men lifted the form of Agent "X". He was permitted to stand up, but so closely was he hemmed in by a ring of threatening automatics that he could not hope to escape. With his own hands, the Ghoul cut the mayor free from the jumping-balloon. Then a man stepped forward at an order from the veiled fiend and linked "X's" left wrist to his own by means of handcuffs.

But "X's" right hand was free to press the switch in his coat pocket. Instantly, he had the nauseating sensation of feeling his right eye twist sharply to the right as the artificial stimulus was applied.

"Now," said the Ghoul, sternly, "you will tell me, China Bobby, why you acted in this way. My plans were perfect The state police were entirely at the mercy of our machine guns. But Raymonds, who accompanied you and Yu'an tells me that you cut the ballast bags and leaped over the wall with Yu'an."

There had been a witness to "X's" action and there was no use denying what he had done. "Perfectly true, master," the Agent replied, "and I admit that I was partially at fault. Yu'an had planned to cheat you. He confided as much to me. In fact, I was admitted into a plan by which Yu'an and I were to kidnap the mayor and share the ransom we obtained. But at the last moment, I could not double-cross you."

"Why?" demanded the Ghoul. "I have never shown you any great kindness, have I?"

Keen judge of human nature that he was, "X" knew that the Ghoul was vain about his power and cruelty. He hung his head. "No," he admitted. "I did not dare be false to you. I am afraid of you. That is why at the last moment, I decided to carry out your instructions."

"And where is Yu'an?" asked the Ghoul.

"With his ancestors," the Agent lied. "I put a knife in his throat."

"You will be conducted back to headquarters," said the Ghoul. "As I drive back to the city, I shall consider what you have done." And the Ghoul stalked majestically toward the road. Two Chinese, who followed him, carried the unconscious mayor between them.

"X" was closely guarded by the gang and forced into a waiting car. Of that long drive back to the city, he remembered little. His companions were silent the entire distance, but the threatening eyes of their automatics never left him. "X" thought he had never worked harder to snare a criminal; yet time after time he had been outwitted by the Ghoul.

The car pulled up at what appeared to be the rear door of China Bobby's restaurant. "X" was forced to get out of the car by goading guns. He was dragged through the door and down a flight of steps that ended in a passage leading to China Bobby's office.

A few minutes later, the Ghoul appeared through a sliding door. Evidently, he had put the mayor in a place of safe keeping, and was determined to settle with the man he believed to be China Bobby.

"I have considered your story carefully," said the Ghoul, addressing the Agent, "and it is a plausible one. However, before you are released, I would like to ask one—"

But the Ghoul's sentence was interrupted by the opening of a sliding panel. Staggering through the door, her blonde hair disheveled, was Drew Devon. The Ghoul wheeled on her. "Where have you been?" he demanded.

She shook her head. "I was drugged by some one. Where's Bill Morgan? Bill Morgan is Secret Agent 'X'."

The Ghoul laughed. "Then Secret Agent 'X' is dead! I killed Morgan with the Amber Death."

DREW DEVON'S mouth was bitter. "Conceited beast!" she

snapped at the Ghoul. "He isn't dead. He escaped the Amber Death. For all your brilliance, he might be in the room right now!"

The man who was linked to "X" by means of handcuffs, said: "Master, it might be wise to ask the lady why, if she was drugged, she was yet able to leave this place and warn the mayor of an attempt to kidnap him."

The Ghoul's thin hand shot out and caught the girl by the wrist. "You did that?"

For a moment, scorn was displaced by terror in the girl's eyes. "No—no. I swear I didn't. I was unconscious in my room all the time."

Another man spoke up. "That couldn't be. The mayor's chauffeur distinctly described the woman who warned the mayor. We all heard him. It could have only been one person—that woman."

Drew Devon screamed her denial. "It isn't true! It must have been some trick of Secret Agent 'X'. If he could impersonate Bill Morgan so that I would risk everything to save—" She checked herself with lip-biting.

"So," said the Ghoul softly, "you saved Morgan, or 'X', or whatever his name is. You saved him from the Amber Death after I commanded that he die. My dear lady, you shall know the maddening torment of the ant pit! When that beautiful body of yours is teeming with tiny, tormenting devils, you will understand the folly of trying to thwart my unalterable commands. Fun-Lo! Gordon! Chang! Take her away to the ant pit!"

Three men sprang forward to do the Ghoul's bidding. In the mind of Secret Agent "X" a battle was raging. It was within his power to check this brutal act. But at what a price? It might mean exposing himself, jeopardizing the progress he had made. Was Drew Devon worth that much? She was a murderess. But no crime deserved the torment of the ant pit. And though she had saved him unknowingly, "X" knew that he would have now been a dead, amber husk had it not been for Drew Devon.

He had long ago resolved that it must never be said that the Man of a Thousand Faces was ungrateful. He had hit upon a plan for gaining time—a ruse that might prevent the Ghoul from carrying out his despicable plan of torturing Drew Devon. He held up his right hand in an arresting gesture. "Stop!" he cried. "Before you sentence this woman to the fate she justly deserves, it might be well to question her concerning Secret Agent 'X'. Undoubtedly, if she warned the mayor she is one of his agents."

A remarkable change came over the face of Drew Devon. A look of cunning crept into her eyes. Hate distorted her features until she was as hideous as a vampire. She pointed a trembling finger at the Agent. "Look at his hand!" she screamed. "He has all his fingers! That man isn't China Bobby! He's Secret Agent 'X'!"

But hardly were the words out of her mouth before "X" had gone into action. A trick he had learned from a Hindu fakir, of compressing the joints of his hands, enabled him to slip free from the handcuffs that linked him with the Ghoul's man. He sprang backward across the room.

Like magic, two guns appeared in his hands—one the revolver he had taken from the mayor, and the other the flare-pistol that Yu'an had given him to use as a signal when the mayor was captured. Those guns swept the company of men before him.

"The first man to move, dies!" he shouted.

Behind his group of menials, the Ghoul shouted: "Knife him! After him, all of you!"

TO a man, the killers moved, surging forward like a human tide of destruction. The arch-enemy of their kind stood before them; their knives were thirsty for his blood. Infrequently, did Agent "X" use lethal weapons, but no man knew better how to use a revolver than he did. Two of the foremost killers were dropped at the Agent's feet by two well-placed shots. Another tripped over a fallen companion and fell upon his own knife. A fourth fired an automatic at close range, the slug landing squarely over the Agent's heart.

"X" dropped to one knee. His bullet-proof vest of finest manganese steel, had stopped the lead. But the impact alone was enough to knock him down. "X" fired again, sprang to his feet and aside to avoid the thrust of a Chinese knife. The butt of the flare pistol in his hand, laid open the head of another man. Shooting carefully, and hacking with the gun in his left hand, he fought through the mob.

But behind the fury of the hand-to-hand encounter, "X" saw a flash of yellow silk. The Ghoul! The Ghoul was escaping through an open door at the rear of the room. The flare pistol in "X's" left hand swung up, pointed at the silken draperies that curtained the door of the closet in which he had concealed the unconscious China Bobby. He pulled the trigger. A faint pop and a red ball of fire shot from the gun and burnt through the silk curtains. Instantly, flames licked upward.

"Fire!" shouted "X," at the same moment sending his last revolver shot at his nearest opponent. To that moment of panic caused by the threat of fire, "X" owed much. Inasmuch as the room was virtually fireproof, no serious damage could be expected from the flaming curtains. But it caused a moment's confusion—one precious second when "X" sprang through the door through which the Ghoul had disappeared.

He ran into the passage, found the tiny button that operated the panel, and pressed it. The steel door slipped smoothly into place. Above the Agent's head, an electric lamp glowed. Holding the flare pistol, which he had effectively used but a moment ago, by its hard rubber butt, he knocked out the lamp. As the metal barrel crossed the elements of the bulb, there was a flash of blue flame, then instantaneous blackness. "X" knew that in one stroke he had captured the Ghoul's mob; for in shorting the electrical circuit he had thrown the electrical mechanism, that operated all the doors leading from the office, out of order. There was no way out for Drew Devon and the horde of killers.

Swiftly and silently, "X" moved down the dark corridor, stopping occasionally to listen to the whisper of footsteps ahead of him. Suddenly, a tiny spot of light shone on what appeared to be a blank wall in front of him. He saw the hand of the Ghoul holding a flashlight and turning the key in the lock of a door. The door opened and closed behind the Ghoul before "X" had a chance to follow. As he approached on tiptoe, a faint hissing sound came out of the darkness. It was a steady hiss like the escape of—

And in another moment, he knew it was gas—poisonous chlorine. He could feel its sting in his eyes and smell its acrid odor. "X" knew that the Ghoul, believing that "X" had in some way managed to inform the police of the gang's headquarters, was deserting his men and burning his bridges behind him. This was his own secret exit, and the quantities of poison gas hissing into the passage had been prepared for just such an emergency.

AGENT "X" held his breath and closed his eyes against the poisonous, stinging vapor. The fingers of his right hand groped across the panel, searching the keyhole. His right hand fingered the bunch of master keys in his pocket. Without a light, it was impossible for him to pick out the exact key that would unlock the door. Finding the keyhole, he tried them one at a time. His lungs were aching; his heart throbbing at his temples. Yet to breathe was to die. At last he found a key that scraped through the eye of the lock. Just as he turned the key, a dull boom sounded hollowly throughout the cellars.

"X" threw open the door and stepped into a lighted room. Evidently this part of the catacombs was on a different lighting circuit than the other part. A ghostly wisp of yellow-green gas followed him into the room. He wanted to cough but dared not. He stepped into the next room. It appeared empty until "X" saw, beneath the yellow silk curtains that draped a doorway, the shoes and trousered legs of a man. Cautiously, he approached. He lifted the yellow curtains. The face of the man on the floor was covered with a yellow silk veil.

Revolver in hand, "X" knelt beside the still form. With the tips of his fingers, he lifted the yellow veil. Beneath was the chubby, red face of unconscious Mayor Grauman.

"Neatly trapped, Agent 'X'," came the Ghoul's cold whisper.

"X" looked up quickly. Standing directly in front of a screen of Oriental design, was the Ghoul—the Ghoul without his silk mask, with only the hideous death-mask of Ah-Fang covering his real features. The automatic held in his unflinching fingers was directed at the Agent's heart.

"I knew," the Ghoul whispered, "that curiosity concerning my identity would prompt you to took beneath the veil that covered the mayor's face. That is why I placed him there as a decoy when I heard you had managed to gain entrance here in spite of my poison gas. In fact, now that the game is over, I think you must admit that I have outplayed you in every hand."

"True," the Secret Agent admitted. "Much as I hate to spoil your good opinion of yourself, I can't resist telling you that I've known your identity for several hours. I was sure of my deduction when, in the guise of Morgan, I fell into your hands in the laboratory. Though your voice came from a reproducer in the ceiling, you were there in person with Vardson and the others. In fact, I might go so far as to say you took an active part in most of the crimes.

"In the laboratory, you were one of those living-dead men ranged along the wall. It is not difficult to fake the Amber Death when you have stained your skin the proper hue. A little lapel-button microphone enabled you to speak through the reproducer in the ceiling, though you were actually in the room. When I attacked your men, you took advantage of the confusion, stepped from the wall and dropped the yellow veil over your face.

"Your actual presence spurred the men to action, just as it did tonight at the mayor's place. Phonograph records of your voice were used for all the Ghoul radio warnings in order that you might be busy elsewhere—busy shifting suspicion from your own shoulders, busy planning new murders in the very presence of the men you intended to murder."

A chuckle sounded behind the Ghoul's mask of mummified flesh. "No one will ever know the truth. Yu'an and Vardson alone knew my true identity. Vardson is beyond sane speech. You say that your knife found Yu'an's throat. Not five minutes ago, I pressed an igniter that fired a charge which will result in the destruction of both laboratories and the Amber Death victims. The formula for the Amber Death will be destroyed. Only Vardson knew it. I have over a million dollars in cash and securities—the reward of my efforts. I have only to step through the rear door of this room, climb steps, and enter a garage where my car is waiting."

Carried away with praise of himself, the Ghoul did not notice that "X" had shifted his empty revolver into the palm of his hand. With a sudden movement, he flung the weapon at the Ghoul's head. The Ghoul ducked to one side, fired a shot that took "X" in the chest. But again the bullet-proof vest saved him. As he leaped, hands extended for the killer's throat, the Ghoul fired again—this time, at the Agent's head.

"X" ducked too late to avoid the shot entirely. It grazed the side of his head, dashed blinking red and yellow lights before his eyes, sent blood trickling into his eyes to blind him. Yet he had reached the Ghoul's gun-hand and clung to it desperately, keeping the automatic turned away from himself.

For a moment, they were locked together, the Ghoul striving to break away from the Agent's hold, and "X" battling to save himself from oblivion. With an unexpected twist of the wrist, "X" disarmed the Ghoul. The automatic clattered to the floor. But in making that desperate attempt, "X" had thrown himself slightly off balance. The Ghoul lunged forward, throwing "X" to the ground.

The shock of the fall seemed to clear "X's" vision. He seized the Ghoul's throat in his right hand. His left came up instinctively to lock over the Ghoul's wrist. For in the Ghoul's hand was something sharp and shiny. Not a knife, but a large hypodermic needle.

"The Amber Death," the Ghoul gasped out. "One more charge of the Amber Death .... All yours." And slowly but surely his hand bent forward, the needle seeking the flesh of the Agent's wrist.

Suddenly, "X's" knees came up, lifting his assailant. Then he straightened, all the strength of his body behind a kick that sent the Ghoul's heels over head across the room. "X" was up in a second. His right hand swept up the Ghoul's automatic from the floor. The Ghoul, completely winded by his fall, attempted to get up, couldn't, and fell back to the floor.

Covering the man with the automatic, "X" seized him by the collar, picked him up, and threw him into a chair. As he did so, he noticed that the chair was one of those peculiar metal chairs similar to the one in which he had sat in China Bobby's office. He saw that a covered cable led from the chair to a generator at the side of the room. Evidently, the Ghoul had used this contraption to torture the truth out of some one. It was a very good idea, the Agent decided.

"X" sprang to the generator and threw over the starting switch. The hum of the generator was drowned out by a shriek of pain and terror from the Ghoul. "X" cut the current slightly. For a moment, he watched the Ghoul writhing in an effort to drag himself from the chair. Then he said softly:

"Let me know when you are ready to sign a full confession. For every moment you delay, I shall step up the current another notch!"

CHAPTER XIII

DEATH-MASK OF AH-FANG

EARLY MORNING SUNBEAMS slanted through the mist rising from the streets of Chinatown when the wail of police-car sirens died in front of the gilt and lacquered front of China Bobby's restaurant

"Looks like a phony tip, Inspector," said a plainclothes man to Inspector Burks as they swung from one of the cars.

Burks glowered at the gleaming front of the restaurant. "If it is, I'll hang the man who gave it by the ears," he growled. Then sighting the lovely form of a young girl who had just stepped from a small roadster parked behind one of the squad cars, he called: "Say, Miss Dale, you're sure that mysterious telephone call that tipped you off said this was the joint?"

"Certain of it, Inspector Burks," replied Betty Dale in her crisp, businesslike voice. She approached the plate-glass front of the restaurant and looked in. Walking beside her was a cheerful, red-headed youth with note book and pencil poised as though he could hardly wait for a big news story to break.

"You two step back, now," ordered Burks. "We're going to break in here if we can't raise the proprietor. Say, Reardon!" he called to one of his subordinates, "you know Chinatown from the sewers on up. Isn't this about where that dope joint used to be back in tong-war days?"

The elderly Reardon nodded. "Used to be known as Hong-Po's catacombs. Cellars and tunnels extended for about a block. But in the last big raid, we sealed up all the catacombs."

"Wouldn't take much to open 'em again," said Burks. He shouted brisk orders to his men, and five minutes later the police were pouring into the restaurant.

"Everything looks on the up-an'-up," one of the detectives was heard to whisper, "and will Burks' ears be red when he gets climbed for raidin' a legitimate joint!"

"Look here, Inspector Burks!" Betty Dale called excitedly. As if entirely by accident, she had located the door at the rear of the restaurant that led down into the opium den.

"Thunderation!" roared Detective Reardon. "I remember that circular staircase! Went down there in a raid once. This *is* Hong-Po's old place. Somethin' in that tip after all, Inspector. I can smell the stinkin' black stuff clear up here!"

"Watch things up, men!" Burks warned. "Maybe this is just a bootleg dope joint. And maybe the tip was okeh when this guy told Miss Dale we'd find the Ghoul here!"

Down the winding staircase, and the squad trooped through the passage that opened on still a larger room. Police searchlights cleaved the tar blackness and gleamed on green and gilt. Light reflected from the baleful eyes of the dragon twining the huge artificial tree; it found here and there, in curtained bunks, the opium sleepers.

"Dope de luxe!" exclaimed Reardon. "This outdoes anything Hong-Po ever put across. Now if the rest of the place was open, there'd be a door over here—" He approached the panel decorated with the lacquered dragon. His keen eyes found the switch-button that centered the eye of the monster. He gave it a push. Nothing happened.

"Looks like somebody put the machinery on the fritz," said Burks. "Malvern, get the acetylene torch and cut through this steel panel."

Reardon's ear was pressed to the door. "Take it easy, inspector," he cautioned. "I can hear people moving around in there. Maybe they won't be in such a sweet temper as the smoky lads in the bunks."

"Be in a damn sight worse temper when we get hold of them," Burks growled. He watched the hissing torch as it knifed through the steel. "That's got it!" The heated panel fell back with a dismal clang. "Let's go, boys!"

AGAIN through smoky blackness, the searchlights cut—this time to find blear-eyed gunmen huddling in the corners of what had been China Bobby's office. A few nervous shots rattled out, but a police Tommy-gun, by way of warning, raked one of the walls high above the heads of the hoods.

"Round them up!" ordered Burks. "We want that girl, too." He kicked through a black charred film that had once been a silk curtain. On the floor of a little closet, he found the yellow-skinned man whom he recognized as China Bobby. He knelt beside the man. "Not dead," he muttered. "Seems to be taking a quiet snooze. Looks like the work of some guy I've met before. Suppose this half-breed's the Ghoul, Reardon?"

The old detective shook his head. "Can't say. We haven't gone halfway through this joint yet. There used to be a sort of dungeon down below that Hong-Po used. Better get that acetylene torch busy again. This room was a sort of center to a spider-web formation of rooms and passages."

But it was only after two hours of arduous labor that the secrets of the catacombs were completely revealed. What had been the Ghoul's laboratories was a mass of wreckage. The explosion had buckled the walls. A yellow, amber-like hand jutting out from a pile of debris told Burks that beneath were bodies made hideous by the Amber Death.

It was the inquisitiveness of the redheaded reporter who accompanied Betty Dale that led the police to find the secret passage that led to the scene of the Ghoul's last stand. And to all appearances, the redheaded youth came very near being asphyxiated by the chlorine fumes that lingered in the passage. Burks, Malvern, and six others ventured up the passage after gas masks had been put on. Though Burks did not notice it at the time, he might have seen that one of his masked followers was the ever-curious redheaded reporter.

"Who's that over in the corner?" shouted Burks. He pointed to a fleshy form in the corner—a man who exhibited signs of life in an effort to wriggle from his bonds and talk through his gag. "The mayor, by all that's holy! Give Mayor Grauman a hand, one of you fellows. I'm going—"

As Burks stepped through the door of the next room, words failed him. Seated in a metal chair in the center of the room was the figure of a man. His contorted yellow face resembled nothing so much as the carved visage of an ugly Chinese joss. He sat perfectly still.

"A Chink!" gasped one of the detectives. "Looks like that Ah-Fang you've been sendin' Keegan lookin' all over town for!"

"Yes, Burks," said the redheaded reporter, "looks as though for once you were right."

"What'd you mean, 'for once'?" Burks sprang across to the chair and snatched up a piece of paper that lay in the lap of the unconscious man. As his eyes skated down the paper, he read:

I am the Ghoul. I freely confess to all the crimes of murder and extortion in which the Amber Death played so important a part.

Burks mumbled an oath. "And it's signed—good Lord!" Burks wiped a hand over his forehead. "And it was reported that he committed suicide in his own home after receiving a warning from the Ghoul!"

THE redheaded reporter had been looking over Burks' shoulder at the note. "I suppose a fellow could easily fake the Amber Death by injecting some harmless yellow dye beneath the flesh of his face. Probably, he switched needles, and used one containing dye instead of the one containing poison that Luigi gave him. Then under cover of dark, he got away with his men and their captives, knowing that if he was reported dead, no suspicion—"

Burks brushed the reporter to one side and snatched the mask of yellow, mummified flesh away from the real face of the Ghoul—a virile face with an impressively high forehead surmounted by gray hair. It was the face of Lionel Gage. He seemed to have been plunged into a doped sleep.

"We should have known," said the reporter softly. "There wasn't any sense to the Ghoul kidnaping Lionel Gage because Gage was broke. Gage admitted as much—told Warnow so in the presence of Malvern. He said Wall Street had stripped him. Yet he continued to live pretty much as he did before. Where did he get the money? Why, from this extortion scheme! And when everybody else could talk only of the Ghoul's fiendishness, Gage kept emphasizing the Ghoul's *power*. He carried vanity, which was the keynote of his character as the Ghoul, into his respectable side of life. He wanted everyone to realize what a master-mind the Ghoul was. Why? Because he was the Ghoul."

"Yeah," Burks agreed. "And Gage kidnaped himself; even gave himself a fake shot of the Amber Death to avoid suspicion. Why, he spent years in China. Knew the ropes." Burks paused. "Say, for a reporter you know a—"

He was interrupted by a faint click. The room was plunged into complete darkness.

"Who turned out those lights!" Burks wheeled around and stood motionless, staring into the darkness. On the wall, directly in front of him, was a steady glow of weird light—a letter "X" drawn in phosphorescent paint on the wall.

Burks' flashlight cut through the darkness and wheeled from one startled face to another. With an oath, he was gone, racing up the passage through which they had come. He burst into what had been China Bobby's office. His eyes were fairly popping from his head as he looked about the room where the police were busily at work.

"Where's that redheaded guy? Miss Dale, who was that reporter who came with you?"

Betty stared innocently at the inspector. "Why, that was Jim Collins of the *Herald*."

"Collins, my eye! That was Secret Agent 'X.' And this time, I've got him. He couldn't get through here without some of my boys seeing him!" And Burks bounded toward the door that led back through the opium den.

But he might have saved his energy. For the redheaded reporter had availed himself of the emergency-exit prepared by the Ghoul. He had hurried in the opposite direction from that taken by Burks and was, at that moment, driving somewhat recklessly down the narrow streets of Chinatown in the Ghoul's own car.

Made in the USA
Coppell, TX
08 November 2025

62785232R00262